TANGLED BEGINNINGS

A WHISPERING PINES NOVEL

ALSO BY KIMBERLY DIEDE

CELIA'S GIFTS SERIES
WHISPERING PINES (BOOK 1)

FIRST SUMMERS NOVELLA SERIES
FIRST SUMMERS AT WHISPERING PINES 1980

TANGLED BEGINNINGS

A WHISPERING PINES NOVEL

Kimberly Diede

Celia's Gifts Book 2

Ebook ISBN: 978-0-9992996-2-3
Print ISBN: 978-0-9992996-3-0

To Rick, thank you for understanding my need to make things up

"Oh, what a tangled web we weave
When first we practice to deceive!"
-Walter Scott

Chapter 1

Gift of Second Chances

Here we go again, Jess Rand thought as she turned to face the gathering of family and friends, smiling through the strong wave of déjà vu that nearly caused her to stumble. This was her second time as matron-of-honor for her sister Renee. Familiar faces smiled back at her. Some of them had been at Renee's first wedding, their faces now lined by two more decades of life experience. Younger faces greeted her as well—children, born out of first marriages, and young men and women who had been mere babies at the last gathering.

Despite being two years younger than Renee, Jess beat her sister to the altar the first time around, so sure her dreams were all coming true. Now her optimism for her own future lay in tatters . . . but regardless, she was just as excited for Renee this time around.

Her sister deserved to be happy. Tragically widowed a decade earlier, Renee had finally managed to beat the odds and find love again—halfway around the globe, no less.

Maybe there was hope for Jess, too. She stole a glance at the man standing before the minister. Matt stood tall and confident in a pale gray suit. Sunlight glinted off silver streaks in his otherwise dark hair, cut short for the special day, and creases spread from his eyes as he squinted against the glare, watching for his bride's approach. He broke into a ridiculous grin as he locked eyes with Renee, who was making her way down the aisle toward him with a serene smile.

Jess peeked at the man to the groom's left, catching his eye. His mouth tweaked up at her and he rolled his eyes, presumably in response to Matt's love-sick face. Jess guessed Ross, Matt's cop buddy from Minneapolis, wasn't comfortable with his friend's display of emotion.

Men can be so shallow.

Still . . . she couldn't help but smile back.

* * *

After the ceremony, the crowd made their way to the large white reception tent. Despite Jess's earlier reservations when Renee suggested an outdoor wedding—at *Whispering Pines* and in *June*—both the weather and the venue were lending themselves to a perfect day.

"Hey, Mom, did I tell you how beautiful you look today?" Lauren asked as she sauntered up to Jess.

"Why yes, honey, you did," Jess replied, "but feel free to tell me again."

Jess caught her daughter up in a hug, the two of them swaying together on the edge of the dance floor as the band warmed up.

The past year had been incredibly tough on them both. Jess regretted the upheaval her split from Will caused her kids, but she had finally accepted that divorce was inevitable. Will, her soon-to-be ex-husband and father to her children, was a selfish man—more intent on living life on his own terms than maintaining their family unit. Now, eleven months into their separation, Jess recognized several basic truths. Will would always value status and wealth over the three of them. He had quit on their family before Jess was even sure he was cheating again. He couldn't be trusted.

Intent on keeping up a festive mood and refusing to let thoughts of that man ruin one more day of her life, Jess gave Lauren another squeeze and stepped back out of their embrace, keeping her hands on her daughter's shoulders.

"I am so proud of you, honey," Jess said. "Graduating at the top of your class, giving the most amazing valedictorian speech that school has ever heard . . . and now college."

Lauren laughed. "Not for two months! And Mom, you have to admit, you're slightly biased on the whole speech thing."

"Maybe just a little," Jess conceded, "but that standing ovation had to mean something!"

Lauren nodded with another quick laugh—a response Jess was used to when trying to give her daughter praise. For some reason, Lauren resisted compliments like water off a duck's back.

"Where's your brother?"

Lauren shrugged. "Don't know. Haven't seen him for a while. He was down by the water with Robbie and Luke after we finished eating. The guys aren't really into all this wedding stuff."

Jess gave Lauren's shoulders another quick squeeze as Renee and Matt approached hand-in-hand.

"You guys having fun?" Renee asked her sister and niece, her ever-present grin still shining from her eyes.

"Of *course* we're having fun, sis!" Jess assured Renee with a quick side hug. "Did you two get a chance to talk to Sheriff Thompson and his wife? He's sure looking better. Retirement must agree with him."

Matt laughed. "Sure did. He says he feels like a new man, now that I lifted all that weight of responsibility off his shoulders. His wife did ask if I might let him come back to work the switchboard a few hours a week, just to get him out of the house. I don't think she was kidding."

"I thought they were going to go south after you took over as sheriff. Didn't they go?" Jess asked.

"They did, but they missed their family and friends back here. Decided to just go for a few months in the winter, after the holidays. Guess they weren't ready to give up on Minnesota year-round quite yet. He stops in the office once every couple of days. I think he misses the action."

"That may be, but I'm glad he was able to get out before his heart totally gave out on him from the stress," Renee said.

Thompson's heart had become so weak that retirement was eventually his only option. Fortunately, Matt accepted the job—an opportunity Jess knew Renee was thankful for, as it allowed him to move closer.

"Can we please have the bride and groom join us out on the dance floor?" the lead singer for the four-piece band asked from the small make-shift stage in the far corner of the tent.

"That's our cue," Renee said, executing a quick pirouette when Matt raised their clasped hands high in the air, her airy chiffon skirt an ivory cloud around her ankles. "Stay close, sister, you're next."

Jess groaned, less than thrilled with the idea of dancing the next dance with Ross, Matt's best man. But she knew what was expected and she would be a good sport about it.

As her sister and new brother-in-law took their first turns around the wooden dance floor as a married couple, Jess took the opportunity to survey the twenty or so tables placed below twinkling white lights, strung across the tent ceiling. She laughed as her dad, George, entertained her mother, Lavonne, and various relatives at one table with what must have been a funny story, if their animated expressions were any indication. Her nieces and nephews sat at two tables nearby, looking bored. She shot a look of disapproval at Renee's son, Robbie, when he glanced up from the phone in his hands. He understood and the phone disappeared into his suit pocket.

Lauren excused herself to grab a glass of punch. One particularly noisy table in a far corner caught Jess's attention and she made her way over to them.

"Jess, you look *beautiful* tonight, girl!" A pretty woman with spiked gray hair stood as Jess approached, extending her hands and giving Jess a quick peck on the cheek. Penny helped lead yoga and exercise sessions at the Whispering Pines retreats.

"And how are some of my favorite ladies doing tonight? Having fun?" Jess asked the energetic group of women seated around the table.

"How could we *not* be having fun?" one of the seated ladies replied, motioning around the tent. "It's a beautiful spring evening full of good food, wine, and music to dance to!"

"I'm glad to hear that, Beth! It was so nice of all of you to come."

"We wouldn't have missed it," Beth replied. "You and Renee are living proof it's possible to survive the curveballs life throws at you. *Of course* we wanted to celebrate with you!"

Jess and Renee first met all of these women through their retreat business right here at Whispering Pines. When Renee inherited the lake resort from their great-aunt Celia a year and a half ago, getting the place up and running became a family affair. It didn't take them long to realize the limited number of cabins wouldn't be enough to financially support Renee's small family, so Jess partnered with Renee to add a retreat business for women. These ladies were a combination of prior guests and staff hired to assist with the retreats.

Penny sat back down and pulled a chair out next to her, motioning to Jess to sit. "You might want to give your feet a rest before you're expected to join Renee out on the dance floor."

Jess sat, a sigh escaping her lips as she slipped her feet out of the confining heels she seldom wore these days. Hoping to catch up a bit before duty called again, she asked, "So, tell me, what have *you* fabulous women been up to since I last saw you?"

"Well, Desiree here was just telling us about her new apartment," an older woman across the table replied, motioning to the youngest woman at the table, directly to her right.

The younger woman nodded, smiling at those around the table. "Liz here was right. Chuck wasn't *ever* going to change. He agreed to go to counseling with me and try AA, but that didn't last long. I finally realized that if I wanted a better life for me and the kids, I just needed to move on without him."

Jess remembered back to when she first met Desiree. Like a few others sitting at this table, Desiree attended their very first retreat the previous November. Jess and Renee were flying blind with that first retreat, learning as they went. Desiree had been very reserved at the beginning of that long weekend, saying little. Jess remembered Renee telling her she was worried the woman wasn't enjoying herself. But Desiree slowly warmed up to the group as the weekend continued . . . until the disastrous night when Chuck, Desiree's extremely drunk husband, showed up uninvited and caused a nasty scene. Matt hauled the man off to jail and Desiree nearly left early, ashamed at her husband's actions. But her new retreat friends convinced her to stay and encouraged her to seek help—beyond just the weekend—to improve her home life.

Now, Jess noticed Desiree fiddling with her naked ring finger, a shadow flitting across her face, replaced quickly by a smile. To Jess it conveyed hope with a bit of resignation over her new living situation. She stood and walked over to Desiree's side, hugging the woman where she sat.

"I'm proud of you, Desiree," Jess said, looking the woman in the eye. "It takes a lot of guts to move on from a bad relationship. I know. I've been living through something similar this past year. But believe me, you *will* get through it and life will start to look a whole lot more promising again."

Desiree gave a brief nod and brushed away a single tear.

Just then, the call Jess had been expecting finally came from the stage.

"We need the rest of the bridal party up here," the lead singer announced.

"Ladies, enjoy the rest of your evening," Jess said, smiling at her friends around the table as she bent down to retrieve her sandals and slip them back on. "Duty calls."

As she straightened, she felt a hand at her waist and turned to see Ross standing behind her.

Having just met the man two days earlier, Jess wasn't yet sure what to make of him. She guessed him to be about forty. He was certainly handsome, similar in height to Matt, with dark hair and broody eyes. But where Matt exuded a certain calm maturity about him, this guy was . . . edgier. Jess hadn't exchanged more than a few superficial statements with him up to this point, but there was something about him that put her guard up.

"Guess that means us," Ross said, motioning toward the dance floor with his other hand.

"Guess so," Jess agreed, making her way toward Renee and Matt, Ross following close behind. She and Ross made up the entire bridal party, which Jess was suddenly hyper aware of as together they stepped out onto the ad hoc dance floor covering the back third of the tent.

The smell of roses tinged the air, perfumed by three large bouquets of pink and white blossoms lining the head table to their right. Between the scented air and twinkling lights above, Jess felt almost transported back to a time and place where everyday worries lost their weight.

The band began to play a love ballad from the 1950s. Jess stepped into Ross's open arms, settling her wrists around his neck. The slow ballad didn't demand much in the way of dancing skill. They swayed together, moving their feet slightly.

When was the last time I danced with a man at a wedding? Jess wondered.

A minute into the song, Ross reached up and captured Jess's right hand, their new position pulling her back slightly so she had to look at the man instead of being absorbed in her own thoughts.

"Having fun?" he asked.

"Actually . . . yes, I am. You?"

"Weddings aren't exactly my favorite gig. But I wanted to be here for Matt."

Jess nodded in understanding. She hadn't been thrilled to plan her sister's wedding either—the past year had completely poisoned her view of romance—but she wanted her sister to be happy and had come to realize that Matt was a good fit for Renee. She hadn't initially thought so. She'd immediately been skeptical of a man who supposedly lived across the world but would suddenly appear, unexpected, at the resort one summer day. Renee had met him while on a trip to Fiji on New Year's—a year and a half ago—but she'd failed to mention him to anyone back home. Matt showed up at a time when their lives were in an upheaval, so it had perhaps taken more time than usual before Jess warmed up to him.

Now, as Jess and Ross danced a few feet from Renee and Matt, she knew her sister had found one of the good ones.

"Have you and Matt known each other long?"

"Long enough" was Ross's somewhat cryptic reply.

Unsure what to make of that, Jess took a different approach. Normally, if someone wasn't in the mood for conversation, Jess happily complied. But since they might be stuck out on this dance floor together for another song or two, she tried again.

"Did you ever get out to Fiji to visit Matt while he was sheriff there?"

"Unfortunately, no. And it wasn't because I didn't get an invite. Matt kept pestering me to come visit—said you couldn't beat the beautiful weather or friendly women. But I just never made the time."

Not missing that comment about "friendly women," Jess gave him her signature look: her left eyebrow raised, conveying her distaste for his comment.

"Oh, relax," Ross replied with a laugh. "I always had the impression Matt didn't do much more than work on that island. He never was much for parties or mindless dating. Too serious if you ask me."

"Oh, so you're more of a Romeo then?"

To that Ross raised their joined hands high in the air and spun Jess in a quick spin then pulled her back against his chest, his arm firm around her waist.

"Feel free to think that, pretty lady."

There was no more conversation after that. Jess felt slightly put off by the man, and Ross seemed content to dance without speaking.

The song ended and the band picked up the tempo, inviting everyone else onto the dance floor. Jess watched her dad make his way out onto the floor and tap her new brother-in-law on the shoulder. Matt stepped back to allow George to take his oldest daughter into his arms then made his way over to Jess and Ross.

"Mind if I cut in, bud?" Matt asked.

"Be my guest," Ross replied, giving Jess a quick nod before he turned his back on her and stepped out of the spotlights trained on the dance floor.

"So, what do ya think of Ross?"

Jess shook her head as she and Matt started a little two-step around the dance floor. She wasn't yet sure what she thought of the man. Finally she said, "Not much of a talker, is he?"

Matt chuckled. "No, not really, at least initially. Took me a while to get to know him. He's leery to share much with someone he doesn't know."

"Seems a bit cynical too."

"He can be. A smart-ass too. But I would trust him with my life. I have, as a matter of fact, more than once."

"Did you guys work together?"

"Yeah, for a couple years, back when we were rookies. He pulled me out of more than one rough spot. Then he transferred up to Minneapolis and I managed to bug him into staying in touch."

The dance floor was getting crowded and the noise level was ramping up, making it tough to hear. Jess gave up trying to carry on a conversation and enjoyed the evening. She danced with Nathan, her eldest, after Matt. He had grown so tall. As he grinned down at her, she couldn't help but be reminded how much he looked like his father.

"All right, let's get everyone out here. You know this one!" a member of the band promised as the first few notes of the infamous "Chicken Dance" rang out.

Jess cringed. *I know it, and I've always hated it.*

Her feet were starting to hurt and she needed some air. The crowd on the dance floor had swelled to the point where a couple of tables were being removed to make more room. Jess easily slipped away from the crowd unnoticed.

She made her way outside the tent and into the darkness. The white canvas tent did little to muffle the racket of noise, laughter, and dancing, so she made her way farther down a paved path. The moon was bright and full, making it easier to see, but Jess wouldn't have needed much light. She knew the paths well at Whispering Pines. She spent summers here as a child and now, having lived here for almost a full year with her sister, she could probably navigate the grounds in her sleep.

She was tired. The week leading up to a wedding is always stressful, especially when you somewhat foolishly volunteer to handle all the details for your sister. A hot bath and her soft bed sounded wonderful at the moment, but that would have to wait. She couldn't be gone long from the dance floor, but she could steal at least ten minutes.

She sank down onto a wooden bench, built to swing with a push. The seat creaked in protest as she shoved off the ground with her right foot. *I'll have to see if Dad or Ethan can fix this old thing.* The bench was her favorite spot anytime she had a rare few minutes to sit with a good book. Kicking off her heels, she groaned in relief—no way in hell would she be able to get the damn things back on now. She should have brought her flip-flops.

Jess closed her eyes and let her head fall forward, a light breeze drying the sweat from the nape of her neck. She hadn't realized until stepping out into the cooler night air how hot and close the dance floor had gotten.

Unfortunately, her hiatus was short lived, interrupted by slapping footsteps on the concrete path.

She grimaced. *So much for a minute of peace and quiet.* She raised her head and strained to see who was coming toward her from the opposite side of the resort. As she squinted into the darkness, the wind picked up noticeably, whispering through the treetops, the faint smell of pine tickling her nose briefly before it was gone.

A beam of light bobbed down the path in tandem with the footsteps.

"Hello?" Jess called out. "Who's there?"

The only immediate response to her question was the moaning of the wind.

I hope a storm isn't blowing in . . .

Figuring it was simply a late wedding guest making their way to the tent, Jess stood, her bare feet cushioned by the damp grass. She didn't want to scare whoever was approaching, sitting there in the dark.

"Hello, are you here for the wedding reception?"

Five more steps and the beam stopped ten feet away, blinding her as the holder now aimed it at her face.

"Oh my God, you scared the hell out of me, Jess! What are you doing out here in the dark?"

Shocked by the voice, Jess's hand flew up to shield her eyes from the beam of light. The flashlight flicked off, throwing them into semi-darkness, the moon their only illumination. Jess didn't need more light. She would know that voice anywhere.

"I could ask you the same thing. What are you doing here, Will? Can't you see there's a wedding going on? And, needless to say, your name is *not* on the guest list."

Jess bristled, furious at her husband for showing up like this, tonight of all nights. She'd managed to avoid seeing Will for months, their only correspondence through their lawyers. He was even a no-show at Lauren's graduation party, claiming he was traveling for work and unable to attend. Instead, he skipped out right after the graduation ceremony and took Lauren out for a fancy dinner later, too immersed in his new life to realize how much his absence from her party had hurt his own daughter.

"Listen, I'm sorry to show up like this, unannounced . . . but I need to talk to you, Jess."

"You aren't just *unannounced*, Will, you're *uninvited*. You aren't welcome here. Now go, get out of here before Nathan or Lauren see you. It'll ruin their evening, and they don't deserve that. You've done enough."

"Jess, come on, just give me ten minutes. This can't wait."

Beyond frustrated and no longer the least bit tired, Jess scooped her discarded heels up, letting the strappy sandals dangle from her fingers.

"Well, I'm not going to stand out here and argue with you in the dark. If I give you ten minutes, will you leave quietly and not cause a scene?"

"Yes, of course. Thank you, Jess. This is important. I wouldn't have come if it wasn't an emergency."

Jess spun on her heel and headed back down the path she had come, but veered left instead of right at the fork in the walkway. She didn't want Will anywhere near the white tent and wedding party.

"The lodge should be open. Hopefully we can talk for a minute in there and then you can leave before anyone else sees you."

Jess led, hustling ahead of the intruder, not willing to walk by his side. The heavy green door of the lodge was indeed unlocked and it groaned on its hinges when Jess pushed against it. She could hear voices back in the kitchen. The caterers would still be cleaning up from dinner.

Great.

She glanced around the entryway, her eyes touching briefly on the wall of old photos lining one wall. The pictures documented previous guests of the resort, dating as far back as the early 1930s. This place had a wonderful history, of which Will wasn't a part. He didn't belong here. She would let him say what he had come to say then get him out of here as quickly as possible and be done with it.

"Come in here," Jess directed.

The small room where they held group discussions during their retreats would be her best bet for privacy. He followed her into the room and she closed the door behind him. There were chairs, but she wasn't going to let Will sit down. She had no intention of giving him that much time to explain himself.

"All right, what was so important it couldn't wait until after my own sister's wedding? Why did you have to come all the way out here, today of all days? Couldn't you have just called?"

That was when Jess finally got a look at Will in the light.

Gone was the immaculately groomed man she had come to associate with the image her soon-to-be-ex always strove to portray. The man standing before her was anything but immaculate. His hair, usually perfectly trimmed and as dark as the day she married him, was now longish and streaked with gray, standing up oddly in places—he'd clearly been running his hands through it in frustration. He wore olive-green cargo shorts, wrinkled and worn, along with an ancient Def Leppard T-shirt Jess would have sworn she hadn't seen since his med school days.

Hiding her initial shock at his appearance, Jess crossed her arms in front of her chest, squinting at Will, waiting for him to speak.

"Jess . . . we have to talk. We're in trouble."

CHAPTER 2
Gift of Solitude

New Year's Eve, six months earlier

"Dad, I know you mean well, but don't worry about me," Jess said. She was trying to convince her father she would be fine out at Whispering Pines, despite the winter storm predicted to blow in by dinner time. George, stubborn as ever, wasn't having it.

"Dad, I have lots of work to do for our January retreat, especially with Renee off gallivanting around Fiji. Besides, I won't be the only one out here. Grant will be around. He hasn't moved home yet, says he enjoys the quiet out here. It gives him a chance to make progress on his novel. He hopes to finish it before spring, you know."

Grant was the twin brother to Renee's first husband. He'd only been part of their lives since the previous winter but they'd all become close. He was a single dad, and with his daughter away at college, he'd stayed on at the resort to use the solitude of winter to write.

"Jess, honey, I do worry about you. All you do is work. Why don't you come in and stay with us tonight? We're going over to your Uncle Gerry's house for some hors d'oeuvres and to watch the ball drop.

She rolled her eyes, though of course he couldn't see that over the phone.

"Oh, gee, Dad, tempting as it is to spend New Year's Eve with my seventy-nine-year-old uncle, I think I'll pass."

Jess paused, afraid she might have gone too far with her snarky comment.

"Come on, Dad, you know me. I've never been a big fan of the whole 'welcome in the new year with a drink in my hand' type of girl. Nathan is already back at college—he could only get three days off from work over the holidays—and Lauren is hanging out with Julie and Grace at their apartment tonight, but I've got Grant. I'll be just fine. And if I'm snowed in for an extra day or two out here, before the plows can come through, I have plenty to keep me busy."

Apparently acknowledging that his daughter wasn't going to budge on this, George accepted defeat, asking only that she be sure to stock some extra food and drinking water in case the storm turned harsher or lasted longer than anticipated.

"Dad, we have enough food in the lodge to feed a small army for a month. I won't go hungry. Now quit worrying about me and go have fun tonight. Tell everyone 'hello' and I'll call you tomorrow, OK?"

Hanging up, Jess uncrossed her fingers, hoping the little white lie she told her father wouldn't come to light. Honestly, she had no idea what Grant's plans were for the evening, and she wasn't even sure whether her friend was back yet from a visit to his relatives in Iowa. Jess simply couldn't stomach the thought of any more forced holiday cheer. The past week had been more than enough for her introverted soul. She was content to spend the evening alone and let her kids, Lauren and Nathan, celebrate with friends.

Her whole family made painstakingly sure to include her in every conceivable holiday event over the past month and a half, this being her first holiday season officially split from Will.

Last year, she had a strong inkling Will was having another affair, but since she kept her suspicions to herself, no one treated her any differently. This year, everyone handled her with kid gloves, probably fearful she was going to fall into the depths of despair over her crumbling marriage.

Too late, guys, she thought, *I've already traveled down that road. I'm so much better off without him.* She quietly admitted to herself that there'd been some tough days since that stormy night last July when she sent him packing, but she was sure she was beyond that emotional rollercoaster now. There was work to be done.

A glance out the window revealed steel-gray storm clouds rolling ominously across the horizon. While sunset wouldn't officially fall until closer to five o'clock, Jess doubted there would be two more hours of daylight today. Zipping her cell phone into her fleece-lined hoodie, she pulled her shin-length parka out of the front hall closet and slipped her feet into the snow boots sitting next to the door. She pulled her new, hand-knit hat down low over her ears and wrapped the matching blue scarf around her neck. Her baby sister, Val, had knitted gifts for everyone this year.

Molly jumped around Jess's feet expectantly, hoping all this preparation meant Jess planned to take her on a walk.

Jess eyed Renee's dog skeptically. "You sure you want to go out there? It's pretty nasty."

Molly's ecstatic response proved she didn't care what the weather was like outside if it meant getting out of this stuffy duplex. Jess shook her head at the spaniel and grabbed a leash off the hook.

"All right, you can come, but I don't trust you to stick close today. Renee would kill me if you took off just before this storm hits."

Jess pushed open the screen door and Molly pulled her through the portal, the dog coughing as her collar cut into her neck. Molly's momentum had her sliding across the porch and scrambling down the steps. Jess resisted, slowing the dog before one or both of them fell on the ice.

I should have cleared this before everything iced over.

"Slow down, Molly! If I fall and break my neck out here, you're going to have to fend for yourself until either Grant gets back or Renee and Matt get back from their vacation. I suspect we would both be popsicles by then, so take it easy!"

Maybe I should have taken Dad up on his offer, Jess considered. *At least I wouldn't spend my night talking to the dog.*

Jess listened as they picked their way down the barely visible path toward the lodge and other cabins. There was little to hear other than the low moan of the wind in the trees. The frigid air froze the hairs in her nose and the wind made her eyes water. Any wildlife in the area must already be hunkered down, their internal systems more failsafe than any weatherman. No lights glowed from Grant's cabin. Looked like she and Molly were on their own—at least for now.

"We'd better get what we need from the lodge and get home, Molly."

As if understanding, the dog turned at the fork in the path, sniffing her way to the back door of the lodge. Jess struggled to pull off her glove in order to insert a key into the lock. Her fingers had already gone numb in the cold, causing her to drop the whole ring into the two-foot-deep snowbank at their feet.

"Crap."

Jess pulled her glove back on and thrust her hand blindly into the snow, her fingers breaking through the crusty upper layer before reaching the granular snow below. She fumbled around for her keys, the fading light not helping her quest. Molly stuck her muzzle into the snow near Jess's fingers, rooted around, and pushed the key ring into Jess's hand.

"That just earned you an extra Scooby snack!" Jess shook the snow off the keys, petting Molly's head in appreciation before driving the key home. Molly continued to sniff around in the snow.

Once inside, she dropped Molly's leash to let the dog wander. Jess strode purposefully back to the kitchen and pulled two reusable grocery bags out of the pantry. She searched the cupboards and fridge, pulling together ingredients to make herself a cheese-and-cracker plate, plus a few other treats to usher in the new year. Molly roamed around the first floor of the lodge, exploring. Jess decided she better find a new book or two from the shelves up in the library before heading back to her place. If the snow did settle in for a couple of days, she would want something to do other than just work.

Upstairs, weak light streamed through the massive windows facing the frozen lake. Jess made her way back to the library in the far corner. The library was, without a doubt, her favorite room at the resort. What book lover wouldn't fall head-over-heels for a room with a cozy fireplace, comfortable couches, and walls lined with books? The shelves were still only partially full but would fill in over time—Jess would see to that.

She found two mysteries she'd heard were page-turners but hadn't made the time to read yet, but as she reached to flip the light off, a small book on the coffee table caught her eye. The cover was a snapshot of a lake with small cabins rimming the shore. It wasn't Whispering Pines, but it looked similar. The title read *History of the Traditional Minnesota Lake Resort.* Maybe there would be something in there about Whispering Pines they could use in their advertising.

You never completely turn off your work mind, do you? Jess asked herself, adding the book to her pile and heading back downstairs to Molly.

They quickly made the trek back to Jess's half of the duplex. The lamp in the living room shone through the picture window, welcoming them home. Renee's half was dark and looked cold and lonely. Jess set her heavy bag of food and books down on the porch before going in, stopping to stomp the snow from her boots and use her glove to brush the majority of the crusted snow out of the crevices in Molly's paws.

"Happy New Year!" Jess hollered to the empty space when they went back inside.

The dog looked at her like she was nuts.

CHAPTER 3

Gift of Bygone Days

*H*appy to be back in her cozy, if still incredibly shabby, home, Jess sat down at the kitchen table with her laptop, her file for their January "New Year, New Beginnings" retreat, and a steaming cup of tea. The aromatic steam tickled her nose with cinnamon and apples, a smell that triggered thoughts of her other home—their family home.

Her definition of "home" had certainly changed since last year.

Exactly one year ago, she had been upstairs in her luxurious ensuite bathroom fussing with hair and makeup, getting ready to go to the annual New Year's Eve party hosted by Will's boss. She'd always despised the annual affair. She remembered she hadn't heard from Will all day but assumed they were still going. He'd always insisted they make an appearance every year.

Last year, by 9:00 p.m., she was sick of waiting for him. As the wife of a surgeon, she should have been used to it—she *was* used to it—but she also knew, at a gut level, the relief she felt to slip off her burgundy velvet dress and climb into her flannels didn't bode well for her marriage.

Will never even bothered to call that evening. He just sent her a text saying something came up and not to wait up. At the time, she'd tried to give him the benefit of the doubt, assuming he was caught up in an emergency surgery, but deep down she knew it was just as likely he was spending New Years with a new squeeze.

Rattling windowpanes brought her back to her small kitchen table at Whispering Pines. She felt an acute sense of relief that Will had never been a part of this place. She didn't mind the "shabby"—she even loved some of its imperfections. Maybe she would have to make a few updates in the spring. To say the oven was unreliable would be a gross understatement, and the fridge often belched out unexplainable sounds, showing its age.

Better knock some things off our checklist for the January retreat, Jess reminded herself, pulling her mind back to the task at hand. She knew Renee felt guilty leaving most of the planning for the upcoming retreat to Jess so she could take a much-needed week of R&R back in Fiji with Matt, but Jess assured Renee she didn't mind. Planning the retreats was fun, for the most part, and it would afford her a needed distraction—and besides, Renee deserved some time with her man. Renee had initially met Matt in Fiji over the previous New Year, so it was symbolic, romantic.

What a difference a year can make, she thought to herself for the umpteenth time.

***

By seven, her stomach was grumbling and her neck felt tight. Standing to stretch out the kinks, she slid the curtains shut against the darkness, surprised to see snow had started falling in earnest while she was lost in her planning. A feeling of total isolation came over her.

The sudden shrill ringing of her cell phone made her jump.

Molly scrambled to her feet, interrupted from her comfortable dreaming.

"It's all right, girl, go back to sleep," Jess assured the dog with a pat as she dug out her phone. She smiled at her daughter's picture on the screen.

"Hi, honey. Happy New Year!"

"Hi, Mom. Happy New Year to you too! What ya doing?"

"Oh, not too much, looking forward to a quiet evening with Molly and a good book."

"Mother, you do know you're kinda boring, right?" Lauren asked with a laugh.

Jess was used to hearing this from her family. The comments didn't bother her. She was perfectly comfortable with her own company, and they knew it.

Lauren went on. "At least you don't have to go to that party with Dad, the one you always hated."

"Funny you should mention that, honey . . . I was just thinking about how much nicer it is to spend New Year's out at Whispering Pines this year. You're so right. I hated dressing up for that stupid party and ushering in the year with a bunch of snobby people I only saw once a year."

"Wait . . . Mom, I thought you were staying at Grandma and Grandpa's house tonight! You're at the resort? Who's out there with you? Don't tell me you're alone."

As a senior in high school, Lauren's horror over the thought of a New Year's Eve night alone—at a remote lake resort—wasn't a surprising response.

"Oh, honey, don't worry about me. We're just fine out here."

Lauren paused. "We? So someone *is* there with you . . . Good."

"Well, actually, I meant me and Molly," Jess admitted, glancing at the dog now sleeping again at her feet. "But Grant might be around."

Jess flicked her gaze to the closed curtains. She doubted anyone would be able to make it to the resort tonight in this weather.

"But, Mom, Julie said it was supposed to storm tonight. Are you sure you're all right out there by yourself? If I would have known you were going to be out there alone, I wouldn't have come over here to Julie's."

Her daughter suggesting she'd sacrifice her own night of fun touched Jess's heart.

"Don't be silly, Lauren. I'm just fine. I am a grown woman, safe and snug at home. You know how I hate parties. You have fun with Julie. What are your plans tonight?"

Julie was Renee's daughter, two years older than Lauren and starting her second year of college. She'd taken the fall semester off after some scary situations with an ex-boyfriend. That ex-boyfriend was now locked up in a mental health facility, but the events were still fresh in Jess's mind.

"We're all staying here. Zoey invited another girl over, too. We're going to watch the ball drop on TV and make a taco bar. Pretty low-key.

"Sounds fun. Tell Julie, Grace, and Zoey 'hi' for me, OK?"

Grace was Grant's daughter, Julie's cousin on her father's side, and a real sweetheart. They hadn't even known of each other until Grant reached out to Renee's in-laws a little over a year ago. Everyone had been shocked to learn that Jim, Renee's late husband, had been adopted as a newborn. His parents had never admitted this to anyone, and Jim never knew he'd been adopted. Grant, Jim's twin brother, reached out because his daughter, Grace, was deathly ill with a disease doctors said would require a transplant. One of Renee's kids, Robbie, turned out to be a match for Grace. The girl was doing much better now, also back in college after time off to heal.

Jeez, our family's turned into a real soap opera, Jess thought to herself, smiling.

"I will, Mom. Are you sure you're all right?" Lauren's concern was still evident.

"Yes, honey, I'm perfectly fine. Thanks for calling. For the last time, don't worry about me. Have fun and I'll talk to you tomorrow. And I love you!"

As Jess expected, her phone rang again within a couple of minutes. This time Nathan's picture smiled back at her from her phone.

"Well, hello there, Nathan. Lauren must have told you your poor mother was home alone on New Year's," Jess teased. "She got that text off to you pretty fast."

"Hey, Mom, how are you?" Nathan asked, apparently refusing to admit that his sister was helping him keep tabs on their mom. "I'm on break. You staying home tonight?"

"Yep. Sure am. For the first time in *years*, I don't have to dress up to go to some stupid party with your father and I am perfectly happy about it."

Nathan gave a little grunt in reply. "Yeah, I know you hated that crap. Do you know what Dad's doing tonight?"

Her son probably asked that simply out of habit, forgetting Jess wasn't in constant contact with his father anymore. She bit back the biting comment that sprang immediately to mind, not wanting to make Nathan feel bad. It had been a tough six months for all of them.

"No, I haven't talked to him. I heard his old boss, McNeal, actually got fired a month or two ago. Some scandal at the hospital. So he must not be going to that annual party. I guess I have no idea what he's up to. What are your plans?"

"We close at ten. I'm going to meet some buddies downtown."

"At the bars?"

"Yeah, for a while at least. And before you start lecturing, don't worry. Since I'm getting a late start, I already told the guys I would be the DD tonight."

Jess sent up a quick word of thanks. If Nathan said he was the designated driver, she could rest assured he wouldn't be getting drunk and doing something stupid. At least she would *try* not to worry . . . much.

"How's work?" she asked.

Jess missed her son. She wanted to keep him on the phone longer. They talked about his part-time job at Barnes & Noble and about his classes. His creative writing course was giving him trouble. Her son had inherited her love for reading. It would be interesting to see where he went with his future career. Unlike Lauren, who was considering something medical, Nathan didn't aspire to spend another decade in school. He was pushing hard to get a degree in four years.

They visited until Nathan's break was over. Hanging up, Jess turned to her only companion.

"All right, Molly, enough of this work stuff. Let's have dinner."

At the mention of food, Molly immediately stood and stretched.

Jess poured kibble in the dog's bowl and threw a plate of cheese, cold cuts, and olives together for herself, then settled on the couch in front of the television.

Molly sniffed at her bowl, looking between her dinner and Jess, as if to say "Really, you couldn't do better than that?" Not bothering to eat anything, the dog instead jumped up on the couch and snuggled against Jess, her muzzle resting on Jess's knee as she sniffed at this much more interesting plate of food.

Jess flipped a piece of cheese to the dog, chuckling. *Am I pathetic or what? Will is probably out with his girlfriend, eating at a fancy five-star restaurant. Here I sit, no one else around for miles—*

The lights flickered.

"Oh no, no, no, no. We can't lose power, Molly."

Jess rose from the couch and hurried to the kitchen. Given this was a working resort—at least when it wasn't the dead of winter—she was well stocked with candles and flashlights for just such occasions. Power lines running through dense woods of pine didn't always mix. She checked her phone, now at only forty-five percent, so she plugged it in to get a little more juice just in case the power actually went down versus quick flicks off and on. With any luck, that wouldn't happen.

She debated between Netflix and one of the books she'd brought over from the lodge, but reading quickly won out—as it usually did for her. She remembered how her brother and sisters used to tease her when they were growing up because she always had her nose buried in a book. Nothing had changed.

The small paperback on Minnesota lake resorts sat on the top of her stack.

Jess grabbed her old white afghan and sat back down to read. She heard the furnace kick in, but the room still felt drafty. The wind was no longer a low, constant hum; intermittent shrieks could be heard, along with what sounded like blasts of sand hitting the windows. Jess shivered, assuring herself it was just wind and sleet. It would be better if it were ten degrees colder outside so it would snow instead of sleet. They would have a mess if this turned into an ice storm. Lower temperatures were forecasted.

Intent on tuning out the sounds of Mother Nature, Jess cracked open the book, wondering how it had ended up in their library. Most books up there were either of the self-help variety or novels meant to entertain or provide an escape from reality. Lauren and Julie helped stock the books with trips to local thrift stores, so Jess decided they'd likely grabbed it then.

The book was older, written in the 1970s. Photos were black and white. Since Minnesota was known as the "Land of 10,000 Lakes," the author would have had plenty of resorts to choose from when deciding which ones to feature. Jess knew Whispering Pines dated back to at least the 1940s, maybe even the 1930s. Celia, her aunt, came here for the first time when she was in college, and she was born in 1923. Celia was enamored with the resort, visiting again and again throughout the years, and eventually managed to buy Whispering Pines.

Jess didn't know all the details, but her aunt's fascination with this place intrigued her. Jess started coming here as a young child with her immediate family, her aunt hosting many of their summer vacations at the Pines. When Celia died in 2015, she left the resort to Renee, which came as a surprise to everyone. She'd been in her nineties by then, so most of the family had assumed Celia sold the place decades earlier. None of them had been out here for years, after all.

Jess suddenly realized she couldn't remember why they'd stopped coming.

Jess and her siblings each received generous bequests from their aunt Celia and all four of them were still figuring out how best to incorporate their gifts into their already busy lives. Part of Jess's inheritance included partial ownership of three small businesses. She knew she'd have to spend more time on all three of the businesses in the year ahead.

Renee inherited Whispering Pines around the same time she got laid off from her company after twenty years, and through a series of events and a ton of family support, Jess's sister made the brave decision to get the old resort up and running again. She took that chance by force and moved her family out here for the summer months. In the past, caretakers Celia hired would maintain the property in the off-season and rent out the cabins during the summer. The resort was only actually closed for one season, but out here it didn't take long for Mother Nature to encroach on things.

Renee, Jess, and the rest of their family worked hard to get things functioning again. When Jess split from Will in July, she asked Renee if she could live in the other half of Renee's duplex. Jess needed somewhere to go and Renee was delighted to have the company. Together they expanded beyond the resort's traditional business of renting cabins to include their growing retreat business. After all, summer rentals alone couldn't cover the cost of running the resort now that property taxes had risen so dramatically.

Jess began thumbing through the book. It was organized first into nine different geographic sections and then alphabetically within each section. Jess was relatively certain the resort had never changed names. While the old wooden sign out on the main road by the turnoff to the resort probably didn't date back as far as the '30s, it did look old enough to have been around when this book was written. Given the hundreds of resorts in Minnesota, Jess didn't expect Whispering Pines to actually be listed in the book, but she was interested to read about others in the same general part of the state.

She flipped two-thirds of the way through the book, to resorts in the center of Minnesota, and thumbed idly through the pictures. The resort two miles north of here was called the Loon's Nest, Jess knew, but it wasn't in the book.

She turned the page and let out a shriek of delight.

"Oh my God, Molly—Whispering Pines *is* in here! I can't believe it!"

Molly didn't even raise her head. The dog simply opened one eye to glance at Jess and gave her tail a wag before continuing her nap.

The section of the book dedicated to their resort was only four pages long, each page partially covered with photos. Jess studied the pictures first. The lodge hadn't changed much. Cars in the parking lot dated the photo. Jess was no expert, but she could hazard a guess that the light-colored Chevy Monte Carlo and dark Ford Mustang in two photos looked to be from the same decade the book was written.

Today, there were five individual cabins at Whispering Pines. The three around the fire pit were right there in one of the pictures. Two of the pictures were taken from a boat, one of the shots capturing a large group of people relaxing on the shoreline and splashing along the water's edge. The stretch of beach in the photo was deeper than what they had now. Time had likely eroded the expanse of sand. Two canoes were pulled up on the sand in the outer edge of one shot.

Jess looked closer and laughed.

"I swear, Molly, these look identical to the old canoe the kids used this past summer. If it *is* one of them, the thing would have to be almost fifty years old. They don't build things to last like that anymore."

Jess studied the remaining pictures. There was Grant's cabin, although it seemed smaller in the picture. His cabin was now the biggest one at Whispering Pines, thanks to an addition built on sometime after the photo was taken. Jess didn't recognize one of the other cabins, but her eye jumped to the last picture.

"Wow . . . look, Molly. This has to be the Gray Cabin," Jess said, holding the book in front of the dog.

Jess practically cackled—she was trying to converse with a dog again!

She took a closer look at the last picture. The size and placement of the cabin was right, but that was where the similarities ended. The cabin in the picture looked new and fresh. A window box overflowing with flowers hung below the single front window. A set of Adirondack chairs sat in front of the cabin. The whole picture exuded the feeling of a peaceful summer setting.

Ironically, if a recent picture of that same cabin was held next to the one in the book, the differences would be striking. The Gray Cabin, as Renee had dubbed it, was a point of pain now. The tiny unit was riddled with problems and had been the site of disturbing events this past summer involving Julie's ex-boyfriend. It was the only cabin Renee had resisted fixing up, now sitting lifeless.

She went back and looked at the other cabin, the one she didn't recognize.

Maybe this picture was placed in the Whispering Pines chapter by mistake . . . ?

It looked similar to the other cabins, but, if this cabin used to be here, it wasn't now. Trees seemed to be closer to this cabin. Maybe it had been set farther back in the woods.

The resort's history, documented briefly in the book, was intriguing. Jess wasn't familiar with some of the lore. According to interviews done by the author, the area upon which Whispering Pines stood was thought to be sacred to the Chippewa, a Native American tribe indigenous to this part of the state. According to the author, some even speculated the land on the northeast corner of the resort might be an ancient burial ground. The land in its entirety was thought to possess special healing properties.

Maybe that's why I feel a sense of calm out here, she thought. *We should use some of this in our marketing for the resort—and especially for our retreats!*

A massive push of wind buffeted the house at the exact moment Jess was thinking back to the many ghost stories told around their bonfires through the years. She vaguely remembered the very first one she'd heard here, about two boys who were said to have gone missing in some cave.

Maybe there is some truth to the stories . . .

The possibility of Whispering Pines sitting on top of an ancient Native American burial ground stayed with Jess for the rest of the evening.

She turned the television on. *I can't go to sleep before midnight,* she thought, despite her drooping eyelids. She stretched out on the old, deep sofa under her hand-knit afghan, the dog snuggled up against her.

The combination of cozy inside and howling wind outside lulled Jess to sleep.

***

Later she would remember snippets of her dreams—glimpses of this land on a vibrant fall day, no cabins breaking the expanse between the edge of the woods and the soft waves lapping the shore line. In her dream, the air was tinged with a smudge of smoke from a low-burning fire on the beach, the air still warm from a bright orange sun, its colors reflected in glorious maple and elm sprinkled in amongst majestic pines. A young Native American woman sat cross-legged before the fire, rocking a small, wrapped bundle in her arms. Silent tears rolled down the woman's brown cheeks. One long black braid draped over the bundle she held, as if offering whatever she was holding in her arms an additional layer of protection. Jess's dream shifted, the land now cold, white, and silent. Only small chunks of charred firewood lay where the fire had crackled before. All appeared deserted. Suddenly a young warrior, his face smeared with bright war paint, strode purposefully out of the woods and into the flat expanse of virgin snow, black eyes sweeping the scene before him. He was searching for something, or someone, a heightened sense of anxiety staining his chiseled cheekbones, although his stoic expression never wavered. He stood motionless for several heartbeats, only his eyes darting over the clearing. He finally threw his head back and screamed a blood-curdling war cry to the frozen heavens above. Hidden flocks of birds took to the sky in protest, their cries joining with that of the man.

***

Jess bolted upright, knocking Molly off her precarious perch on the couch, the dog narrowly missing Jess's snack plate on the coffee table. That high-pitched screech came again, the glass in the windows rattling in protest.

"Aw, come here, girl," Jess said, again making room for Molly. "I'm sorry. I didn't mean to knock you down. Man, this storm is really picking up."

Molly glanced toward the blackness beyond the windows, ears twitching but tail down low. She let out something between a bark and a growl, more like a nervous groan as she jumped back up next to Jess. The dog wasn't a fan of storms, summer or winter.

"Hey, look—we didn't miss the ball drop after all, Molly."

Vowing to stay awake for the last ten minutes of the year, Jess turned up the volume. A scantily clad popstar was trying to belt out a jazzed-up version of a classic Christmas carol, but in Jess's opinion she looked ridiculous in her skimpy outfit surrounded by partygoers in parkas.

"If her teeth weren't chattering so much, maybe her brain would actually remember the words," Jess said, her sarcasm met with a bland stare from the dog.

I am pathetic. Sitting here, talking to my sister's dog on New Year's Eve because I'm too stubborn to listen to Dad. Renee and Matt are probably back on their beach in Fiji right now . . . while I keep her dog company.

The countdown began and Jess ushered in the new year with her first resolution: "I will do everything in my power to make this year *way* better than this last year of disasters!"

Chapter 4

Gift of a Nudge

$\mathcal{S}$ now fell steadily throughout the night while Jess slept, and the blizzard delivered twelve more inches than originally predicted. By morning, the concrete-colored clouds and roaring winds were miles away.

Jess woke to a damp doggy nose pushing against her cheek. She was disoriented, buried far under the bedding. Frigid air enveloped her when she threw back the covers. Her eyes slammed shut in protest against the bright sunlight streaming in.

"How can it be so bright and so friggin' cold at the same time? I hope the furnace didn't go out, Molly."

Thankfully she had jumped into bed seven hours earlier still wearing her sweatpants and wool socks. Still, she scooped up her heaviest hoodie from a nearby chair and pulled it on over her T-shirt. It was so cold in the room the warmth from her breath and face fogged her glasses when she put them on.

Shivering and rubbing her hands together in a futile attempt to warm up, Jess skipped down the stairs with Molly on her heels. She started to cross the living room toward the basement stairs to go down and check the furnace but the dog stopped in front of the door and yipped.

"Sorry, girl. You can't wait, huh?"

Molly yipped again in response.

Jess sighed. "Let's get this over with."

She jammed her stockinged feet back into her heavy boots and again bundled up from head to toe, fully expecting to step out into bitter cold. She pulled the front door inward but had to shove hard on the outer screen door. Six inches of snow lay tight up against the house, the roof over the small porch only partially protecting against last night's wind. Grumbling, Jess waded through the snow to the shovel propped against the far wall of the porch. She needed to clear the porch and stairs.

Molly bounded down to the grass, the snow as high as her back in places but not quite solid enough to slow her down. After taking care of business, the dog played around in the fresh drifts.

"Stay close, Molly," Jess warned as she cleared her way to the top step.

Suddenly, Molly stopped her frolicking and faced the lodge, barking. She kept at it long enough for Jess to look up to see what had Molly so uptight. In the summer, trees blocked much of the view between the duplex and the rest of the resort, but naked trees in winter allowed for a less obstructed view. Jess squinted in the direction of the lodge. Sunlight glinted off something red and out-of-place on the road leading up to the lodge parking lot, catching her eye.

"Molly, what *is* that?" Jess propped her shovel back up against the porch railing and waded down the stairs to try to get a better look. Now the little sliver of red grew to a whole vehicle.

"Oh my God, Molly, that looks like Grant's car! Come on."

Jess hurried toward the four-door sedan. Trudging through the snow was tough. Even though it was more powdery out in the open, it was almost thigh-high in some places, only an inch deep in others—a testament to the massive winds of the night before.

The car sat a hundred yards short of the lodge parking lot. The passenger side faced Jess and Molly as they approached. The snow was drifted as high as the bottom of the window. All was eerily quiet.

"Grant?!"

Jess reached the car and trudged around the front of it, trying to peer into the windshield. The snow on the driver's side barely covered the ground. Jess couldn't see anyone in the car, but yanked open the door to double-check, starting to panic just a little.

Where's Grant . . . ?

The car was empty. No footprints, either, other than new ones she just made.

"Doesn't he know better than to leave his vehicle if he gets stuck in a snowstorm?" Jess asked, her voice rising along with her concern.

Oh shit . . . what if he got lost in the storm and froze to death?

Jess spun in a circle, falling into a full-blown panic as she scanned the area for any sign of her friend.

Molly's only response was to continue sniffing around the surrounding area, not appearing to have any answers.

Jess walked out farther from the stalled car, looking around frantically. She knew it was stupid to panic and so tried to take deep breaths to calm down.

"Grant . . . Grant Johnson . . . where are you?!"

Her voice echoed back at her, but nothing else. She tried again.

Finally she heard a response: a slamming screen door.

"Hey, what's all the yelling about, Jess? Give me a sec, I'll be right over!"

Limp with relief, Jess sagged against the car.

At the sound of the familiar voice, Molly ran over to the cabin back along the edge of the woods—Grant's cabin. The dog waited until he came out a minute later, pulling on a jacket.

He jogged over to where Jess stood next to his car, the snow slowing his progress.

"Oh my God, Grant, you scared me to death. What happened? Did you get stuck? Don't you know better than to leave your vehicle in the middle of a storm?"

Grant broke through the last snowbank to stand a few feet from Jess, his blue eyes shielded by a Twins baseball cap, bare hands in the pockets of his jeans. Those eyes were the only thing about Grant that resembled his twin brother Jim. Over time, Jess came to recognize similarities between Renee's late husband and Grant, but it was in their mannerisms and personalities more than their physical appearance.

"Sorry, Jess. I didn't mean to scare you. I didn't figure anyone else was out here in that weather last night. The closer I got to Whispering Pines the harder the wind blew, and I regretted my decision to make the trip before the storm moved out. The drive was brutal. It was snowing and blowing so hard. I *almost* made it," he said, motioning to his stuck car.

She wasn't letting him off the hook that easily. "So you left your car in a snowbank and walked to your cabin. Could you see *anything?*"

Now Grant leveled a look at Jess.

"Hey, relax, I made it, OK? You can stop lecturing me now."

Jess pushed off the car and stepped closer to Grant, wrapping her arms around his waist and resting her forehead against his chest.

"All right, truce. Sorry. You scared me."

He hugged her back. "I truly am sorry about that, Jess. Hey, I just made a pot of coffee. Why don't you come over and I can fill you in on my little adventure?"

Jess pulled back, shivering as the adrenalin wore off and the cold seeped in despite her heavy winter gear.

"Sounds good. It's freezing out here."

The three of them trudged back over to Grant's cabin. The homey smell of coffee met them at the door as they stomped the snow off their boots (and paws) and stepped into the welcoming warmth.

"It feels and smells like *heaven* in here," Jess said. "I think my furnace went out last night. I woke up to an icicle hanging off my nose this morning."

Grant glanced back at her as he pulled coffee cups out of the cupboard and filled each cup.

"Really? Did you check the pilot light?"

Jess moaned in pleasure as she took the full cup Grant handed her, inhaling deeply and warming her fingers against the ceramic mug.

"I was headed that way when Molly had to go out. Then we saw your car stuck in a snowbank and we got a little distracted." The sarcasm was back in her voice, masking the relief she felt at finding her friend unharmed.

"Again, sorry about that. Here, sit," Grant said, pulling a chair out for her before taking a seat on the opposite side. "Believe me, I know I made more than one stupid decision last night. I shouldn't have driven out here in the first place, given that storm. I was *so* close, too. One minute I could see the old streetlight by the lodge, then it was gone. The snow was disorientating. The car just bogged down and that was it. I couldn't get any traction and knew I was stuck."

Grant paused to take a sip of his steaming coffee.

"And . . . ?" Jess prodded.

"*And*, my final stupid choice of the night was to leave the car. I *do* know better. But it was the weirdest thing. It was like there was a lull in the storm. The wind laid down and I could see the cabins nearest the fire pit in the headlights. I figured if I left my headlights on, I would know which direction to walk and I'd be able to find my cabin without any trouble, even if the wind picked up again. If I stayed in my car, I worried I might run out of gas before the storm cleared—and I would get awfully cold, awfully fast, if that happened."

Molly gave Grant a little bark, her tongue hanging out to the side as she panted. He got up, filled a cereal bowl with water, and set it down for the dog before continuing.

"I thought I would turn off the car, start it again with my remote start, and use the headlights to find my way home. Then I'd turn off the car with the remote so the battery wouldn't get totally drained."

"So did it work?"

"Well . . . not exactly. Once I turned off the car, it wouldn't start again. Then I had to decide whether to try finding my cabin in the dark, since the headlights only stay on for less than a minute after the car is turned off, or stay in a cold car that wouldn't start. Since the wind had calmed down, I thought I could make it home without too much trouble . . ."

His voice trailed off.

"I sense a 'but' there."

"I made it as far as the lodge parking lot when the wind started howling again. The light from my phone didn't do much. Guess I got a little turned around. I walked for quite a while, thinking I had to be close, when I saw a set of steps in my wimpy little light. But it wasn't my cabin. It was the Gray Cabin, locked up tight."

"So how did you find your way from the Gray Cabin to yours in the storm? I know how dark it is back there, even on a good night."

"I had to sit for a minute and catch my breath. My eyes stung from the blowing snow, felt like little needles jabbing me in the eyeballs. By then I realized this could have a very bad ending if I wasn't *really* careful. I offered up a quick prayer and stood, knowing I didn't dare sit too long."

Jess shivered, an unwelcome image of a frozen Jack Nicholson at the end of *The Shining* morphing into Grant, frozen to death on the steps of the Gray Cabin in the crisp morning light. She pushed the awful vision away.

Grant paused, rose from his chair, and grabbed the coffee pot, topping off their mugs. He appeared to consider his next words carefully.

"It was the weirdest damn thing, Jess. I hate to even admit this out loud . . . but it was as if something showed me the way. When I stood up, everything was a mass of swirling white in the weak little beam from my phone. I took about three steps in what I thought was the direction of my cabin when I heard something crash behind me. I turned toward the sound and something pushed me in that direction instead. It was like . . . like there was a little hand pushing against my back, nudging me forward. I suppose it was just a blast of wind, but it felt more substantial at the time. Without any better options, I trusted the sign. I tell you, it was like walking into a white abyss. I was starting to lose hope again when I heard another banging sound right in front of me. A few more steps and *bam*, the toe of my boot hit something solid. Damned if it wasn't another set of stairs—*my own* this time. I gotta admit, I could have cried I was so relieved."

Jess reached across the table and clasped Grant's hand.

"Oh my God, Grant . . . I hate the thought of you wandering around out here last night, lost, while I was holed up all cozy in the duplex. Why didn't you call?"

Grant gave Jess's hand a return squeeze before releasing it and sitting back in his chair, rolling his shoulders.

"I honestly thought I was all alone out here. I never dreamt you would be out here in this weather, on New Year's Eve, all by yourself. I figured you were at George and Lavonne's or with your kids somewhere. Besides, I got myself into that mess. What could you have done, besides get lost out there in the snow with me, if I'd've called you?"

"I guess you're right," Jess acknowledged. "And everything turned out fine, thank God."

Grant nodded in agreement but quickly changed the subject.

"By the way, what exactly *are* you doing out here by yourself on New Year's?"

"Being stubborn," Jess laughed. "Dad invited me over, but I had work to do and thought a quiet evening at home sounded good. There's still lots to be done for our retreat in a couple of weeks. Work is busy, too— plus, I'm trying to get a better handle on the businesses Celia asked me to look after."

"You know, Jess, you don't have to work *all* the time."

"I know. Honestly, I like to lose myself in the details. Nice escape from the mess the rest of my life has become."

"I get it," Grant said. "When Grace was so sick, I would sometimes lose myself in my writing for hours on end. Gave my brain a break from the worry."

Jess nodded and stood, circling the table to give him a quick side hug. "Thanks for the coffee. Don't ever scare me like that again," she warned, a smile taking the bite out of her words. "I better go figure out what's going on with the furnace. What are you going to do about your car?"

"I already made a couple calls. The guy from the garage in town gave me the name of another guy that does snow removal. He's coming out with his tractor this afternoon to clear the road. After that's done, they'll send a tow truck out to pull me out and get my car running again."

"Hmm, thanks for lining that up. I hadn't even thought about how to get that road cleared yet. This is the first big snow of the winter."

Grant waved off her thanks. "I may need to think twice about trying to ride out the whole winter out here in this cabin. Unlike the duplex, it wasn't really meant to be year-round."

"I know Renee was worried about that, too. Man, can you imagine if it storms like this again when we have people here for a retreat?"

"Something to keep in mind," Grant agreed. "I'll feel better when Matt's back in the area. Their office has access to better weather reports. We'll have to be sure to put a little scare in Renee for how nasty it can get out here when it storms. She isn't going to want to put anyone in danger." Grant stood as well, pushing his chair back under the table. "Need help with your furnace?"

"Thanks for the offer, but let me try to see if I can figure it out. I'll call you if I can't get it going. I need to learn how to handle these types of things if I'm going to be on my own." Jess walked to the door. "Not that Will would have bothered to figure out how to get a furnace going. He'd have just called someone. I've got a few hours of work to do, but I planned to throw together a meatloaf for dinner later. If you're bored, come over to eat about six."

"Sounds good, Jess, I'll probably take you up on that. That'll give me time to get another chapter done."

Jess let herself out. Molly followed close behind.

Thank God Grant found his cabin last night . . . That could have been horrible.

Trudging back home, she was careful not to drop her phone in the snow as she Googled how to ignite a pilot light on a furnace. She didn't want to freeze to death, either.

CHAPTER 5

Gift of a New Address

*T*hree days later, Molly went crazy at the front door, barking like mad. The noise pulled Jess out of deep concentration. She stood up from her computer, arching her back and tossing her glasses down on the kitchen table.

"Are they home, girl?" Jess asked, although the dog's actions had already confirmed her masters' arrival. They were due back from their holiday trip to Fiji.

Jess was halfway to the door when it swung inward and Renee came through, dropping to her knees and catching Molly up in a hug. Standing again after greeting her pet, Renee kicked off her ankle boots and swooped into the living room, catching Jess up in a big hug as well.

Jess hugged her sister back, laughing. Renee had always been more of a hugger than Jess.

"I'm surprised you're in such a good mood," Jess said, taking a step back. "Thought you'd be depressed coming home to all this snow. Looks like you worked on your tan. How was Fiji?"

"Even better than last year," Renee said, peeling off her jacket and tossing it on her sister's couch. "Got any coffee?"

"Sure, let me flip it on. It'll just take a second. Where's Matt?"

"He's unloading the car."

As if on cue, Jess could hear heavy footsteps trudging up the stairs on the other side of their adjoining wall. She smirked at her sister as if to say *What, you can't help?*

Renee held her hands up in defense. "He insisted. He knew I would want to see you."

With that, Renee pulled off her stocking hat, light reflecting off her left hand.

"Oh my God, what is *that*?" Jess asked, grabbing her sister's hand.

There, on Renee's ring finger, was a large solitaire. That particular finger had been naked for years.

"Want to help me plan a wedding?" Renee asked, grinning from ear to ear.

Jess, ever the cautious, conservative sister, didn't reply with a scream or another round of hugs. Instead, she leveled her sister with a thoughtful gaze.

"Isn't that awfully fast, sis?"

Renee laughed, undeterred by her sister.

"Jess, I'm a big girl. I know Matt has only been here a few months, but *technically* I've known him for a year now. He gave up his job in Fiji to be closer to me and the kids. These last few months have proven to me that we *belong* together, Jess. Now, come here and give me another hug. Don't be such a cynic."

Jess let herself be caught up in another hug, giving her sister a quick squeeze in return. She was facing the door when Matt appeared, his broad shoulders filling the entryway as he stepped inside.

"I see Renee didn't wait long to share our news," Matt said with a grin that said he was fully aware Jess might not be thrilled the two of them had decided to take the next step.

Jess pulled out of Renee's embrace and approached the man her sister seemed set on marrying, stopping a few feet from him, hands on her hips.

The previous year, after losing her job and vowing to make the most of her unexpected time off, Renee took Julie and Robbie on a last-minute trip to Fiji. Jess remembered Renee telling her that shortly after boarding the plane for their tropical trip, she'd nearly fallen into a panic attack. She'd felt reckless and irresponsible. But she'd run into Matt on their first day on the island when she locked her keys in their rental and he came to their aid. She couldn't have known what a blessing that stupid mistake would prove to be.

"Matthew . . . I have to say I am more than a little surprised. I do admit, though, I haven't seen Renee this happy in a *very* long time. But I'm warning you—if you break her heart, you will have *me* to answer to."

Matt laughed and strode the few additional feet into the room to come eye to eye with Jess. Knowing the woman probably wouldn't appreciate another hug . . . he hugged her anyway. Then he pulled away and held out his hand, still grinning.

Jess looked from his hand to his eyes, seeming to search there for assurance he would take care of her sister. With a sigh, Jess shook his hand.

"You do know I'm serious, right? She's been through a lot and she deserves to be happy."

Matt nodded in agreement, growing serious. "I have every intention of making your sister a very happy woman and growing very old with her."

"See that you do," Jess said, finally giving a little laugh and surprising Matt with an unprompted little hug. "Because if you don't, I know people," she whispered, for his ears only, and Matt let out a belly laugh.

"I consider myself adequately warned. Now, why don't I let you two catch up? I need to bring in a few more things from the car and I should probably call into the office." And with that, he made his exit. As the local sheriff, Matt would have plenty to catch up on now that they were back.

Jess shook her head at him as he left, then went back to the kitchen and made Renee that cup of coffee.

"Have you told Julie and Robbie yet?"

"No," Renee said. "We thought we would get unpacked first and then drive over to pick up Robbie from Mom and Dad's. We'll get Julie on the phone from there and tell everyone at the same time."

Jess busied herself with getting out an herbal tea bag—she didn't need more caffeine at the moment, but Renee's surprise announcement had her nerves on edge. While Renee took her coffee out to the living room and sat down to pet Molly, Jess took a minute to gather her thoughts. She suspected her niece, Julie, would be happy for her mom. She was away at college and would probably like the idea of her mother having a man in her life again. Robbie, on the other hand, might not be so thrilled. He was already facing big changes, switching schools mid-year. Renee had let him attend his old school back home for the first semester of his sophomore year and stay with family friends, but she didn't want to be apart from him for the second half of the school year. He was upset he wasn't getting to play basketball with his old team, but since he broke his arm in a scrimmage game in his friend's driveway before Christmas, he wouldn't have had much playing time anyhow.

"How do you think the kids will react?" Jess asked her sister as she joined her with her own cup.

"Well, I'm hoping they'll be happy about it. They both like Matt. They might have the same reaction you did, though . . . thinking it's a little fast. I hope they'll be supportive. It's been just the three of us for so long, I know it might take some getting used to."

"I think they'll be fine with it eventually, maybe just surprised at first. Robbie is the one you might need to handle a little more carefully. He's facing lots of change right now, especially for his age."

"I know," Renee said, concern showing in the worry lines on her face, dimming the glow from her eyes. She'd always be a mother first.

Jess forced a smile. "So, tell me about your trip."

***

Jess struggled to concentrate on the spreadsheet in front of her. Her mind kept wandering back to Renee's big announcement. Her sister was getting *married*. Again. How would that change the dynamics at the resort? Jess already considered this place home. She still technically owned the house with Will—at least until their divorce was final—but she'd moved most of her things out months ago. She didn't think there was much left in the house she wanted to keep.

Lauren had tried to live in their house with Will when school first started back up in the fall. It was her senior year of high school, and no one wanted her to have to switch schools so close to graduation. The resort was over an hour away so it wasn't practical for Lauren to stay with Jess during the week. While not ideal, it should have worked.

But, like so many "should haves" in their lives these days, it didn't work out as planned.

Less than two weeks into the school year, Lauren called Jess in tears. Will's new girlfriend, Tiffany, had been staying at the house every night. After the initial shock of learning the woman existed in her father's life, Lauren had mistakenly assumed she might run into the woman once in a while and she would just have to try to tolerate her until graduation. Then Lauren could move back to the resort with Jess for the summer until leaving for college in the fall.

Instead, the woman all but moved into Jess's former home. So far, Jess had managed to avoid meeting her, but based on things Lauren shared, Jess understood why her daughter wasn't comfortable at home and was staying with George and Lavonne most nights.

The situation with Lauren weighed on Jess. She would have given anything to allow her daughter to have a "normal" senior year—a year that was supposed to be full of friends, happy memories, and the usual anxious moments over graduating and moving on to whatever would come next. Instead, Lauren found herself sharing her childhood home with her father's mistress, a woman fifteen years younger than him.

The woman apparently acted like she'd won the lottery. Jess wondered how long it would be until Tiffany figured out she actually won the "booby prize"—she'd told this much to Lauren, who'd laughed.

Unfortunately, it'd probably be a while. Will could be charming when he wanted to be. After all, he'd fooled Jess for years and she considered herself a pretty good judge of character.

Sighing deeply, Jess forced herself to focus on the financial report lying on the table in front of her. Her wandering mind struggled to make sense of the numbers she was attempting to follow, but she needed to figure this out. Her aunt Celia had high expectations of Jess's business acumen. After all, she'd chosen to leave most of her stock and business portfolio to Jess upon her death. Jess hoped she was up for the challenge, but if today was any indication, Celia's trust might have been misplaced.

The financials she was attempting to understand were the preliminary year-end results for a house-cleaning service called Homes Sparkle, Inc.

Two sisters ran the company, and according to notes Celia left to Jess about the business, neither woman had an aptitude for numbers. The women's parents, Joyce and John Robins, started the company nearly thirty years earlier and Celia had been one of their first and most loyal customers. When they struggled to make payroll in the early years, Celia provided them with financial backing and business advice in exchange for a twenty percent ownership. Once the Robins reached their late sixties, they decided to pass the business on to their daughters and spend their winters down south. They'd hoped their girls were equipped to handle the various aspects of running Homes Sparkle, but . . .

The older daughter, Wendy, had managed their team of housekeepers for the five years leading up to her parent's full retirement. It was demanding work keeping track of the logistics behind scheduling multiple homes for cleaning every day, made even more challenging by the often transient nature of their staff. Jess knew within minutes of meeting Wendy that Celia would have found a kindred spirit in the woman.

Celia, an extremely successful businesswoman in her own right, always had a soft spot in her heart for others struggling to find their way. She used to provide financial support to both of the women's shelters in town and even spent time teaching classes, trying to help the women get on their feet. Always having been single herself, she was a firm believer in helping other women be self-sufficient. Wendy shared the same commitment.

Jess glanced up from her work at the sound of a knock on her door. Not waiting for an answer, Renee let herself in.

"What are you up to?" she asked.

Jess removed her glasses, stuck them on top of her head, and pushed back slightly from the table.

"Trying to understand these numbers for Homes Sparkle."

"Ah, yes, one of Celia's pet projects. Did they have a good year?"

Jess considered how best to respond. "Well . . . things looked all right when I reviewed their third-quarter numbers. But these show a little different story," she said, motioning to her laptop and the mess of papers spread across her kitchen table. "The expenses seem higher. At first glance, things look a little strange."

"Well, sis, if I know you—and I do, last I checked—you'll figure it out. That's why Celia left so much of her actual ownership interests to you."

Jess hoped Renee was right. Some days it all felt overwhelming. She was trying to balance so many things, between her day job, helping Renee with the retreats, and the small handful of businesses Celia had still been actively involved in up until her death. Not to mention her two kids and the mess her separation was turning out to be. But the woman had been over ninety when she last worked on these, for crying out loud! Who still worked at that age? Celia, of course, but not because she had to. Their aunt thrived on staying active and helping others, right up until the end.

I can't fail her now, Jess thought. If her aunt could handle all of this at more than twice her age, Jess certainly could too.

"You're right, I'll figure it out. I just need to spend more time with these numbers. What brings you over?"

"Since our 'New Year, New Beginnings' retreat starts in a few days, I thought we should double-check everything to make sure we're ready."

Jess nodded, her brain already switching gears. "Good idea, let me grab my file real quick."

***

The two reviewed their plans for the next hour, making calls and setting up schedules.

Jess was aware of Renee the whole time, pacing Jess's small kitchen.

"For God's sake, Renee, would you sit? You're making me dizzy just watching you," Jess said. "What has you so wound up? Seems like we're in good shape for next week."

Renee helped herself to a glass from the cupboard and filled it with tap water before answering. She took a few sips and dumped the rest down the drain, returning to the table and plopping down in the old chair.

"I know, I know . . . I think the retreat will be great. I just . . ."

"Renee? What is it?"

"It isn't the retreat I'm worried about."

Jess never let anyone beat around the bush too long. "Well, come on, then—spill it."

Renee eyed Jess for another second before replying.

"Have you heard from Lauren or Nathan today?"

Renee's question confused Jess, but her mother's instinct was already tingling. "It's the middle of the day on a Tuesday. They're both in school. Why would you think I might have talked to them today?"

Renee pulled her purse off the back of her chair and dug out her phone. She fiddled with it for a second before handing it to her sister.

"Looks like Will's girlfriend had their baby."

CHAPTER 6

Gift of an Innocent

*J*ess studied the picture on Renee's phone for a minute before replying. She'd known this day was coming, had dreaded it since Will first told her he was going to be a father again, months ago.

That tiny person looks an awful lot like Lauren did, Jess thought.

She had to admit, if only to herself, that the baby was beautiful—all rosy and pink, not wrinkled like some newborns. But the woman holding the infant was on an entirely different level.

"If that woman is the mother, she looks like she visited the salon before she allowed anyone to post any pictures," Jess said aloud. "Who the hell looks like that right after giving birth?"

"I hate to break it to you, but she *is* the mother," Renee confirmed.

"How do you know? Maybe she's an aunt or something."

"Lauren posted a picture of herself, Will, and some woman on Snapchat last fall. I figured it had to be the girlfriend. I think it was back before Lauren decided she hated the woman, too. That's her," Renee said, motioning at her phone, now lying on the table in front of Jess as if it were too hot to touch.

"Why am I even surprised?" Jess asked. "Of *course* anyone Will hooked up with would be just as concerned about appearances as he is."

Renee laughed. "You know, sis, you can vent all you want to me. But you might want to cool it a little when you talk to your kids. That baby is their half-sister."

"Don't remind me," Jess said with a groan. "I can only imagine how this is going to complicate things. It's one thing to have your husband cheat on you with another woman. But to have him start a new family with her, before his divorce is even final with yours truly? It stings. A lot. I'm just glad it's her and not me. She can deal with his shit now. I'm done with it all."

"But you *will* play nice around your kids, right?" Renee persisted.

"I'll be sweet as honey, sugar," Jess answered sarcastically, her fake Southern drawl thick enough to get them both laughing.

It's laugh or cry, Jess thought, aching inside.

***

Jess did cry, but she managed to keep the tears bottled up inside until Renee left to throw something together for dinner. Matt was coming over, she said, and invited Jess to join them, but Jess begged off, claiming she had too much work to do.

The floodgates opened the moment she heard Renee banging cupboard doors next door. Jess made her way upstairs to her bedroom, threw herself face down on her comforter, and allowed herself a good old cry.

I've earned it, she told herself. *That man put me through hell and I'm almost all the way through the crap. Now I just have to push through this last insult, act like this isn't killing me inside, and come out at the other end of all this drama to the point where I'm actually,* finally, *happy without him.*

Eventually, there were no more tears.

I vow I will never *shed another tear over that man again,* she promised herself.

But if she was going to be honest, she figured there was only about a fifty-fifty chance of actually pulling that promise off.

***

She must have dozed off at some point, because she was startled awake by the ringing of her cell phone.

Well, here we go, she thought as her son's face looked back at her from her screen. *Time to put my game face on. Or at least my game voice.*

"Hey honey, what's up?"

"Hi, Mom. Thought I better give you a call. Talk to Dad yet?"

Jess sighed. It was obviously going to take more time before Nathan was acclimated to the fact his parents weren't exactly on speaking terms these days.

"No, I haven't talked to him for a few weeks. But I suspect you're calling with baby news?"

"Oh. You already heard, huh?"

"Renee was over and she saw it on Facebook. She showed me."

"Crap, I'm sorry, Mom. I didn't want you to find out that way."

Jess slipped into her protective mother mode. "Nathan, don't worry about it. I'm a big girl and we've all known this was coming for months. I'm honestly relieved this part is over. Now maybe your dad will stop dragging his feet over stupid little technicalities in the divorce settlement and move on. Besides, the baby is cute. You have a new little sister."

She tried to muster an ounce of excitement in that last part, but she wasn't sure Nathan was convinced. He didn't immediately reply, but Jess could hear him sigh.

"Yeah ... baby sister ... how weird is that? But wait, back up. What did you say about Dad dragging his feet?"

"Oh, never mind, it's nothing."

Jess could have kicked herself. She tried hard not to pull either kid into the mess of their divorce. Will's hesitancy to sign the final papers had her confused as well, but she didn't want either of her kids to worry about it. She had been so concentrated on pretending not to be phased about the baby news she'd neglected to keep the rest of the bitterness out of her words.

"When are you going to go see the baby?" Jess asked, trying to steer the conversation in another direction. "Do you know her name yet?"

"Harper."

Jess cringed. *Damn, that's cute.*

"Are you going up to the hospital to see her?" she asked again.

"Nah. Dad called, but he said they would have us over in a couple of weeks. Said it was crowded up at the hospital. Guess *she* has lots of visitors."

Given the emphasis Nathan placed on "she," Jess suspected he meant Tiffany had lots of visitors, not necessarily Harper. And it gave her hope that her son didn't like this new woman either. But something else he said suddenly registered.

"What do you mean, 'they'll have us over'? Is that woman at the house all the time now? Have you talked to Lauren?" She didn't bother censoring herself with the "that woman."

"I talked to her right before I called you," Nathan replied. "She sounded relieved that Dad didn't seem to expect us to come up to the hospital, pretending to be the perfect family."

"Did she seem upset?" Jess was concerned this was going to have a much bigger impact on Lauren. Nathan was away at college.

"You know Lauren. She tried to act like she was fine, but her voice had that edge to it she always gets just before she loses it."

Jess knew exactly what Nathan meant. Lauren often tried to act like nothing bothered her, but she wasn't very good at hiding her true feelings.

"I do appreciate your call, honey. I better call Lauren quick, make sure she's OK."

"Yeah, all right, Mom, but wait. Do I have to buy the baby a gift or something?"

Jess's heart broke a little bit more.

"No, honey, you don't have to. If you want to pick up a little something, that's fine. But don't feel obligated. This is all just a tad bit bizarre."

"You can say that again. I'll call you tomorrow, I gotta be at work in fifteen."

Relieved she'd been able to hold it together with her first kid, she braced herself for what might be a tougher phone call. She dialed Lauren's number, but the call went straight to voice mail. Unable to resist, she opened Facebook and scrolled through recent posts.

It didn't take long to hit a picture featuring her ex's smiling face above a bundle in his arms. There were more, but she couldn't look at them for long. Nathan was right: the photos showed a crowded hospital room full of people, but she only recognized one.

It was all so surreal. Pictures out there for the world to see. Twenty years ago, Will's actions would have appalled most, and a new baby, born out of an illicit affair, certainly wouldn't have been paraded out in the open. Now, no one seemed to think anything of it.

Except, of course, the family he left behind.

***

When Lauren still hadn't called her back by 7:00 p.m., Jess was getting concerned. She called her mother. Lavonne picked up immediately.

"Hi, honey, how are you?"

Jess could tell from the tone of Lavonne's voice she'd heard the news.

"I'm fine, Mom. Is Lauren there? I can't get ahold of her."

"She is. She came home about five and is up in your room. Said she had lots of homework and she'd already eaten. She didn't come down when I let her know dinner was ready."

"Is she upset?"

"Probably, but she isn't about to talk about it. You know our Lauren."

Jess had to laugh. "I know exactly what you mean. I'm just so relieved she's there with you two. I had visions of her sitting in her room at the house, all alone, dreading the moment her father would bring that woman and Harper home."

"Harper?"

"Yes. You do know Will's 'friend' had her baby, right? Nathan said that's what they named her."

Lavonne sighed. "Renee called to warn me. She said you were really upset and she thought Lauren might show up, since she's here most of the time anyhow."

Jess balked. "Why would Renee say I was upset?"

"Honey, I hate to break this to you, but apparently that wall between your side of the duplex and Renee's is rather thin. I'm sorry. I know you deserve your privacy. I shouldn't have let on that Renee heard you crying."

"So much for me having *that* to myself. Guess I'm no better than Lauren at hiding my feelings."

"That's where you're wrong, dear. You hold *way* too much inside, deep down. I'm never sure if you really are all right or if you're just pretending."

"Whew, what a relief. I thought I was starting to slip." This time Jess wasn't being sarcastic. She really did work hard to keep her feelings private. "Thank you, again, Mom, for being there for Lauren. I'm sorry my split with Will is impacting you like this."

"Don't be ridiculous! You *must* know how much we love having Lauren here. This is a special time. She'll be gone before you know it, off to college and then the world of adulthood. We're lucky to have her."

Lavonne, ever perceptive, recognized what she'd said the minute it was out of her mouth.

"Oh, honey, I'm so sorry. That came out all wrong. I know you would give anything to be spending this time with Lauren. I didn't mean to be insensitive."

Jess shrugged her shoulders and shook her head, despite the fact her mother couldn't actually see her through the phone. "Don't worry about it. I'm fine, and you and Dad are amazing. Hey, will you please ask Lauren to call me if she ever comes out of her hiding spot? I really do want to make sure she's all right."

Lavonne assured her she would. "But, you know, honey, Lauren is growing up. She needs some space to process this too. Try not to worry too much. I'll keep a close eye on her and I'll give you a call if I sense anything I think you should be worried about."

"Thanks, Mom. What would I do without you?"

CHAPTER 7

Gift of New Skills

*J*ess chewed on her lip to keep from laughing at the ragtag line of women stretching out ahead of her. So far, their first retreat of the new year was proving to be a success, but she wasn't convinced she would be able to bring everyone home safely from this *particular* excursion.

The previous evening, two different guests pulled her aside, individually, to thank her. One had been moved by Jess's heart-felt sharing with the group after dinner; the woman recently separated from her spouse and expressed appreciation for Jess's candor and honesty. Both guests felt inspired by the energy of the group as a whole. Renee reported a few others also made positive comments to her, so the sisters knew they were on the right track.

They wanted to get everyone out for some fresh air this morning and had rented cross-country skis for those interested. Since their theme for the weekend was to *Open Yourself Up to New Possibilities*, a few brave souls in the group were taking that advice. They'd obviously never done this before. Jess grimaced as one woman fell over on her side—hard—and not for the first time.

We'll be lucky if we don't get sued over this, Jess thought.

She left her post at the back and glided up to the woman struggling to rise out of a snowbank.

"You all right, Marnie?" she asked, stooping to give the woman a hand.

"You bet. Nothing hurt but my pride," came the reply, although Jess suspected Marnie would be in pain by the next morning if she wasn't already.

"Do you want to go back?"

To this Marnie let out a bark of laughter. "Are you kidding? I may suck at this, but it's a beautiful morning and I don't want to be stuck inside. Give me a minute, I'll get the hang of it."

"OK," Jess replied, "but just let me know if you change your mind."

She skied back to the end of the line, and by the time she turned back around she was happy to see the guest right behind Marnie was sharing some pointers with her—hopefully the stubborn woman would listen.

The eight women eventually got into a bit of a groove, making progress on the trails. The air was crisp and the sunlight bright. Peggy, their yoga instructor, was branching out—leading the group over the groomed path. Her voice echoed high into the treetops as she started singing "Fight Song" by Rachel Platten, a very appropriate song given the reason they were all gathered. Jess would have to remember to suggest to Renee that they look into the copyright issues with possibly making it their retreat's anthem.

By the time they looped back to the resort, it was well after one o'clock. The aroma of grilled meat and vegetables met the famished skiers. Jess and Renee's younger sister, Val, stood next to the source of the divine scent. Val's skill around a barbeque was already legendary and the unexpected surprise of outdoor cooking was another one of her contributions to the retreat.

"All right, ladies," Jess announced loud enough to get everyone's attention. "Why don't we leave the boots and skis here, against the side of the lodge, and head inside? That was quite the workout, and if you're all as sweaty as I am, we should strip out of these clothes quick and put on something dry and comfortable so we can eat!"

"I'll need about fifteen minutes to get lunch set out," Val confirmed. "Go ahead, ladies."

***

The hungry crew ate everything Val had prepared, which turned into a great segue for her afternoon session on healthy cooking. Jess knew, based on earlier conversations, that every single woman in attendance wanted to get healthier in the year ahead.

Val handled all the questions thrown at her with ease. When they found themselves an hour over the scheduled time for the class, Val raised her hand to quiet the group.

"I'm so glad we've had such wonderful participation this afternoon, but if we don't wrap this up pretty soon, I won't have the food ready for tonight's celebration!"

"But, Val, I still have so many questions," one guest said, her disappointment evident while the others laughed.

"Hey, don't worry. Catch me any time before you leave tomorrow or send me an email after you get home. I promise to answer all your questions," Val reassured the group.

Jess stepped in while Val got back to cooking. "We've kept you all busy since sunrise today, but our initial promise to you was to be sure to give everyone time to kick back and relax. Take the next couple of hours for yourselves. Nap, read, or whatever. And get ready for one hell of a send-off party tonight!"

The women cheered.

***

Their guests sat in rapt attention, listening to the evening's speaker, Nicole Lee, as she bared her soul.

"Two years ago, I lost my best friend in the world: my twin sister Melissa. We were only twenty-six years old. She was my rock. Growing up, our family unit was sadly dysfunctional. My father was born with a chip on his shoulder. In his mind, he was destined for greatness, always getting involved in the 'next big thing.' Trouble was, he worked hard on each new project, but only for a little while, then lost interest. When he was still excited about something, he was all in, ignoring everything else—including his own family. By the time he lost interest, depression would set in and he'd hole up in his home office with a bottle of Jack Daniels. Sometimes we wouldn't see him for days on end.

"Mom hated the fact Dad never followed through on anything. She, too, thought life owed her so much more than she ever got, but she never worked hard for anything herself. When Dad went on his binges, Mom would spend all her time with this circle of girlfriends she'd grown up with. The women were terrible influences—nothing like our group here."

The listening women laughed, smiling at one another.

"These friends spent all their time drinking and partying," Nicole continued, "which left me and my sister and our little brother to fend for ourselves most of the time. When we turned sixteen, Dad bought a Jeep for us to drive. It was our job to drop Alan, our brother, off at school every morning and pick him up in the afternoon. That way Mom was off the hook, which was a good thing, since she was usually so hung over she would forget to pick him up anyhow.

"One day I had hockey practice after school, so Melissa dropped me off and picked up Al. We lived in northwest North Dakota and it was an icy, blustery afternoon. Melissa liked to drive faster than she should, and the roads were in bad shape. Jeeps can be top-heavy.

"I'll never forget that day. Practice was just wrapping up. Two police officers came in and talked to my coach. Coach called me off the ice and the officers asked me to follow them. They took me into the deserted office and proceeded to tell me, as kindly as possible, that there had been an accident. A *bad* accident. They refused to give me any details other than I needed to get to the hospital right away and did I know how to get in touch with my parents. All I knew was Dad was on a business trip to South Dakota and Mom should have been home. She wasn't. Since Melissa dropped me off for practice, I didn't have a car at the rink. The officers gave me a ride."

The room was silent, as if the women were holding their breaths.

"Our minister was waiting for me when one of the officers walked me in. No one had been able to reach our parents. I knew from his expression something was terribly wrong. He sat me down in a quiet corner to tell me Alan hadn't survived the accident. Our little brother, only nine years old, was thrown out of the Jeep when it rolled. He wasn't wearing his seatbelt. Melissa was in critical condition with serious back and head injuries.

"The next few months after that day are still no more than a blur to me. Melissa was in the hospital for six weeks. She never did regain her memory of the actual accident, but to say she was traumatized would be a huge understatement. She needed pain meds for her back injury. Eventually she was able to walk again, but the pain never went away entirely.

"My parents couldn't accept what happened. They divorced and both moved away. Last I heard, Mom was in San Diego, living with two other women and attempting to publish her life story. If there is any truth to it, that would be an incredibly depressing book."

A few nervous chuckles.

"Dad, on the other hand, trusted the wrong people in one of his get-rich-quick schemes and he's currently spending five to ten in state prison in Ohio.

"My sister and I lived with our grandparents for our junior and senior years of high school. I will forever be grateful for their love and support. If not for them, we might have wound up in the foster care system. After graduation, we moved to Minneapolis, thought it sounded like an adventure. Grandma and Grandpa had done enough for us, we decided, and we wanted that adventure we felt was owed to us.

"We rented a cheap apartment with another girl, waitressing our way through part-time college classes. I did all right, but Melissa struggled. She still had significant trouble with her back, but we couldn't afford medical insurance. Unbeknownst to me, Melissa started dealing to earn enough money to afford the drugs she had become addicted to. I hate that I didn't realize what was happening. She somehow found a source for the meds and she was both selling them and taking them herself. I guess she thought she knew how to self-medicate. After all, she'd been needing the medication for almost ten years by then.

"I'm sure you can probably guess how Melissa's story ends. One day, she overdosed. She was home alone in our apartment and I found her when I got home from class. Her body was already cold when I found her."

Nicole paused to take a moment to collect herself. Even after all this time, it clearly affected her. Finally, she continued, her voice little more than a whisper now, but the women were hanging on every word.

"I was absolutely devastated. My grandparents came back and helped get me through the darkest days. They invited me to move south to live with them, but that didn't feel right to me. I had some serious decisions to make, the first of which was that I didn't want my sister's death to be in vain.

"The opiate epidemic is out of control in America. More people need to be sharing the story about the dangers these drugs pose to the public. My sister was *not* a drug addict. At least she didn't start out that way. But in the end, whether the drugs were legal or illegal, it didn't matter. They killed her. My goal is to speak to as many groups as possible. I want to share some of the signs I missed with my sister in the hope more lives can be saved."

There was no applause, only awed silence. Renee walked up to the front of the room, handed Nicole a Kleenex, and hugged the younger woman.

"Thank you so much for sharing your incredible story with us, Nicole. We can only imagine how painful it is for you to relive those parts of your life. You are very brave." Turning to the retreat guests, Renee wasn't surprised to see more tears. "What questions do you have for Nicole?"

A number of guests weighed in. Some thanked Nicole for opening their eyes to this very real problem. Two shared their own stories of losing loved ones to opiate addictions. One brave woman even spoke to her own battle against addiction to painkillers following shoulder surgery.

Jess surveyed the room full of women. She was again amazed at the impact one person can make when they share from the heart, as Nicole had just done. The love and support being offered up by their guests was staggering. Jess now understood why Nicole was doing this. Not only was she making an impact and doing things in an effort to save others, she was receiving the strength from others she needed to get through her days without her sister or brother.

If Nicole can find a way to move on from her staggering losses, Jess resolved, *I can certainly survive and thrive despite this chapter in my own life.*

CHAPTER 8

Gift of Vulnerability

*W*ith the retreat over, other responsibilities claimed her attention and January passed in a blur. Jess set up an appointment with Wendy and Patricia at Homes Sparkle for late February to finalize the books for their tax accountant. She'd have to find time to review the numbers again before their meeting. She'd hoped to meet with them sooner, but Patricia was in Mexico on vacation.

Jess sighed. *Why is everyone taking tropical vacations while I sit here in the snow and cold, busting my butt?*

In the meantime, Jess needed to get back out to visit the two other businesses Celia had remained involved with and had expected Jess to keep in contact with going forward. One was a small bookstore and the other a shop that dealt with both architectural salvage and stained glass. Jess was concerned about the viability of the bookstore. Frank and Virginia Fisk, the couple that owned and ran the bookstore, worked hard to keep the shop open, but the truth was that in the age of ebooks it wasn't easy.

Jess searched through her contacts in her phone and placed the call. She needed to stop in to see the elderly couple so she could at least try to help them like Celia used to. If business didn't pick up, they wouldn't be able to stay open much longer.

"Hello," a hoarse voice came over the line.

"Frank, is that you? You sound terrible."

"Yes, unfortunately this is Frank."

"Frank, this is Jess Rand. Are you all right? You don't sound like yourself."

"Ah, Jessica. I've been fighting this blasted cold for a month now."

Jess could picture Frank, his already bulbous nose red and chapped, a white linen handkerchief in his hand.

"I was hoping to stop over and pick up a copy of your year-end financials. Will you guys be around? Or do you want me to wait until you feel better?"

"No, actually, we planned to close up a little early today. We're going over to visit old friends for the weekend."

Jess sighed. Closing the shop early wouldn't help business, but she also knew they couldn't afford part-time help and Frank and Virginia deserved to have a life outside of the shop.

"No problem," she replied, flipping ahead in her planner. "How about next Thursday afternoon. Will that work for me to stop by?"

"Hold on a sec, let me check."

Jess tapped her pen as she listened to Frank holler at Virginia, probably in the back of the store.

"Yep, that'll be just fine, Jessica," Frank replied when he came back on the line.

He was the only one who'd ever called her by her proper name. He was a formal type of man, never having quite lost his scholarly personality, especially not while surrounded by books.

"All right. I'll see you Thursday then. Feel better, Frank."

After hanging up, Jess sat back and contemplated whether or not she was up for a visit to the architectural shop. She'd been out there a few times over the past year but always seemed to butt heads with Seth, the shop's owner.

The man was stubborn. While Jess understood why Celia enjoyed working with both the Fisks and the Robins, her aunt's relationship with Seth Lindell left her perplexed. She vaguely remembered that they'd met when Celia made a significant donation to her church to have the stained glass windows refurbished. Never one to blindly give away her money, she would have insisted on being involved in the hiring and supervision of the company making the repairs. That still didn't explain how Celia became a partial owner in the man's business. When she'd asked Seth about it, he offered little in the way of explanation, muttering something about Celia's tendency to take in strays.

Deciding she didn't have time to let a little personality conflict stand in the way of Celia's wishes, she found Seth's number in her phone and placed her second call.

"What do ya need?"

Jess was instantly irritated he couldn't even utter a proper hello. He sounded offended, like she'd interrupted his day.

"Hello, Seth, it's Jess Rand. I thought we should probably touch base now that we're past the end of the year and need to get the taxes done. I was wondering if I could stop out this afternoon."

Her request was met with a grunt and then nothing.

"Not a good time?" she asked.

"It's never a good time to stop what I'm doing and bother with the damn numbers. Look, I've got enough in checking. I'm good to go for at least another month."

And this was what irritated Jess most about Seth Lindell. His priorities were way off.

"Seth, as you know, if you don't pay your taxes, you don't get to keep doing what you like to do ninety-five percent of the time. You actually get to go to jail instead." Jess knew it was a condescending thing to say, but something about this man just rubbed her the wrong way.

"Oh for Christ's sake, don't you think that's a bit overdramatic?"

"That depends on how long you plan to put me off. If we miss deadlines, I'd say it isn't dramatic at all."

This time a heavy sigh came over the phone.

"Fine. Look, I've got about one hour this afternoon but I'm leaving town by 4:30. Will that work?"

It was Jess's turn to sigh.

"Yes, that'll be fine. See you in an hour."

At least I won't have to spend much time with him, she thought, scooping up her keys and heading for the door.

***

The road from the highway to the architectural shop was pitted with frozen ice and gravel. Jess bumped along, careful not to slide off the shoulder into the steep ditch. Once there, she parked next to a sign that read:

SAVING BITS OF HISTORY

How quaint, Jess thought with a smirk. The man couldn't come up with something more unique?

She stepped down out of her Land Rover and kept a tight grip on the door to keep her feet from flying out from under her. The drive was solid ice. She slammed the door, took two steps—

And fell flat on her back.

Air whooshed out of her lungs when she hit the ground. She lay there, stunned. The sky above was a brilliant blue and ice crystals floating in the frigid air reflected rays of sunshine.

Too bad the sun's not strong enough to melt this damn ice.

As the cold started to seep into her backside, Jess pushed up to a sitting position.

Footsteps approached from behind.

"New feet?"

"Really? You have to be a smartass at a time like this?" Jess shot over her shoulder, having no doubt who was now standing behind her.

"Sorry, guess you wouldn't find that funny given your current predicament."

"Jeez, ya think?" Jess pushed up to her knees.

"Here, let me help you," Seth said as he offered his hand.

She batted it away. "I can get up myself. Ever heard of a shovel or a little ice melt? Someone could break their neck out here. Like I almost just did."

"It's a losing battle. Too much ground to cover. Besides, don't get many visitors out here this time of year."

Jess straightened slowly, painfully. Even though there were a few layers between her skin and the ground, she suspected she would find scraped elbows and a black and blue bottom when she got home. But she refused to let him see she was banged up.

She turned to him, wishing for the umpteenth time that his pleasant features extended to his attitude. Instead, the man provoked her ill temper. "Come on, let's get this over with. Don't you need to be somewhere?"

"Yep, as a matter of fact I do. You've got twenty minutes."

This time, Jess made it safely inside. She knew the way to his office despite only coming around when she absolutely had to, and weaved her way back there now, carefully stepping around piles of what looked like reclaimed lumber and an old scale of some kind. She stopped short at the office doorway, dismayed by the mess on Seth's vintage oak desk. It was piled high with manila folders and pink, yellow, and white invoices. She felt a headache coming on.

"I see you didn't take my advice and use the filing system I set up for you last time," she said, spinning on her heel to face him.

He stopped a few feet from her, lifting his ball cap off his head a couple of inches to brush back the reddish curls that had fallen across his forehead. He squinted bright green eyes at her, partially obscured by a pair of wire-rimmed glasses.

"I don't have time for that shit. I told you that last time," he said, but tempered his response with a small grin. "Isn't that what you're for? Celia had no problem straightening up this mess for me a couple of times a year."

"Well, my dear aunt also didn't have quite as many irons in the fire as I do," Jess retorted, spinning back toward the desk and approaching it reluctantly.

Is that actually true? she wondered to herself. *Celia had an awful lot going on. Why would she waste her time with this infuriating man?*

Seth said nothing more. Jess did not understand the man. She'd done some research on him and knew he was well regarded for the quality of work he did. Ethan, Jess's brother, owned his own construction firm. He knew of Seth and said he had a good reputation—spotless, even. What confused Jess was why a man with so little regard for the *business end* of his business could keep his doors open.

Reminding herself she was doing this for Celia, she took a deep breath and faced Seth.

"All right. Truce," she uttered, although she couldn't quite bring herself to make eye contact with the man. "Do you have an empty box around here? I'll go through all this and organize it, but I'm not going to do it here. I can take it home with me, go through it this weekend, and bring it all back early next week. Will that work for you?"

Another shrug. "I guess. I'm heading over to Rogers now. There's a dilapidated county building in town they're going to demolish on Monday. I have the weekend to pull as much out of there as I can before they knock the sucker down. I won't have time to do anything with this over the weekend," he said, motioning to the disarray on his desk. "I'll get you a box."

After he'd left to find a container, Jess plopped herself into the old wooden desk chair with a sigh. Guess she wouldn't have time to start that new novel she'd picked up—it would take her most of the weekend to sort through this mess. She pulled open a large bottom drawer on the left-hand side of the desk. There were the files she'd organized in October. It didn't look like they'd been touched since.

At least he hadn't messed *those* up, too.

She pushed the drawer closed. It slid easier than she expected and banged shut. The force popped open the drawer above by a few inches and the corner of a photograph peeked out.

Curious . . .

Jess glanced at the door. Not seeing Seth, she gave herself permission to snoop a little, as Seth's comeuppance for not maintaining his icy parking lot. She slid the drawer out farther so she could see the whole snapshot.

She was surprised to see it was Seth with a young girl, maybe ten years old or so. Both were laughing for the camera. Seth's arm was draped over the girl's shoulders and her arm was at his waist. She'd never seen an easy smile like that on his face before—barely even any smile, in fact. She lifted up the photograph to see if there were more pictures underneath.

"Find what you were lookin' for?" Seth asked from the doorway, his displeasure apparent on his face.

"Sorry," she stammered. "I was just . . . looking for a pen."

He met her eye, then glanced at the cup full of pens at her right elbow before again looking her in the eye.

"You can do better than that," he said.

Deciding to ignore his taunt and distract him instead, Jess stood. "Find me a box?"

Seth continued to watch her for a second and then stepped farther into the office, dropping a plastic storage tub onto the cluttered desktop.

"Thought this would work better" was all he said.

She took the tub and started transferring the piles of paper and file folders from the desk into the container as quickly as she could. "Do you have the bank statements from the last quarter?"

He sauntered over to her side of the desk, gave her a look that said to move, and pulled open the center drawer once she got out of the way. He pulled out a stack of envelopes, dropped them into the box, and snapped the plastic lid on top. Without another word, he hoisted the now full tub off the desk with a slight grunt.

"Don't want you falling on your ass again on the way to your car," he said as he left his office.

Jess zipped up her winter jacket, looped her bag over her shoulder, and followed. She felt like a child, scolded by the teacher for some infraction.

God, that man infuriates me was all she could think about as she followed him out to her vehicle. Then: *I just need to put him out of my mind. The weekend will still be fun.*

She reminded herself Lauren was coming out to Whispering Pines to spend the weekend with her. Jess climbed back in her Land Rover and headed for the grocery store. A can of chicken noodle soup wouldn't cut it for dinner when her daughter was home.

***

Jess collapsed on the gold velour sofa, exhausted from an afternoon of cross-country skiing with Lauren. Unlike her earlier outing during the January retreat, today had been fast-paced and unforgiving. Together they'd covered miles of scenic trails, and now every bone and muscle in Jess's body felt like Jell-O.

"God, Mom, that was *amazing!*" Lauren said as she set the lid of the crockpot to the side and scooped out a ladle of steaming chili. She filled an old stoneware bowl to the brim and carried it, along with a bag of crackers, over to the kitchen table. "Are you going to join me?"

"I would if I could get up," Jess said with a groan.

"Aw, come on, a little skiing never bothered you before."

"That was not just a *little* skiing, girl," Jess declared, laughing. She rolled off the couch to her feet, one of her wool socks nearly sliding off and creating a trip hazard. Jess kicked it off and shuffled into the kitchen, filling a bowl for herself. She grabbed two cans of soda out of the fridge and joined Lauren at the table.

"Thanks for today, Mom," Lauren said as she nibbled on a cracker. "You know I love Grandma and Grandpa dearly, but I missed you."

Jess reached across the table to squeeze her daughter's shoulder.

"I missed you too, honey. Are things going OK?"

Lauren shrugged. "I guess. I met Harper a few days ago."

Jess stopped mid-bite at this announcement. She slowly set her spoon back in the bowl, her appetite deserting her.

"And how did that go?"

"All right, I guess. Nathan drove home and we went over to the house for dinner."

Jess was swarmed with visions of *her* family around *her* dining room table, minus herself, plus a new stand-in and a newborn.

Could this get any more bizarre?

"What did you eat?"

Lauren looked at Jess like she'd lost her mind.

"Really? I tell you I met my sister for the first time and you ask about the menu?"

"*Half*-sister," Jess corrected.

Lauren just glared.

Jess reached up with both her hands to massage the back of her own neck, giving herself a minute to collect her thoughts.

"Sorry, honey, I don't know where that came from. How was the baby?"

Lauren resumed eating. "Harper was sweet. She's still tiny. She *was* pretty fussy, though."

Jess hated to ask the next question, but she had to know. "How was your dad with her?"

"With Harper?"

"Yes, with the baby. How was he with her?"

"He was good with her. Actually, since you asked, I noticed he was lots better with Harper than her mother was. Tiffany acted really nervous around her. When Harper cried, she'd try to settle her down, but if she didn't stop crying right away, Tiffany would just hand her to Dad."

Why does it feel so good to hear that?

"Tiffany doesn't have any other kids, does she?"

"No," Lauren replied with a shake of her head. "Not that I know of, anyhow. It's not like we talk much."

"Maybe she's just not used to being around babies."

"Maybe . . ."

"Do you think the two of them are living at the house now?" Jess asked. She'd given up trying to sound casual.

"Seems like it. There's a crib set up in Dad's old office but it doesn't really look like a nursery. I don't exactly know what their living arrangements are right now, Mom. I just know I'm not comfortable being there much."

Jess pushed her bowl away even though she'd only eaten a couple of bites.

"I hope you know how sorry I am about this, honey."

Lauren stood up in a rush, her chair skidding away across the linoleum. She slammed her hands down on the tabletop and leaned in toward Jess, who had jumped in shock.

"You *have* to quit apologizing, Mom! This is *not* on you. I am not a child! I know Dad cheated and it probably wasn't the first time. I mean . . . it can't get more obvious than having a new kid to show for it, can it?

Quit acting like you had anything to do with this mess our lives have become!"

With that, Lauren picked up her bowl, stomped over to the sink, and dropped it into the basin. Jess cringed but remained silent.

Lauren stood glaring at her mother, hands on her hips, face red and eyes swimming with emotion. "This is all on Dad. And I, for one, am sick of playing a part in his little game of 'house'! That woman doesn't belong in our home. *We* do! Why did he have to go and ruin everything?"

This time Jess simply gave her daughter the smallest of head shakes and a shrug of her shoulders. What more could she say?

To that, Lauren groaned, spun, and headed for the stairs. "I have homework. See you in the morning."

Jess dropped her head onto the tabletop.

For the most part, Lauren was right. Will had ruined everything. Of course, it takes two to make a marriage work, and if Jess were being totally honest, she hadn't been making much of an effort to hold their family together in recent years either.

But I never cheated.

Over on the counter, her phone gave a ping.

Better clean up this mess, she thought with a grimace, her overexerted muscles groaning in protest when she stood and went to check her phone.

Everything OK over there?

Great. Renee had heard Lauren's outburst.

These damn walls really are too thin.

Knowing Lauren, she wouldn't be down again until morning. Desperate to get her mind off the mess of her personal life, Jess struggled to hoist the heavy tub of Seth's paperwork onto the kitchen table after she'd cleared up dinner. Her evening was already shot—she might as well muscle her way through more bad news.

CHAPTER 9

Gift of Letting Go

Be nice, be nice, she kept telling herself. *Benefit of the doubt, Jess.* "How did the weekend go?" she asked Seth as she lugged the heavy tub back into his shop on Thursday afternoon. "Were you able to save some good things out of that old building?"

Seth stopped what he was doing and set down the drill in his hands. He quickly walked over to Jess, taking the large container out of her hands.

Jess almost complained about him being too presumptuous but bit her tongue. *I promised to play nice,* she reminded herself. *Besides, he's just being a gentleman.*

"Managed to not fall on your ass today, huh?" he shot at her over his shoulder.

So much for being a gentleman.

"No, wore sensible boots today," Jess replied through gritted teeth. She wouldn't allow herself to snap back at him.

"How'd things look?" he asked, nodding his head at the tub now sitting in the middle of his still-cluttered desk. Under it were a few new invoices that hadn't been there the previous Friday, Jess noticed.

"I think you're doing all right, for now, but your receivables are growing. What policy do you have as far as late payments and interest on balances due?"

Seth simply looked at her with a blank expression.

"Let me guess. You don't have a policy for late payments."

He shrugged unapologetically. "Never needed one. People pay . . . eventually."

"Well, 'eventually' is costing you money. Your revenue is about even with last year but your cash flow is down. Seems like people are getting more lax in making those payments to you. You might want to consider charging some interest if they go past thirty days."

To this Seth simply grunted and walked back to the project he'd been working on when she got there.

"Do you need help figuring out how to do that?"

"Listen, lady, I'm not going to charge my customers interest. I've got better things to do with my time and, besides, they'll pay when they can."

"Then you might expect to be a little short in your checking account to make your quarterly tax payment," Jess informed him, still gritting her teeth.

He seems grumpier today . . .

"I'll be fine."

"Not at this rate you won't."

"How short?"

She thought back to the estimations she'd done on Sunday. "A few thousand at least."

He fired up a grinder and sparks flew. She waited.

Eventually, he set the power tool down and turned back to face her.

"I'll figure it out."

To this she shrugged. "All right. Let me know if you need help. Taxes have to be deposited on time. *That* isn't negotiable."

Seth turned back to his project and Jess took it as her cue to leave.

Driving home, she rolled her shoulders and stretched her neck side to side, keeping a cautious eye on the road. There were scattered slippery spots, and the way her day was going, she better be careful. Hopefully her visit with the Fisks tomorrow would go better. She hoped this past holiday season was busy for them. She needed a win.

***

Grant wrestled a cardboard box into his trunk as Jess pulled into the Whispering Pines parking lot. He slammed the trunk shut and waited for her.

"What are you up to?" she asked when she opened her door and stepped down to the gravel.

"Packing up," Grant replied.

"What do you mean?"

"Listen, Jess, I've been meaning to catch you. I've decided to move back home."

Grant's announcement shocked Jess. She slammed her door and hurried over to his side.

"But why? I thought you liked it out here!"

"I do. In fact, I love it out here. The peace and quiet, before the place starts to fill up with summer renters again, is a perfect place to do my writing. Well, *almost* perfect . . ."

Jess was so disappointed her friend was leaving. Another tally to her losses. "Do you have time for a drink before you go?"

Grant checked his watch and then glanced up at the sky. "Sure, but just a quick one. And make it a Diet Coke. I've gotta drive."

"You got it," Jess assured him as she grabbed her purse and phone. Together they walked back to the duplex. It didn't look like Renee was home.

"Just toss your jacket over the back of the sofa," she suggested as she went into the kitchen and grabbed two sodas out of the fridge. "Have a seat."

"Sorry I didn't have a chance to talk to you about this, Jess. I made up my mind a few days ago and you've been gone quite a bit."

"But you *did* talk to Renee, didn't you?" Jess knew Renee and Grant had a special bond—after all, Grant was the twin to Renee's late husband and their kids were cousins. Having him at Whispering Pines since the previous summer had been a lot of fun.

"Of course. I can't thank her, or you, enough for all your family did for Grace, for both of us, over these past months. I just think it's time to get back home. I have a few other writing commitments I've been neglecting, staying out here and working on my novel. With Grace back at college, it's time. Besides, it gets damn cold in that cabin when the temp starts to flirt with zero."

Jess gave a little laugh, sure it *did* get cold—the cabin wasn't well insulated.

There was something else she'd wondered about but never dared bring up with Grant. Now she felt compelled to ask.

"Grant . . . are you sure those are the only reasons?"

Grant eyed her carefully. "What do you mean?"

"I may be off base here," she said, "and please, tell me to mind my own business if you don't want to answer. Is the fact that Renee and Matt came back from Fiji *engaged* influencing your decision to leave at all?"

"Why would that make a difference?" he asked.

He was either a good actor or she'd been wrong about Grant's feelings for Renee.

"I just thought . . . you know . . . maybe you were interested in more than just friendship with Renee."

Grant showed no initial reaction to what Jess was suggesting, but, ever so slowly, he started to nod his head. "You know, Jess, you're pretty good at reading people. You see things but you don't necessarily let on that you've noticed. All right. I admit, I had a bit of a crush on Renee when we first moved out here. But . . ." Jess didn't jump in when Grant paused. He squirmed in his chair a bit, clearly uncomfortable with the whole conversation. "It didn't take me long to realize she didn't think of me in those terms. Maybe because I was Jim's brother—even though he and I never even met."

"That might have had something to do with it. But remember, she *did* meet Matt on that winter trip with her kids, a month or two before she even met you."

"Yeah, I know . . ." He looked up and smiled in a sad way. "Funny how things work out, isn't it?"

Jess reached out, taking his hand. "One thing I do know for sure, though. Renee considers you a dear friend. We all do. I wish you weren't leaving. It's been fun having you around. Promise you'll come back to visit?"

Grant gave her hand a squeeze, drained the last of his soda, stood, and tossed the can in the recycle bin near the back door. Jess stood as well and Grant walked back to her, arms open. They hugged, each sorry they wouldn't be seeing as much of each other in the future.

"I already have that cabin reserved for the second week of August," he assured her with one last squeeze before stepping away and grabbing his coat off the sofa. As he shrugged into it, he looked back at Jess, now grinning from his confession about Renee. "Did you ever wonder if the two of *us* could ever be more than friends?"

Jess laughed along with him. "Honestly, it never occurred to me until I thought you might be *dead* in some snowbank after that New Year's Eve storm. Up until that point, I was sure you only had eyes for Renee, although I feared, for your sake, it would never go anywhere. The thought crossed my mind that morning when you stepped out of your cabin, alive and well, that *maybe* there could be more."

"Do you still wonder?"

Jess had to laugh again. The man was tough to read. She couldn't tell whether he wanted her to still think about it or not. So she decided honesty would be best.

"Grant, you are a great guy and fun to be around. I count you amongst my dearest friends—and, not being an overly social individual, I don't have many. With that said, I worry that opening ourselves up to a different kind of relationship might just screw it all up, and I'm not willing to risk losing you like that. Besides, I'm still, unfortunately, a married woman."

"Jeez, woman, aren't you about done with that mess yet?" he asked with a laugh, apparently not upset with Jess's reply.

"*God*, I hope so."

***

Jess pulled into a diagonal parking spot in front of a vintage store whose window display was in a state of transition. Valentine's Day was right around the corner, so there was Virginia Fisk, standing on a ladder inside, stringing paper hearts in front of the window. The shiny red paper hearts spurred memories. Jess used to love helping the kids figure out what kind of Valentine's boxes they'd create to take to elementary school for their classroom parties. Her favorites included an elaborate castle—complete with a moat—that Nathan spent hours on, and Lauren's circular box that looked like a huge, brightly striped lollipop. There was even one shaped like a bird. She used to help them write out their tiny Valentine's cards— one for every child in the class so no one was left out. They'd use Scotch tape to attach little pieces of candy to each Valentine. During their party, they'd walk around and deposit the cards in each kid's box.

Jess jumped at a light tap on her window.

"Coming in?" the man asked her when she rolled down her window.

"Hi, Frank. I am. Be there in a second," Jess replied, feeling sheepish at getting caught daydreaming.

Frank went ahead of Jess into the old bookstore. Jess grinned when she saw him go immediately in Virginia's direction. She didn't need to hear his words to know he was scolding his wife for climbing up on that ladder by herself.

Jess followed Frank, but paused inside the door, letting the nostalgic feel of the place seep into her. Old bookstores have a smell all their own and a naturally hushed atmosphere, like libraries, markedly different from larger, more modern bookstores. This was the one business interest Celia left to her that brought her true joy. She only hoped she would be able to help the Fisks keep the doors open for now and find a way to maintain the store when they finally retired for good.

"Well, if it isn't our favorite customer, stopping for a visit," Virginia greeted Jess as she gingerly climbed down from the ladder, her husband's hand on the small of her back, guiding her. "What brings you out this way today, child?"

With a laugh, Jess set down her purse and briefcase so she could clasp both Virginia's hands with her own. "Hello, Ginny. I'm forty-four years old, you know. I don't think I qualify to be called 'child' anymore."

Virginia dismissed the idea with a wave of her hand. "Dear Celia always talked about her little niece Jess and how much you loved books and reading. To me, you will always be that child."

Jess knew better than to argue. "Don't you remember, Virginia? I was stopping by today to help with your year-end receipts and to discuss how your holiday sales held up."

"Oh, no, dear, I don't recall that," the older woman replied, a hand going up to lightly adjust an imagined hair out of place. From the looks of things, Virginia recently had a rinse and set. Her hair sported a pale pink hue, perfect for the upcoming holiday of love.

"This way, Jess," Frank instructed, leading her to the back of the store to a cluttered desk in a far corner. "I remembered for the both of us. I've got things pulled together for you."

"You two go talk figures," Virginia said. "I need to finish up this front window. I need to get these glorious romance novels properly displayed so we can sell them in time for Valentine's Day."

"Stay off the ladder, dear."

Jess looked around the small shop. Shelves still appeared to be well-stocked. Not exactly what she was hoping to see after the holiday rush.

Frank settled in behind their desk and Jess pulled up a chair from nearby.

"So, Frank, did you have a busy Christmas season?"

Frank sat back in his chair and seemed to ponder his reply before speaking. He always kept a finger on the pulse of the store, knowing what it took to keep things afloat—unlike his wife, who never acknowledged the fact that it wasn't easy to keep a shop like this going these days, faced with stiff competition and changing reading habits.

" 'Bout average, I suppose," Frank said, glancing around with an expression that said otherwise. "Maybe down a bit from last year. I'm sure you'll tell me when you get a chance to go through the receipts and make some comparisons."

He handed her the records from fourth quarter. They'd be well organized and easy to review, Jess knew. Frank took pride in keeping clean records. She may not like the numbers themselves, but she never had to worry about them being inaccurate or incomplete.

"I'm not sure how many more holiday seasons we have in us, Jess," he said, keeping his voice low so Virginia couldn't hear him. "Ginny loves it here, never wants to retire, but I have some concerns. I wanted to let you know . . . I think our main focus this year should be on finding a buyer. If we don't have anyone by the end of the year, we'll probably have to close the store."

Jess had suspected something like this was coming, but she'd hoped it wouldn't be for a few more years; she was just getting to know the Fisks better and learning about this end of the business of reading. While she appreciated Frank wanting to look beyond this, given their age, she hated the thought of the store closing. She didn't hold out high hopes of being able to find a buyer. The sad truth was that small, independent bookstores were a dying breed.

"I understand, Frank. You have my promise that I will help you figure out a way to both keep this store open and allow you and Virginia to have more time for other things."

Frank leveled an unwavering look at Jess. "I'm serious, Jess. We're about done here. I know you love this place. I do too. But I don't want this to be the end of our story." He glanced toward his wife, who was humming as she adjusted the display up front. Quieter yet, he added, "I worry . . . you know? Ginny has always been a bit, shall we say 'eccentric'? But she seems a bit more detached from reality than usual these days."

Jess nodded sadly. She needed him to know she still held out hope. "I really do understand, Frank. You're serious about this. But let me see what I can come up with for possible options first. Do you trust me to do that?"

"All right, missy. I do trust you. But I don't want to have this exact same conversation a year from now."

CHAPTER 10

Gift of Laughter

*R*enee and Matt's wedding was less than three months away. Plans were coming together, but Renee still didn't have her dress. Seeing an opportunity for everyone to get a break from work and school, Jess quickly pulled a girl's weekend together. Minneapolis was the logical destination.

"I talked to Laura, Matt's sister, like you suggested. Her daughter has a gymnastics meet, so she can't come. I'm disappointed. It would be fun to get to know her better," Renee reported back to Jess.

"Darn it. I wanted to meet her, too. But I thought you said her name was Macy?"

Renee laughed. "I probably did. Matt uses both interchangeably. I guess her real name is Laura Macy, but his mom's first name was Laura, too, so growing up, she was always Macy. Once their mom passed away, their father insisted on calling his daughter Laura. A little bizarre, but she goes by either."

"Oh. OK . . . that is a little weird, but whatever. Are Mom and Val coming?"

"Yes," Renee confirmed. "And so is Julie. Can Lauren come?"

"She wouldn't miss it," Jess said. "That makes six of us. We'll need two hotel rooms. Let's let the girls have their own room. Then we can share the other one with Val and Mom. Just like old times."

***

"I could get used to this," Julie declared as they all lounged in leather recliners at the spa. She was clad in a fluffy pink robe, her newly polished toes stretched out carefully in front of her so they wouldn't get smudged.

"Don't go getting spoiled now, missy," came Lavonne's quick reply.

"Grandma, you look too pretty in your pink robe to be grumpy. Don't you think this is *fun?*"

"Of course it's fun, honey, but we only do this on *very* special occasions," Lavonne said, a smile lighting her face. "You know I love being with all my girls. I think the last time I had a pedicure was when your Aunt Val got married."

Val, situated at the end of the row and dressed in a similar pink robe, let out a loud snort. "For God's sake, Mom, that was twelve years ago. No wonder your feet look like that!"

The woman working on Lavonne's feet, quiet up to that point, let out a loud laugh and said, "That explains a lot!"

Lavonne didn't take offense; their morning of pampering, which included massages and now pedicures, had everyone in a good mood. She laughed along with the rest, then resumed picking a color for her toenails.

"I just want to thank you, Jess, for arranging this weekend," Renee said. "I've dreaded dress shopping. I don't have any idea what I want to wear. But you've made it so much more fun than just another task to check off the list. To spend the weekend with my favorite ladies in the world . . . it doesn't get any better than this."

As she reached over to squeeze Jess's hand, her tears started rolling.

Jess tried to stifle a chuckle. "I hope those are happy tears," she said as she squeezed back.

"*So* happy! Can you believe this is happening? I'm getting married! Again! It wasn't that long ago when I thought I was destined to be single for the rest of my life. Now here we are . . ."

Julie laughed and tossed a tissue at Renee when her nose started dripping along with the tears.

"Now it's officially a 'girl's weekend,' " Val said, "complete with tears and nail polish. Next stop, shopping! Now all we need to do is talk about sex and we've hit all the requirements."

"Valerie! There are children present!" Lavonne reprimanded her youngest, trying to keep a straight face.

Everyone else busted out laughing again.

"Grandma, you really need to stop treating us like kids," Lauren said. "Julie's in college and I'm close. I think we can handle it."

Lavonne shook a finger at her granddaughter, but the wink ruined any chance of being taken seriously.

"So who has a good sex story to share?" Renee asked, willing to play along in such a relaxed state. "How about you, Jess?"

Jess glared at her. "Now *that* is just plain mean."

"What?" Renee shot back in mock innocence. "Whatever do you mean?"

"You know I currently have the love life equivalent to this nail file," Jess countered with a sigh, waving an emery board in Renee's face.

"At least the shape has promise," Julie chimed in before she thought better of it. She slapped her hand over her own mouth, cheeks staining a bright red.

"Julie!" Now it was Renee's turn to scold her daughter, but she couldn't keep a straight face for long, falling into hoots of laughter.

"What about that cute Seth Lindell you've been spending so much time with?" Lavonne asked, wiggling her eyebrows at Jess two chairs down the row. "*He's* single."

Jess's face screwed up in confusion, maybe even distaste. "Mother, you have *got* to be kidding," Jess replied when she could find her voice again.

Has Mom totally lost it?

"That man is awful. Stubborn, ornery . . . a huge pain in my side. Besides, he's *way* too young for me. How do you even know Seth?"

"I've known Seth since he was a child."

"You're kidding!" Jess said, shocked. "I thought Aunt Celia met him when she had the church windows redone. Did she know him since he was a kid, too?"

"Sure. He's Ruby Poole's grandson," Lavonne said, as if that would explain everything.

When she didn't elaborate, Jess asked, "Who is Ruby Poole?"

"Come on, Jess, you remember Ruby. She was your aunt's oldest and dearest friend. Jack Poole's mother?"

The dots started to connect for Jess. "Jack, as in Celia's lawyer? So is Seth Jack's son?"

"No, no, Jack's an old bachelor—no kids, no wife. Jack had a sister, Shirley, and she was Seth's mom."

"Was?"

"Yes. It was terrible. Shirley and her husband—I think his name was Ron—they were both killed in a car accident about fifteen years ago. On Valentine's Day, as a matter of fact. I'm not sure if Seth was even twenty yet. He was a bit of a handful, but he was Ruby's only grandchild, and she was simply crazy about him."

Jess slumped back into her chair, feeling pity for Ruby and the young man who had grown to be so bitter. "What a shame. That might explain why he has such a bad attitude."

"No, I don't think so," Lavonne countered. "Ruby was good for Seth, and he was great with her as she aged. He chauffeured her all over the place after she couldn't drive. Ruby was one *active* woman. She played bridge, loved to volunteer, and was president of the local Historical Society for years. Every bit as active as Celia, that woman was. If I remember right, that's how Seth first got interested in old architecture."

"What do you mean?" Lauren asked.

"Celia told me once that Seth started sitting in on their meetings. He was often there because he dropped Ruby off and picked her up again afterward. He started to help out on some projects. Once, there was a beautiful old theater the group wasn't able to save—there had been a fire and repairs were too costly. It needed to be demolished. The city allowed the Historical Society to go in and take what they wanted out of the building before they knocked it down. Someone suggested Seth should be the one to pull out anything worth saving . . . probably since he was fifty years younger than most of the other members."

Lavonne paused to catch her breath before continuing with the story Celia shared with her years ago. Jess was riveted—and more than a little relieved the conversation had steered away from her sex life.

"He could sell the items he salvaged, keep half the profits, and give the rest to the Society for their funding. And from that point on he was in business."

"So . . ." Jess began slowly, processing everything her mother shared, "at what point did Celia also get involved in his business?"

Lavonne blew on her fingernails—the technician having skillfully painted them while she'd been reminiscing—taking her time before responding to Jess.

"I just remember Ruby asking Celia to watch over Seth when she found out she had cancer. She hated the thought of him with almost no family and knew he and Celia shared a love of history and old buildings." Lavonne gave Jess a sly look. "You'll have to ask Seth if you want to find out more about the business end."

"Like he'd tell me anything," Jess murmured.

"So does that mean you don't anticipate having sex with this Seth guy anytime soon?" Val asked from the far end of the row, to which everyone burst into laughter and Jess only grunted.

CHAPTER 11

Gift of Obligations

$\mathcal{T}$he last months leading up to Renee and Matt's wedding were chaotic.

The dress shopping trip to Minneapolis had been successful. Renee came home with a simple, classic chiffon gown that flattered her figure and would be comfortable enough for a long day of celebrating. Since Jess was standing up for Renee, she felt compelled to splurge on a summery dress they found in a fabric and style like Renee's (but pale pink, instead of the ivory color reserved for the bride).

In addition to all the last-minute wedding preparations, Jess also planned a graduation party for Lauren. Her daughter was graduating at the top of her class, and Jess couldn't have been prouder. The party was a success. Many of Lauren's classmates stopped by to wish her well, in addition to all of Jess's family and various friends and teachers. Only Will was absent during the open house—something neither Jess nor Lauren had forgiven him for yet.

Missing the graduation party was only one of the items on the ever-growing list of frustrations Jess was compiling related to Will's behavior over the past year. Now, standing before him in the lodge at Whispering Pines, demanding to know why he dared show up uninvited on Renee's wedding day, Jess could barely stop herself from throwing her hands up in surrender and walking out on Will.

What could possibly be so important that it couldn't have waited until tomorrow? Will had always been the one to use the term "emergency" more often; Jess usually considered Will's *emergencies* to be mere inconveniences. She could still hardly believe Will had the nerve to show up at Renee and Matt's wedding.

"Will, what do you mean, *we're* in trouble?" Jess repeated for the second time.

Will turned his back on Jess, running his hands through his hair, and paced to the closed door and back. Jess was still shocked by how disheveled he looked; given how insistent he'd been to talk to her, his hesitancy now notched up Jess's concern. He turned back to face her, a hard glint in his eye, jaw set. She'd seen that look before and it never boded well.

"I don't even know where to start. First of all, you should know the money is gone. If it weren't for that damn aunt of yours, I probably wouldn't even be in this position."

Her jaw dropped. "Whoa, back up. What do you mean, 'the money is gone'? And what aunt?"

Will adjusted his stance, hands on his hips, feet set out wide, chin thrust in Jess's direction.

"Who do you think? Who takes care of all her relatives except me? *Celia*, of course. I've never even *met* Lavonne's sister, I only know *Celia*."

This was going nowhere. Jess was more confused than before he'd opened his mouth.

"She'd never give me a dime. I could have used a hand, but she never even considered it. Then she goes and dies and gives it all to the rest of you."

"*That's* what this is all about?" Jess asked, incredulous.

Has this man lost his frigging mind?

"You're mad because Celia didn't leave you anything when she died *a year and a half ago?*"

"Oh, honey, I wish that was all there was to it." Will crossed his arms over his chest and his lips turned up into a menacing smile, spots of color staining his cheeks.

"Don't you dare take that tone with me," Jess shot back, eyeing the door behind Will and seriously considering using it.

"The money is *gone*, Jess," he repeated. "Almost every penny. The house is mortgaged to the hilt, our investments tanked, and there isn't much left in the kids' college funds. Just"—he splayed his fingers as if he were performing a magic disappearing act—"*poof.*"

Her jaw dropped for the second time. Will was a surgeon and made good money. They'd been in their house for almost ten years. "But . . . how can that *be?*"

Will breathed in deeply, obviously working to gather his composure. He let his arms drop to his sides and started again, contrition in his voice. "I had some lapses in judgment and made some poor choices. Now . . . Jess, I'm headed to prison."

For once, Jess was momentarily speechless. She fumbled behind her for a chair and dropped into it, never taking her eyes off her husband.

After a longer pause, Will said, "Jess, did you hear me? Prison."

She blinked. "That sounds like more than a *lapse* in judgment."

"I suppose."

He pulled a chair around and sat facing her. They stared at each other. Jess was fighting to comprehend everything this man was saying—a man who was so much more of a stranger than she ever would have guessed.

"What did you do?" she asked, bracing herself for the answer. "Why are you going to prison?"

"I'll explain everything," Will said, "but I have an even bigger problem."

"What can be bigger than going to *prison?* Are you dying of some devastating illness?" she asked, her sarcasm flooding in to protect her from the awful things Will was saying.

"Believe me, I might have welcomed that lately, the way things have been going. I know I'm in absolutely *no* position to ask you to do this, but you have to believe me when I tell you I have no other choice."

Jess threw her hands up in frustration. "For God's sake, if you aren't going to tell me *why* you're going to prison, just say what it is you need me for already, Will."

"OK, here it goes." Will took a breath. "I'm sure Lauren and Nathan have told you about Harper, my baby daughter . . . ?"

"After I saw pictures on Facebook? Yes, they mentioned it."

He had the decency to cringe, but then he charged on. "Tiffany, the baby's mother . . . she's been struggling with severe postpartum depression. Never really bonded with Harper. Now she's gone."

"What do you mean she's *gone*? Who has Harper?" Jess looked around as if she thought Will had brought the baby and left her lying somewhere nearby.

Will said nothing. He just stared at her.

"Will, I'm only going to ask you this one more time. Where's the baby?"

"With a sitter, for now."

He continued to simply watch her as her mind raced through a dozen scenarios, landing on the most bizarre one she could dream up. *If this man expects me to take that baby—a baby conceived with another woman while he was still married to me—he is sorely mistaken!*

She glared at him. She held her voice level despite her racing heart and sweating palms. "Tell me you aren't considering asking me to take Harper when you go to jail?"

He didn't look away. "Jess, there's no one else."

Jess was on her feet before he could finish speaking. She made a break for the door, her mind on overload, anger clouding her vision. He grabbed her arm when she tried to pass, pulling her to an abrupt stop. She tried to yank her arm away but he was too strong.

"Jess, I need you. *Harper* needs you," he said softly, releasing her arm.

She stormed out, unable to stand being in the same room with him for one more minute.

***

Somehow, Jess made it through the rest of the reception. She busied herself with things the caterers or clean-up crew could have handled—that was why she hired them, after all—in an effort to block all of the horrible things Will had said to her out of her mind. Lauren laughed when she saw

Jess clearing nearly empty champagne flutes from some of the tables, accusing her mother of avoiding the dance floor.

"No, honey, I . . . just don't want any of the kids drinking these," she improvised, holding up a half-emptied glass. "That happened at a friend's wedding and she had tweens out on the lawn, throwing up. We don't need to end our night that way."

"Whatever, Mom. I know what you're really doing. I'm going to go catch these last couple of songs before the band wraps up. You need to live a little," her daughter shot over her shoulder as she sauntered back to the dance floor, barefoot—her shoes were probably lying under a table somewhere.

Jess set the two flutes back down on the table she'd been clearing before Lauren caught her cleaning up. Her daughter's comment snapped her out of the fog she'd allowed herself to sink into since Will dropped his bombshells. She watched as her daughter joined her cousins on the dance floor, oblivious to the new storm clouds hovering on their horizon.

If any of what Will told me tonight is true, how am I going to protect Lauren and Nathan from more pain?

***

She didn't turn in until well after two in the morning. There was nothing more to do after having overseen clean-up. All that was left was the tent itself; the rental company would be by on Sunday to collapse it and haul it away.

Despite the exhausting day and the gamut of emotions she'd experienced, sleep eluded her. She couldn't have slept more than two hours, tops, before she woke with a dull headache. Her phone vibrated with an incoming text. Her headache increased when she saw it was from Will.

We have to talk.

Jess considered how best to respond, then typed:

Meet you at the house at 3:00.

She turned the ringer off and left the phone on her dresser. She went downstairs quietly so she wouldn't wake Lauren or Nathan. She paused to grab a cup of coffee and took it outside.

The air was heavy with humidity and the bright sun of yesterday was hidden behind a heavy bank of clouds. The weather reflected her mood. Seeing no one about, Jess made her way down to the water and out onto the dock. She sat down and dipped her toe into the lake, causing circular ripples to radiate out over the water.

Kind of like how Will's news last night is going to affect all of us, she thought, still unable to fully grasp the magnitude of it all.

If she were honest with herself, she'd have to admit his legal problems didn't come as a huge shock. His moral compass hadn't been pointing due north lately—something that was painfully obvious—but she hadn't considered he would do anything that would land him in jail. Jess remembered his boss lost his job not too long ago due to some scandal. Maybe it was related.

I let him off too easy last night. Today he will *tell me why he is going to prison.*

She could kick herself for not keeping a closer eye on their financial situation. Jess had worked ever since they married, even after Will graduated from med school. She'd always insisted on keeping separate checking accounts and they each took care of certain monthly bills. Given Will's salary was higher, he'd been responsible for paying off his student loans, the mortgage, and feeding into the kids' college funds. Since they'd been in their house for so long, there should have been equity. She shouldn't have trusted him on that one—hell, she shouldn't have trusted him on any of it.

How am I going to help Nathan through his last year of college? What about Lauren? She's supposed to start college in the fall . . . and it won't be cheap.

Jess shuddered at the thought that her daughter may have to switch colleges to something more affordable. Lauren had worked so hard to get into that school . . . but if the money was truly gone and Will was off to prison, it would fall to Jess to help the kids.

At least she did have other investments Will couldn't touch—complements of Celia, something he apparently was bitter about—but they weren't something she could easily convert into cash.

She cringed when she remembered her conversation with Seth the previous month. As she'd predicted, he ended up short on cash when his quarterly tax deposit was due. He'd come to her—sheepishly, since he'd ignored her warnings—asking for a $10,000 loan to get him through. Not knowing of the financial tornado blowing toward her, she'd been comfortable taking her annual earnings from Homes Sparkle and lending the money to Seth. It seemed prudent at the time, but now she might need that money, and he was in no position to pay her back right away.

Jess eased back down onto her forearms and gazed into the clouds above. A lone eagle looped in a silent circle high above, oblivious to Jess's troubles.

I need to think more about what to do about Will's baby. She's the most troubling part of this whole fiasco, Jess admitted to herself. There was usually a way to figure out money problems, but this?

"Mom? What are you doing down there?"

Jess pushed back up and looked behind her, up the shoreline toward her daughter's voice. She smiled at Lauren but didn't say anything as her youngest walked across the dark sand beach and stepped onto the dock. She was barefoot, just like last night on the dance floor, and Jess felt a sudden ache in her heart.

"Man, it's sticky out here," Lauren said, plucking at her tank top, pulling it away from her skin. "Glad it didn't feel like this yesterday."

"I know, it's really humid. Feels like there's a storm coming."

And not just a thunderstorm, she thought to herself. *How am I going to tell the kids about their father going to prison . . . and everything else?*

Lauren ambled down the length of the dock. She looked tired. Yesterday's wedding had made for a long day for everyone.

"How'd ya sleep?" Jess asked.

Lauren sighed as she sat down and dropped her feet into the water below. Her legs were longer than Jess's—a trait she'd gotten from her father. "All right," she said, looking closer at Jess for the first time. "Um, sorry to say this, but you look terrible this morning, Mom. What time did *you* finally go to bed?"

"I think, like . . . two o'clock? But I couldn't sleep."

"Too wound up?"

"You could say that," Jess replied, keeping her comments vague as she pondered whether to say anything to Lauren yet.

Lauren rested her elbows on her knees and her chin on her fist, gazing into the clear water below. "Hey, what's that?" she suddenly asked, pointing at something below.

Jess bent forward at the waist, trying to see whatever it was Lauren was pointing at. "What?"

"Right there. Can't you see it?"

"I just see a bunch of rocks and three little minnows."

Lauren stood up and walked back off the dock, leaving wet footprints down the length of the bleached wood. She waded into the water, heading back toward the end of the dock, this time from the water side.

"Lauren, what are you doing? You're going to get soaked!"

"I think I see an arrowhead. Those are *so* cool. Robbie found a couple last year," she said, referring to her cousin. "I'm hot anyhow, I don't care if I get wet. I need to go take a shower pretty soon."

Lauren made her way cautiously toward her discovery, side-stepping when sharp rocks poked her feet. The sand gave way to a jumble of clay and rocks halfway to the end of the dock. The water reached her chest when she rounded the corner. She tried to pick up the small rock by pinching her toes. When that wasn't going to work, she gave a quick shrug to her mother and dove under.

"You are crazy!" Jess hollered at her now-submerged daughter, laughing despite herself.

Lauren soon surfaced empty-handed, took another gulp of air, and tried again. This time her hand broke the surface of the water first, a triangular rock pointing toward the clouds clutched tight in her fingers.

"Got it!" she said as she swiped streaming water from her eyes with her free hand.

"I can't believe you did that," Jess laughed, wishing for a moment she could be spontaneous like that. *Oh, to be young again.* She'd been feeling anything but young and carefree lately.

Lauren hopped over to her mother and handed her the arrowhead before making her way back out of the water and up onto the dock. She shimmied her whole body as she walked, trying to shake off as much water as she could, but a large puddle still formed around her when she sat back down, wetting Jess's shorts in the process.

Jess sat staring at the chiseled stone she held in her hand. It was two inches long, wider on one notched end and angled up to a point on the other. Such a shape was obviously manmade.

Lauren held out her hand and Jess gave it back to her. As Lauren studied it, Jess decided to loop Lauren in.

I guess now is as good a time as any to tell Lauren what I know to this point.

She took a steadying breath. Things were going to start moving fast.

"There's a good reason I couldn't sleep last night, honey. A few good reasons, actually."

Something in Jess's tone caught the girl's attention.

"Is something wrong?"

Jess focused off to her right, out at the woods encroaching on the water's edge, then back at her daughter.

"Yes. I talked to your dad last night."

"When did he call? You were busy with the wedding all night."

"He didn't call."

Lauren's face screwed up in confusion. "Well, how did you talk to him, then? Dad wasn't here last night."

"Actually, he was."

Lauren stared at her mom. "*I* didn't see him."

"I know, honey. I went outside for some air and met him just as he was coming up from the parking lot. Thank God I caught him before he got to the reception tent. I would have hated for there to have been a scene."

"OK . . . why was he here? I mean, I know he wasn't invited, but it wouldn't have been a big deal if he just stopped by. Why didn't he talk to me . . . or to Nathan?" She paused. "*Did* he talk to Nathan?"

"No, sweetie, he came to talk to me," Jess assured her daughter. "He looked pretty haggard, so I knew something was up right away."

Lauren squirmed, her wet clothes squishing. "What did he want?"

"Oh, babe . . . I'm not even sure where to start."

"Mom, come on, already, quit with the drama."

Jess gave her daughter a soft smile at the irony of her comment—Lauren was usually the family drama queen. "To quote your father, he had some 'serious lapses in judgment.' Now it seems he's in a *world* of trouble."

"What kind of trouble?"

"I don't know exactly . . ." Jess paused, struggling to explain. She rubbed the back of her neck; she could feel a tension headache gathering. "He promised to explain everything eventually. But the crux of it is . . ."

Here goes . . .

"Your father's going to prison."

Lauren's eyes bugged wide and her jaw dropped. "Are you *shitting* me?"

Jess winced, but let the swearing pass unremarked. "Believe me, honey, I'd give almost anything to be kidding. And given how upset and deadly serious your father was last night, I'm willing to bet this isn't something that's going to just blow over, either. I'm going over to the house to meet with him this afternoon to find out more."

After a long moment, Lauren asked softly, "How long?"

"What do you mean?"

"How long is he going to prison for? What's his sentence? How can we just be hearing about this now? Doesn't there have to be a trial or something? Did he hurt someone? I know Dad has a ton of faults, but I don't think he'd ever hurt anyone." Lauren's voice was taking on a hint of hysteria. A lone tear trailed down her cheek.

Jess held up her hand to stem the questions. Once Lauren hushed, Jess put her arm around her shoulders to offer what little comfort she could. There was so much more she still had to tell her.

"We'll get answers to all of that, I promise you. I can't imagine Will would ever hurt anyone physically. If I had to guess, it's probably somehow related to his work."

The two sat side by side on the dock, the sun hot on their backs as it left cloud cover and climbed higher, each lost in her own thoughts, contemplating what this would mean for their family.

I can't tell her about the money yet, Jess decided after much internal debate, *not until I know more. I don't want to scare her about school. But I've got to talk to her about the baby. I need her input.*

"Lauren . . . when was the last time you saw little Harper and her mother?"

This snapped Lauren out of her stupor. She swiveled her whole body to face Jess.

"Oh my God, is Harper OK?"

"Calm down, Lauren. Yes, as far as I know, Harper is fine. But when was the last time you saw her and Tiffany?"

"Well . . . I saw Harper right before finals. I went over to the house because Dad asked me to babysit for a couple of hours. He had to run in to work. Tiffany wasn't around and I really didn't care *where* she was, so I guess I didn't ask." Lauren shrugged, a small smile on her lips. "I had fun with Harper."

"Can you remember the last time you actually *saw* Tiffany?"

"Oh, man. Um . . . it's been a long time. Probably back in April? She was so uptight. Little Harper cried and cried. It was like she didn't know what to do with her, with her own baby. Dad would pick Harper up and she'd settle down. It was kind of weird. And I could tell Tiffany didn't like me seeing them like that. Why all these questions about Tiffany?"

"It sounds like she took off," Jess answered.

"What do you mean, *took off?*"

"Again, I'll get more of the story from your dad this afternoon . . . at least I better . . . but he said she was suffering from severe postpartum depression and she's gone."

"Gone, like . . . *dead?*"

"Oh, for God's sake, no! At least, I don't think so. I just meant he said she left."

Overwhelmed, Lauren shifted back to face the lake but then flopped down onto her back, her left arm flung over her face to shield her eyes from the sun—and maybe from any more bad news.

Jess waited for the reality of what she was saying to sink in. It didn't take long.

Lauren slowly sat back up. "Mom . . . if Dad has to go to prison and Tiffany is gone, what's going to happen to Harper?"

Jess didn't answer immediately. Her eyes were locked on a fishing boat out on the water, but her mind was fabricating different scenes: Jess holding a screaming infant in the middle of the night . . . Jess wiping a snotty nose as she dropped a toddler off at daycare . . . Jess attending a high school graduation wearing orthopedic shoes and dentures.

I can't do all that again! *I'll be old by the time Harper is eighteen.*

Lauren grabbed Jess by the upper arm and shook her, bringing her back to their conversation. She asked again, "What will happen to Harper, Mom?"

Jess sighed. "Your dad asked me to take her. Said he didn't have any other options. I don't know exactly what he meant by that—if he just meant until he can make other arrangements, until he gets out of prison, or . . . forever. Can you imagine? Him asking *me*, of all people?"

Now it was Lauren's turn to pause. Jess could almost hear the wheels turning in that brain of hers. Jess gave her time. She needed to know what Lauren thought about the baby.

"Mom, you have to do this."

No, I don't, whispered a panicky little voice in Jess's mind.

"Why?" was all she managed to utter out loud.

"Well, for one thing, you're the best mom *ever*," Lauren said without pause, and Jess melted a little. "Harper would be lucky to have you. She'd turn out way better than if she were raised by that flake, Tiffany, I can promise you that."

And there you have the rationalizing mind of a seventeen-year-old, Jess thought as she stared at her daughter in amazement. *She'd have me ignore all the mind-blowing complications this whole situation represents and take the baby because I did all right parenting my own kids the first time around?!*

"Lauren . . . honey . . . think about what he's asking me to do. He had an *affair*, while married to *me*, and had a *baby* with the other woman, while *still* technically married to me . . . and now he's asking *me* to care for that baby?"

Lauren pulled her knees up to her chest, folded her arms on top of them, and dropped her forehead down to rest on her wrists, deep in thought. This was heavy stuff. Eventually, she raised her head and again turned to face her mother squarely.

"You're absolutely right, Mom, and that all really, really sucks. And I know it isn't fair to ask you to do this. But remember, you're always reminding me life isn't fair." Lauren looked Jess right in the eye and continued. "She's my sister. If we don't take her, and Dad's in prison, and Tiffany is gone, she could be placed into the system. Dad told me Tiffany hadn't talked to anyone in her family in, like, ten years. I don't think we have any choice."

Jess noticed how Lauren was starting to substitute "we" where Jess had been thinking "me." *But she's leaving for college in two months. It'll almost all fall on me.*

"Lauren, this will change everything. I'll be starting over with another baby."

Lauren gave one solemn nod of her head. "I know. But Mom . . . everything is already changing anyhow. You can't *not* do this."

CHAPTER 12

Gift of Teamwork

"Where are you?" Will asked quietly into his cell phone. A car door slammed outside, loud compared to the hush pervading the inside of the house.

"Wait, I gotta go. She's here." He paused, listening. "I know, I know, I'll make it right. But I gotta go—I don't want the doorbell to wake Harper. Call me back later."

Will dropped his phone into the pocket of his jeans and rolled his shoulders to release the tension. He regretted how he'd handled things with Jess the night before. He should have kept his cool. He needed her help with the baby, yes, but he couldn't afford her snooping around.

He scooped up the paperwork spread across the dining room table, took it back to his office, tiptoed in, and stashed it in the only drawer that wasn't already full. He quietly slid the drawer closed, pulled the ring of keys out of his pocket—carefully so they wouldn't jingle—and locked the wooden filing cabinet. The baby in the crib in the corner of the room stirred but settled again without waking. A quick glance around the room confirmed nothing else was out that shouldn't be, so Will tiptoed back out again and gently shut the door behind him.

He could hear footsteps approaching the front door but spared a second to glance at his reflection in the hall mirror. *Much better,* he thought to himself. *Shouldn't have let her see me like that last night.*

He reached for the door knob, opening it before his wife could ring the bell.

***

The door swung inward before Jess could insert her key, surprising her.

Here was Will, and gone was the bedraggled man from the night before. *Looks like he cleaned himself up,* she thought, eyeing the man she'd known and loved for more than twenty-five years. He almost looked like his old self. Almost.

She gave him a second to invite her in. Instead, he glanced back over his shoulder, into the shadowed house.

"Are you going to let me in?" she finally asked.

"Well, I'm wondering if we should talk out on the porch. Harper is taking a nap and I don't want to wake her."

Jess glanced inside, then rolled her eyes.

"Will, she's a baby. We can't very well stand out here and have a lengthy discussion—because God knows there's plenty to talk about—and leave her alone inside. You need to be able to hear her when she does wake up. We can keep our voices down."

Will seemed to consider this, finally letting out a sigh and stepping back with a motion for her to come in. She set her purse down on the floor in her usual spot, put her keys in the tray on the front hall table and slipped off her sandals, everything done out of habit. She headed to the back of the house, to the kitchen, where they would be least likely to wake the sleeping child.

She filled the teapot with water and set it on the burner to heat. She settled on one of the stools and glanced at Will expectantly. Today wasn't a day for small talk.

"Now, why don't you explain what's going on," Jess said. It wasn't a question.

"You never waste any time, do you, Jess?"

Jess knew her husband had come to dislike her straightforward nature, but she also knew that she wasn't going to feel sorry about that anymore.

"Will, your little show last night has the potential to implode my world. I don't have time to exchange niceties with you."

Jess kept her gaze on Will, doing her best to avoid looking at the clean baby bottles drying on a rack next to the sink and the highchair in the corner. Their own children had been eight and ten when they moved into this house. Baby things looked out of place.

Will pulled up a stool. "Where do you want me to start?"

"I guess that depends. Why don't you start at the beginning of the story? What came first? You spending all of our money, or you doing something terrible enough to land you in jail?"

"I guess I deserve that. First, let me apologize for last night. I didn't handle that very well. I never should have showed up at Renee's wedding and upset you. I could have picked a better time."

You think? Jess thought, but she bit her tongue and simply gave him a brief nod to continue. If she addressed every little thing he said, they'd be here all day.

"I suppose it all started with the money. I guess I thought all my years of schooling and work would afford me, would afford *us*, the kind of life I've always wanted to live. You know I hated that house I grew up in. It sucked growing up on the wrong side of the tracks, everyone assuming you weren't going to amount to anything. I thought I had to have a beautiful home, nice cars, exotic vacations, all the trappings of success. If I wanted to *be* successful, I needed to *look* successful."

Jess was taken aback. She'd known this about Will, but she'd never heard him actually verbalize any of it.

"By the time I finally started making decent money, there was so much debt, I never felt like I could get ahead. When you wanted to buy this house so badly, I struggled to scrape together the down payment. I was embarrassed to tell you we couldn't just write a check for it."

The man is delusional, Jess thought as she listened to him. She remembered it completely different. She'd have been perfectly content to stay in their starter home, closer to their kids' school, and full of wonderful memories despite its small size and cookie-cutter layout. It was *Will* who insisted they needed something more "suitable."

"I even went to Celia to ask her if she would help," he continued, his voice turning a shade bitter. "But she turned me down, of course."

"You did *what?*" Jess asked, her voice rising. She'd had no idea Will had approached her wealthy aunt. She would have been mortified if she had known.

"Shh," he hissed. "You'll wake the baby."

Jess closed her eyes and tried to calm herself.

"You did what?" she asked again, keeping her voice down this time.

"Jess, Celia was always helping other people. So I thought she'd be happy to help us, too. But she put a stop to our conversation pretty quickly. Said we were smart, able-bodied people and should live within our means. I went home with my tail between my legs."

"Did she think *I* put you up to that? My God, Will, you better have told her asking for money was all your idea."

Now Will rolled his eyes, clearly exasperated, and the bitterness in his voice grew. "Don't worry your pretty little head, Jess. Dear Auntie Celia thought you could do no wrong. I told her I wanted to surprise you. She said you wouldn't appreciate a surprise like that."

Jess chose to ignore his condescending tone, immune to it after all these years. She was relieved Will hadn't told Celia asking for help was her idea—if he was being truthful, that is.

Will rose quickly when the teapot started to gurgle, grabbing it off the burner before the shrill sound could start. He pulled two mugs out of the cupboard, dropped in tea bags from the canister on the counter, and set one of the mugs in front of Jess.

"Look, I'm sorry Jess. I'm sorry I ever asked Celia and I'm sorry I kept it from you. I know she was a good woman and she helped a lot of people. I guess I'm just a little bitter she never felt compelled to help *me.*"

"Will, Celia appreciated people who could fend for themselves when they had the means. I'm sure she thought you had everything under control and didn't need her help, outside of that one time. Otherwise, she would have helped."

"Yeah, you're probably right," he conceded. "Anyhow, we bought the house and life went on. It got to a point where I decided I needed to find a way to supplement our income. It seemed like no matter how hard I worked or how many surgeries I did, the hospital just kept finding ways to pocket more of the revenue I earned for them."

"Will, you have *got* to be kidding. You make more money in a month than most people make in a year. The fact that you can't live on that salary is beyond ridiculous."

Will shrugged, saying nothing.

"So what did you decide to do?" Jess asked. In no way did she find his justifications for whatever he did anything less than deplorable, but she needed him to get to the heart of the matter.

"Well, I saw the crazy prices our patients were being charged for medications I prescribed. Everyone was getting a piece of that pie except me."

"And let me guess," Jess interjected. "You found a way to get your own piece of that pie."

Will narrowed his eyes at her. "As a matter of fact, I did. Why should everyone else get rich off a broken system except the doctors and nurses that bust their asses every day, trying to heal the sick and patch up the wounded? Why, Jess?"

Jess waited.

"There was this guy," Will started to explain, but he was interrupted by static on the baby monitor followed by a loud wail. Harper didn't sound like she'd be going back to sleep anytime soon. He stood and walked over to the monitor, snapping it off. "Just a minute," he said, and left the room.

Jess sipped her tea, anxious about what would come next. She knew she was about to meet little Harper for the first time—and probably find out why her husband was going to prison too. *Maybe I should just leave, before I have to do either,* she thought, but knew that really wasn't an option. She waited. Her hand slipped into her pocket and she stroked the arrowhead with her thumb. Lauren gave it to her before she left to see Will, telling her she hoped it would protect Jess from more heartbreak. As she rubbed the old rock, Jess didn't know how that was possible.

When Will didn't immediately come back with the baby, she went to check on them, remembering Lauren said there was a crib in Will's office.

She stopped short at the doorway. There, on the floor, was Will, kneeling with his back to her, wrestling with what looked to be nothing but arms and legs on top of a blanket. A small stack of diapers, a tube of ointment, and a box of wipes lay on the carpet next to them. Will was grunting and little giggles met her ears.

"Need some help?" Jess asked, hesitant to enter the room uninvited.

"Christ, yes, I swear this kid is half monkey," Will replied, reaching for the infant as she squirmed and rolled away bare bottomed.

Jess couldn't help but laugh. Will hadn't shied away from helping with their kids when they dirtied their diapers, but that had been years ago. He wasn't as young anymore either, and probably not as quick as he used to be. Bracing herself, she took three steps into the room, scooping up the baby before she got far.

Harper squirmed in the strong arms now surrounding her, her giggles turning into grunts of frustration when she realized she wasn't going anywhere. She pushed against Jess's arms and then shifted to look at who was holding her. She settled, unsure how to act when she realized she was gazing at a stranger.

Jess, surprised to find herself eye to eye with this little human whose existence she'd resented since she'd first learned Will's girlfriend was pregnant almost a year ago, gazed back, neither of them moving for a second. Harper, oblivious to anything but her own desires, decided she did not like being constrained and let out a loud cry of protest, arching her back and throwing her head, trying to escape.

Jess laughed. The girl was spunky.

She set the child back down in front of Will and, together, they were able to get her into a diaper and a dry outfit. Will carried her back out to the kitchen while Jess tossed the dirty diaper in the diaper pail and did what she could to set the mess straight. Realizing she was stalling, she followed them back out to the kitchen.

Will attempted to fill a bottle with one hand while he held Harper in his other arm. Again, Jess's instincts kicked in and she took the baby from him so he could fill the bottle faster. This time Harper simply eyed her, sucking on a pacifier, waiting to be fed. Once the bottle was ready, he held it up in front of Jess, silently asking if she wanted to feed the baby. With a negative shake of her head, she handed Harper back and went to her stool. Jess loved feeding babies, but she knew, deep down, she needed to keep her defenses up. Lots of things still needed to be decided and she had to keep a cool head.

This time Will sat in a more stable kitchen chair, angling the five-month-old across his lap to allow her to drink the bottle in a comfortable position.

He's been doing lots of this, Jess observed.

Once Harper was settled, he continued, although the harsh tone of his voice was gone, replaced now with the sound of regret.

"I did some stupid things, Jess," he said, shaking his head as he gazed down at his baby daughter. "I got involved with people at work who were illegally dispensing prescriptions to people and pocketing the money. Not only that, but I pulled Tiffany into the whole ugly mess. She hadn't known about it for long, hadn't really gotten involved much yet, when everything blew up. I had to protect her. If I went to jail, she'd have to take care of Harper. So I told no one. When the Feds came, I never *ever* mentioned her involvement. But someone must have said something . . . because they started snooping around."

Jess was enthralled with his story despite herself.

"Tiff was already acting really strange, never comfortable around Harper. She started drinking. Too much, too often. She wasn't ever able to breastfeed the baby. At first I thought it was just a physical issue, but looking back, I can see she never wanted to have much to do with her." Will's voice cracked as he looked upon his daughter's upturned face.

He looked across the room at Jess, held her gaze, his eyes misting over.

"How could I have screwed up so badly?"

Jess felt something tug at her heart. Despite everything, she'd given her heart to this man and built a life with him, shared two children with him. She'd be a monster not to feel some of the pain he was feeling right now.

"I don't know, Will. To be honest, I don't feel like I know you anymore. I haven't truly understood you for years."

He nodded. "I know. It's been rough. Please know how sorry I am about all of it. I'm sorry I wasted our money on stupid, inconsequential things and then turned to last resorts—crimes, if I'm being honest—and putting us in this position. I'm sorry I was so stupid and I'm sorry I cheated. But I can't be sorry about Harper. She's an innocent in all of this."

Jess couldn't take her eyes off the baby, sipping on her bottle, content to be held and fed. *She has no idea what a terrible hand she's been dealt,* Jess thought in despair. Will's other daughter, Lauren, came to Jess's mind. Her words on the dock rushed back to her, and she felt the arrowhead in her pocket.

"All right, Will, I'll help you out with her *for now.* But we need to figure this mess out."

He lifted his gaze from his daughter's face to stare at his wife.

"Thank you."

CHAPTER 13

Gift of Routine

*J*ess still felt like she had more questions than answers, but things kept moving and she allowed herself to be swept up in it all.

Will told her he'd taken a plea deal. He'd said he wanted to avoid anything that would implicate Tiffany—not because he was in love with her, but because he still held out hope she would start acting like a mother to Harper. And for what it was worth, Jess didn't care whether or not he was still in love with the woman. She did believe his concern for the woman was tied to Harper.

Will shared more about Tiffany's departure. She'd left Harper with Will one afternoon, saying she needed to run to the grocery store. When she didn't come back, he started to get worried and then, later, suspicious. She didn't call and he feared she might be gone. Given her mental state, he was worried about her safety, but he didn't dare report her as missing. He had to hope she was all right.

When a detective called and asked for her, Will tried to convince the man Tiffany wasn't involved, but it did little good. They still wanted to talk to her. They looked for her, too, but they probably didn't put many resources into the search. They already had Will and others from the hospital. Tiffany had worked at the hospital for less than a year. Their fraud ring had been going on much longer. No one was intent on finding Tiffany.

When Jess asked if he worried something might have happened to Tiffany, he told her he did eventually talk to her. Tiffany called him but wouldn't tell him where she was, just that she was sorry about the baby but she didn't feel she was strong enough to take care of her and she would come home when she was better. From Will's voice, Jess wasn't sure he believed that last part.

Jess couldn't comprehend what type of woman would desert her baby; despite all the reasons *Jess* had to turn her back on the whole situation, she couldn't walk away. No one would have blamed her if she had . . . but Lauren was right. Fate had placed Harper's well-being in Jess's hands.

At least for now.

***

At first, Jess told no one other than Lauren what was happening—not even Nathan. She knew she wouldn't be able to keep it quiet for long, though, since Will had to report to the prison on July 5th.

Matt and Renee took a short honeymoon after their wedding. When they returned, Renee only had to take one look at her sister to know something was terribly wrong. That night, at Jess's kitchen table (and over two bottles of wine), Jess shared the whole sordid tale. Needless to say, Renee was furious with Will. She'd never been a big fan of his, and this confirmed many of her earlier suspicions about his lack of integrity.

"How can he put you in such an unfair position?!" Renee asked, repeating the same question Jess had been asking herself all week. "That man is a slime ball. A jackass. He is pure *evil*."

Jess finally grabbed her sister's hand and pulled her back to the table. Lauren was in the basement, changing laundry loads, and Jess didn't want her to hear Renee busting on her father. Jess doubted her daughter would argue with any of her aunt's points, but she hated to instill any more dislike in her kids for their father. He'd already done plenty of damage himself in that regard.

Renee wasn't surprised when Jess said she'd decided to take Harper, at least for the time being. "We don't think there will be any *legal* issues with her staying here," Jess explained. "Will is her biological father, and he *wants* me to keep her. He obviously can't take care of a baby from prison. I'm still his legal wife and the mother to his other children. Tiffany abandoned her, and as far as Will knows, the woman has no contact with her family, so no one should come around on Tiffany's behalf, either."

"But Jess," Renee said, as seriously as the wine and the anger would allow, "you do realize there is the very real possibility Tiffany *will* come back at some point, right? What if you get attached to the baby and then her mother comes and takes her away from you? It could break your heart."

"What do you think keeps me up at night? That worries me more than anything else. The rest of it . . . the late nights, the fevers when she gets sick, the things I'll have to give up . . . none of that bothers me as much as the risk I'm taking in getting attached."

There was a moment of silence in which they both took another sip of wine.

"But Renee . . . at the end of the day, that's not what really matters. Harper is an innocent child, involved in this mess without her control, and she deserves to be in a safe, loving home. I can give her that. I don't know who else can at this point."

Renee sat back in the chair, her head tilting back. She gazed at the ceiling as she appeared to consider her sister's words, then brought her head back up with a sigh and reached across the table for Jess's hand.

"Please know we'll help in any way we can. You've done so much for me, helping me get Whispering Pines up and running again and joining me with the retreat business. I owe you more than I can ever repay."

"Don't be ridiculous, Renee, you don't *owe* me anything. You gave me a safe place to land when my world blew apart last summer. That's what family does. But I *will* take you up on that offer of help. I have a feeling I'm going to need it."

"Are you going to move back to your house, now that Will won't be there anymore and you'll have Harper?"

"I'm not moving back into that house. *Ever.* This place is home now. That will never be home again. It's tainted. Besides, I have an extra room here."

They both took a moment to look around them at the duplex.

Renee smiled. "Honestly, it's a relief to hear you say that. I wasn't sure what you would want to do, and I'd hate for you to leave."

"Lauren will have to watch her when I'm working this summer. I'll find daycare before Lauren goes to school later next month. But we'll be OK for now."

"Have you told Nathan yet?"

Jess drained the last of her wine and grimaced. "No. He's camping with buddies right now. He's due back Sunday afternoon. I'll go to his apartment, update him on everything. He's going to be so mad at his father. He was already fed up with him."

"This is all so unbelievable," Renee said with a shake of her head.

Jess was supposed to pick up Harper from the house the next day. Never in a million years would any of them have guessed they'd have a five-month-old living at the resort with them this summer.

***

A baby was crying. Jess knew she had to find the baby, but her feet felt like they were stuck in cement. She couldn't move and the crying was getting louder. Jess started to panic.

Her eyes snapped open to total darkness. The cry came again.

Oh my God, it wasn't all a dream.

Jess moaned as her sleep-fogged mind began to clear. She reached for her glasses on the side table and checked the alarm clock. Its glowing digits read 3:22 a.m.

"I'm too old for this," she muttered as she threw her legs out of bed.

In the next room, Harper was sitting up in her crib, tears streaming. Her little body shook with emotion. The nightlight emitted a soft glow. When Harper saw her, she reached her little arms up to Jess. The tears didn't stop.

"What's wrong, honey?" Jess cooed as she lifted the baby out of the crib. The child was sweaty, her light cotton sleeper damp. She was soaked through on her bottom. "Oh, that can't feel good, baby girl, let's get you cleaned up."

Jess changed Harper's diaper and put her in a dry sleeper, saying little more in the hopes the baby would fall back to sleep. She laid her back down in the crib and left the room, softly closing the door behind her. Jess crawled back under her own covers, crossing her fingers in the hope she'd get two more hours of sleep.

She didn't get two more minutes. Harper started whimpering in the next room, her complaints quickly escalating to wails. Jess threw her own covers up over her head, hoping the child would settle back down.

"What have I gotten myself into? I didn't plan to get up during the middle of the night with another baby until I was a grandmother!" she complained to her empty bedroom.

Resigned, Jess tossed back the covers and made what was becoming a familiar trek back to the baby's room. They went downstairs, Jess prepared a bottle, and together they sat down in the recliner in the living room, gently rocking while the baby ate.

At one point, Harper reached up and touched Jess's face. Jess's irritation dissolved. It was impossible to stay frustrated with the little imp.

***

Within a few weeks, their new family unit had found their rhythm. Once Harper got used to her new surroundings, she started sleeping through the night. Lauren watched her during the day so Jess was able to work. Nathan came out and spent a weekend with them, and, never having been around babies much, seemed surprisingly comfortable with his little sister.

As she'd expected, Nathan was furious with his dad, even refused to visit Will before he had reported to prison. Jess couldn't blame their son. Will had broken trust with all of them too many times.

Jess would have preferred to take a similar stance as far as Will was concerned, but couldn't because of Harper. As the days ticked by, she worried *she* would be Will's long-term solution to caring for the child. Jess still hoped it would be temporary, so she needed to work with Will.

The following week, Jess finalized the necessary paperwork so she would be able to visit Will. She was scheduled to see him Friday afternoon. She didn't tell Lauren where she was going and her daughter didn't ask. She probably assumed Jess was going to meet with one of her small businesses.

I do need to get back out to see all of them soon, too, Jess thought as she drove to the prison. She was struggling to keep up with everything now that Harper was in the picture.

She pulled into the prison parking lot. As soon as she turned off her vehicle, heat from outside seeped in. It was a hot, cloudless day, the temperature already in the low nineties. Jess gave herself a pep talk before getting out, gazing up at the formidable building filling her windshield. *I could have gone my whole life without ever visiting a prison,* she thought as she reached for the inside door handle, *and now here I am, married to a convicted felon. If I had just left Will years ago, I wouldn't be in this mess.*

Jess marched across the tacky surface of the parking lot and entered the cool interior of the penitentiary. She produced the necessary identification and made her way through various metal detectors and locked doors. The experience was similar to what she'd expected.

Eventually, she found herself in a cafeteria-style room, across the table from Will. Gone were his designer clothes. He sat across from her in standard-issue prison garb.

At least it's not bright orange, Jess thought. There was to be no touching—which Jess was perfectly fine with—and there was a heavy guard presence around the room's perimeter. The tables were all occupied.

"Thanks for coming, Jess ... I'm so sorry to have put you in this position," Will apologized for the umpteenth time.

Emotions roiled in Jess's stomach as she glanced around the room, but she kept a cool mask of indifference plastered on her face. Was that guy over there, two tables down, a murderer? How about the tattooed man just to their left—what had he done? It occurred to Jess that Will was now forced to live among these people. How far he'd fallen from the Will who was a respected surgeon, making his rounds in his white lab coat, to this. Despite how badly he'd treated her, she'd never have wished this on him.

"How are the kids?" he asked.

"Adjusting. Lauren is doing great with Harper when I have to work. I don't know what I would have done without her. I still need to figure things out for fall. Nathan came last weekend and had fun with the baby, too."

"And how are *you* doing with Harper, Jess?"

She shrugged. "You don't forget how to care for a baby. It's ingrained in you. Muscle memory. She had some trouble sleeping at first, but now she sleeps through the night most of the time. So that's getting better."

"Really? I don't think she did that once for us. I mean . . . for me," Will stumbled.

And there it was again. The impossibly odd situation she now found herself in.

"We need to start figuring some things out," she said, choosing not to comment on his faux pas. "I think we have to sell the house."

Will didn't immediately reply, but his jaw clenched. She waited.

Eventually, his face relaxed.

"I suppose you're right. I could be in here for a few years, and the mortgage has to be paid whether it sits empty or not." He paused. "Say, you haven't considered moving back home, have you? Now that I'm not there, you could be comfortable there again. Maybe you could use some of the income off your investments from Celia to make the mortgage payment."

Jess knew him well enough to know this was a prepared speech, meant to look like it was an idea that just occurred to him. Maybe he really did belong in here.

"Will, you may not have ever bothered to notice, but I never really felt comfortable there, even before all of this happened. How many times did I tell you it was way bigger and fancier than we needed? No, I have no desire to live there again. And no, I won't be using the income from my investments to make *your* mortgage payment. Any income I'm getting from those investments will be going toward the children, now that their college funds are almost gone and I suddenly find myself with *another* mouth to feed."

"Fair enough," he said, the preparedness dying from his tone. "Just thought it was a question worth asking."

"You might want to think a bit more before posing those types of questions to me, given our current reality," Jess shot back. She'd hoped he wouldn't get under her skin, but he still knew exactly how to do it after years of practice.

She glanced at her watch. They'd already used up half their allotted time and accomplished nothing.

"As I was saying, we need to get the house sold. Anything I need to keep in mind or have repaired before I list it? I'll use Gerald again, but do you have a price range in mind?"

They proceeded to have a civil discussion and made decisions. By the time a guard announced visiting hours were over, Jess felt comfortable proceeding with selling the house.

"Can you come back again next week?" Will asked when she made to leave. "Maybe bring one of the older kids with you?"

"Unless I have paperwork you have to sign for the house, I won't be back right away. And the kids can choose to visit you on their own terms. I'll be in touch."

With that, Jess turned her back on Will and walked out, the heavy metal doors slamming shut behind her.

***

Back in the parking lot, she collapsed into the driver's seat of her Rover. The inside of the vehicle was as hot as a sauna, but it took time for her to stop shivering. *What an awful, depressing place.* She wished she'd never have to go back, but she knew she wouldn't be that lucky. Like it or not, she was still tied to that man. Those ties still needed to be untangled before she'd be free of him.

Once her nerves calmed, she drove to the old house. She'd had an idea, sitting across from Will, but kept it to herself; she should have thought of it sooner. She needed to change all the locks on the house. Tiffany probably had keys to it, and the last thing she wanted was for that woman to come back and make herself at home.

Will had assured her he'd done everything he could think of before he left so the house could sit empty for a while. He'd tossed the food, given away any indoor plants, and arranged for a service to check on the property once a week. Lawn-care was contracted and paid for through fall. *And I thought he was broke.*

She used her door opener to get into the garage. *Need to change the code on that, too.*

Two vehicles sat in the three-stall garage. Jess suspected the Lexus might be in danger of repossession, but the other vehicle was hers, free and clear. *At least it better still be free and clear,* she thought. It sat underneath a tarp: her 1978 Volkswagen Beetle convertible she'd owned since high school. Even when they were struggling to make ends meet, back when they were first married, she'd never once considered selling it. She'd always loved that car.

She entered the house through the garage. Inside, it was cool, but it felt . . . empty. She peeked into the cupboards and fridge. All were stripped bare. Jess wandered from room to room. Most of it still looked as it had when she lived here. The kids' rooms were getting bare—many of Lauren's things were now either at Jess's parents' house or at Whispering Pines; Nathan had been in an apartment for three years, so he'd taken most of his belongings.

Jess stopped at the door to her bedroom. She refused to go in. Today she felt like anything still in there could be burned for all she cared. But she knew that if the house sold, she'd need to figure out what to do with everything.

"That son of a bitch!" Jess yelled in frustration to her empty house. "Will is sitting in jail, probably reading or lifting weights, and I have the gargantuan task of getting this McMansion sold and emptied."

Infuriated, she decided now might be the perfect time for a little detective work. She stomped down the stairs to Will's office. She'd spent little time in this particular room. The antique cherry-wood desk sat in the middle of the room, surely positioned as Will would imagine the office of any important, wealthy man's office. *What a poser,* she thought as she rounded the desk and sat down in the matching chair. Pleather, probably.

She rummaged through all the drawers but found nothing interesting. Most of the papers she glanced at related to his work—his *legitimate* work—at the hospital. There was a slim laptop in a bottom drawer. She pulled it out, plugged in the cord strung up through the desktop, and fired up the computer. She tried different possible passwords until it locked up. *No getting that thing open,* she thought. *At least not today.*

What she really needed to do was find the files related to the house. The realtor would have questions when they set up the listing. Maybe those were stashed in the wooden file cabinet in the corner. Jess tugged at the top drawer, but it didn't budge; her hand slipped, chipping her nail off.

"Really?" she asked aloud to the empty room, sucking the tip of her stinging finger. "This thing is never locked."

Jess went back to the desk and rummaged through the top pencil drawer, hoping to find the key. She vaguely remembered the vintage cabinet came with two keys when they bought it years earlier. She'd kept one in her jewelry box just in case they ever wanted to lock it. Unfortunately, her jewelry box was now at Whispering Pines instead of upstairs in her old bedroom. Will must have hidden the other one. It probably made sense to lock important paperwork when the house sat empty.

Speaking of locks—I need to get a locksmith over here for the doors.
She'd have to remember to bring her key back with her.

CHAPTER 14

Gift of a Gale

Saturday, August 12, dawned clear and sunny. Jess, having lots to do, was up with Harper in time to see the sunrise. Jess was excited for the weekend. Nathan should be in by noon; Grant and Grace would arrive for their week of vacation; all the other cabins were rented to family; there would be no strangers here and they wouldn't have to cater to anyone. It promised to be a fun week before all the kids had to start heading back to school.

"I'm going to have all kinds of help with you this week, aren't I?" Jess asked Harper in her baby voice. Harper was in her highchair, wearing almost as much of her pureed carrots on her face as Jess had managed to get her to eat. She kicked her legs and replied to Jess, although it was all in baby-speak. Jess kept up her end of the conversation, telling Harper about all the people she would meet.

"On Wednesday, I'm going to take advantage of all the extra babysitters around here and do some work. I need to make my rounds to see Seth and the Fisks. Luckily, I made it over to see Wendy and Patricia at Homes Sparkle last week, so I don't have to squeeze them in."

Jess used a warm washcloth to clean the baby's face. Harper babbled back, appearing to enjoy their conversation despite the communication gap and the wipe down.

"You're a better listener than your brother and sister, I'll give you that," Jess said, ruffling the baby's hair.

She pulled a crockpot out from a lower cupboard. She needed to make her special bean dip for their cookout that evening, and the longer it simmered, the better. She set the hamburger on the stovetop to brown, opened the numerous cans of beans, and pulled out the ketchup and brown sugar. Once she had it all dumped together in the crockpot, she remembered the bacon. She ripped open the bag of pre-cooked bacon, tore it into small pieces, and tossed it in the pot with everything else.

"Shh, don't tell anyone I'm cheating," she said to the baby, her finger to her lips.

Harper made a ruckus in reply, banging her hands on her metal tray. Her giggles added to the noise and it wasn't long before Lauren joined them in the kitchen.

"You two *do* realize it's only 7:30 on a Saturday morning, don't you?" she murmured as she entered the room, her long chestnut hair piled on top of her head in a messy bun. "Whatever happened to sleeping in on the weekend around here?"

"We've got lots to do and no time for lazing around today, babe. I made caramel rolls if you want one. Have some coffee, that'll help you wake up."

"Hmm," Lauren grunted as she shuffled toward the food and caffeine. "What time is everybody coming?" she asked, already perking up at the smell of the coffee.

"Not sure exactly, probably throughout the day. I'll need you to jump on one of the lawn mowers. Robbie is already out there getting started, but he shouldn't have to spend his whole morning working on the grass by himself. Matt's on duty, and I don't think Julie is back yet. If your brother gets in before you're done, he can grab the weed-eater and trim things up."

"Seriously? All I do is work around here!"

Lauren's whining earned her a look from her mother. "Actually, all *I* do is work around here," Jess said. "You find plenty of time to play. Finish your breakfast and get out there. I don't want to hear another word about it."

Arguing with her mother never got Lauren far. She finished her roll, licked her fingers, and headed for the stairs with her coffee in hand. "I gotta go change. I'll be down in a minute."

"See that you do."

"Da, da, da!" Harper hollered, probably trying to mimic Jess, but the words sounded close enough to *Dada* to stop her cold.

***

By six that evening, everyone was settled and steaks were grilling. Different groups of cousins were busy fishing on the dock, trying to get three turtles to "race" across the beach, and playing in the sand. The oldest few sat on the end of the dock, catching up.

"Those kids are going to be starving. Good thing we have plenty of food!" Lavonne laughed.

A ring of lawn chairs covered a large portion of the grass between the cabins and the beach. Normally, when the resort was full of paying guests, Renee wouldn't set any picnic tables or chairs there because it obstructed the view and hampered access to the water. But with only family around—friends who felt like family, anyway—they'd made an exception. This way they had easy access to each other's cabins and could keep an eye—multiple eyes, in fact—on the kids.

Val's husband Luke and Grandpa George were on grilling duty. The other food was ready, stacked on a nearby table and covered with a spare tablecloth to keep the flies away.

"About done over there, hon?" Lavonne asked her husband as he stood a few feet away from the grill. The August day was winding down, but the thermometer hadn't budged yet and the combination of high temperatures and a hot barbeque had George wiping his brow.

"Patience, woman," he grunted, motioning with his spatula to the large roaster sitting nearby. "We already have that baby half full of hotdogs and burgers. We need about twenty minutes and the steaks will be ready, too."

"Here, sit down and relax, Mom," Jess said, motioning to an empty chair next to Matt as she brought two bags of buns to Luke to toast. "Let the guys do the cooking for a change."

Lavonne sat down. Unfortunately, the ground beneath her chair was uneven; Matt had to make a grab to keep both the chair and Lavonne from toppling over when she sat down.

"Oh Lord! Thank you! A broken bone would have put a damper on the week," she exclaimed. Once her chair was stable, she asked, "So, what's new around here, Renee?"

Renee, seated on the other side of Matt, turned toward her mother. "Well, we've been thinking about moving."

"What?!" Jess screeched when she overheard her sister, bringing all side conversations to an immediate halt. All eyes were on her. "You can't be serious! Can't I have just *one* stable thing in my life? Are you thinking of selling Whispering Pines?"

"Relax, Jess," Renee replied with a laugh. "Of course I'm not going to sell the Pines. I just meant . . . well . . . now that Matt and I are married and Robbie is back here full-time, we're feeling a little cramped in the duplex."

"Cramped, huh?" Val asked with a wink.

"Oh, shut up," Renee shot back at her youngest sister. "Yes, *cramped.*"

"So you wouldn't live out here full-time anymore?" George asked.

"Actually, we're playing around with the idea of maybe clearing a little bit of land somewhere out here and building. On the perimeter."

"Thank God," Jess said as she slumped back in her chair. "I'm just about ready to sell my old house. If I had to leave here, I don't know where Harper and I would go."

"That won't be necessary, Jess," Renee assured her sister. "You're welcome to live in your half of the duplex as long as you want."

Ethan was bouncing Harper on his knee, quietly listening to the exchange between his sisters up until that point. "Renee, have you thought about converting the duplex into a single unit instead? Wouldn't be that tough," he said. A contractor by trade, and a good one, he would know what he was talking about.

"Hey there, bro, you're not helping my cause one bit, you know," Jess scolded Ethan. While he might have a point, that solution would displace her, too.

"We talked about it briefly, but ultimately we don't want to do that. Whispering Pines is such an awesome gathering place for family, and if we converted the duplex into one home instead of building another one, we'd lose two spots out here. Besides, it'd be kind of fun to have something all our own that we can build to meet our needs. I've never gotten to do that before."

"What are you thinking, Matt?" Luke asked, bringing his new brother-in-law into the conversation.

"I'm with Renee on this. I've done the whole massive remodel thing more than once back in my construction days. It's hell to live through, expensive, and we'd be losing space instead of gaining it."

Grant, who had wandered up to the circle of chairs in time to catch the tail end of Matt's comments, asked, "What are you guys thinking about doing?" After Matt quickly repeated the high points of their conversation, Grant gave a nod and scanned the area around them. "Where have you thought about building? Would you knock the Gray Cabin down, maybe tuck a new house back a little farther behind where it sits now? You don't seem to want to make use of it, Renee, and it's really getting shabby."

Renee eyed the small cabin that had become her nemesis.

"Hmm, I hadn't really thought about that," she said. "You're right, though. It is an eye-sore, isn't it?"

Jess followed Renee's gaze. As she studied the shabby little cabin, a more polished picture of the structure during earlier days popped into her brain. She jumped up out of her lawn chair, tapping her forehead at the same time.

"Oh hey, I forgot to tell you about this book I found up in the lodge library," Jess said. "It's an old paperback featuring Minnesota lake resorts. I was looking through it and almost *flipped* when I saw Whispering Pines was featured."

"You've got to be kidding," Renee said in surprise. "What do you mean, *featured?*"

Jess nodded. "There were a few pages of pictures and a brief history of the place. I can't believe I forgot to show it to you! I found it over New Years. Guess it slipped my mind when you got home from Fiji with your big news. Want me to go grab it? I think it's still in the end table in my living room."

"Well, yeah, of course we want to see it. Go get it, will you?"

"Yep, I'll be right back," Jess said, hopping up and starting toward the duplex. She pulled up short and turned back to Ethan. "You OK with her?" she asked, motioning to Harper, now asleep in his lap, clearly worn out from the day's activity.

"Of course, she's fine. I am raising three of my own, you know. Go!"

Jess was only gone a few minutes. She handed the book to Renee.

"Hey, Jess, I'm sorry about that," Ethan apologized as she went to sit back down.

"About what?"

"I shouldn't have said that about 'raising my own.' I know Harper isn't *technically* yours, but I figure you can use all the help you can get."

His comment hadn't even registered with Jess. "No need to apologize. Look—and this goes for everyone, not just Ethan. I know the situation with Will and Harper and everything is *beyond* weird, but I don't want anyone worrying about saying something that will offend me. I've got thicker skin than that. We're just doing our best with a crummy situation."

"All right, then," George said, perking up at the opening Jess had given, "as long as you brought it up, honey . . . then how are you *really* doing? Come on, you can be honest, you're amongst friends here. You've taken on *so* much over the past year, what with your split from Will and helping Renee out here, then the new businesses Celia left you—not to mention the most significant additional responsibility of all," he said, motioning to the sleeping child.

"I'm not going to lie . . . it's hard," she said. "Most nights I fall into bed completely exhausted, but I'm getting by. If you don't get hung up on all the work that comes with a baby, having Harper has been more of a joy than I could've ever expected. I don't know how this will all pan out, long-term, but for now it's working. I love living out here. Helping Renee with the retreats has been a blast. In my opinion, they've been a huge success!"

"Are things going all right with work?" Lavonne asked.

"My day job is fine, Mom. The team I'm on is working on a big system upgrade. I've been doing it for so long, I can do my portion of the task list in less time than the new people. Plus, I'm lucky. They're flexible. As long as the work gets done on time, and done well, that's all they care about. It doesn't matter what time of the day I work on things.

"You do know how rare that is, don't you?" Luke asked.

"I do know. It's why I approached them to figure out a way to stay with them when I moved out here. It's worked out great."

Lavonne said, "What about those businesses Celia left to you? There were, like, three or four of them, right? You seemed to think those would take up some of your time every month, too."

Jess, used to her mom's inquisitive nature, gave a little laugh. She knew her mother's interrogations meant she cared.

"Yes, there are three. I'm learning a ton. Each one is so different. We already talked some about Seth and his architectural salvage business when we were on our girl's trip in Minneapolis."

"Oh, right, right. Are you getting along any better with Seth? I know your aunt really liked that boy."

"Actually, yes. Things are a little better with him. I've given him some business advice that, once he got over his stubbornness and gave it a try, has been working well for him. I think that earned me a few brownie points in his eyes. At least he isn't quite so crabby every time I stop out there. Which I do at least a couple times a month to help him keep his books up. The other two businesses don't need as much help on that end, but Seth does. He thinks keeping the books is a waste of time."

Renee laughed at this. "Well, that would explain why the two of you don't see eye-to-eye on things. Sounds like you fall on opposite ends of the analytical spectrum."

"You might have a point there," Jess agreed.

Jess went on to update her family on how things were going with the other two businesses, Homes Sparkle and Book Journeys. Now that she'd figured out the bookkeeping error that gave her trouble with the cleaning business's year-end results, her only complaint with them was their reluctance to try any ideas she offered to help with their expansion plans.

When she went on to explain the struggles the Fisks were facing to keep their small bookstore afloat, George suggested Nathan might be able to give them some pointers since he worked at Barnes & Noble. Jess loved the idea and decided she'd try to get Nathan to come along when she went out to visit the Fisks mid-week.

"I remember when Virginia was another one of Celia's projects," Lavonne said, reminiscing.

"How was Virginia another one of Celia's projects? I hadn't figured out the connection there yet. You know, how she got involved with the bookstore in the first place."

"Well, you'd probably have to ask Virginia or her husband to get the whole story, but I do remember that it all began a long time ago. Virginia's mother, Helen, was a close friend of Celia's."

"Wait, isn't that how she met Seth, through another friend?"

Lavonne laughed. "It sure was. But you have to remember, Celia never had a husband or kids of her own. So her friends were very important to her. She had resources at her disposal, as you know, and sometimes she used them to help either those friends or their families."

"I wish I would have thought to talk with Celia more about her life outside of our family," Renee said. "I hate that so much of that history is now lost, forever."

"Hey, *we're* still here!" Lavonne said with a laugh, motioning at George.

"I know, but you know what I mean, Mom. You were like, what . . . twenty years younger than Celia? You probably don't know it all either."

"You're right. I was her sister-in-law, but the age gap did make a difference, though we were good friends nonetheless. But I've probably forgotten at least half of what I did know through the years, too. Anyhow, back to Virginia. If I remember right, it all started when she failed to live up to her parents' *high* expectations."

"What do you mean?" Jess asked.

"I always thought Helen was a bit of a snob," Lavonne explained. "Celia tolerated it, but if I'm being totally honest, Helen was the one friend of your aunt's I didn't much care for."

Renee laughed. "Mom, that's not like you."

"Well, she was a *piece of work*, if you know what I mean. Now, do you want to hear the story or not?"

"Yes, yes, go on."

"Anyhow, Helen had four daughters. Quite the handful, as you can imagine. Virginia was the youngest. Because Helen thought wealth and standing in the community was of the utmost importance, her goal was to marry all her girls off to rich men." Lavonne lifted her nose in the air to imitate Helen. "Imagine how mad she was when only one of the four achieved it. The oldest taught high school French, took her students on a field trip to France and fell in love with a Frenchman, but never had any intention of marrying him. One turned out to be a lesbian and, given the stigma back then, was completely cut off from the family. Virginia was a dreamer. She wanted to be a writer. She was a beautiful girl and fell madly in love with a guy. I think his name was Bryce-something."

Lavonne had most everyone's attention with her story until the grill lid slammed shut.

"I hate to interrupt, folks," George announced. "But the steaks are ready."

"We can't stop now, Dad," Jess said. "Mom's on a roll, and this is too interesting. Can you toss them in the roaster with the rest of the meat?"

"Seriously?" he asked, aghast. "You want me to ruin a pile of perfectly good T-bones?"

"They'll be fine, George. I'm almost done," his wife assured him. "Now, where was I?"

"Virginia was in love," someone offered.

"Yes, right. So Bryce-something wasn't exactly what Helen had envisioned for her youngest, but Virginia couldn't be dissuaded. In reality, Bryce was an unemployed pothead who liked to paint a picture once in a while, but Virginia didn't see that right away. She ended up pregnant, and since she wasn't on speaking terms with her parents, the couple went down to the courthouse and got married."

A nightmare for any mother. Jess knew how devastated *she'd* feel if she thought, as Helen likely had, that one of her own kids was making a huge mistake.

"I bet *that* made Helen mad," Jess said with a sigh. "There's got to be lots more to this story, since Virginia is married to dear old Frank these days."

"There is lots more to the story, yes, but I'll make it quick so we can eat. Baby Karen was born, and it didn't take Virginia long to realize she'd made a terrible mistake marrying Bryce. The home they lived in was like a commune, strangers staying there all the time and lots of drugs. Bryce refused to work. When there eventually wasn't enough money for diapers or baby food, Virginia took the baby and left, vowing they'd never return. Bryce was never a strong man, and when they left him, he grew despondent. Eventually, he committed suicide."

"Oh God . . . I didn't see that coming," Renee said.

"Yeah, that was awful. At Bryce's funeral, Helen and her husband made an appearance for appearances' sake. They refused to help Virginia or acknowledge Karen—at least at first. Celia was at the funeral, too. She'd always thought Virginia was a delight, with her dreamer ways and kind heart. Celia took pity on her and allowed her to come rent her basement apartment, I suspect for next to nothing."

"That sounds like my sister," George said.

"Virginia worked as a librarian for a few years, writing a novel and raising Karen on her own. Eventually, she met her current husband, Frank Fisk, at some writers' meeting held at the library. They dated and eventually married. Karen was around eight by then, I suppose. Frank adopted her."

"I've met Karen," Jess said, nodding. "I like her."

"So where does the bookstore come in?" Renee asked.

"It had always been Virginia's dream to own a bookstore, a place she could showcase lesser known authors, local authors and such, alongside the big names. Frank was a college professor, taught creative writing. They didn't have much money, but Celia helped them get the bookstore off the ground. So she's been part of it since the beginning."

"That is so cool," Jess said, appreciating the history of the old store.

"The one thing I always found a little odd," Lavonne said, "was the relationship that eventually developed between Karen and her grandmother, Helen."

"Oh really? I thought she wouldn't acknowledge her."

"She wouldn't, not at first, but when it became apparent she would be the only granddaughter Helen would ever have, the old woman reached out. Her one other married daughter only had boys—and the teacher and the lesbian weren't going to give her any grandkids. Anyhow, little Karen loved her Grandma Helen. She'd spend weekends over there. I think Helen had a lot of influence over Karen because eventually Karen married a local man. I've met him. His family owns the local bank. Seemed to me he had the personality of a rock. Celia agreed. I remember Celia telling me that she thought since Helen wasn't able to get Virginia to follow her wishes, she instead got to Karen. Anyhow, far as I know, they're still married."

"I thought Karen seemed like a perfectly nice woman when I met her," Jess shared.

"She's probably just fine, and I shouldn't be repeating idle gossip. So, that's about all I can remember about Virginia, the bookstore, and how Celia fit into that whole puzzle."

"You know, Celia continues to amaze me. Can you imagine how different Virginia's life, and Karen's, could have turned out if she wouldn't have helped them?"

***

The weather held for three more days, during which the family had plenty of fun at Whispering Pines. Tuesday evening, the weather took a turn for the worse. A thunderstorm rolled in just as they were getting the younger kids bathed and ready for bed. Matt called Renee from work to let her know their area was under a tornado warning. A funnel had already touched down on the other side of their lake. He didn't yet know if there was any damage or injuries, but he wanted Renee to get everyone over to the basement in the duplex.

She immediately called everyone, and within five minutes, twenty-one people crowded into the duplex basement, some on Renee's side and the rest on Jess's. They watched the radar on their phones as the worst of the storm passed overhead, the actual sound of the storm muffled, underground as they were. It passed quickly, as summer storms do.

Their first problem was power. Lights flickered and then went out during the height of the storm. Luckily they had a stash of extra flashlights; Jess opted not to hand out the candles, deciding it was too risky with the kids.

Everyone except Renee, George, and Ethan were to stay downstairs until the three of them could assess any damages. Renee crossed her fingers as she came up out of the basement and met the guys on the front porch. Lightning continued to flash off in the distance, but it did little to dispel the darkness. George used his flashlight to check the rain gauge.

"Wow, three inches. That's a *lot* of water in a *very* short time," he said, wandering farther into the front yard. "I'm surprised we didn't get any in the basement."

"Cross your fingers it doesn't seep in yet," Renee said with a grimace.

Ethan circled the yard and used his heavy-duty flashlight to inspect the outside of the duplex as best he could. "Some decent-size tree branches down back here, and from the looks of these shredded leaves, there was hail, but I don't see anything too bad at this point."

"I hope the power isn't out for long," Renee said. *And I hope none of the cabins or lodge were damaged,* she thought to herself. *We've worked too hard to get this place up and running to have a setback now.* Aloud, she asked her father and brother to follow her. "We need to check the other buildings. Make sure they're safe for everybody to go back to tonight."

Together they checked the buildings—at least what they could see of them with so little light. They didn't find anything significant other than a broken window in the Gray Cabin.

"But of course," Renee said with a sigh. "It would be the Gray Cabin with a busted window."

Ethan shook his head. "Look, you need to let that shit go, sis. It's just a cabin, same as all the rest. Polish it up, put a little life back into it, and start renting it out. You letting it sit here, all ugly and rundown, just serves as a reminder of things you'd rather forget."

Renee shivered, still struggling to forget what happened in the Gray Cabin the previous year. Someone broke in and holed up inside, watching them, watching her daughter Julie. The night of their Halloween party, a deranged young man kidnapped Julie and held her in the back bedroom of the dilapidated cabin. The whole ugly situation still haunted Renee's dreams.

She opened her mouth to argue, but stopped when she saw Matt's cruiser pull into the lot. Her cell rang at the exact same time. She glanced at the screen but didn't pick it up.

"Hey, Ethan, call Jess back for me, will you? I'm sure she's looking for updates. I'm going to go let Matt know we're not in too bad of shape out here." She gave the Gray Cabin one last look, then headed toward the lot.

***

Whispering Pines fared better than two of the neighboring resorts on the lake. There were scattered power outages, and Matt and his team had been fielding calls. Once he was sure things were under control at Whispering Pines, he headed back out. He wouldn't be getting any sleep for a while.

Ethan and George found a piece of plywood and nailed it over the one broken window they'd found. It should do the trick for a while, keeping out critters and any more rain that might fall. Ethan didn't want to deal with another family of squirrels like the one they'd found squatting in the lodge when they first came back to the resort after Celia's death.

Renee went back to the duplex and helped Jess get everyone settled back in their cabins. Val's four young boys were loving the excitement of it all.

"I'll be lucky if they're asleep before two. Just because the power's out, Noah and Dave think they need to pull the bedding off their beds and make tents in the living room. And you know what?" Val asked, to whoever was listening in all the commotion. "I'm gonna let 'em. They won't forget this night. I bet they stay up an extra hour telling ghost stories inside their tent. Logan will scare the three younger ones to death and Jake will probably crawl into our bed in tears."

Renee laughed at Val's prediction. Her sister was spot on. *Nights like this make for the best childhood memories.*

CHAPTER 15

Gift of New Interests

*M*orning brought clear skies above and, on the resort grounds, a mess below. The power still hadn't come back.

Even though she didn't have to get up with the baby—Harper was still sound asleep at seven, the excitement from the previous night throwing her off schedule—Jess woke out of habit. *What I wouldn't do for a cup of coffee,* she thought, pushing the button on her Keurig, even though she knew it wouldn't work.

She went out the front door, trying not to wake anyone. The air smelled fresh and damp. She sat on the top step of their shared porch, surveying the yard. Renee's poor flowers were flattened, petals stripped away. Jess hoped some would spring back. Nature had a funny way of rejuvenating incredibly fast. *Unlike the rest of us,* she thought. Given the storm damage, Jess worried she might not be able to keep her appointments with Seth and the Fisks in a few hours.

The sound of a screen door grated and Matt sank down beside her, handing her an extra bottle of water. He was still in his uniform.

"I know, coffee would be better, but this is the best I can do."

"I'm guessing from the stubble on your face and circles under your eyes that you haven't been to bed yet," Jess said.

"Good morning to you, too," Matt replied with a tired grin.

"So, how bad is it around the area?"

"Could have been worse. We didn't have any injuries reported. Pelican Cove did lose roofs off three of their cabins. And that other one—oh, man, I can't remember the name, straight across the lake from us . . ."

"You mean Walleye Way? That resort's been around as long as Whispering Pines. It was featured in that book I found about Minnesota resorts, too."

"Yes, that's it. By the way, what kind of name is that?" Matt asked with a shake of his head. "They had a bunch of boats damaged and a jet ski is missing. It'll probably show up today, if there's anything left of it."

"Any word as to when power might be restored?"

"It could be another day."

"Crap," Jess sighed. "At some point we'll need to start worrying about the food in the refrigerators and freezers."

"If nobody opens them, we might be all right. Do you have most of the food in the lodge? Because we could look at getting the generator running if we had to."

"It's split between your place, mine, and the lodge right now. The other cabins probably have some perishables, but not much. We can look at moving it all into the bigger units in the lodge if we have to."

"Maybe the power will be back on in time so we don't have to mess with all that."

"Might be an 'ice cream for breakfast' day?" Jess suggested. "The kids would love that!"

***

Power came back on before eleven—late enough for the kids to have their pick between vanilla, chocolate, or cookie dough ice cream for breakfast, but early enough that it didn't interfere with their plans.

"This is great, Aunt Jessie," Jake proclaimed. "I've never had ice cream for breakfast before. I *love* the lake!"

Jess laughed at her youngest nephew as he shoveled in his chocolate ice cream. "What'd ya think of the storm last night? Did you guys tell ghost stories later and get all scared?"

"Honestly, I was a little scared," the boy admitted through a mouthful of ice cream. "Logan told us about the two little boy ghosts that wander around the woods and sometimes play tricks on people. I stayed in the tent all night, because I'm a *big* boy, but I made sure I was in the middle. Aunt Jessie?"

"Yes?"

"Were those boys real?"

"Yes, there were two little boys that died in a tragic accident in these woods, but honey, that was many years ago. They died before I was even born. I've heard that ghost story, too, but I've spent lots of time at Whispering Pines, even when I wasn't much older than you, and I've never seen them."

Not that I ever admitted to anyone, at least, Jess thought—but she wasn't going to share that little tidbit with her nephew.

"But just because you can't see something doesn't mean it isn't *real*," the boy pointed out in a voice that just screamed *Duhhh!*

Jess considered this. "I guess you're right, Jake. But if they *are* out there, I think they must be good ghosts. I've never heard of them scaring people. Maybe they're more like . . . you know . . . guardian angels."

"Hmm," Jake said, considering. "I like that better. Can I have some more ice cream? Since I'm a big boy now, I can eat a lot!"

***

With power restored and many hands around to clean up the debris, Jess got the green light to keep her afternoon appointments. Val wanted to watch Harper—she said she "needed a baby fix," to which her husband Luke rolled his eyes.

"Don't go getting any ideas, Val," he warned. "We talked about this. After four boys, we can't afford to keep trying for a girl."

"I know, I know. Don't get your panties in a bunch—I just want to *play* with one for an afternoon," she assured him.

Jess headed back to the house to grab her things. Nathan was just coming outside.

"Hey, bud, you look ready for the day," Jess said to him, taking in his just-showered hair and clean, although slightly shabby, lake attire. "Have any plans?"

"Not really," he said. "I was going to see if Grandpa or Luke could help me figure out why the weed eater won't start. Maybe do a little fishing. What are you doing?"

"Actually, I'm going to work a little this afternoon. I hate to leave everyone, but I just need a few hours to make a couple visits, and I've got plenty of willing sitters here for Harper. I'm going to swing by the bookstore and then stop by Seth's. I should be back in a few hours. Want to join me?"

Nathan paused, considering. Jess knew he'd been wanting to check out the old bookstore. "Can I wear this?" he said, motioning to his bedraggled outfit.

"Sure. You'll just look like a tourist if anyone stops in at the Fisks' while we're there, and anything goes at Seth's shop."

"Then . . . yeah, I want to go with you. Fishing's probably off from the storm anyhow."

"Great! It'll be fun to have a little time to catch up, too. I just need to grab a few things and we can go," Jess said, delighted to have the company.

***

"Hello?" Jess called out as they entered the bookstore, the heavy old door triggering the jingle of a welcoming bell. *It's those little things,* Jess thought, inhaling the unique smell of the store, a combination of old building and thousands of books.

No one replied.

"That's odd," Jess said, noting neither Frank nor Virginia seemed to be around. She wandered toward the back while Nathan walked around, acquainting himself with the store and its layout.

Footsteps came up the basement stairs. "Well, hello, Jess," an older woman in a flowing gauze dress came into view. The aqua color of her outfit accentuated her white hair and brilliant blue eyes. "I thought I heard the bell," she said, sounding a bit winded.

"Hi, Virginia. It's good to see you. What were you doing downstairs?"

"Oh, we have a bit of a mess down there," she explained, pulling a chair out and taking a seat.

"What kind of mess?" Nathan asked, coming up to stand beside Jess.

Virginia looked between Jess and this young man she'd never met. "Hello. Can I help you?" she asked, assuming he was a shopper.

Jess put her hand on Nathan's shoulder. "Virginia, I'd like you to meet Nathan. Nathan is my oldest. He goes to college in St. Cloud. He's home for the week, taking a little break before school starts again. I thought he'd enjoy seeing your place. He's a book lover, too," she added, knowing that one statement would earn Nathan plenty of points in Virginia's eyes.

"Oh, such a handsome young man," Virginia said, extending her hand to Nathan. "I didn't realize you had a grown child, Jess."

Nathan shook Virginia's offered hand, gifting her with the smile so like his father's. "Nice to meet you, ma'am."

That smile will melt hearts, Jess thought with trepidation.

When Nathan released the older woman's hand, she waved it in the air. "Call me Virginia. My mother is a 'ma'am,' but I prefer to pretend I'm not mature enough for the title."

Jess laughed at this, remembering Lavonne's recounting of Virginia's relationship with her mother, Helen.

"Anyhow, we were downstairs because we got water down there from last night's storm. Half the floor is wet and, unfortunately, some boxes of books were on the floor. Karen came over to try to help us clean it up."

"Oh, no! I'm sorry to hear that," Jess said. "Can we help?"

Virginia looked over at Nathan and back to Jess. "I don't think Frank would argue with having a strong young back help lift a few things off the floor down there, if you're sure you don't mind?"

"Of course we don't mind," Jess replied.

"Not a problem," Nathan confirmed. "We've got books to rescue. Show me the way."

Virginia began to hoist herself out of her chair, but Jess stopped her. "Why don't you stay here and help any customers that come in? I'll show Nathan down to the basement, introduce him to Frank and Karen, and then I'll come back up here so we can catch up."

"Bless you," Virginia said with a sigh. "Those stairs aren't getting any easier."

Jess led Nathan to the basement. The air cooled as they descended the stairs and the smell of mildew met them. *I don't think today is the first time they've had water issues down here,* Jess thought, keeping a hand on the railing.

A scene of organized chaos met them at the bottom of the stairs. There were tables set around the perimeter of the first room, loaded with stacks and stacks of books. Two similar rows also ran down the middle of the room.

"Man, check out all these *books*," Nathan said, a hint of wonder in his voice. "This damp air can't be good for 'em."

"You're probably looking at thirty-plus years of unsold inventory right here," Jess replied, her voice grim.

Nathan walked down one aisle, eyes and fingers skimming the visible spines. The sucking sound of a shop vac led them to Frank and Karen in a back room in the east end of the basement.

"Frank, Karen, it's Jess. Need some help down here?" Jess hollered, trying to be heard over the whirling of the vacuum.

The vacuum switched off. Frank appeared in the opening to the back room, wiping his brow with a white handkerchief. His dress pants were wet at the knees and one tail of his white dress shirt hung loose from his waistband. "Hey there, Jess, am I glad to see you! We could use another set of hands back here."

"So I hear. And it's your lucky day . . . well, other than having water in your basement, that is. I brought my son Nathan along today. He wanted to check out the shop. I bet his strong back will come in handy if you have any heavy lifting."

Nathan wandered up behind his mother. Frank glanced his way, grinned widely, and extended his hand.

"Well, my goodness, you are right, Jess. It might just be my lucky day at that. If you'll follow me, son, I'll show you what we're dealing with back here."

Jess had been down in the basement before, but never ventured back this far. The room Frank entered was one step farther down.

"Watch your step," Frank instructed. "Hope you're not wearing your favorite shoes today, because they're going to get wet. Karen, we've got reinforcements."

A woman, similar in age to Jess, wearing a plain gray T-shirt, jeans, and bright pink Hunter rain boots, turned to face them after setting a cardboard box onto a plastic table. The table wobbled under the weight of the box and water dripped back down to the floor; the box was obviously saturated at the bottom.

"Oh hey, Jess. Good to see you again," the woman said—although Jess didn't think she sounded as grateful as she should have at the prospect of more help.

"Good to see you, too, Karen. Looks like you're dressed better for this work than your dad over here. I don't think I've ever seen you in jeans before."

Usually you're dressed like a high-powered CEO. Women like you make the rest of us working women look like slobs when we prefer business casual, Jess thought with a twinge of jealousy.

Karen gave a little laugh. "You know how it is, always have to dress the part! And my 'part' doesn't usually include manual labor. But Mom called and asked me to come over and help clean up this mess."

"Nice boots," Jess said, motioning to the bright, shiny rain gear that probably set Karen back $150. *She must not struggle financially like her folks.*

"First excuse I've had to wear them," Karen said, and then paused when she noticed Nathan enter the room behind Jess.

Jess stepped to the side and made introductions. "Karen, this is my son Nathan. Nathan, this is Karen. She's Frank and Virginia's daughter."

Karen smiled at Nathan.

Looks like she has more faith in Nathan's ability than mine to help clean up this mess.

"Nice to meet you, Nathan. Now, if you two don't mind, do you want to help us get these boxes up out of this standing water?"

Her question snapped everyone into motion. Frank directed Nathan to the other end of the basement where there were a few additional tables not currently being used. Nathan brought them over. Water barely covered the floor where they were standing, but stood a couple of inches deep against the outer wall.

"These old buildings settle," Frank offered in explanation as he caught Jess sizing up the situation. "I could kick myself for setting these boxes on the floor this past winter. When things were slow, I tried to get organized down here. I had every intention of setting tables up in this room, like we have out there," he said, motioning to the front room, "but I forgot. I hope we can save some of the books in the boxes."

"Let's try," Jess said, and they all got busy.

It didn't take long to get all the boxes off the floor. Nathan, Jess, and Karen worked on that while Frank, whose back wasn't up to the task of lifting heavy boxes, ran the shop vac. They started the process of emptying the wet boxes, removing the books not directly touched by the water and placing them onto an additional table they'd set up in the front room. Unfortunately, there wasn't room for the excess merchandise on the main floor.

"I don't recognize any of these authors," Nathan said to Frank as he juggled a stack of paperbacks.

"Most of these boxes back here were from our 'local authors' section upstairs. Like I said, I was trying to get organized. Your comment makes me think you're a reader, like your mom."

Nathan set the stack of books down, careful to fan them so they could dry completely in case they were damp. "I do like to read, but I don't have much time these days, between my classes and my job."

"Where do you work?"

"I actually work at Barnes and Noble in St. Cloud."

This surprised Frank. "Well, I'll be. That would explain why you don't recognize these. Those stores don't cater much to lesser-known authors. Helping them get started has always been a passion of Virginia's," he explained, pointing toward the ceiling and his wife upstairs.

"Really? That's pretty cool," Nathan replied as he got back to work emptying the rest of the boxes. Jess saw him flip through a couple of the books, looking intrigued.

The books on the bottom layers of the boxes were soaked through. They filled three dented aluminum trash cans with the ruined books. Books are heavy to start with, and water makes them even more so; it took all Nathan's strength to wrestle the containers up the stairs and out to the back alley.

Within a couple of hours, they'd done what they could. They set fans out to try to rid the air of the damp and dry the floors better than the shop vac could do on its own. Jess suggested they invest in a couple dehumidifiers. Bars covered the basement windows, but they could still be opened, so Nathan went outside and tugged them open after Jess threaded her hand through the bars bolted to the inside walls to unlock them.

"I wouldn't leave these open too long," Jess warned Frank. If there were ever screens over these windows, they were long gone. A person couldn't crawl through them, but small animals or birds could.

The four of them made their way back up to the shop, dirty and hungry. Virginia directed them to the apartment upstairs. No one lived up there anymore, but they did use the kitchen from time to time, and she'd gone over to the small grocer on the corner for bread and sandwich fixings. Karen declined, needing to go home and clean up so she could make a client appointment in an hour.

Revived with food and lemonade, they went back down to the main bookstore. Virginia had just finished up with a customer, a young woman with the latest paperback from a popular series tucked under her arm.

"I swear, there's no accounting for taste these days," Virginia said before the door was even completely shut behind the woman.

"Virginia," Frank said, a slightly scolding tone to his voice. "We've talked about this. Don't say things to insult our customers. We don't have enough of them to start with—you don't want to chase away the ones we do have, do you?"

"Don't worry, honey," Virginia said. "I just have to smile and wink at them and they'll assume I'm a crazy old woman and pay me no mind."

Jess laughed. "You are anything but a 'crazy old woman,' Virginia."

"Some days I wonder," was Virginia's only reply as she stared out the front window, a concerned look on her face.

Nathan chimed in. "Why don't you show me around your store?" he asked Virginia, extending his arm to the woman.

He can be a charmer, just like his dad, Jess observed, wondering whether she should be concerned. *God forbid he turn out like his father. And I need to stop thinking about that man.*

Virginia appreciated the attention, and her signature smile came back. She lightly grasped his arm and proceeded to give Nathan a tour, pointing out how she had the different sections organized and why it made perfect sense the way she had everything laid out. Nathan gave Jess a discreet wink at one point, appearing to be enjoying himself.

Jess and Frank took a look at the sales results and expenses while Nathan kept Virginia busy. Jess was glad to see the summer tourist season had helped business a bit.

"Are you still working on finding us a buyer?" Frank asked when Virginia was out of earshot. "I'm getting more concerned about Virginia's memory. This is too much for her anymore."

"I'm working on it," Jess assured him—although in reality she'd had no time to start looking for one.

***

"So, what did you think?" Jess asked as they drove to Seth's shop. "I'm sorry they put us to work."

"No problem, Mom. That's a cool store, and I liked Virginia. She's . . . different. Not sure how to explain her."

"I'd call her *eccentric.* Your grandmother said Virginia was a bit of a hippie back in the day."

"That wouldn't surprise me."

They rode in silence for a few miles. Nathan fiddled with the radio.

"We should help them figure out some ways to drive more business. Like I said, it's a cool place."

"Actually, if you have any ideas, I'm all ears. Don't say anything to Virginia, if you talk to her again, but Frank really thinks they need to either sell soon or close the store. Within the year."

"Oh man, that would suck if a great old place like that closed."

"It sure would, honey, so if you have any brilliant ideas, I'd love to hear them."

***

The gravel in Seth's lot was much smoother this time of year as she pulled in and parked. Seth's one-ton pickup was parked off to the side. Another vehicle was parked closer to the door.

"Come on, I'll introduce you to Seth. Hopefully he isn't in his usual jovial mood today," Jess said, her voice dripping with sarcasm.

Nathan grinned. "Not always a cheerful guy?"

"Not always," Jess said, deciding not to say any more and let Nathan draw his own conclusions.

Jess led the way into the cool interior of the shop. Seth gave her a small nod of acknowledgment, but he was busy showing a man and woman a long section of intricate wrought iron fencing.

Nathan paused next to Jess so his eyes could adjust after the bright sunlight outside. He let out a low whistle as he took in their surroundings. Jess allowed her eyes to follow a similar path. She usually headed straight to the office when she came out. She'd never actually taken the time to do any exploring. She looked at her watch.

"We need to be home before too long. We took longer than I expected at the bookstore. Looks like Seth might be a while. Why don't you go ahead and wander around, check things out? I'll go get started on things in the office. Don't touch anything."

"Jesus, Mom, I'm not three years old anymore."

"Noted," Jess said with a laugh and left him to explore. She was pleasantly surprised at the state of Seth's desk—either things had been slow or he was starting to file the invoices away as she asked. When she checked a couple of folders, she was happy to see he was finally starting to take her advice. She fired up his computer, used the key he'd given her for the large bottom drawer, and pulled out the check register. She'd recorded two weeks of deposits and a few checks into QuickBooks when Seth strolled in.

"Hey, who's the kid you turned loose in my shop out there?"

"That 'kid' is my oldest son," she answered, not looking up from what she was doing. "And he's probably only a few years younger than you."

"Jesus . . . Jess, how old do you think I am?" Seth asked, taken aback by her comment.

Now she looked up. "Um . . . I guess I don't really know. I never gave it too much thought. Like . . . maybe . . . thirty?"

"Try thirty-seven."

Now he had her full attention. "Really? It must have been your juvenile attitude that threw me off."

"I guess you just tend to bring out the best in me," he snapped back. "And for the record, I would say I'm not the only one that can be a bit *immature* at times."

"Cute."

Their banter was cut off by the sound of crashing metal.

"For Christ's sake, now what?" Seth said as he spun on his heel. "I'm not liable if your kid lost a finger out here."

Jess was right behind him. "Nathan? What happened? Are you all right?"

More metal clanged and there was the scraping sound of something being dragged across concrete. Seth and Jess rounded a corner together and found Nathan surrounded by scattered ceiling tins. He looked up sheepishly.

"Aw, sorry about that, bud," he said to Seth, his face burning red. He stepped cautiously out of the middle of the mess and approached them, his hand extended. "I'm Nathan Rand."

"Seth Lindell," Seth said, eyeing Nathan up and down as he shook his hand.

"Look, I'm real sorry. We just came from this cool old building with a ceiling covered in these things," Nathan explained, motioning to the rusty metal squares now lying all over the floor. "I was looking through your stack to see if you had any like theirs. For replacements."

"Are mine damaged now, too?" Seth asked, squinting at Nathan. If he was trying to intimidate Nathan, Jess could see it wasn't working. Once Nathan got an idea in his head, he got laser-focused.

Her son laughed at Seth's comment. "Dude, these look like they've got a few *decades* of damage on them. But don't worry, I'll stack them all back, nice and neat, like you had them."

Seth paused, probably trying to tamp down his irritation. "Better not. I'll do it later. You can't be moving these things without gloves on. The edges are sharp and there's always old nails sticking out of 'em. Don't want you getting hurt on my property."

Seth's tone finally seemed to catch Nathan's attention. "You are uptight, aren't you?"

"Been talking to your mother about me, I see," Seth replied, but there was a hint of a laugh now. "Anything else you want to wreck around here, or can we go get this blasted paperwork done? I still have to get my truck unloaded before I can call it a day."

"I've got an idea," Nathan said. "Why don't you let me make it up to you for making a mess? I can help you unload your truck while Mom does her thing."

This seemed to surprise Seth.

Good move, Nathan, Jess thought. *That's the quickest way to get into Seth's good graces—if that's possible.*

Seth considered Nathan's offer. "Sure you got the back for it?"

"I'm sure. Got another pair of those gloves laying around?" he asked, nodding toward Seth's gloved hands. Jess seldom saw the man without gloves on.

Seth turned back to Jess. "Need me in there?"

"Don't think so. I'll find you if I have a question. Go get your truck unloaded while you have a willing assistant."

***

"So what exactly do you do out here?" Nathan asked, pulling on the gloves Seth had found on a nearby workbench. Seth walked outside and Nathan followed.

"I salvage structural pieces out of old buildings, usually right before they're scheduled to be demolished. Clean it all up and sell it to people to use somewhere else."

"Didn't know that was a thing. Can you make a living at it?"

"That's what I've been doing."

Seth dropped the tailgate on his truck and rolled the tarp back. Inside were rows of neatly stacked wooden spindles and other pieces. He was glad to see his straps held everything in place. He didn't need any of this damaged. He already had a potential customer in mind.

Nathan waited while Seth undid the straps. "Wow, where'd all this come from?"

Seth wrestled with a particularly tough knot. *This kid talks as much as his mother.* When he finally worked the strap loose, he pulled the closest stack of wood out and turned to Nathan. On cue, Nathan held out his arms, taking the heavy bundle from Seth.

"An old church about an hour from here. The place got to be too much to maintain, so the congregation decided to demolish it to make way for something new."

"How do you find out about these in time?"

"Unfortunately, I don't *always* find out in time. You'd be amazed at the beautiful things that are lost forever in the name of progress. But sometimes I get lucky. I keep my ears open, make sure the different historical societies around the state have my name on file."

"Sounds like you're pretty passionate about saving this old stuff," Nathan said, nodding to the full truck box as Seth filled his arms with another pile of railings.

"I guess so."

The two worked in silence after that, just as Seth preferred. He'd never been one for small talk.

As they set the last stacks down on the pallets inside, Nathan pulled his gloves off and pointed to a room in the back. "I saw you had some stained glass back there. Do you work with that, too?"

"I do."

"Do you do repair work?"

"I do."

"I should have Mom talk to you about her old bookstore. That place needs some TLC and you seem like the man for the job."

Seth grunted. "Your mother probably gets enough of me out here. In case you didn't notice, we tend to rub each other the wrong way."

CHAPTER 16

Gift of Moral Support

"Well, isn't this a surprise," Will said to the woman sitting across from him. She was the last person he'd expected to show up on visitor's day. Probably the last person he *wanted* to see.

"I just couldn't stay away any longer," Tiffany said. "I was too lonesome. I missed you and Harper too much."

More likely you ran out of money, Will thought, but he was careful to keep his face a pleasant mask of surprise. He would play along.

"I've missed you, too, Tiff," he said. His brain was moving fast, trying to decide how best to play this. He had a lot to lose if he wasn't careful. "I've been worried. What happened? Where did you go?"

"I'm *so* sorry, Will. I just couldn't take the pressure anymore. I don't know what was wrong with me. I was always so blue, so tired. The baby, she made me so nervous, and then that just made her uptight, which just amped up my nerves even more. You're so much better with her. So comfortable with her. And then with everything going down at the hospital . . ." Tiffany took a dramatic pause. "I just couldn't take the stress of it all anymore. I needed space."

"We talked about this, Tiffany. What you suffer from is a real medical condition. Postpartum depression can be treated. But, instead, you ran. I wish you wouldn't have left like that, Tiffany. You scared me." Will was careful to keep his tone even and non-confrontational. He couldn't say anything that would put Tiffany's guard up. He needed to know why she'd come back.

She wiped at her eyes as if sweeping away a tear—but as far as Will could tell, she was as dry-eyed as him. The woman wasn't as good an actress as she thought she was.

"Do you forgive me, Will? I'm much better now. All I needed was some rest. I . . . I'm ready to be Harper's mom again."

Being a mother isn't something you can just turn on and off as you feel like it, Will thought. The woman sitting before him had turned out to be such a disappointment. He shouldn't have let her attractiveness and youth blind him to her lack of character. She'd never be half the mother Jess was. How could he have been so stupid?

Tiffany sat up straighter in her metal chair. "I'm ready to take Harper back," she repeated. "Where can I pick her up?"

Will couldn't help himself. *This woman is unbelievable.*

"Tiffany, you can't just swoop in here and expect to take Harper. That's not how it works. How do I know you're fit to take care of her? What happens if you start to feel overwhelmed again? It's not like you can dump her off on my doorstep next time."

Tiffany squirmed in her seat. She seemed to have a hard time meeting his eye. Finally, she looked back at him.

"I get it, Will. I was irresponsible and you're right to question me. But I have a better support system now. I miss my baby . . . I never want to be separated from her again."

"And what, exactly, does that support system look like?"

"I moved in with my cousin, Alysa, in Chicago. I'm working the night shift in an emergency room. Alysa will be with Harper when I'm working."

"Who will watch her when you sleep? You have to sleep sometime."

"A neighbor girl in the apartment building. She babysits all the time. She's willing to help out. So, see, I've got it all worked out. I just might need a little money—you know, to help pay the babysitter and part of our rent. I can cover most of it."

And there it is, he thought. He was tempted to tell her there wasn't much money left but decided to wait. *I need to warn Jess that Tiffany is back and wanting to take Harper. I need to convince Jess to keep the baby. Harper wouldn't be safe with this woman.*

Tiffany babbled on, "I so appreciate whoever's been helping with Harper while you're in here, until I could feel strong enough to take care of her." She glanced up at him tentatively. "Who did you line up?"

Will stared evenly at her. He couldn't help but test her reaction to what could very well have happened if Jess hadn't stepped up. "What if I told you, Tiffany, that she went into the foster system when I took the plea deal—which I did to protect *you*? I couldn't very well take care of her from prison."

All the color drained from Tiffany's face. "Oh my God, Will, tell me you didn't let that happen? I don't want Harper with *strangers!*"

"Maybe you should have thought about that before you left, knowing full well I was facing some very serious charges." After a moment of letting her squirm, Will added, "But . . . you can relax. We got lucky. I asked Jess—my *wife*—to take her. And because she's an infinitely better person than either you or I, she agreed."

Tiffany released a sigh of relief, but Will could see the moment his response fully registered. She narrowed her eyes at him.

"Wait . . . what are you talking about? Don't you mean *ex*-wife? I thought you were almost done with all that legal crap. Aren't you divorced yet?"

"Not quite."

Tiffany sat back and chewed on her thumb nail, absorbing the news, then finally said, "Thanking her might be a bit awkward."

"Oh, you have no idea." *Jess could rip your fragile psyche to shreds in one conversation,* he thought. "You better let me talk to Jess first. I don't want you showing up on her doorstep. This is going to come as quite the shock to her."

"Well . . . OK, then. But I have to be back in Chicago by Wednesday for my next shift at the hospital."

Will almost laughed. "Jeez, Tiff, that's only five days away!"

She shrugged and pushed her chair back, the metal grating on the institutional tile at their feet. "You don't want me to lose my new job, do you?" A pause. "All right. Can you talk to her soon?"

"I will."

"In the meantime, do you mind if I swing by the house? I need to pick up more of my things." She stood to leave.

"That's fine. You have a key. Just don't help yourself to anything that doesn't belong to you," he warned.

"Seriously, Will? You don't have to worry about me. I'll be back on Monday. Please have things arranged with Jess by then."

As Tiffany walked away, Will thought, *What the hell am I going to do now?*

***

Jess had just finished a conference call early Thursday afternoon when her cell phone rang. She didn't recognize the number. Often, she let those calls go to voice mail, but she answered this time.

"Hello, this is Jess."

Not hearing a response, Jess repeated herself. She started to hang up when she heard someone on the other end.

"Jess Rand?"

"Yes, this is Jess Rand. How can I help you?" She thought maybe it was a customer from one of their retreats, so her voice instantly took on a helpful-businesswoman tone.

"Um . . . Jess, this is Tiffany. Harper's mom."

Jess almost dropped her phone. *Oh my God!* Her brain clicked off. *What could this woman possibly want?* Then the worst entered her mind and Jess looked around her, saying, "Where are you, Tiffany?"

"Actually, I'm at the house. Where are you? Do you have my baby?"

Struggling to maintain her composure, Jess stood and started pacing around her small kitchen.

"What are you doing at the house? Do you mean *Will's* house? Technically *my* house?"

"Yes, of course. What other house would I mean? I needed to pick up some of my things. I stopped to see Will during visiting hours earlier today. He said it was all right for me to swing by the house. He wanted me to wait to talk to you until after he had a chance to tell you I was here, but when my key wouldn't work, I decided to call you directly. I don't have much time. Can we meet?"

Is this lady for real? "When? Where?"

"Can you meet me at that Starbucks on 111th? We have a lot to talk about."

Jess paused, her brain still locked up. *Do I really have a choice?*

"Jess?"

"All right," she said finally, "but I need an hour. I'll be there at four."

Jess hung up and dropped to the scarred linoleum. After a few moments, the shock of Tiffany's phone call began to wear off. She closed her eyes, furious. She'd dreaded this day, known it could come. Harper was no longer the object of her hatred due to her husband's infidelity; she hadn't been since the first time she saw Will struggling to change the baby's diaper. Harper was an innocent in all of this, and she already had a piece of Jess's heart—a piece that grew with every day.

How could Will put her in this position?

She hoisted herself off the floor and went over to Renee's. Thank God her parents and other family had gone home that morning; Renee could maybe help, but Jess would have had a hard time telling everyone about this right now. Not bothering to knock, she let herself in the front door.

Renee and Matt jumped apart. They'd been standing just inside the front door and now they looked guilty.

"Jeez, Jess, can't you knock?" Renee complained, but she quickly saw something was wrong. "Jess? What happened?"

"Tiffany called."

"Oh . . . God . . . OK. Come in," Renee said, grabbing her sister's hand and pulling her toward the couch. Matt was in uniform. He must have just gotten home. Renee's eyes met Matt's for a split second.

"I'll give you two a minute," Matt said, kicking off his shoes and heading up the stairs.

"Tell me everything," Renee said, tugging Jess down to sit beside her.

"There isn't much to tell," Jess said. She gave her a quick summary of the brief call. "Renee . . . do I have to take Harper with me?"

"Of course not," Renee assured her. "But I don't want you going alone. Where's Harper now?"

"Napping. Lauren is home too. I can ask her to watch her."

"Yes, yes, do that. We need to find out more before we let that woman see Harper again. What about Will?"

"Tiffany said she saw him but he asked her not to reach out to me until he'd had a chance to talk to me first. She doesn't follow instructions very well."

Renee was trying to keep up. "So Will doesn't know you've talked to Tiffany? That you know she's back?"

"It didn't sound like it. I'm supposed to go see him tomorrow. I need to get his signature on the listing agreement for the house."

"Why don't you go tell Lauren we need to run an errand? Don't tell her Tiffany is back. Not yet. Not until we know what that woman is up to. I'll go tell Matt real quick, so he knows where we went, and we'll go. Does that work?"

"Yes . . . thank you, Renee."

Renee stopped on her way to the stairs leading up to Matt. "For what?"

"For helping me keep my sanity."

***

Jess was too shook up, so Renee drove.

"Do you think Tiffany is back for Harper?" Renee asked as she turned off the gravel road leading away from Whispering Pines.

Jess shrugged, still feeling disoriented by the surprise call. "Either that or she needs money. Will has made enough comments about her for me to think she has champagne taste. She might be out of money by now if Will was supporting her." She let her head fall back against her seat, closing her eyes to the trees rushing by outside. "Oh, Renee . . . what am I going to do?"

"Let's not get ahead of ourselves, Jess. If it's money she wants, Will can deal with that. But if she wants to take Harper . . . how do you feel about that? You told me going in that you wanted this to be temporary, you having Harper."

"I know I did. Maybe I still do. I don't know . . . it's all *so* confusing. But that woman abandoned her baby, Renee. She walked away and has been gone for months. The thought of her taking Harper now . . . it chills me."

They rode in silence for a time. The drive seemed endless to Jess. Her mind skipped back over her time with Harper. She now felt a strong sense of protectiveness toward the child.

But Tiffany is her real mother, she kept reminding herself.

Finally, Renee pulled into the Starbucks parking lot, but before she could get out of the Toyota Jess grabbed her hand.

"What if . . . what if she *does* want to take Harper?"

Renee squeezed her hand back. "One step at a time, Jess. One step at a time."

***

Jess recognized the woman immediately, sitting at a corner table, watching them with wary eyes as they entered the coffee shop. She stopped Renee just inside the door with a touch on her arm. "Can you give me a minute with her first? Then join us?"

"If you're sure," Renee replied, looking questioningly at Jess. "I can get us a cup of coffee and give you a minute to introduce yourself. Remember, I'm right here. I've got your back."

Jess nodded to Renee but never took her eyes off Tiffany.

The woman stayed seated as Jess approached.

"Tiffany?"

The woman nodded, motioning to the seat across from her. She looked as nervous as Jess felt. She was obviously younger than Jess, her blond hair and light complexion so different from Jess's own appearance. In her own mind, Jess had built this woman up to be "the enemy." But the woman before her now seemed . . . fragile.

Once Jess was seated, Tiffany gave her a weak smile. "Thank you for meeting me," the woman finally said. "I'm sure this is all a bit shocking for you."

"A bit," Jess replied, reminding herself about the promise she'd made to Renee to be civil to this woman—the woman who had stolen so much from Jess. It was important to find out exactly what she wanted.

I know Renee's right . . . but I hate this woman to the very depths of my soul.

"Thank you for taking care of my baby while I've been gone and Will's been . . . unavailable. I don't know how much Will shared with you, but I'm feeling so much better now. Stronger."

You don't look strong to me.

At that moment, Renee approached with their coffee. Jess pulled out the chair next to her and took one of the paper cups. Renee sat and Jess made introductions.

"I was hoping you'd bring Harper," Tiffany said. "I miss her so much."

"She had a fun day today playing with our daughter, Lauren, so she was napping," Jess said, unable to resist getting a dig in. She wanted to remind the woman of the family Will had *before* she entered the picture. She'd do her best to behave, but that didn't mean she had to make it easy for Tiffany.

Renee shot her sister a warning glance and took over the conversation. "We thought it would be more appropriate, for this first meeting, to leave Harper home. What we need to know first is what exactly you are doing here, Tiffany. You've been gone for months."

Tiffany blinked. "I came to get Harper."

Renee shook her head. "It's not going to be that simple, Tiffany. Will asked the courts to assign guardianship to Jess when he went to prison. Harper is an infant. She needs constant care by a capable, responsible adult. Last I heard, you weren't up to providing that care."

Tiffany visibly bristled at the comment, but seemed to be trying just as hard as Jess was to keep things civil. "Fair enough. I admit, I found myself in a very dark place. But I feel so much better now. I have a place to live and a new job in Chicago. Will won't get out of prison for years. I need to move on . . . but I can't do that without my child."

The hell you can't, Jess thought. She took a sip of her coffee, but it tasted bitter. Renee started to respond, but Jess cut her off. "So you think you can waltz right in here and whisk Harper off to *Chicago,* just like that?"

Renee reached over and squeezed Jess's knee, hard.

I need to stay calm, Jess reminded herself, giving Renee's hand a reassuring pat—a commitment to behave.

"Why don't we take a step back," Renee suggested. "We all need to keep a level head here. What's changed, Tiffany? Why do you feel able to take care of Harper now, when you couldn't before?"

"I've started to get some things figured out. My cousin is willing to help out with Harper. I think I can do it this time. As long as Will can help with child support, I've found people that can watch her while I work."

Jess considered Tiffany's words while she drank more of the coffee, though she'd lost her appetite for it. "And you shared this plan with Will?"

"Of course."

"And he agreed to everything?"

Tiffany looked away. She took a moment before responding.

"No . . . I wouldn't say that. He had some of the same concerns as you do, like whether or not I could *really* take care of Harper now. I assured him I could."

"Did you mention the part about him paying you money?"

"Of course—but I'm sure he expected to. After all—and while I appreciate how painful it is for you to remember this—we *are* Harper's parents. *Together.*"

"Believe me, that fact is never far from my mind," Jess said, her words laced with sarcasm. She took a breath. "I'm scheduled to visit him tomorrow. I have some papers he needs to sign. We *will* be discussing all of this *in detail.*" While Tiffany kept glancing away, Jess's eyes never wavered from the other woman's face.

"Well, good. The sooner we can get all this figured out and I can get back to Chicago with Harper, the better. I have to be back for my next shift. When you see Will, ask him why my key won't work. I couldn't get into the house."

"You can ask *me* that question," Jess said.

Tiffany looked surprised at this. "OK . . . why didn't my key work?"

"Because I changed the locks."

"But how can you do that? You don't live there anymore. It's Will's house."

This woman is not very bright, Jess thought. *What did Will ever see in her, other than maybe the fake eyelashes and even faker breasts?*

"Tiffany," she said, speaking slow and clear as if to a child, "we're not divorced yet. The house is an asset we own jointly. In fact, the papers I need him to sign tomorrow are for the listing agreement."

Tiffany just stared back. "I don't understand."

"We're selling the house."

"But . . . why?"

"Because the money is gone. We can't afford it."

***

"Did you see the look on her face when you told her the money was gone?" Renee asked, laughing so hard her eyes watered as she drove out of the parking lot.

"Oh, I saw it. Renee, how can you laugh at a time like this? This is serious!"

Jess's emotions were through the roof, but Renee's laugh was contagious, and Jess finally tipped into gales of laughter herself.

"That *bitch.* She's just after Will's money!" Jess said. "Probably has been since the beginning. I thought she was going to fall out of her chair when I told her there was none left."

Jess fought against her roiling emotions and stopped laughing. None of this was funny.

"Renee ... Tiffany probably can do whatever she wants as far as Harper goes. She's the baby's biological mother. Will may be her father, but he isn't exactly playing from a position of strength right now. I don't know how binding the guardianship is if Tiffany is back in the picture."

Renee sobered. "You may be right. I don't know how the law works either. I'll ask Matt when we get home. He probably has a better idea than we do as to the legal aspects of all of this."

"And I'll talk to Will when I see him tomorrow. Renee, what am I going to do if she really does insist on taking Harper? It'll kill Lauren and Nathan to lose their little sister. It just might kill me, too."

CHAPTER 17

Gift of a Reprieve

*J*ess held Harper extra close two nights later, rocking her long after the baby was asleep. Lauren was next door, spending her Saturday night watching a movie with Julie and Robbie. Renee and Matt were at some law enforcement function. ("Just have to make an appearance," Matt had said, looking less than thrilled to be going.)

The book she'd read to Harper, before giving her a bottle and rocking her to sleep, sat on the end table. Jess's eyes rested on the family favorite: *Goodnight, Moon.* She used to read the very same book to both Nathan and Lauren when they were babies.

Life can be so funny sometimes, Jess thought, staring down at the peaceful child in her arms. This baby wasn't her flesh and blood, but she still felt a connection to her, clear down to her soul. *I promise I'll keep you safe, little one.*

Aside from the surprise appearance by Tiffany, it had been a fun week with the family. Everyone was back home now, and new renters had arrived (as they did every Saturday in the summer). Renee had made sure everyone was settled before she'd left for the evening.

Tomorrow Jess would take Harper to see Tiffany. They were set to meet at the house. As far as Jess knew, Tiffany was still hoping to take Harper to Chicago on Tuesday because she had to be back to work Wednesday.

Jess thought back to her visit with Will the previous day, and she felt the crack in her heart spread open a tiny bit further.

***

She'd been late getting to the prison on Friday afternoon. The realtor held her up and she couldn't leave to go meet Will until she had the listing agreement for their house in hand. By the time she got there, visiting hours were almost over.

Will looked almost as disheveled as he had when he first came to her in June, the night of Renee's wedding. He took the papers out of her hand and set them to the side, then grabbed both her hands and pulled her down into the seat across from him.

A female guard was instantly at his side. "Rand! Hands to yourself. You know the rules. No touching. I'm not going to tell you again."

"Sorry, sorry," Will apologized to the guard, holding his hands up where she could see them and then putting them back down on the tabletop, slowly.

The guard gave him another stern glare and took her place behind them, along the wall.

Will turned back to Jess. "I was afraid you weren't coming."

"You knew I was coming. We have to sign those papers," Jess reminded him, nodding to the folder he'd set aside.

"I meant because of Tiffany."

Jess sighed. "Quite the prize you found yourself there, Will. You've outdone yourself this time."

Will groaned and lowered his head into his hands. "You don't have to remind me," came his muffled reply.

"Did you know she called me? Renee and I met her at Starbucks."

Will sat back up. "She already came back here today. She told me she saw you. I swear, Jess, I told her to stay away from you. *I* wanted to be the one to tell you she was back. To warn you."

"That's beside the point now, Will. Do you honestly think she can handle raising Harper? She seemed normal enough yesterday, although not real bright." Will didn't respond, so Jess went on. "Damn you, Will. We've all gotten too attached to that baby. I haven't dared tell Lauren and Nathan that Tiffany is back. If she takes Harper away, takes her to Chicago, they'll be devastated. They don't need any more *heartache*." She emphasized that last word, her hard stare reminding him he was the source of too many broken hearts already.

"Jess, you have to believe me when I tell you how truly sorry I am. For all of this. You have done so much more than anyone would have ever expected you to do. None of this is fair. I honestly don't know if she's capable of raising Harper, and I'm afraid to find out. I love that little girl and I want her where she's safe . . . I want her with *you*."

"Will, I'm tired of hearing you say how sorry you are. That word is meaningless now. We need to put our heads together and figure out what to do about Tiffany."

"Do you want me to call my cousin? He'd probably know someone."

"For God's sake, Will," Jess said in a forced whisper, "don't even *joke* about that."

Will *did* have a cousin they'd always suspected had ties to organized crime. It had been a fun little joke earlier in their marriage—"Uh oh, better call the cuz!"—but now it just made Jess sick to her stomach.

"You're right," Will said. "Not cool. Sorry, again. It's just . . . part of me thinks all she really wants is money and she's using Harper to try to get more out of me. I can't have her stirring up any more trouble."

"How do you think we should fight her?"

"Don't you see, Jess? That's the problem. I don't know that we *can* fight her. She's Harper's biological mother. Sure, I'm her father, but I'm in jail. I don't know whether or not the fact you and I are still married will carry any weight."

"I don't know either. Renee was going to talk to Matt about it, see what he might know, being in law enforcement. Do you think I should call a lawyer? I decided last night, after seeing Tiffany, I probably should find one that specializes in custody situations."

Will appeared to consider her question before he answered.

"No, no, I don't think that's necessary yet. I'm hopeful, now that she knows there's no money, that she'll take off again. Let's cross our fingers she'll choose herself over Harper. I can't believe she wants to be a struggling, single mother—she's already proven she's not the maternal type. Maybe the best we can do is pray she'll change her mind."

***

Jess struggled to keep the days straight in her head as she continued to rock Harper. Tiffany had showed up on Thursday. Both Jess and Tiffany paid Will separate visits on Friday. Tomorrow would be Sunday, the day she'd reluctantly made plans with Tiffany to let the woman see her baby. They'd arranged to meet at Will and Jess's home. Jess didn't want Tiffany coming anywhere near Whispering Pines. Will didn't belong there and neither did she.

Renee refused to let Jess take Harper to meet with Tiffany by herself; Matt had the day off, fortunately, so they all agreed it would be best if he went along this time. Renee had already met Tiffany at Starbucks, and Matt wanted to form his own opinion. Given the uniqueness of the situation, it couldn't hurt to have someone in law enforcement present, even if he couldn't be considered impartial.

After she finally put Harper down in her crib, Jess couldn't fall asleep herself. Her mind kept playing over conversations she'd had during the past few days with both Tiffany and Will. She couldn't get a good read on Tiffany and wasn't sure if the woman *really did* want her baby back, or if it was a play for money. As for Will, something he'd said bothered her. He said he "couldn't afford for Tiffany to stir up any more trouble."

How much more trouble could there be? He's already in prison!

Something wasn't quite making sense.

She tossed and turned. If she slept at all, she couldn't remember, and after what felt like an eternity she was up and showered before Harper started to stir in her crib.

By nine, they were ready to leave. Matt planned to drive separately because Jess had some things she needed to work on at the house, after Tiffany left. Even though they were taking two cars, he insisted on following her. Jess secretly really appreciated this. She didn't want to get to the house before him and end up alone with Tiffany.

Jess rushed around to gather up the diaper bag and all the other things she'd need for the day. They were almost out the door when she stopped and called Matt back.

"Can you hold her for a sec? I forgot something upstairs."

"Sure. But Jess, you need to relax. I know this whole thing has you beside yourself, but you don't want Harper to get fussy if she senses something's wrong."

Jess stopped with her foot on the first step and looked back at Matt and Harper. "I know. You're right, of course. I'm usually not so scatterbrained. I need to chill. Besides, maybe she won't even show up. Will thinks she might change her mind now that she knows she can't get much money out of him anymore."

She was only gone for a minute. They got on the road, and all too soon they pulled into Jess's old driveway. Tiffany was due to arrive in fifteen minutes. The three of them went inside and got settled. It was a beautiful day outside, and since Tiffany wasn't there yet, Jess suggested Matt take Harper out to the backyard. A baby swing hung from an old oak tree. Harper loved to swing.

"Just make sure it's sturdy enough before you put her in it, all right? It's been there since before we moved in. Lauren used to swing her dolls in it."

"Have no fear. We've got this, don't we, Harper?" Matt declared as he scooped Harper up from where she was sitting on the kitchen floor. "Do you want to join us while we wait?"

"I'll be out in a minute," Jess said, again peeking out the front curtains. Now Tiffany was late. The wait was stretching Jess's nerves.

It didn't take long before she could hear Harper's delighted squeals and Matt's laugh. It was a shame Matt hadn't had children of his own, Jess thought. But Renee and Matt had no intention of having kids together at their ages. And besides, he was doing a great job as a father figure to Renee's kids. Robbie had only been five and Julie eight when Renee's first husband died.

Twenty minutes later, Tiffany still hadn't showed up yet. Jess couldn't help but hope maybe the woman had changed her mind about taking Harper. Unable to stand the pressure of waiting, Jess called back the number Tiffany had called from a few days earlier.

"Hello?"

"Tiffany, is that you? This is Jess."

"Oh, hi, Jess. Yeah, it's me. What time is it?"

Jess thought Tiffany sounded like she'd been sleeping.

"Tiffany, where are you? It's almost 10:30. We were supposed to meet at ten o'clock, at the house, so you could see Harper."

Silence.

"Did you change your mind?" Jess asked.

"No, no, I didn't really *change* my mind. I've been doing lots of thinking, that's all. When you told me Will didn't have any more money, I honestly didn't believe you. But now he's telling me the same thing. I don't know what to do." Tiffany's voice took on more of a whine. "I had it all planned out. And everything would have worked, if only Will could help me out a little on the financial side. You see, I have to work, I know I do. But I don't *make* enough to pay for daycare *and* to live on."

Sorry, honey, you're not unique in that respect, Jess thought.

"Are you still coming over?"

Jess heard Tiffany sigh. "I'm sorry, Jess. I should have called and told you I need more time. I'm not feeling well this morning. I was so upset, I called an old friend and we went out last night. I needed *someone* to talk to."

Jess tried to tamp down the excitement she felt at Tiffany's words. "So do you think maybe *now* might not be the best time for you to take Harper to Chicago? Maybe you want to get more established first? No one would blame you for that, Tiffany. Raising a child, especially raising one *alone*, is *so* difficult," Jess said, hoping she was reading the situation right. She'd say anything to convince Tiffany she shouldn't take Harper away, even if it meant pretending to understand the dilemma Tiffany thought she was finding herself in, instead of telling her to grow up.

"I don't know, Jess. You're alone, too," Tiffany pointed out.

"Well, I don't have a man in my life, but I do have lots of other help around. Lauren and Nathan are practically adults, and they love helping with Harper. You wouldn't have as large of a support system in Chicago."

"Maybe you're right . . . maybe I just need a little more time. Would it be all right if I left Harper with you for a little while longer, maybe a few more months, until I got on my feet?"

Jess had the feeling Tiffany was the kind of woman who liked to think everything was her idea. If Tiffany felt like it was *her* idea to leave Harper with Jess for a while longer, she'd be all in.

"If you're sure that's what you want, Tiffany, I'd be happy to help. Do you think Will would approve?"

"I think he'd understand," Tiffany said. "After all, he wants what's best for me. And of course what's best for Harper, too. You're older. More settled. You have more time to take care of all the day-to-day things babies need."

Jess would have bitten her tongue until it bled if she'd been the least bit tempted to set Tiffany straight in her warped way of thinking. But Tiffany did get one thing right: Will wanted what was best for Harper, and he knew that meant Jess. She'd only asked Tiffany that question to let the woman believe this was all her idea.

Jess hated to ask the next question, but she knew it would be an important indication of how Tiffany truly felt about little Harper.

"I understand you can't take her back to Chicago yet . . . but do you want to come see her now? She's growing so quickly."

"Oh no, no, I couldn't do that," Tiffany stammered. "That would simply be too hard on both of us. Harper would be *so* confused if she saw me again, *bonded* with me again, only to have to say goodbye. You do understand, don't you?"

"Of course. I understand completely. I wouldn't want us to do anything that would be difficult for Harper," Jess assured her.

"All right, then," Tiffany said, the relief evident in her tone. "Give Harper a kiss for me, and I'll be in touch."

Jess stared down at the phone in her hand. *Did that just happen?*

Jess wasn't usually one to get overly emotional, but this time merited a little celebrating. She ran from the house to Matt and Harper in the backyard, yelling the whole way. "She's not coming! She's going back to Chicago . . . *alone!*"

Matt slowed the swing and turned toward Jess as she flew across the yard at them. She scooped Harper out of the swing and hugged her tight, relief flooding over her.

"What?" Matt asked, surprised to see his new sister-in-law so emotional. "What are you talking about?"

"When Tiffany was late, I decided to call her, see where she was at. She answered my call, but she sounded kind of out of it. I think she might have been hung over," Jess said, still slightly out of breath. "But anyway, I think the reality of Will's financial situation is finally registering with her. I told her Will doesn't have any money left, but she didn't believe me. When she saw Will again on Friday, he told her the same thing. Maybe the friend she went out with last night helped her to realize how hard it would be if she took Harper now, without financial support from Will. I steered the conversation so she'd think it was her idea to ask me to keep Harper for a while longer, until she was better established in Chicago. And she bought it, hook, line, and sinker."

"Really," Matt said, eyeing her with some doubt.

"Yes, really!" Why wasn't Matt as excited as she was?

"And just how long do you think this manipulation you just pulled off will stick? It seems like you might have just kicked the can a little farther down the road, maybe put off the inevitable."

Jess dropped down to sit in the grass and let Harper crawl. It was comical to watch her reaction as the grass tickled her skin.

"Come on, Matt. You know me well by now. I'm a realist. I understand this is not a permanent solution, but it gives us time to try to come up with one. If that woman had taken Harper to Chicago now, who knows what might have happened?"

Matt sat down in the grass, too, directly in front of Harper's trajectory, turning the baby back toward Jess.

"Good point. Do you want me to do some discreet digging into her background?"

Jess shrugged. "It probably wouldn't hurt." She dropped back onto her elbows, thinking.

Harper saw her opportunity and crawled right up onto Jess, causing Jess to collapse and roll with the child in a fit of giggles. Not to be deterred, Harper quickly started crawling off in another direction. Jess turned the baby around so she was crawling toward Matt. Harper would be willing to play this game for a while, and Jess was still excited enough to play along.

Matt pushed himself up to standing and brushed off the loose grass stuck to his jeans. "Well, listen, I should probably get back out to the resort. Renee wants to start looking for a spot we might be able to build on out there."

"Oh, that's exciting. Are you thinking you might want to try to get something framed in before the snow flies? You might be pushing it."

Matt shrugged. "Whatever the little missus wants."

"Oh Lord, spare me," Jess said with a laugh. "Hey, I got that book out for Renee and then I forgot to show it to her when everyone was here."

"What book?"

"That book about Minnesota lake resorts," Jess explained. "I think we put it over at your side of the duplex after steaks on Saturday night. Whispering Pines is in there. It's pretty cool."

"Oh yeah, I remember Renee mentioning something about that."

"When you get home, ask her to show it to you. You'll be surprised at how nice the Gray Cabin looks in there. The weird thing, though, was there was a picture of another cabin within the section on the Pines. I didn't recognize it. Something must have happened to it—unless someone put it in the wrong chapter in the book. Not a big deal, but since you're going to be snooping around out there anyhow, see if you can see anything."

"Will do. You know me. I always love a little mystery. Are you heading back, too?"

"Nah, not right away. I have some things I need to work on here first."

"What about Harper?" he asked, motioning to the little diaper-butt making her way across the wide lawn.

Jess ran over and scooped her up, again, and settled her on her hip. "We'll be just fine. I brought some lunch. I think we'll have a little picnic out here in the grass and then I'll see if I can get her to take a nap in the playpen inside."

"Sounds good. See you later then. Call if anything comes up, I'll be around. And Jess, just to be on the safe side, keep the doors locked when you're inside, all right?"

"Um, OK ... but why? Trust me, Tiffany is not coming around today."

"Just humor me, all right?"

"Yes, sir!" Jess replied with a mock salute. "Seriously though, thank you, Matt. I appreciate you giving up your morning. I hope it wasn't too big a waste of time for you."

Matt smiled. "Hey, when I get to have a little outside play time with a princess, it isn't a waste of time."

***

Getting a seven-month-old to settle down enough to eat while seated outside, in the grass, proved to be hopeless. Instead, Jess used the baby swing as a makeshift highchair, and in that way they still had a picnic of sorts. When Harper started rubbing her eyes, Jess took her inside and laid her down. Worn out from the fresh air and play, she was asleep in minutes.

Now's my chance ...

Jess dug around in her purse and pulled out a small silver key on a Disney World keychain. She'd been dying to find out what Will had locked in the old wooden filing cabinet in his office. She doubted he even knew she had a key for it, which gave her a certain level of satisfaction.

"Why do I feel like a thief in my own house?" she whispered, wanting to break the silence but not disturb the baby sleeping down the hall.

The key easily unlocked the cabinet.

The top drawer contained the type of paperwork she'd expected to find, including the bank statements for their joint account. Since they'd split a year ago, Jess had only used her own, separate account. As long as Will kept up on paying his bills, she hadn't cared about the joint checking account; she didn't want any more of his money than was absolutely necessary to cover their mutual commitments. Given the financial mess they were in now, that had been a terrible decision on her part.

She pulled the statements out of their still-sealed envelopes—obviously Will wasn't keeping close tabs on the details of the account. She put the statements in order since last July, when they'd separated. She wasn't looking to pick them apart or try to account for every dollar, but she *was* curious.

She could see his hefty bi-weekly paychecks from the hospital. *That man made a good salary.* The fact they were now broke was mindboggling to Jess. She noticed a few large withdrawals start to show up early last winter. She couldn't see a pattern as far as either dollar amount or timing. Maybe he was just funding Tiffany's lifestyle. She would have been in the picture then.

"Oh Lord, I probably shouldn't even be looking. I don't really *want* to know what he's been doing with his money."

Or do I? Why should her and her kids be in a financial bind now, through no fault of their own? She opened up the April statement. As expected, Will's paychecks stopped appearing. *Funny how they stop paying you when you get fired for running an illegal operation out of their hospital.* At that point, the balance was large enough that it should have funded their normal, monthly bills for over a year—even the mortgage. But somehow that was no longer the case, at least according to Will. *Where's the May statement? Or June?* April was the last one in the drawer. *Maybe he switched them to online only when he was going to prison. I'll need to get copies.*

Finding nothing more of interest in the top drawer, she checked the second one. It was full of medical journals and work-related papers, same as his desk. Boring.

The third drawer had more papers in the front portion, but the back contained what looked like old computer equipment. A dusty keyboard, a wired mouse, even a ten-key calculator. The papers in front were the kids' investment accounts for college. She glanced through them, but seeing the physical evidence of what Will had already told her made her sick to her stomach.

She slammed the drawer in frustration. Harper whimpered in the next room. *Whoops.* She'd be hollering for some attention before too long. Jess had to hurry.

The bottom drawer looked to be full of office supplies: boxes of pens, reams of paper, and new manila folders were all stacked inside. Jess dug a little deeper and was surprised to see some kind of box on the bottom, near the back of the drawer. She pulled it out. It was square and about one foot across, made of light gray metal, and locked up tight. Her instincts told her she wasn't meant to find this.

Her instincts also told her she needed to find out what was inside the box.

Jess set the box on top of Will's desk, unsure what to do with it. Harper picked that exact moment to let her know she was lonesome and tired of being confined. Knowing she wouldn't have any more time to snoop, she locked the cabinet back up, minus the small box. The box was coming home with them.

CHAPTER 18

Gift of a Fireside Chat

"*J*ess, can you come out here?"

Jess and Lauren were in the kitchen cleaning up the supper dishes, and Harper had the lower cupboard open and was pulling out the plastic containers as fast as Lauren could try to put them away. Renee's voice had come drifting through the screen on Jess's back door.

"Sure, I'll be out in a sec!" Wiping her hands on a dish rag, Jess turned to Lauren. "Got her?"

"You bet. We'll finish this and then Harper can come help me pack."

Jess laughed. "Don't expect to get much packing done, but thanks."

Jess found Renee and Matt in their shared backyard.

"What's up?"

"We think we found where that old cabin used to be. You know, the one that you mentioned to Matt that's in the book but not here now? We thought you'd want to see. Come on," Renee said, heading back in the direction of the lodge.

Matt and Jess fell into step next to her, and Jess instantly felt a rush of excitement over the possibility of solving this particular mystery. "What did you find? I've never noticed anything that could have resembled another cabin before."

"You wouldn't if you weren't looking for it," Matt said.

Renee led them toward the three cabins ringing the fire pit, on the southwest end of the resort. She continued walking, behind the cabins, heading farther south. Forty feet behind the cabins they came to a thicket of trees.

"I can honestly say I've never been back this way before," Jess said, walking behind Renee but ahead of Matt as they weaved their way through the trees. The lake was off on their left-hand side. "How far back does your land go, Renee?"

"I'm not a hundred percent sure, but I think to where the shore curves in. See, up there a little ways further. I need to find out the exact property lines."

"Careful now. This brush is really thick," Matt warned as they walked another twenty yards farther back, away from the water.

"Here it is!" Renee said, excited.

Jess looked around, but she saw nothing but trees and a sliver of water back in the direction from which they'd walked. "Here's *what?*"

"Come here." Renee took a few more steps and knelt down. "Look at this."

There, almost completely obscured by overgrowth, was what looked like two pieces of broken-off boards, forming a right angle just above the ground.

Renee stood back up. "See, if you go down this way, you can see some other little bits of something sticking out of the ground, too. Together they form a rough rectangle about the same size as each of the three cabins by the pit."

"You've got to be kidding. Way back *here?*"

"I know, that's exactly what we thought, too. But it sure looks like it could be an old foundation. Of course, we can't be sure it's the same cabin from the book, but it's possible."

Jess wandered the perimeter Renee had pointed out. "Something was definitely back here . . . but this is so far from the water."

"It is. But who knows, maybe it wasn't meant for guests. And some people enjoy the woods more than lakefront. And these trees around here . . . they don't look quite as old as those back over there. Maybe it didn't used to be this overgrown."

Matt stood in the center of what might have been the old foundation and faced the lake. "If some of this brush and these trees were cleared away, you could still have some view of the water, and it would be completely private. We might have to put this spot on our list of *maybes*," he said, looking to Renee for confirmation.

"I agree, this is really neat back here," Renee said.

Jess started jumping around and swatting at her arm. "Oh my God, *gross*, get it off me!"

"What?!" Matt asked, crossing quickly to her side and grabbing her arm. He started to laugh. "That? Jess, that's a tick."

"Don't you think I *know* that?" she asked, nearly hysterical. *"Get—it—off—me—NOW!"*

Matt plucked the offending little insect off Jess's arm and flicked it into the grass. "They only hurt you if they latch on and start sucking your blood. That thing was barely attached. I'm surprised to see one this late in the summer. They're *way* worse in the spring. That's when you really have to watch for them," he teased.

Jess squirmed. "Now I feel like they're crawling all over me!" She tried to calm herself and looked around again, albeit more guarded this time. "OK, well . . . nice spot. Cool that you probably found the missing cabin. Now let's go back to where the grass is short and the ticks aren't so bad."

***

Three hours later, after Jess had Harper bathed and asleep in her crib, she joined Renee, Matt, and the older kids around a smaller fire pit in their backyard. Julie was talking about the new apartment she was moving into in a week, once school started back up again after Labor Day.

"Hey Julie, you still rooming with Grace and Zoey?" Jess asked. Julie roomed with both of them up until this past spring, when they gave up their old apartment to move home for the summer.

"Yep, it's the three of us plus one new girl. Zoey had a couple of classes with her and says she's nice. I hope we'll all get along. I'm sure we will. I can't wait to get moved in." Julie was beaming, clearly excited to be getting back to college-life after working at the resort all summer.

Always there to needle his sister, Robbie said, "Hmm, four girls in a two-bedroom apartment. Can you say *drama*? What could possibly go wrong?"

"Speaking of drama," Jess said, looking to her nephew. "Last year must have been a little crazy for you, right? Going to your old school the first half of the year and then shifting to school here for the second half."

"Yeah, that kind of sucked," Robbie said.

Renee, sitting next to her son, reached over and squeezed his shoulder. "I'm sorry last year was so tough. This year *will* be better, I promise. Do you think you want to play basketball? Now that you have the green light from the doctor? He said your arm looks good. I can't believe you're going to be a junior in high school already."

"Yeah, I'll try out at least. Their team is pretty good, might be tough. As far as school goes, I'm glad I got to know some of the guys last year. A couple of them were pretty cool." Robbie shrugged, trying to play it off. "It won't be a big deal if I can't make the team."

"What about you, Lauren, how's the packing going?" Renee asked. "Freshman orientation . . . that's always exciting."

"I haven't done much as far as packing goes, but I've still got time," Lauren said, giving her mother a sheepish grin. "I keep *starting*, but then I get distracted."

"*Are* you excited?" Julie asked her cousin.

"I am," Lauren said, "but nervous, too, since I don't know anyone there yet. My roommate seems nice. I've talked to her on the phone a few times, but we haven't met in person yet. Fingers crossed she doesn't turn out to be some psycho."

"Don't worry, no one ever *really* meets psychos their freshman year of college. Oh, except for *me*, that is," Julie said with a nervous laugh, referring to the boyfriend she'd met at the beginning of her freshman year—the same guy who'd squatted in the Gray Cabin last year. He'd turned out to be an extremely imbalanced individual who stalked Julie and had the whole family living in a nervous state for months.

"Come on, Julie, don't tease her like that," Matt scolded his stepdaughter. "What happened to you isn't the norm." He turned to Lauren. "I promise."

"You're right, Matt. Sorry, Lauren. I shouldn't even joke about that. Just be careful if you date. If they seem at all controlling . . . run far and run fast."

"Got it, cuz. I'll keep that in mind," Lauren said. "Hey, you guys want to go watch Netflix? I heard about this new sci-fi series, it's supposed to be pretty good."

"I'm in," Julie said, pushing up out of her lawn chair.

Robbie slapped at a mosquito on his face. "Me too. These things are starting to eat me alive."

"Hey, watch over at Renee and Matt's, will you?" Jess asked, waving the baby monitor she'd stowed in her pocket. "The baby is sleeping and I don't want you to wake her up."

After the kids were gone, only Matt, Renee, and Jess remained.

"So," Renee said, breaking the silence, "now that you've had a few days to process everything, how are you feeling about what happened with Tiffany?"

"Well, relieved, of course. I know this could just be a temporary breather, but I'll take what I can get. I called Will to tell him Tiffany decided not to take Harper back to Chicago. Oh, and he changed his mind about talking to a lawyer—now he says he's going to call his to see if there is any way I can be given legal custody of Harper while he is incarcerated. But get this: Will thinks it may complicate things further if we were to finalize our divorce."

"You're kidding! If you want to keep Harper, you might have to stay married to Will? That seems like an awfully high price to pay. Don't you want to move on with your life?"

"Of course, I do. And who knows . . . that's just what Will thinks. Maybe whether or not we are still married won't even matter. We just have more questions than answers at this point."

"Are you and Will getting along all right?" Matt asked.

"We're trying, for the sake of the kids. Lauren and Nathan still haven't agreed to go visit him, and I know that bothers him. But this is all his fault, so there isn't much he can say about it. We're trying to get the house sold. I've been doing a little more research into Will's finances. I told myself it was just so I would have a better feel for how long before there isn't enough money left to make the house payment, but . . ."

"But *what?*" Renee asked, Jess's hesitation catching her attention.

"I don't know. It's just a *feeling*, really. Maybe I'm reading too much into it."

"Jess, this is *Will* we're talking about here. If your gut tells you something's up, you should probably trust it. He's screwed you over enough times for you to know when he might be up to something."

Jess pulled a bag of marshmallows and a roasting stick out of the basket she'd brought out earlier. She skewered the white puff and held it over the fire, the activity giving her time to decide how best to articulate what she was feeling.

"I just can't understand how the money can all be *gone*—or almost gone, anyway. Will made a good salary. I started looking through his bank statements I found in his office today . . . and up until he got fired, there was a lot of money coming in every single month. I just find it all a little too hard to believe, you know? And then the other day, when Tiffany came back around, he made some comment about how he 'couldn't afford to have her stir up any more trouble.' It struck me as odd at the time . . . and my mind keeps going back to that."

Matt pointed to the end of her stick, chuckling. "You might want to check that. It's looking like a piece of charcoal at this point."

"Oh crap," Jess said. She shook the burned little ball into the fire and tried again.

"Did you find anything suspicious when you were looking through the statements? Or any other paperwork?" Matt asked. "I'm guessing that's what you wanted to 'work on' when I left you at the house the other day?"

"I didn't take a ton of time to study things . . . but there was one thing that seemed really odd."

"What?" Renee asked.

"The bottom drawer in Will's filing cabinet was filled with office supplies, nothing interesting—at least that's what I thought, until I dug a little deeper."

"What did you find?" Matt asked.

"A small metal box, tucked back in the very bottom of the drawer. I pulled it out, but it was locked. I have no idea what's in it or how to open it."

"Do you want to go back over there tomorrow and see if we can bust it open?" Matt asked.

"That won't be necessary," Jess said sheepishly. "It's here, under my bed."

"Should we play 'thief' and see if we can break into it tonight?" Renee asked, always game for a little adventure.

"Tempting as theft with my cop brother-in-law sounds . . ." Jess yawned and glanced at her phone. "Oh man, it's almost midnight. Why don't we see if we can't get into it tomorrow? Whatever's in there will keep another day."

CHAPTER 19

Gift of Indignation

*J*ess didn't have a chance to try to break open Will's metal box the next day; she spent the morning doing tasks for her job, and around noon, she received a call from Patricia over at Homes Sparkle.

"Hello, Patricia. What's up?" Jess was surprised Patricia was calling. They'd met and reviewed some of the year-to-date results just the previous week.

"Jess . . . I think we might have a problem."

The woman does not have much in the way of social skills, Jess thought, bracing herself for whatever Patricia wanted to gripe about now.

Patricia recently earned her business degree from a local university, having graduated last December as an older-than-average student of thirty-five. Now she was determined to prove her worth to her parents and grow Homes Sparkle's reach beyond the local area. Jess tried to give her advice but, more times than not, Patricia seemed to just resent her input.

"What kind of problem?"

"I just ran across something I don't like. I don't want to get into it over the phone. We should meet, in person. Do you have time this afternoon?"

Jess rolled her eyes. "I did have another appointment."

"You'll probably want to reschedule it. We need to talk."

Jess considered Patricia's request. It was a bit rude, sure, but Seth would probably be more than happy if she canceled on him.

"All right, if you really think it's that urgent. Where do you want to meet?"

"At my office. Can you be here by 2:30?"

Jess checked her watch. "I can if I hustle. If I'm a little late, you'll just have to sit tight."

"Fine."

Irritated at Patricia's usual gruff tone, Jess called Seth—her other gruff business partner—to let him know she could stop by either later this afternoon or tomorrow. She needed to pick up his paperwork; she still didn't have second quarter results done yet. She couldn't catch his exact response, as the connection was poor and he cut in and out. She thought he agreed either was fine, but she suspected he wouldn't care even if she'd misheard him.

***

Patricia's desk was covered with spreadsheets, as was the table in the corner of her office. The slightly younger woman appeared frazzled, even a bit shaky. This was new.

Jess set her laptop bag down on the floor and took a seat in the chair across the desk from Patricia. She pushed up her sleeves, slipped her glasses on, and readied herself for whatever had Patricia so uptight.

I hope she's not going to tell me they're in a cash crunch, too . . . I won't be much help if that's the case.

"OK, I'm here, so why don't you fill me in on what has you so concerned?"

"I'm missing money," Patricia said, angling her body toward Jess as she spoke. "I mean, the *company* is missing money."

Jess hadn't expected this. "You're going to have to be a little more specific, Patricia. Why don't you start at the beginning? Why do you think money is missing? Do you mean cash?"

"No, no, I don't think that's it," Patricia replied, her brow furrowed. The makeup around one of her eyes was badly smudged, like she'd rubbed it without mercy. "So you know I've been trying to convince Mom and Dad we should open another office or two, expand our reach out into the state. Even though they are supposedly retired, they keep pretty tight reins on us girls."

Jess nodded, finding Patricia's reference to *girls* humorous, since both she and Wendy were in their thirties. Jess had been working with both long enough now to understand why Mr. and Mrs. Robins still kept their hands in the business. Wendy was great with customers and employees but didn't have a head for business; Patricia showed promise on the business end, but some of her grandiose ideas were risky, to say the least.

"I know they've stayed involved to some degree," Jess confirmed, "but what does that have to do with your concerns today?"

"Nothing other than the fact I was digging way back in our financials—I wanted to start making my case for expansion . . . you know, show where we've had growth, where we seem to be stagnated, that kind of thing."

"How far back did you go?"

"I could find some financial information back as far as 2009."

Jess nodded. "I wonder where the older books are stored. Homes Sparkle has been in business for what . . . like forty years, hasn't it?"

"I don't know, but I'm going to ask Dad."

"So did you see something in the older books that has you concerned?"

"I most certainly did. I think I've stumbled upon a huge problem."

Jess was tired of waiting for Patricia to get to the point. "For God's sake, spit it out! What do you think you found?"

Patricia blinked, and her jaw set. "I think someone embezzled from this company for years and years . . . and I think it was Celia, your aunt."

***

"Seth! Seth, are you here?!" Jess yelled as she searched his shop. She'd already checked outside, in the office, and all over his large shop for him. His vehicle was parked outside and the door was open. He had to be close.

There were stairs leading up in a back corner of the building, but Jess had never been up there. She hadn't even realized there was an upstairs. With nowhere else to look, she ascended the stairs, yelling his name the whole way.

She entered into what looked like simple living quarters. It wasn't a big area: there were only a few pieces of furniture, a tiny kitchen, and a television. No one was in the room, but there was one door at the far end and she could hear an old AC/DC song blaring from that direction. Upset as she was, she didn't stop to consider it might not be wise to barge through that door.

Walking quickly, she grabbed for the knob and pulled the door open, yelling for Seth as she went.

Everything happened at once. Hot steam rolled out the door, enveloping Jess in moisture. The music was so loud she could barely hear herself yell. Seth spun away from the mirror, wearing only a towel, his shocked face half covered with shaving cream, a razor in his right hand. The bathroom was so tiny, Jess's one step into the room brought her right up against him. He grabbed blindly at her waist with his free hand to steady himself.

"Jesus Christ, Jess! What the hell are you doing? You scared the hell out of me!"

Jess froze. All her befuddled mind could think of at that immediate moment was an old cliché she'd heard her mother say more than once: she'd just jumped out of the frying pan and into the fire.

Seth was still holding onto her. "Jess, is everything OK? Why the hell would you come barging in here like that?"

Remembering why she'd come, how furious and shocked she'd felt when Patricia had voiced her allegations against Celia, layered on top of all the other stresses in her life as of late, she cracked. There, in that cocoon of steam and song, she did something she rarely did. She cried. She let her head fall forward, rested her forehead on Seth's bare chest, and cried.

Seth didn't move, at least initially. The towel around his hips didn't offer much coverage and his hands were now full. As Jess's crying jag continued, her arms crept around his waist of their own accord. He dropped the razor into the sink behind him, loosened his grip on Jess's waist, and pulled her in closer, rubbing her back with his other hand, offering some semblance of comfort, as awkward as it may have felt.

Reality slowly seeped back in for Jess. Pulling her head back, horrified at what she'd done, she held Seth's gaze. Once she'd gotten her mom's phrase about fire out of her head, *I owe this poor guy an explanation* was all she could think. She pulled her arms back in, but his were still wrapped around her, so she rested her hands on his chest, pushing back slightly.

"God, I am *so* sorry, Seth," Jess began. "I had to talk to you, and I knew you had to be here because your truck was here, but I couldn't find you, and then I saw the stairs, but I didn't know what was up here, but I *had* to find you, and . . . and . . ."

"Whoa, slow down. Why don't we do this," Seth said, cutting off Jess's agitated ramblings. "How about you close your eyes for a second, let me adjust this towel that is very close to falling off and embarrassing the hell out of both of us"—Jess chuckled awkwardly—"then give me a second to throw some clothes on and we can talk. Does that work for you?"

Jess squeezed her eyes shut and her face turned a mottled red. *Could this day get any worse?*

"All right," Seth said, after he'd had a chance to secure the towel again. "Wait for me down in the office, will you? I'll be down in a minute."

Jess nodded her head but didn't open her eyes again until she had her back turned to Seth and was marching toward the stairs. As she pounded down the stairs she thought how wrong she'd been.

Seth actually has a compassionate side . . . and he looks good in a towel.

***

Seth watched Jess run toward the stairs and disappear.

What the hell just happened?

He'd known Jess for over a year now, and he'd never once witnessed her show any extreme emotion—other than annoyance at him. He'd been skeptical of her at first, coming in here with her analytical mind and sarcastic mouth. Other than the fact she looked a bit like Seth imagined Celia would have when she was younger, he'd thought any resemblance between Celia and Jess ended there.

Over time, however, Seth started to recognize Jess's commitment to the well-being of his business. It was as if Jess couldn't let him fail because, to her, that would mean she'd failed Celia. Month after month, she worked on his financial records and offered advice. Now he could see he probably should have listened to her sooner. He'd hated to go to her and ask for a loan when he was short on cash when taxes came due, just as she'd predicted he would. But she hadn't hesitated. Having her help, her assistance, was giving him more confidence that he could keep this dream of his going long-term.

Seth was also quite conscious of the fact that he had a tendency to annoy the hell out of Jess. But for whatever reason, he couldn't seem to help himself. He found some twisted pleasure in annoying the woman but wasn't sure why.

And then that just happened, he thought, swiping the razor as fast as he could over the remainder of his face. Jess actually *cried.* In his arms. With barely a towel between them. A crying woman usually had him running in the other direction, but with her, it hadn't thrown him into a panic. Instead, for some bizarre reason, he just wanted to comfort her, to make her stop crying.

He refused to acknowledge the fact he'd also wanted to kiss her in that steamy bathroom.

Now I know I've lost my mind.

When he got downstairs—now fully clothed in his ratty, albeit favorite, jeans and the only clean T-shirt he could find—Jess wasn't in the office.

A crack of thunder drew his eyes to the window and outside. He saw Jess out there, sitting on the top rail of the wooden fence on the south side of the building, staring off into the distance. As he turned to leave, he heard a phone vibrate. Her purse sat, forgotten, in the middle of his desk.

Whoever it is can wait, he decided.

***

Jess heard him approach. She hoped the steady wind had cooled her face and dried her tears. She was mortified with herself. Talk about crossing about a dozen boundaries.

Seth walked around the far end of the fence and came to stand near her, his back leaning against the old wood, his eyes on the storm clouds on the horizon. He didn't say anything.

Uncomfortable with the silence, Jess tried to explain herself. "Look, Seth . . . I'm sorry. That was incredibly rude of me to barge in on you like that. This will certainly rank right up there as one of my top ten most embarrassing life moments."

Seth looked over at her, one eye squinted against the glare of the sun, just beginning to set. He seemed to be weighing how best to handle the situation.

"Tell you what," he finally said, pushing off the fence and turning to face her. "Why don't we forget that little episode in my bathroom ever happened. *I* should have locked the door and I shouldn't have had the music so loud. *You* should have knocked—or better yet, *called* before coming over—but what's done is done. What I really want to know is why you're here. When I told you I was busy, I thought you'd come tomorrow. More importantly, why don't you tell me what has you so upset? What was so important that you had to find me *immediately?*"

"You're busy? Oh, man . . . I'll admit, I couldn't really hear what you were saying earlier." Jess shifted her body to jump down from the fence railing.

Seth held up a hand to stop her. "It's fine. No big deal. I was just going to meet some friends for darts. I'll skip this week. Believe it or not, I'm finding this more entertaining."

Jess kicked him lightly with the toe of her sandal. She *did* appreciate his efforts to lighten the mood. "I'm afraid you're not going to like what I have to tell you, though. Why I came over."

"Try me."

Jess let her mind go back to the meeting in Patricia's office. "Are you familiar with Homes Sparkle?"

"Hmm, sounds vaguely familiar. Why?"

"Homes Sparkle is a family-run cleaning business. They mainly clean homes but do some office buildings, too. They're another business Celia had an ownership interest in and passed to me."

"Maybe that's why it sounds familiar. She must have mentioned them at some point. Do you do their books, too?"

"No, not really. Patricia, the original owners' daughter, has been keeping the books for the last year or so, and they also have an outside accountant who they use for taxes and such. I offer more of a consultative role with them."

"So all the hand-holding you do with me isn't the norm?"

Jess gave a little laugh. "No, thank goodness. There aren't enough hours in the day to do this much with all three of Celia's businesses."

"Oh yeah, there's that old bookstore too, right? I remember your boy mentioning something about that."

"Right. The current owners, the Fisks, have been struggling, so their daughter has been helping them where she can. Anyhow, I'm getting off track. So I got a phone call around noon today. It was Patricia, wanting to meet right away. She was persistent enough that I thought I better reschedule with you and meet with her. You have to understand—Patricia can be a bit *overdramatic* sometimes. She's new to the business end of Homes Sparkle. She just got her degree and has big plans for the company, but she has to convince her parents her ideas are solid."

Seth resumed his previous stance, his eyes on the clouds now moving closer.

"Is all this somehow related to your barging in to my bathroom?" he asked. "Just wondering."

Jess laughed. "Unfortunately, I'm getting to that part. So I headed over to Patricia's office to see what was up. I got there and she was all . . . I don't know . . . *flustered*, I guess you could say. She had reports and spreadsheets spread all over her office. She started out by reminding me of her master plan to expand—open up at least one more office, hire a bunch more people, and grow. Even though her parents are retired, they keep close tabs on things and still have the final yea or nay when it comes to big decisions like that. So she decided she was going to put together a business plan. Compare old financials to now, see if they've had any growth, where they might be stagnated, that kind of thing."

"Jess, how does any of this relate to me?"

"Believe me, you're going to want to hear this. Stay with me now. I know all this business talk bores you to tears, but I need to give you this background."

Seth gave an exaggerated sigh but nodded.

"Patricia went back in the records as far as she could, as far as she could find the information in their company office. I think she said she had back to 2009."

"Jesus, she went digging around into accounting records from eight years ago? I'd rather someone stuck a needle in my eye!"

Jess gave another little laugh. She didn't doubt his statement one bit. "Anyhow, within minutes of me getting there, she started saying she was missing money."

Seth was silent, waiting for her to continue, but his eyebrows had shot up.

Jess nodded. "I had the exact same reaction. She told me she started reconstructing things—you know, annual trends and such. She only has paper to look at for the stuff back then. The reports were done on a computer, but who knows where those files sit all these years later. Things weren't adding up. Some of the payroll reports weren't matching up with the P&L or the tax returns."

"Hold up. Keep this in English."

Now it was Jess's turn to sigh in exasperation. "Just because you don't like accounting doesn't mean you don't understand the basics. I know you do. She's convinced there are discrepancies in the books. It's too early to know for sure, but some of the things she pointed out did start ringing little warning bells. The upsetting thing is—and this is why I needed to talk to you—that Celia's initials were on some of the statements."

Seth shrugged. "Well, that makes sense. Celia was still around and really active eight years ago, despite her age. Hell, she helped me build my financial tracking from scratch."

Jess nodded. "I know. But here's the kicker. Patricia thinks Celia might have been embezzling from them."

"What?!" Seth cried, bolting upright and spinning to face Jess again. "That is the most ridiculous thing I've ever heard. Celia was the most honest, *trustworthy* person I ever met."

Jess held up her hands in defense. "Hey, you don't have to tell me that! That's the same Celia I knew, I grew up with. No *way* would she ever do something dishonest, let alone steal. But Patricia is insistent. Very few people would have been involved in the bookkeeping process. Mostly her parents, and they wouldn't steal from themselves."

"Did this Patricia woman even *know* Celia? Did she ever meet her? Because if she did she would know this is ludicrous."

"She knew her, but not necessarily in a business capacity. Celia was involved in Homes Sparkle since the early days, when the Robins were just starting out. Celia started out as a customer, but when they ran into some hard times, she helped them out."

"That was kind of her MO," Seth acknowledged.

"Right. I think Patricia used to clean Celia's house, back when she was younger. So she knew her, at least to some degree."

"So, how developed is this ridiculous theory of Patricia's?" Seth asked. It was his turn to be flushed. Crimson circles spotted his cheeks, evidence of his anger, despite how rigid he held himself. Jess suspected he was having the same internal reaction she'd had. Celia was *not* the kind of person that would do something like this.

"She really doesn't know yet. But she suspects there could be thousands missing over the years. I don't know why she called *me* right away, before she has her facts straight. If there really are funds missing, a lot more work needs to be done to figure out how the money was taken, and more importantly, *who* might have been involved."

"This is insane. Where did you leave it with her? Did you get a chance to dig into the books, see what she was seeing?"

"Not yet. I asked if I could take some of the records home with me, study them, but of course she thought that was a *terrible* idea, given I was Celia's niece and Celia is Patricia's prime suspect. She wants to find the records dating back before 2009 and then talk to her dad. He's in Baltimore right now, visiting family, but will be back next week."

Jess looked at him. "Seth . . . she even mentioned going to the police, in case this means there are issues with the IRS. Even though Celia's gone, maybe *because* she's gone, Patricia sees no harm in pulling her into this whole fiasco. Seth, this could *ruin* Celia's reputation, and she's not here to defend herself. Hell, if money is missing, it *could* have been Patricia's folks trying to avoid paying taxes. Or maybe Patricia is totally off base and nothing is missing at all. I don't know, but her accusations totally rocked me. I hate the thought of telling my family about this. They'll all recognize it as the BS it is, obviously, but I don't even want to put that little germ of doubt in anyone's mind."

"I get it, Jess. Really. I'm so mad that anyone would say that about Celia, I can barely think straight."

Jess gave a little laugh. "I figured as much. Maybe that's why I came here, to commiserate with you. You're a bit more impartial than my family will be, but I get that you were good friends with Celia. Will you help me with this?"

"Absolutely. I'm not going to allow anyone to speak ill of Celia. But what can I do?"

"Well, for starters, I wanted to check through your books. You know, make sure they're clean. Celia did your books for years, right?"

Seth looked surprised by her request. "Do you suspect Celia might have done something inappropriate?"

"Absolutely not! I want to show she wouldn't have done what Patricia is claiming. I'll ask if I can do the same with the financial records for the Fisks' bookstore. If everything is clean, that could help show evidence of Celia's integrity. Does that make sense?"

"Kind of, I guess," Seth said, not sounding entirely sure. "God, Jess, I don't know. But of course you can do whatever you think might help clear Celia's name, before this all gets blown out of proportion. I will never believe that she had anything to do with something illegal, *stealing* from someone. Celia would never have done that."

CHAPTER 20

Gift of Fresh Air

*J*ess said nothing about Patricia's claims to anyone but Seth. At home, she tried to pretend like nothing was wrong: she helped Lauren pack and started taking Harper to a daycare center, wanting the baby to get acclimated to her new caregivers before Lauren left for college the Tuesday after Labor Day.

Jess wasn't sure what was happening over at Homes Sparkle, but she knew she would hear something soon enough. In the meantime, she spent her mornings on her job, and when time allowed she spent a few hours at Seth's in the afternoon, poring over his old records. She started back at the beginning. Records were neatly stored upstairs at the shop, organized in plastic tubs. (Jess knew this was Celia's handiwork and sent up a prayer of thanks to her great aunt. If it would have been up to Seth, the records would have been a mess.) It would take her a while to get through everything. She'd start now and ask Seth if she could take the rest of the tubs home to review over the weekend.

She compared bank statements first to the financials and then to Seth's tax returns. Celia had done all of the work except the tax returns, which were prepared by an accountant. When she asked Seth about it, he said the guy was "Uncle Jack's buddy." Jack had also been Celia's long-time lawyer; Celia had trusted him to handle her many business dealings. Jess figured anyone Jack recommended had to be reliable.

Because Seth was a one-man show, the books were pretty straightforward. She wasn't sure where he'd gotten his startup funds, but figured that was none of her business. He would have been in his mid-twenties when he first started, and his initial years were lean. She wasn't sure how he'd been able to live off the meager earnings.

"Anything weird in there?"

Jess jumped and let out a yelp.

Seth chuckled. "Sorry, didn't mean to scare you."

"I didn't realize you were around. Guess I was concentrating," Jess said, embarrassed. "So far, everything looks fine. I'll probably take some of these home with me when I leave and keep working on them this weekend, if you don't mind. But hey . . . I have to ask. How did you make it through those first couple of years? Financially, I mean."

Seth pulled his gloves off, ambled farther into the office, and sat down facing Jess.

"It wasn't easy," he finally replied, resting his elbows on his wide-spread legs, his hat dangling from one hand. "I did some bartending to supplement our income. I almost gave up on this place . . . more than once."

"*Our* income?"

"Yeah, our income. Life looked different for me back then. But Ruby and Celia kept pushing me, kept assuring me I'd regret it if I gave up on my dream to make a go of this place."

Jess said nothing, hoping he'd share more.

Eventually, he nodded at the desk between them and said, "Remember that picture you found when you were snooping in my desk?"

"I wasn't snoo . . . oh, all right, maybe I was snooping a little," Jess acknowledged, again pulling open that same drawer. New junk was on top, but when she dug a little deeper, she found the picture and pulled it out. "This one?"

Seth reached across the desk and Jess handed him the photo. He studied it, his face unreadable.

"Who is the girl in the picture, Seth?" Jess prodded.

Seth dropped the photo on the desktop and met Jess's gaze. "My daughter."

It was Jess's turn to think before replying. "Why haven't you mentioned her before?" she asked gently.

Seth shrugged and shook his head. "Her name's Kaylee. Her mother and I, we met at the bar I was working at. She waited tables. Hey, listen, you don't have time to hear about my younger years. I'm sure you have better things to do, like finish up here and get home to your family."

"Oh no, you don't get off that easy. I've shared a little with you about the troubles with my ex and the fact I'm raising a baby he had with another woman. I think it's time you aired a little of your dirty laundry, too." Jess stood, walked around the desk to Seth's side, and held out her hand.

He looked at it, clearly unsure how to react.

She wiggled her fingers in front of him, impatient. "Come on. Let's go for a walk."

"You are a hard one to figure out, Jess Rand," he said, reluctantly taking her hand.

She tugged and he stood, following her out of the office, their fingers still loosely linked. She led the way out of the cool, dark interior into the brilliant afternoon sunlight of a hot August afternoon. Jess dropped his hand and walked over to her vehicle to grab her sunglasses. He'd already put his hat back on, the brim shading his eyes.

"Where should we walk?"

Seth looked at her like she was more than a little nuts. "You do realize it's like eighty-five degrees out here and no wind, don't you?"

"And we will look back on this afternoon in six months and wish it were *still* eighty-five degrees outside," she assured him.

"Guess you're right about that. Come on, follow me," Seth said, leading the way now, heading around the back side of the shop.

They walked in silence, across an old pasture. Seth made his way toward a grouping of trees, his boots easily traversing the hard ground. It was slower going for Jess. The long grasses caught in her sandals. At one point, Seth stopped and turned around to check on her but said nothing as she waved him on.

My idea, Jess reminded herself. *But I was picturing more of a nice walking path.*

She heard running water. Seth stepped into the trees ahead and Jess welcomed the cool shade as she followed him in. Ahead was a small stream. Rocks, a few large enough to sit on, lined the water's edge. Seth perched on top of one and motioned to another slightly larger one right next to him. Jess kicked off her sandals and stepped carefully up on the rock. She dangled her now bare feet over the edge of the stone, trailing them in the water. The cool water erased the itch she'd felt walking across the prairie.

"Nice," she said.

Seth looked down at his own feet, still encased in heavy work boots, and then at the cool water. "I'm going to regret this when I have to put these damn things back on," he said, unlacing his boots.

She smiled. "So, Seth, why don't you go back to the beginning? Tell me more about how you got started in your business. And of course I want to hear about Kaylee."

"You are nosy, aren't you?" he said, dipping his feet into the water next to Jess's.

"I've been accused of worse."

"All right—since you seem so intent on this, I'll give you some glimpses into my sordid past. I do understand why you want to know more about this place," he said, hitching his thumb over his shoulder back toward his shop. "Where to start . . . well, with this, I suppose: my grandmother Ruby and your aunt Celia were friends—*best* friends, I'd say."

Jess nodded in encouragement. She already knew some of this from Lavonne, but she'd let him talk now and fill in the blanks. She didn't need him knowing he'd been part of their girls' weekend conversation—especially the part where her mother pointed out how handsome he was.

Thanks for putting that *in my head, Mom.*

She pulled her attention back to what Seth was saying.

"My folks died in an accident while I was away at college. Suffice it to say I didn't handle things very well after they died, but Ruby did her best to keep me alive and out of jail."

"I'm sorry, Seth. That must have been awful. Did you finish college?"

"Barely. My grades sucked, but I managed to get out of there with a diploma, thanks in large part to Ruby. My degree was in architecture, but I wasn't cut out for all that. I was always happier getting my hands dirty in buildings instead of using them to draw schematics or blueprints, stuck inside all day. So I bounced around from odd job to odd job, Ruby helping pay my rent the months I was short. I was still living like a kid, not taking things seriously like I should have."

"How did you get involved in architectural salvage then?" Jess asked, curious at how closely her mom had gotten the story straight.

He laughed. "Ruby loved old buildings, and it was her mission in life to save as many of them from the wrecking ball as she could. She'd been to Europe and loved all the amazing old buildings and architecture there. She had her work cut out for her here, where the tendency is to knock anything down that starts to get a little patina to it and build new. As she got older she didn't drive anymore, so I took her to her meetings at the historical society. Sometimes I hung around and listened if I didn't have anything better to do. Met Celia there, too."

Seth went on to relay a story very similar to what Lavonne shared about the first building he dismantled.

"Guess I had the bug after that. It finally felt like I was doing something worthwhile. Ruby and Celia encouraged me to find a way to reuse things I'd taken out of the old theater. Some of it I sold as is, other pieces I hung on to until I figured out a way to retro-fit them into something folks could use."

Jess thought back to all the amazing pieces she'd seen in his shop. She understood the appeal.

Seth leaned over and picked up a loose rock from the ground next to his makeshift seat, turning it over in his palm.

Probably trying to figure out how much to share about his daughter, Jess speculated, watching him skip the smooth rock across the water's rolling surface.

Eventually, he began again. "It was fun and all, but I didn't make much money. I worked at it when I could, but I kept my paying jobs, too. That's how I found myself bartending. And that's where I met Dawn."

"Dawn?"

He nodded. His smile seemed to reflect a mixture of emotions. "Kaylee's mom."

"Did you get married?"

"No, it wasn't like that. Dawn and me, we never really had that kind of relationship," he said with a shrug. "A one-night stand resulted in another little human being, and my days of doing whatever the hell I wanted were at an end."

"So what did you do?"

"Even though Dawn and I were never a *real* couple, we were friends and we committed to doing our best—whatever that ended up looking like—for Kaylee's sake. We even tried living together for a little while, but that didn't work."

"What did Ruby think of all that? Was she old-school and judgmental?"

"Hardly," Seth replied, grinning. "The woman was unbelievable. She loved Kaylee. I just wish Kaylee could remember her. She was only four when Ruby died."

Jess's heart went out to him. So much loss for one person to endure.

They sat quietly for a few minutes, both lost in their own thoughts.

A bird squawked overhead, breaking the silence.

"My grandmother had cancer," Seth shared. "She used the time leading up to her own death to make sure I wouldn't be alone in the world. She left what she had to me and Kaylee, as far as material goods, but she also did all she could to keep throwing Celia and I together. I guess she saw how much we had in common. When Celia told her she was working with a church to refurbish old stained-glass windows in the sanctuary, Ruby saw it as another opportunity for us to work together. After Grandma passed, Celia and I just continued with our strange working relationship. I started struggling to keep up with all the paperwork and Celia offered to help. I couldn't afford to pay her, so we figured out a way to convey a twenty percent interest in the company. I wasn't a charity case," he said, his voice tinged with frustration.

"No, I'm sure you weren't. Don't forget, I knew my aunt well. She was an astute business woman. She probably saw it as a wise investment."

Seth gave Jess a bland smile at her comment. "You don't have to pump up my ego, Jess. I suspect she promised my grandmother she'd keep an eye on me. Help me out now and then. Like I said, they were best friends. You know Celia would have done everything she could to keep that promise."

"That I do," Jess agreed. "Celia was fiercely loyal. So, that helps me understand where you got your start here, and how Celia was involved . . . but why have you never mentioned Kaylee until today? We've been working together for quite a while now. Does she not live around here anymore?"

"No, and I'd be lying if I said it's been easy. Short of it is, Dawn met someone and they got married. Her husband had an opportunity to move back to Texas and work in their family business. I hated for her to take Kaylee, but I knew that was really the only option. I wasn't equipped to be a single dad, without much family around to help. Uncle Jack isn't exactly the type to step in and babysit on a moment's notice, you know?"

"I know exactly what you mean," Jess agreed with a small laugh. Celia's lawyer was the suit-and-tie type, always professional and kind, but not very grandfatherly.

Abruptly, Seth said, "Hey, listen, I better get back. I've gotta meet someone down at the old courthouse at five."

He dried his feet as best he could and forced them back into his boots, then jumped down off his rock and turned back to Jess, offering her a hand. She slipped her sandals back on as he helped her balance. She jumped down and landed inside his personal space. Resisting the temptation to step back, she instead stood her ground.

"Don't you get lonely, Seth?"

He angled his body in a hair closer. "I didn't until you came along."

Moving slowly, Seth brought his hands up and rested them at her waist, holding her gaze.

"You know this isn't wise, right?" he whispered, tilting his head ever so slightly.

"Of course it isn't *wise* ... but maybe we could both use a little companionship," Jess said with a barely perceptible shrug of her shoulders, softly tossing the question back at him.

With a soft groan, Seth pulled Jess up against his chest, his arms wrapping around her. Their kisses were tentative at first, searching. Jess's hands came up to rest on his chest—that chest she'd crashed into days earlier and the memory of which, if she were being honest, had cost her sleep. The accusations leveled against Celia weren't the only things keeping her up at night.

When Jess didn't back away, Seth deepened the kiss and her hands traveled upward. She stretched up on her tiptoes to run her fingers into his hair, knocking his hat off. Neither noticed. Jess pressed the whole front of her body against Seth, both to keep her balance and because it felt like the most natural thing in the world.

Seth's hands slipped under Jess's lightweight blouse and caressed her bare back, his hands pausing at the clasp of her bra.

Jess broke the kiss, dropping her forehead to his heaving chest, working to catch her breath. "I thought you needed to be somewhere," she said against his shirt, still stunned at what they'd just done.

Seth, the man she'd have sworn existed only to test her patience, gently placed a finger under her chin and brought it up so their eyes met.

"You OK?" he asked.

She inhaled deeply, the scent of both the beauty around her and the man in front of her calming her racing pulse. "I am."

Now Seth did step back, adjusting her shirt as he did so. He glanced at his watch. "I think I'm going to be a little late."

Jess grabbed for his wrist and checked the time for herself. "Oh my God, I'm a terrible person," she screeched, whipping around and taking off in the direction of the shop. "I'm supposed to pick Harper up in twenty minutes and it's a thirty-minute drive! We haven't even gone there a week and I'm already going to be late!"

"Oops," Seth said with a grin, breaking into a jog behind her.

When they reached the gravel lot, Jess skidded to a halt at her vehicle. "Crap!"

Seth opened her car door and waved her in. "I know you wanted to take all those records with you. Why don't I bring them out to Whispering Pines tomorrow? Celia used to talk about her resort. I'd like to see it sometime."

"Really? You'd do that?"

"I would. Now get going," he said as she jumped into the driver's seat and he slammed the door.

She rolled down the window. "Do you know how to get there?"

"I'll figure it out," he said, and he leaned through the open window and gave her a hard kiss.

CHAPTER 21

Gift of Rapport

*L*auren left early the next morning with Julie. She was looking forward to helping her cousin and friends change apartments and wouldn't be back for a few days. Robbie was at his buddy's house in Minneapolis for the weekend, so Harper was the only non-adult at the resort, outside of some young guests over in the cabins.

Jess heard Lauren and Julie leave but wasn't out of bed yet. She had been up with Harper for an hour during the night, and as long as the baby still slept, Jess planned to try to do the same. But then she heard voices outside. Renee was talking to someone. Acknowledging she wasn't going to be able to fall back asleep, she kicked her tangled covers off and got out of bed.

Why is it so stuffy in here? She used the bathroom and brushed her teeth. *Yep, definitely stuffy,* she thought as she tossed off her pajamas and pulled on a tank and shorts.

Harper must have heard her, because she started making rustling noises in her crib next door. Jess took a minute to slide her bedroom window open. Sure enough, a breeze of cooler air came wafting in.

Now Harper was babbling, looking for someone to come give her some attention.

"Hello there, sweet pea," Jess coed at the sight of the baby standing up in her crib, gripping the railing. "It won't be long until you're walking and running all over this place, will it?"

Harper lifted her arms to Jess, her little grin now including two little pearls on her bottom gums. Jess lifted her out of the crib and set her on her hip.

"Eww, you're sweaty too, aren't you?" Jess said in dismay. "And you need a dry diaper."

Jess dropped a blanket onto the carpet and kneeled down, trying to get Harper to lay down to get changed. As soon as the diaper was off, the kid flipped up onto her hands and knees and made a break for it in nothing but a onesie, the tail of the now unbuttoned garment trailing after her.

"Oh no, you don't, little one," Jess laughed, pulling Harper back onto the blanket. She tried again, but Harper successfully wriggled away.

"OK, let's try plan B. I think we both need a bath before Seth gets here. This is going to be tricky, but we need to get cleaned up. Then I have to figure out why its cooler outside than it is in here. The AC is *supposed* to be on."

It took some maneuvering, but Jess managed to get them both rinsed off without dropping the slippery little girl. She put a lightweight romper on Harper and caught her baby-fine, white-blond hair into two tiny pigtails.

"Now you won't look like a fuzzy little duck in this heat," Jess said as she secured the second tuft with a miniscule rubber band.

Once Harper was ready for the day, Jess stepped into a cool sundress. She ran a towel through her own hair, brushed it into a ponytail, and slicked a little mascara on. Glancing in the mirror, she cringed but accepted what she saw; it was too hot to fuss, and she supposed she might as well let Seth see how she really looked without her usual makeup and hair-styling. Harper needed breakfast—and she needed coffee.

After the baby had eaten, she took her outside. Renee was in the front, deadheading her flowers.

"Hey, those don't look too bad, considering it's almost Labor Day—not to mention that beating they took a few weeks ago."

Renee straightened, using one hand to shield her eyes from the sun. "Yeah, I wasn't sure if they'd come back." Harper stretched for the bud Renee held in her hand. Renee held it closer so she could touch it, but didn't give it to her. "I know right where that pretty yellow flower is going to end up if I let you take it, peanut," she said. "And you won't like the taste of it. Even deer and bunnies don't like the taste of marigolds."

"You are getting heavy, little lady," Jess complained, and she set Harper down on her bottom in the grass. "Stay." Jess went to set her coffee down on the step and Harper rolled to her knees and was off like a flash. "What are we going to do with you when you start walking? *Running?*" Jess asked, her feigned dismay partially real. "Here, sweetie, hold my hands."

Jess helped Harper get up on her little bare feet and take a few steps.

"Don't encourage her then," Renee observed, turning back to her flowers.

"You know as well as I do that they'll walk when they're ready, and whatever we do or don't do with them doesn't make much difference."

"I suppose that's true. What are your plans today?"

"Actually, I'm going to work on Seth's books."

"Again? Haven't you been doing an awful lot of that lately?"

Jess wasn't ready to tell Renee about Patricia's claims—or about her recent tryst with Seth—so she improvised. "He's thinking about going to the bank for a loan. He might want to expand. I'm helping him get everything in line."

Pretty good for on the fly, she congratulated herself.

"What are you going to do with Harper? Are you taking her with you?"

"Um, actually . . . he's coming here."

This caught Renee's attention. She had heard both Jess and her mother talk about Seth, but she'd never met him. "Really? Why?"

Jess swung Harper back up onto her hip as the baby was starting to resist her guiding hands. "I guess I always go out there, so he offered to come here. He thinks I'm doing him a favor, helping him with this on a Saturday. Plus, you know he and Celia were good friends. She'd told him about Whispering Pines, but I guess he's never been here. I think he kind of wanted to see it. Now that I think about it, I wonder if Ruby, his grandma, ever came out here with Celia. They were close friends."

"I bet she did, then."

"How about you?" Jess asked. "Do you and Matt have plans? Robbie is gone for the weekend, right?"

"Robbie is gone. Matt's on duty. So, after I get the cabins turned, I'm going to relax. Maybe read a *real* book. Can you imagine?"

Jess laughed. Renee worked every bit as hard as she did and deserved an afternoon off—or at least a couple of hours—to read a book or do whatever she wanted. "That sounds wonderful," she said, unable to remember when she'd last had a chance to read for fun. "Oh, that reminds me—I think the air is out on my side."

"Oh *no*," Renee groaned. "How can you tell?"

"How do you *think* I can tell, sis? The thermostat is set at seventy-two degrees but it's showing eighty, and my sheets were stuck to my back when I woke up this morning."

"Well, you don't have to get snippy about it. I hate to call a repairman on a Saturday . . . can I have Matt look at it when he gets home? I don't know the first thing about air conditioners."

"Sure. Or maybe Seth can look at it. He's pretty handy."

Renee grinned. "He is, is he?"

"Cute," Jess said, turning away from her sister and taking Harper inside, mumbling something about needing to get the baby out of the sun. She hoped Renee didn't see her blush. Her astute sister would have been all over that.

It was already getting hotter inside. Jess opened all the windows on the main and upper levels and started fans going. It immediately felt better. She puttered around in the kitchen for a while and let Harper play with the Tupperware. *Babies don't need toys, just plastic dishes.*

Not knowing when Seth would show up and hating to spend the whole day inside, she pulled out Harper's wagon, loaded it with beach toys, and took her down to their beach. A heavy coating of 50 SPF sunscreen and a big floppy hat should protect Harper's delicate skin; the swim diaper under the baby's one-piece swimsuit would let her splash around in the water a bit, too.

Jess plopped down in the sand next to Harper, hoping she wouldn't ruin her sundress. Together they scooped sand into buckets and dumped them out time and time again. When Jess dug a canal in the sand and dumped a pail of water into it, Harper delighted in splashing around until she was covered in wet sand. Jess was just reaching for a towel to wipe the baby's eyes (before Harper's tiny, sand-covered hand tried to do the same and she ended up with grit in her eyes) when Seth walked up.

"Hey there," Jess greeted him. "I didn't hear you pull up. How did you find us?"

"I could hear her from the parking lot," Seth said, grinning at Harper. Harper grinned back just before she slammed both her hands back down into the sandy puddle again, spraying the concoction in all directions and screaming in delight.

"I better get her cleaned up," Jess said, watching the messy little imp make more mounds of wet sand. "Adding the water was probably a bad idea."

"Oh, I don't know, looks like fun to me," Seth countered as he squatted down.

Harper had a fistful of sand and threw it straight at Seth's face.

"*Harper!* That's not nice. We don't do that," Jess scolded.

The little girl's face scrunched up and her bottom lip began to quiver.

"And here come the waterworks. Come on, little one, let's go get you cleaned up."

Jess held Harper under her arms and Seth did his best to brush the sand off her with the towel—not an easy task given the greasy sunscreen.

"Guess it's time for bath number two of the day," Jess said as she set Harper back down in her wagon beside her sandy toys and towel.

Seth grabbed the wagon handle and pulled it across the sand. Jess kept one hand on Harper's shoulder until they reached the smoother walking path he would have initially followed from the parking lot.

"Which way?" Seth asked.

"Sorry, I forget you haven't been here before. We'll get the baby cleaned up and then we'll give you the grand tour."

"Sounds good to me."

***

The tour had to wait. Jess took Harper upstairs for a quick bath while Seth brought tubs of paperwork in from his pickup. She fed the baby two jars of baby food and then let her play with big plastic blocks on her highchair tray while Jess made sandwiches. By the time they'd finished lunch, Harper's little head was starting to bob from the gravity of sleep. Jess put her down for a nap and then joined Seth again in the kitchen. He was standing at the screen door, looking out at the backyard and the woods beyond.

"It's nice out here," he said, not turning when she came in. "I see why you like it. But I bet winter can be tough."

"Very," Jess said as she put the lunch dishes away.

An awkward silence filled the room.

Finally, Seth turned around and walked back toward the table where Jess was pulling files out of a tub he'd set on a nearby chair. He stilled her hand with his own. "Look, Jess, I was kicking myself the whole way over here for letting that happen yesterday."

There it is, she thought. *He regrets getting too personal with me . . . kissing me. I'd do well to remember we're business partners and not get all caught up in a messy situation with this man.* She should have felt relief at his words. The fact that she didn't would be something she'd wait to analyze when she was alone.

She eased her hand away. "Look, how about we agree to forget yesterday ever happened, and go back to being business acquaintances?"

"Business acquaintances, huh? Well, all right . . . I wasn't going to go quite that far, but if you insist. I was thinking *friends* would be more appropriate. I think Celia would have preferred that . . . don't you?"

Now I'm being an ass, Jess thought, mad at herself for overreacting.

"I'm sorry . . . you're right. It's just been a long time since a guy swept me off my feet. I guess I'm a little rusty."

Seth laughed out loud, the tension gone. "Oh, I 'swept you off your feet,' did I?" he joked.

"Forget I said that!" Jess cried. "That didn't come out right."

"How about we call a truce?"

"Perfect. The last thing I'd want to do is wreck this . . . whatever the heck *this* is," Jess said.

She was struggling to articulate what she wanted to say, but Seth seemed to understand. He nodded, smiled, and got down to business. Harper slept for two and a half hours, giving them time to comb through most of the remaining records. They didn't find anything out of the ordinary or even remotely questionable.

Finally, Jess sighed and said, "I do have to say I'm impressed, Seth."

"With what? My ability to sit at this table and look at books for hours on end when you know I'd much rather be out there doing *anything* but this?"

Jess wasn't offended by Seth's words. She knew he was referring to the task they'd been working on and not her personally. At least she hoped that's what he'd meant.

"Well, that too," she acknowledged, "but I meant with the way you've been able to build something real out of nothing. Starting at the beginning of it all and walking through it with you, it really makes me realize how far you've come."

Seth stilled, seeming unsure how to take the compliment. Jess decided to give him a break.

"I think we've done about all we can here," she said, motioning to the mound of papers now covering the tabletop. "I'm just not seeing any irregularities. You know I didn't expect to, but we had to check."

"Jess, I . . ."

But he was interrupted by a knock at the door.

"And I suspect that's my sister," Jess said, pushing away from the table and heading for the front door. "I know she wanted to meet you."

Before Jess could get to the door, it opened and Renee stuck her head in. "Hi, you guys busy over here?"

"No. In fact, we were just finishing. Why don't you come in and I'll introduce you?"

"OK, if you're not busy," Renee said, giving Jess a discreet wink as she headed straight for Seth, her hand extended. "Hi. I'm Renee Blatso, Jess's sister. It's nice to finally meet you. I've heard a lot about you."

I can't believe she just said that, Jess thought with an inward groan as she watched the two of them shake hands. She scrunched her face up at

Seth when he wriggled his eyebrows at her as if to ask, *"Have you been talking about me?"*

"You've got a great place out here," he said to Renee. "At least what I've seen of it so far. Jess promised me a tour, but Harper decided it was nap time."

Renee looked around the kitchen and living room area. "Where is she? Is she still sleeping?"

"She is. She had a busy morning."

"Perfect," Renee said, looking between Seth and her sister. "Why don't you take Seth on that tour now, if you like, and I'll stay here? I was just going to read for a while. I can do it here as well as over on my side."

"I don't know if she'll sleep much longer," Jess warned. She hated for Renee to feel like she had to give up her downtime to help with Harper.

"That's fine. My book isn't real great, to be honest. If she wakes up, I'll take her home with me and we can hang out for a while. Besides, it's cooler on my side."

"It is getting pretty warm in here, now that you mention it," Seth said, plucking his shirt away from his body.

"My air conditioning went out last night, or this morning. I don't know what's wrong with it."

"Want me to take a look?"

"Do you know anything about air conditioners?"

"Not much, but maybe I'll get lucky. I've been known to be handy."

Jess tried to ignore Renee's smirk.

"Point me in the right direction and I'll at least look at it," Seth said.

"All right," Jess said. "It's downstairs. Do you want anything to drink before we go? A beer or a water?"

"Water would be great," he said as he let himself into the basement.

Once they were alone, Jess spun on Renee. "I can't believe you said that!"

"Said what?" Renee asked, trying to sound innocent, but the glitter in her eyes told Jess she knew exactly what she meant.

"I wouldn't have taken you up on your offer to watch Harper, except now you owe me."

"Yeah, I guess I do," Renee laughed. "I loved the look on your face. And when he said he was *handy* . . ."

Jess stuck her tongue out at her sister—the only way she could think of to show her frustration but stay quiet at the same time.

"You know you failed to mention he was gorgeous."

"Seriously, Renee, you are a newly married woman. You shouldn't be noticing things like that."

"*Seriously*, Jess," Renee mimicked her sister. "I do still have eyes, you know. My own husband is the hottest thing I've ever encountered, but this guy has potential for you."

"Would you just knock it off, Renee!" Jess hissed. "He might hear you."

"Who cares? He has a mirror," she said, clearly loving this chance to tease Jess about a man.

The door to the basement opened, and Seth walked back in. "Yep, froze up."

"What does that mean, exactly?"

He looked at Jess and laughed. "Honestly, I don't know. But I thought it sounded good. I'm pretty handy, sure, but not when it comes to things with motors. That's not really my forte. I think you probably need to have a repairman come out and look at it on Monday."

"I thought you might say that," Jess said. With a sigh she grabbed two bottles of water out of the fridge and ushered Seth out the back door before her sister could come up with anything else embarrassing to say. "You sure this is OK?" she asked Renee on her way out the door.

"Absolutely. Go, have fun. Take as long as you want. We'll be fine," she said in a normal voice, and then added, "and I'll be forgiven," for Jess's ears only.

***

Jess showed Seth around Whispering Pines. Most of the cabins were rented out, so she took him into the lodge. He was impressed with the updates

Renee had done, particularly the wall of windows facing the lake and the library she'd added upstairs.

"Yes, the library is my favorite place at the resort," Jess said, wandering around the perimeter of the room, her fingers trailing along a row of books.

"Are you a reader?"

"Normally, yes—I *love* to read—but life hasn't allowed for much reading lately." Jess was careful to keep her tone neutral. No one liked to listen to people complain about being too busy.

"Do you ever think maybe you're taking on too much with all of this, Jess?"

"I don't have to wonder. I *know* I'm taking on too much. But, Seth, what choice do I have? I have a responsibility to help maintain Celia's business interests, I can't afford to quit my real job, and I can't let Harper go to someone that won't love her and take care of her like we will. It won't be forever . . . but it's my life right now."

Seth simply nodded. What more could he say?

He followed Jess back downstairs. She showed him the bedrooms and bathroom, installed when Renee came up with her plan to offer retreats at the lodge during off-season.

"You should have seen the mess we found in here when we first came back out to Whispering Pines after Renee inherited it from Celia. The resort had been closed for a year or two. When we checked out the lodge, I opened the door to the old bathroom and almost had a heart attack—there was an honest-to-God family of squirrels making their home in the sink! I probably gave them a heart attack, too, with all my screaming."

Seth laughed at Jess's animated telling of her story about the squirrels. "Remind me not to bring you on one of my 'business trips.' Critters holed up in old buildings comes with the territory."

The wall of photos caught his eye as they made their way back to the door. He stopped to study them. Jess did the same. She'd never really taken the time to look closely at any of the pictures.

"Are they in any kind of order?"

"I don't know," Jess replied. "They look pretty jumbled to me."

"Is Celia in any of these?"

"Again, I don't know. I haven't really looked at them very closely."

Seth shot her an incredulous look that spoke volumes. She tended to forget what a history buff the man was. He studied each photo, starting at the top right and making his way over and down. It didn't take long for him to stop and point.

"Look—there."

"What? Is it Celia?" Jess asked, straining to see the picture. Seth's height gave him an advantage.

"Can I take it down, so we can see it better?"

"Sure, be my guest."

The picture came off the wall easily. The paneling behind the photograph wasn't faded like the rest of the wall—the frame had obviously hung in that same spot for a very long time. Seth carried the picture over near a window for more light.

"Oh, that has to be Celia!" Jess exclaimed in delight.

"And that's Ruby," Seth said, his smile bright.

Jess leaned closer to the old black and white photo. "I wonder who all the other people are in the shot . . ."

"I don't know," Seth said with a shake of his head. "But I bet there are lots of stories behind that group."

They studied the picture a bit longer and then Seth hung it back in its rightful place.

"I'll have to be sure to show my family that one," Jess said. "Maybe Mom or Dad would know some of the other people in the picture."

Their tour of the lodge complete, they went back outside. A family was grilling next to one of the cabins and a group of kids splashed around in the water near the dock.

"Well, I suppose I maybe should head out," Seth said, eyeing the sun, which had just begun its descent. "You probably have things to do."

"Not really. I was actually going to take you back and show you something Matt and Renee found, back in the woods a little ways. You might think it's cool. I know I did."

Seth stopped, looking at her as if surprised. "If you have time, I suppose I can stay a while yet."

Jess was enjoying herself and didn't want to see their day end. "Come on," she said, heading back to the spot she wanted to show him. "Watch for ticks. I got one the last time I went back here."

He followed her into the woods, and her mind skipped back to the thicket of trees they'd visited on their walk the day before. She felt the same sense of isolation. *No worries,* she assured herself, *he's made himself perfectly clear that he doesn't want that to happen again. So I'll put it out of my head.*

"Where are we going?" Seth asked.

"Almost there," she said over her shoulder, walking on. When she reached the spot she stopped and knelt down. "Look."

Seth followed her lead. He immediately saw the outline of whatever used to be there, barely visible to most. He found a stick and used it to dig a little deeper around the wood that peeked out of the ground.

"This looks like an old foundation."

"That's what we thought, too."

"How did anyone find this, way back here?"

"Well, it was kind of a fluke. Matt and Renee are thinking about building a home somewhere out here and they thought this area might be nice. Close enough, but still tucked back here to give them some sense of separation from the resort itself. I think Renee said she actually stubbed her toe on one of the ends of these old planks when they were walking through here."

"That's almost what it would take to notice it," Seth said, still intent on studying the ground.

"I found an old book that has some pictures of the resort in it. There's one picture of a cabin that isn't here anymore. Do you think this might be an old foundation from a cabin?"

"Could be. The size would be about right."

Seth got back down on his hands and knees and made his way around the outline.

Leave it to Seth to crawl around on all fours to get a better idea as to what used to be here. He's not afraid of a little dirt.

"You're going to scrape up your knees doing that," Jess admonished. "Besides, the mosquitoes are getting bad. Let's get out of these woods. I thought you'd like seeing this, though."

"You know me well, Jess," Seth said as he stood and brushed off his knees.

When she swatted at a bug on her cheek, he nodded and followed her as she made her way back toward the water. When they got back to the lawn surrounding the resort, she took him over to show him the Gray Cabin.

"Now, this little place has become a bit notorious," she explained as they approached the decrepit structure. She gave him a brief history of their troubles with the Gray Cabin, including Julie and her stalker boyfriend and Grant's more recent blizzard episode. "Renee's convinced herself it's cursed and has refused to fix it up."

Seth studied the old cabin. "Some places do seem to have a . . . I don't know . . . certain *presence* about them. I've seen it before."

Jess glanced at him. "You really believe in that kind of stuff?"

"One hundred percent," he replied, not taking his eyes off the cabin.

Jess gave a nervous little laugh and bent down to turn over a rock next to the stairs.

"Tricky," Seth said. "Hide-a-Key?"

"Yep. Nothing much in here for anyone to steal, but the place does seem to be a magnet for trouble, so we keep it locked."

Jess opened the front door and entered the cabin, Seth following close behind. It smelled stale and stuffy inside. It took less than five minutes to show him the interior. He said nothing until they were back outside.

"It would make sense to fix the place up and start renting it out. There aren't that many cabins out here to begin with. But I tend to agree with Renee. Something about it feels off."

Jess looked at Seth with some surprise. She wouldn't have expected him to be bothered by anything mumbo-jumbo.

"Is that it? Have I seen everything?"

"Pretty much. Man, it's a beautiful evening. Want to go down on the dock? It looks like all the kids must have went in to eat."

Seth nodded and silently followed Jess out onto the dock.

"Man, look at that water," he said. "It's so still. Like glass. Perfect night for a boat ride."

Jess surprised herself by saying, "Would an old canoe suffice? We have one, but I've never gone out in it. Want to give it a try?"

CHAPTER 22

Gift of Caution and Clues

The paint-faded canoe glided easily over the glass surface of the lake. A loon's mating call echoed off the water. Seth dipped his paddle in, side to side, and guided them out farther.

"Thanks for coming out today," Jess said, her voice joining the loon's. "It was nice to be able to stay home."

"Happy to do it. It was fun to finally see Whispering Pines instead of simply imagining what it was like based on Celia's stories."

"So what do you think? Is it what you expected?"

Seth nodded as he continued to paddle, but he didn't immediately elaborate. Jess peered over the side of the canoe, the water below so clear she could see small fish swimming under them. If the sun would have been higher, she suspected she would have been able to see the bottom.

When Seth finally spoke he said, "The resort itself is similar to how I pictured it in my head. What I didn't expect was how calming it feels. There's a solitude about it."

"I guess you're right," Jess said. "I never really thought about it like that. Sometimes, when we have lots of people around, it's anything *but* calm. But other times, like now, it does allow you to relax. Slow the pace down a bit, ya know?"

Seth nodded. "So, now that we've gotten through my books and everything looks good, what's our next step?"

"I still think I need to do the same thing over at the bookstore. Look through their records. Of course, much as I hate to, I need to call Patricia, too, and find out what she's been up to."

"Wouldn't that mean you'd have to tell the people at the bookstore *why* you want to dig back through their old records? Are you sure you want to do that?"

"If it was anyone other than Frank, I probably wouldn't, but he was fiercely loyal to Celia, too. She basically saved the lives of his wife and daughter, long before he was even in the picture. He'll want to do anything he can to help make sure nothing tarnishes Celia's reputation."

A fish jumped, the disturbance causing ripples to move out across the otherwise calm surface of the lake.

"The more people we involve, the more likely it is your family's going to find out. You still haven't said anything to them, have you?"

"No. It's just so ugly to even talk about. But I am feeling a little guilty. Maybe I should tell some of them. At least my folks and my sisters, maybe my brother. What do you think?"

Seth laughed dryly. "I'm probably the last person you should take advice from on family dynamics, but if keeping it from them feels wrong, you need to tell them. Who knows, maybe they'll have ideas as to how to get to the bottom of this."

"I suppose. I've just given them so many other things to worry about, I hate to pile on top of all that."

"Like what?"

"Like that little girl back at the duplex, for one."

"Jess, what you're doing for Harper takes amazing strength. I admire you for it. Hell, I didn't even fight for my own daughter when her mother wanted to take her away. And here you are, caring for your ex's baby."

"Well, thank you for that. But there's more. Will screwed up royally. I've told you some of it. He won't be out of prison for years. Apparently, in addition to being a rotten husband, he was also a rotten money manager. While I was trying to rebuild my life after I left him, he was busy spending our money, all the way down to our kids' college funds and our retirement. There's almost nothing left."

Seth stopped paddling and set the oar across his legs. The canoe slid silently through fingers of shadow now stretching across the water as the sun dipped behind tall pines that fanned back from the shoreline.

"Wait, didn't you say he was a surgeon? How long has he been practicing?"

"Plenty long to have the financial burdens of med school far back in the rearview mirror. He's had almost two decades of working under his belt. There should be plenty of money."

"So you know for a *fact* the money is gone, or he just *told* you it's gone?"

"Well, the bank statements I've seen prove those accounts have very little left in them. I'm even having to put our old house on the market, because I can't afford the hefty mortgage payment."

"And is the man always straight with you?"

Jess dropped the oar she'd been balancing across her knees into the bottom of the old boat. The clatter echoed outward, disturbing the quiet. She swung her legs around so she was facing Seth instead of the lake ahead.

"Actually, the man is rarely straight with me."

"So you, a smart business woman in your own right, are willing to just take his word for it?"

Jess kicked at Seth, her bare toe catching him in the shin. The canoe rocked under her movement, causing Seth to grip the sides to keep it balanced.

"Ouch! What did you do that for?"

"Because I'm too much of a wuss to kick myself. *Dammit.* You're right. Will always lies. He's probably lying now, too. But I haven't been *completely* gullible. I started doing a little digging because this niggling little voice in the back of my mind kept saying, 'Really?' "

"Have you found anything yet?"

"No. Oh, except for a locked metal box in the bottom of a locked drawer in the filing cabinet in his office."

Seth raised an eyebrow. "That's an awful lot of locks."

"Yes. Yes, it is, isn't it? It's probably a good thing I didn't leave it in his office."

"What do you mean?"

"Well, first of all, that cabinet never used to be locked," Jess said, going on to explain how she had to find her spare key to get into it in case there was any paperwork inside that she'd need. "When I found the small metal box, also locked up tight, it set off warning bells for me. As you say, an awful lot of locks. Since I'm listing the house, strangers will be traipsing through there. I thought it would be best to bring anything important back here."

"So what was in it?"

"I have no idea."

"Didn't you open it? You like to snoop."

"Cute. But no . . . not yet. I mean, Matt was going to help me break the lock, but it was late so I said we'd do it the next day. And that's when Patricia called."

"Aren't you dying to know what's inside that box?"

"Yes . . . and no." She expelled a heavy sigh. "Seth, what if I find something in that box I don't want to see? Something I don't want to know about? Remember, he's in *jail* now. God only knows what all he got himself into."

"I get what you're saying, what you're worried about. But Jess, this is your life we're talking about here. Or at least, things that could significantly impact your life. I think you need to see what's in the box."

"I'm scared."

"I think you need to suck it up, buttercup."

Jess cracked up, her laughter echoing across the lake. "Buttercup?!"

Seth smirked at her. "Dawn used to say that to Kaylee all the time. It seemed to fit this occasion. But seriously, Jess, not knowing is probably worse than whatever is actually in the box. At least I hope it is. Where's the box now?"

"Under my bed."

"Do you want me to see if I can help you break into it?"

Jess sat for a moment, watching Seth closely. "You have to promise me that no matter what we see in that box, you'll keep it between us. If it's bad, you have to let me deal with it and you can't tell another soul."

Seth reached over and took Jess's hand in his. "I can do better than that. I'll help you open it, but I don't even have to look inside unless you want me to." He winked and added, "I won't go snooping through *your* stuff."

Jess squeezed Seth's hand and a smile slowly curved her lips.

"Well then, what are we waiting for?"

***

The sun sat poised on the edge of the horizon, ready to dip out of sight as they pulled the old canoe off the lake. Together they tugged it far enough up the shore that it couldn't float away, even if bad weather came through. They could see a group of people around the large fire pit and hear muffled conversations and laughter. It sounded like a summer evening should. Seth followed Jess back to the duplex. Lights shone through the windows on Renee's side, but Jess's half was dark.

I need Renee to keep Harper just a little longer, until we can get that box open.

"Shh," Jess said, walking quietly up the front porch stairs and easing her own front door open.

Seth followed her lead, carefully closing the door behind them—and bumping into Jess as she fumbled for the light switch. She pitched forward, his arms coming out instinctively to catch her before she tumbled. Maybe it was just her imagination, but Jess thought she felt his arms tighten around her waist for a brief moment before he let her go.

"Sorry," he whispered.

Jess giggled and flipped the light over the stairs on. "I feel like a kid, sneaking back into my own house."

"Do you have any tools?"

"Tools? For what?"

"How do you plan to break the lock?"

"Good point. Just a minute." And she disappeared into the dark kitchen, coming back a minute later carrying a small metal toolbox that had seen better days. She held it up for Seth to see, then motioned him to follow her upstairs.

Once they were both on the upstairs landing, she flipped the light off again, their path now lit by weak moonlight. The sun had set. Jess reached behind her and found Seth's hand, leading him back to her bedroom. She didn't need light to find her way. She pulled him into her room and gently closed the door behind them. A fan stirred the air and her curtains danced inward. She slid the window shut, pulled the curtains closed, and turned on her bedside light.

Seth still stood next to the closed door, surveying her room.

Jess looked around in dismay. *The one time I don't make my bed,* she scolded herself, but then a realization struck her: *I brought a man to my room,* In her haste to open the box, she hadn't even realized what she was doing. *Maybe Seth won't think anything of it.*

But as she took in his rigid stance and the quick glance he gave her unmade bed, she feared he was very much aware of it as well.

Jess chose to ignore it. "The box is under here," she said as she dropped down to her knees and dug underneath her bed. Her hand found the cardboard box she'd stowed the smaller box in and pulled it out. She set it up on the bed next to the tools. She examined the lock, pulled a screwdriver out of the toolbox, and tried to pry it open.

Seth stayed where he was.

Finally, she looked at him and held the screwdriver up. "Are you going to just stand there or are you going to help me?"

He covered the distance from the door to her bed in three long strides and took the tool out of her hand. "Let me see it," he said.

Jess got up and moved out of the way. He picked the metal box up, examined the lock and sat down on the edge of the bed. He held the box in his lap to get more leverage.

"Do you have a better light? God, it is so dark in here. Couldn't we have done this down on the kitchen table where we could see something?"

Jess snickered, still feeling silly to be sneaking around in her own home—and more than a little nervous about having Seth in her bedroom. "I'm sorry. The kitchen shares a wall with Renee's place, and I was afraid she'd hear us and bring Harper over. Here, I have a flashlight in my drawer."

She grabbed the flashlight and aimed it down on the lock, helping Seth to better see what he was doing. He asked her for a couple of other tools, otherwise working silently to break the lock. Finally, with a grunt of satisfaction, the lock snapped. Seth opened the top just far enough to be sure Jess could get into it and then shut it again. The mangled lock wouldn't be any kind of barrier now. He stood and set the box back down on the bed.

Jess stepped forward to thank him, but he took the flashlight out of her hands, flipped it off, and dropped it onto the floor, pulling Jess up tight against him in one fluid movement. His mouth came down on hers, catching her completely off guard. With no time to think, her body responded to his without hesitation and she was swept up in the kiss.

Too soon, Seth pulled back and stepped away from her. "Don't ever bring me to your room again unless you mean it," he warned her, his intense gaze boring into her. "I've gotta go. See ya later."

Jess found herself alone, painfully alone, with only a box of mysteries taunting her from her bed.

***

Jess left the unlocked box on her bed and went over to Renee's. She knocked once and let herself in. Matt was standing in the kitchen by the sink, still in uniform, eating something out of a bowl. He held a finger up to his lips, motioning for Jess to be quiet. He took another bite and set the dish in the sink.

"Renee and Harper are both asleep in the rocker upstairs," Matt said, pointing to the ceiling. "I didn't want to wake them, so I came back down and heated up some dinner."

"I hope she's not mad," Jess said, keeping her voice down. "I didn't expect to be tied up with Seth for so long."

He cocked an eyebrow. "Seth?"

"Oh, he's a guy from work. I mean, I'm working with him now, since Celia left me an ownership interest in his business," Jess tried to explain.

Matt nodded. "I saw a guy drive away when I pulled in. Thought it was one of the cabin renters. Must have been your Seth."

"Let's be clear," Jess said, raising a finger in the air to emphasize her words. "He is not *my* Seth. We're just trying to figure something out, and Renee was helping me out with Harper."

Matt gave her an odd look but said nothing more.

"I'll run up and grab the baby, let you guys call it a night."

Jess left Matt in the kitchen and headed upstairs. Their place was a mirror image of her own, although not quite as shabby. Upstairs, she poked her head in Julie's old room. A night light bathed the room in a soft glow. Harper's eyes popped open when Jess stepped inside. She'd been resting her head on Renee's shoulder. Jess's sister was sound asleep.

"Hey there, peanut," Jess whispered to the baby, Harper's sleepy smile warming her heart.

" 'Hey there' yourself," Renee replied, giving the rocker another push as she shifted Harper into a sitting position in her lap. "I guess we dozed off." Harper reached up and touched Renee's lips. "We had fun, didn't we little one?"

"Renee, thank you so much for watching her. I'm sorry it got so late." Jess reached down and took Harper.

Renee yawned and stretched. "Not a problem. What did you guys do?"

"I just gave him a tour and then we decided to take the canoe out. It was such a beautiful evening."

"It sure was. Did you have fun?"

"We did."

Jess offered nothing more and Renee didn't push, for which Jess was grateful. She was still trying to sort out her own feelings about Seth's actions and abrupt exit. *For a man regretting that kiss, he sure was intense tonight.* He . . . confused her.

"Hey, we'll see you tomorrow. I'll take her home now and let you go to bed. Matt's home. He's downstairs eating."

"Oh good, send him up, will you?"

***

Jess changed Harper and put the baby down in her crib, careful not to talk to her or get her riled. She tiptoed out of the room, worried Harper would object, but the little girl just stuck her thumb in her mouth, rolled to her side, and stilled.

Renee must have worn her out, Jess thought, heading back to her own room.

She pulled up at the sight of the box, somehow looking ominous sitting on the edge of her unmade bed.

"I'm not going to be able to sleep until I look," she whispered. She picked up the box she'd taken from Will's and her battered old toolbox and carried both down to the kitchen table. She stowed the tools back under her sink, poured herself a glass of wine, and sat down at the table, staring at the box.

She drained half the glass, set it off to the side, and slowly opened the lid.

A black three-ring binder sat inside. She took the binder out and set it on the table. There wasn't much else except an envelope with some cash in it and a key-ring with two common keys. Nothing else.

Jess counted the cash—all twenty-dollar bills—and came up with $960. She set the money aside, an emergency stash maybe, and picked up the keys. They looked too small to be house keys, but she was only guessing. Putting both items back in the box, she opened the binder.

The top sheet was some kind of computer-printed spreadsheet. All numbers and a few letters, no words or names. The column on the far left was dates; the other columns were just numbers. The top of each was labeled with a combination of numbers and letters. The page was three-fourths full and the most recent date, at the bottom, was June 20, 2017.

Renee's wedding had been on June 17.

What am I looking at?

Jess flipped to the next page. She noticed a row, between May 31 and June 5, with larger numbers—maybe subtotals or something. There were eight to twelve rows per month. Subsequent pages looked similar and the stack of papers in the binder was roughly an inch thick. The very last page in the binder was the oldest. The earliest date listed was 9/12/07, almost ten years ago.

Jess flipped all the pages back into place and closed the cover of the binder. Maybe she was just too tired to understand what she might be seeing. She laid the binder back in the box, on top of the cash and keys, and closed the lid. She knew she was too exhausted to try to figure any of it out tonight. She dumped out the rest of her wine and went upstairs to put the box back under her bed. She needed sleep.

The day had left her emotions raw.

CHAPTER 23
Gift of Allegiance

"Patricia, it's Jess. Can you talk?"

Jess paced, barefoot, on the beach down by the water. Harper was at daycare and Renee was a safe distance away, mowing. While Jess hated to pick up the phone and call Patricia, she needed to find out where things stood and she wanted to make the call from somewhere she knew no one would overhear.

"I can talk," Patricia replied. Short and to the point.

"Listen . . . I can't stop thinking about the things you shared with me about your suspicions, but I haven't heard a word from you since. Have you been able to find any answers? Do you still suspect Celia might have done something wrong?"

"Hold on a second." Jess could hear rustling in the background. "I wanted to shut my door. Wendy is sitting at her desk, talking with one of our team supervisors. I haven't called, Jess, because I don't have any answers yet. I've been trying to make heads or tails of the numbers, I really have, but things still aren't adding up."

"Are you sure you don't want me to take a look at them with you, Patricia? Maybe I could help."

"Jess, don't you think that would be a little bit like inviting the fox into the hen house?"

Stay calm . . . stay calm. The woman could be so infuriating, though. Jess knew exactly what Patricia was insinuating but wanted to make her say it out loud.

"What do you mean?" Keeping all emotion out of her tone.

"I mean, if your aunt was up to something, you aren't going to want to help me find proof. You'd probably try to steer me in another direction just to protect her."

"I don't appreciate you insinuating that I'd be dishonest . . ."

Stay calm . . . stay calm . . .

". . . but I suppose if I was in your shoes with the same suspicions, I might say the same thing. Have you talked to your parents about your concerns?"

"No. I don't want Dad to brush me off. He'll only give me one chance to make my case, and I don't want to blow it. Unfortunately, our tax accountant is out of town for a few weeks so I haven't gotten any help from that avenue, either. Something about a family emergency. Can you believe it?"

Leave it to Patricia to find someone else's emergency an inconvenience for *her.*

Patricia continued, not expecting an answer to her rhetorical question. "I really need to find the older records. I've looked everywhere around here and even over at Mom and Dad's, but I can't find them anywhere."

"I thought you said you hadn't mentioned anything to your folks yet?"

"I haven't. I have a key. I went over there when they were gone for the weekend. But there was nothing."

"Maybe older records weren't maintained. The IRS can only go back seven years if they have questions or concerns. Maybe there was no space to keep the older documents and someone thought it was OK to toss them."

"Well now, *that* would be convenient, wouldn't it?"

Jess didn't even bother to reply to that comment.

"Look, Jess, I'm sorry. I hate that this is happening. But something isn't right. I feel like there hasn't been enough money flowing to the bottom line for a long time, based on the revenue coming in and what I know of our normal expenses. If someone actually cooked the books, I just don't know who else it could have been if not Celia. She was the only other one that had access to the books on a regular basis—other than Mom and Dad, and they certainly wouldn't have stolen from themselves."

Jess tried to interrupt, but Patricia was a steamroller, continuing, "I don't *want* to believe Celia did anything wrong, but I need to be *sure.* I hope you understand."

Jess waited to make sure the woman was done. If in fact Patricia's parents weren't guilty of some "creative accounting," Jess suspected there was nothing wrong with the books and that Patricia was simply underestimating how much it costs to run a labor-intensive business such as theirs, but she also knew she wasn't in a position to convince Patricia of this.

She settled by saying, "So . . . we're basically on hold, then?"

"Unless you can find the old records . . . yes."

***

After lunch, Jess drove over to pick up Seth. During their time in the canoe they'd agreed he would go along to Frank's with her. Frank was available to meet now, so Jess had sent Seth a text, asking if he still wanted to come along. She knew a text was the chicken way out, but she seemed to step all over herself when it came to Seth. Maybe it would be better if she minimized their communications. His response made her feel silly, though.

Sure, pick me up at two.

She sighed with relief and thought, *All right, nice and straightforward. I can do this.*

As she pulled into the lot in front of Seth's, he came out, locking the door behind him. He was back in his usual attire—jeans, work boots, and a navy T-shirt with his logo on the back. His surly attitude was back, too, and he said little after he jumped up in the passenger side of her Land Rover.

"The bookstore is about half an hour from here," Jess informed him, to which he simply nodded. She stole a quick glance at him, but he was looking out the window, his face giving nothing away. She turned up the radio and drove, doing her best to ignore him.

There was little traffic. In Seth's continued silence, Jess let her mind wander back over the past twenty-four hours. Patricia was still convinced something was wrong in their books, dating back years; with Seth's help, she'd gotten into Will's box, but the contents told her nothing; and now, with him sitting next to her, she was having a hard time blocking out the memory of Seth kissing her last night.

"Watch out!"

Jess automatically hit the brakes, careful not to lose control of her vehicle, her right arm shooting out in front of Seth. Thanks to his warning, the dog that ran in front of them kept running, oblivious to the danger. Shaken, Jess pulled over to the side of the road. No other cars were around. She glanced quickly at Seth and then back out at the road, taking deep breaths to slow her racing heart. He'd scared the *crap* out of her.

"Thanks," was all she said.

"No, thank *you*."

Something in his tone rubbed against her already-raw nerves. She spun in her seat to face him. "What is *that* supposed to mean?"

"I appreciate you saving me from injury," he said, keeping his face straight.

"You don't have to be a smart-ass about it," she said. "If you're going to act like a child, I'll treat you like one."

OK, so maybe that was a bit much, she scolded herself.

Her natural reflex to protect her passenger was born from driving with a kid in the car much of her past twenty years. Frustrated with the whole situation, she let her forehead fall down to her steering wheel, waiting for his comeback. When none came, she sat back up and looked over at him. He was studying her.

"What?!" she said, uncomfortable under his gaze.

"How long are we going to keep doing this?"

"Doing what?"

"Come on, Jess, knock it off. You know exactly what I'm talking about. Ever since you barged into my bathroom, we seem to keep finding ourselves in these situations."

"What do you mean, 'these situations'?"

"These situations where we're either totally pissing each other off or having a hard time keeping our hands off each other. It's a freaking rollercoaster, and it's exhausting."

This turn in the conversation was making Jess highly uncomfortable. She knew he was right—their interactions *had* been a rollercoaster—but she didn't know what to do about it or why they'd so quickly gone from just starting to be civil to each other to this. All she could do was shrug, at a loss for words.

"Can you at least acknowledge that *something* is happening here? Between us?" He made a circular motion with his hand.

"Yes . . . but I don't know what to do about it."

"Look, Jess, I said it before and I'll say it again: I think we might be making a mistake if we let this turn into something more. But I'm *also* starting to think maybe we might not have a say in it."

"What are you talking about, 'not have a say in it'? We're both adults. We can choose what kind of relationship we want this to be." Jess copied his motion with her own hands.

"I used to think so."

"Seth, I'm still married. I have no room in my life for a man right now. Besides, I'm way older than you. It would never work."

Seth laughed, but he didn't sound happy. "Jess, you're only a few years older than I am, and at our age that hardly matters anyway. I have to tell you . . . I've never run across a woman who managed to bug the hell out of me one minute and . . . and . . ."

"And what?"

"You know what I mean. I'm just not good at talking about it."

Jess sat quietly for a minute, her mind mulling over what he'd said. He'd made the same mistake she had, underestimating her age. *I'll let him go on thinking I'm only forty.* Finally, she said, "If I'm being honest, I don't still *think* of myself as a married woman. The only reason I'm still married is because Will dragged his feet. Over the years, he threw my heart back at me so many times, he no longer has any piece of it. So there's that. I admit, too, there's something between us. I don't *want* there to be."

Seth grunted.

"Don't take that personally," she added. "It's not you. It's me. I'm a friggin' mess."

And now I'm starting to sound like a character in a cheesy movie.

Seth surprised her by draping his left arm across the back of the seats, his hand on her headrest, his fingers gently caressing the nape of her neck. "Jess, I'd say we're both a bit of a mess. Why don't we try to set all this on the back burner for now? Call a real truce this time. We need to figure out what the deal is with Celia and Homes Sparkle. You need to iron out some wrinkles in your personal life, too. I don't want to say *never* when it comes to you and me, but how about if we say *not yet?*"

Jess was afraid he was right. Whatever this was between them, it wasn't likely to just go away because they wanted it to.

"All right. Truce," she said.

"Can I kiss you to seal the deal?" Seth asked, leaning toward her with a grin.

Jess held up her hand to stop him. "Not yet."

Still grinning, he said, "But not never, either."

***

The rest of their drive passed quickly, with their rollercoaster ride now on an even keel. She filled him in on what she'd found inside Will's box after he left and how she had no idea what it all meant. He told her about an old church he needed to check out the following day.

Frank was at his desk when they entered the bookstore. There were no other cars out front and a quick glance confirmed there weren't any customers browsing. Frank came around the counter and approached Jess and Seth. He gave Jess a friendly, one-armed hug and waited for her to introduce Seth.

"Frank, this is a friend of mine, Seth Lindell. Seth, this is Frank Fisk. He and his wife Virginia own this amazing little establishment."

Frank held out his hand to Seth. "Lindell . . . sounds vaguely familiar."

Seth shrugged. "Do you know Jack Poole? He was Celia's lawyer. He's my uncle. My mom was Shirley Lindell and she was Jack's sister."

Frank nodded, continuing to study Seth. "Sure, I know Jack. Maybe that's where I've heard the name before."

Jess intervened. "It'll make more sense once we have a chance to talk about why we're here. Is Virginia around?"

"No, actually, she and Karen are out of town. Jess, you must have heard of Helen before, Virginia's mother?"

"Sure. She was a good friend of Celia's, wasn't she?"

"Yes," Frank said. "Unfortunately, Helen passed away a couple of weeks ago. Come on, let's go sit back here and get comfortable. I can't stand for as long as I used to. I've got the coffee on, too."

Frank led the way to a small alcove in the back of the store. Four comfortable armchairs formed a circle. The smell of coffee wafted out to meet them. Seth offered to pour, and once they were all settled with steaming mugs in hand, Jess turned to Frank.

"Why don't you start? What happened to Helen?"

Frank gave a small nod and sipped his coffee. "Well, Helen was a tough old bird, lived to be ninety-five. Her husband, Virginia's father, died twenty years ago. But Helen was a bit of a force to be reckoned with—she wasn't about to go easily. But eventually old age simply caught up. Pneumonia's what did it, and it happened quickly."

"So if she died two weeks ago," Seth asked, "why aren't they back yet?"

"Helen still lived in the same house Virginia grew up in. She and Karen decided to stay and get things taken care of so the house can go on the market. Virginia had three other sisters, too, but one died a few years back and the other two don't want the house. Virginia hopes to be back in a couple more weeks."

"I'm sorry, Frank," Jess said. "It's difficult to lose a parent, no matter their age."

"Yes, it is. In this case, it's been really hard on Karen. Karen is our daughter," he added for Seth's sake.

"Were they close?" Jess asked, already suspecting they were, based on comments from her own mother Lavonne.

"Very," Frank confirmed. "Virginia and Helen were two very different people. Their relationship was always a bit strained. But not Helen and

Karen. They were extremely close. I suspect they still talked nearly every day, right up until the end. I love my daughter dearly, don't get me wrong, but she does have a bit of Helen in her—and that isn't a compliment."

Jess, knowing Frank wasn't the type to talk ill of anyone, had to stifle a laugh of surprise. "What do you mean?"

Frank got up, walked over to the coffee pot, and topped off his mug. He offered more to his two visitors, but they declined. Sitting back down, he continued.

"Helen always liked the finer things in life. Things Virginia never cared about. That was a big part of the rift between them. Helen always thought Virginia *settled* in life, failed to live up to her potential. To be blunt, Helen was always a snob—and she managed to pass some of those tendencies on to Karen."

This surprised Jess. "I've met Karen. She seems perfectly nice."

It was Frank's turn to laugh, but he didn't stifle his. "Of course Karen is *nice*. She takes wonderful care of us. I've just always felt like Karen made some important life decisions poorly based on Helen's influence."

"What kinds of decisions?" Jess glanced over at Seth to try to gauge whether or not this conversation was boring him, but he seemed to be listening.

"You must be catching me on a particularly chatty day, Jess. I don't normally talk about these kinds of things. Let's just suffice it to say I think Karen selected her husband more for what he could offer her than how he made her feel. There hasn't been much laughter in their home, more like a business relationship than a love affair. Helen's marriage to Virginia's father felt a bit like that, too, at least to someone looking in from the outside."

"But Karen works. It's not like she married for money and stays home and eats bonbons all day."

"Oh no, of course not. She's always been ambitious. I just wish she seemed happier. But enough about all that," Frank said. "That's not why the two of you came all the way over here today. Why don't you loop me in?"

Jess contemplated where to start. "Well . . . something has happened that could tarnish Celia's good name, or worse. And I'm not about to let that happen."

Frank sat taller in his chair when he heard this. "Are you serious, Jess? Celia was one of the best people I knew. Why now? How can her reputation be called into question? The woman has been gone almost two years now."

"Our thoughts exactly," Seth interjected. "We need your help to put this ridiculous notion to bed."

"What notion?"

Jess said, "You know Celia was involved in a few other businesses other than your own, right?"

Frank nodded.

"Are you familiar with Homes Sparkle?"

"Sure. They clean our house. I knew Celia worked with them as well."

"So John and Joyce Robins started Homes Sparkle many, many years ago. When they retired, they left the business to their daughters Wendy and Patricia. Patricia is wanting to expand the business and was trying to pull together some trending information. In the process, she thinks she's uncovered something in the books, thinks money is missing from the company. In her mind Celia is the obvious culprit, since she had access but isn't family."

"That is the most ridiculous thing I've heard in a *long* time," Frank exclaimed.

"Of course it's ridiculous," Seth said.

"And how do you fit into all this, young man?" Frank asked Seth.

"I run a small architectural salvage and stained-glass company, Saving Bits of Time."

Frank blinked in response, likely meaning he'd never heard of it, so Jess added, "Seth's grandmother, Ruby, was another good friend of Celia's."

"Oh, of course. I met Ruby a time or two. Forgot she was Jack's mother and that she and Celia were friends."

Seth nodded. "My grandmother and Celia, they encouraged me to start my business. When Ruby died, Celia stepped in as kind of a surrogate grandmother to me and helped me keep my business afloat."

"And now," Jess added, "similar to our business relationship here at the bookstore, Celia passed on her ownership rights in Seth's business to me."

"Frank," Seth said, "I would have gone out of business a long time ago if I wouldn't have had Celia's help. So you must understand that I can't stand around now and do nothing when someone levels such claims against her."

"I can't either," Frank agreed. "How can we help?"

"That's what brought us here today, Frank," Jess said, relieved to sense a level of camaraderie between the two men already. "I've gone through Seth's books cover to cover, careful to check for anything unusual. Celia was more involved in the bookkeeping end at Seth's than with you here or Homes Sparkle, but I suppose the *opportunity* was there for Celia at any of your businesses. It's our job to prove she did nothing wrong at any of her businesses, which means you're next."

Frank nodded firmly. "I couldn't agree more."

"So I would like to go back in your records, too—as far back as you have, at least—and prove there was nothing inappropriate going on. Would you mind?"

"Of course not. You have my permission to do whatever you need to do to help build a case for Celia."

"Great. Tell you what," Jess said, glancing at her watch. "It's probably too late to get started today, but can I come back Tuesday afternoon? I have to get Lauren settled at college this weekend."

"Please do," Frank said, hoisting himself out of the armchair and gathering their coffee mugs. "The sooner we put these ridiculous rumors to bed, the better."

"You know, Frank, you've got a great old building here," Seth commented, looking around him. "I don't suppose you'd give me a quick tour before we leave?"

"She's pretty," Frank acknowledged with a chuckle and a shake of the head, "but just like with the rest of us, her upkeep is getting lots more expensive with age. Sure, I'll show you around."

Jess came along for the tour. She'd loved the quaintness of the old building since she first saw it, but going through it with Seth gave her a new perspective. He pointed out things she'd never really noticed before. In the basement, for example, Seth mentioned that the old cistern may be behind some of the water issues the Fisks faced; the ceiling in the main level, covered with antique ceiling tins, was in need of some repair.

"That must be what Nathan was referring to when he was digging through the ceiling tins at the shop," Seth said to Jess, pointing to the damage in the upper north corner.

Jess cringed, thinking back to the crash Nathan had caused with his digging. "I'm *sure* it is."

As the tour wrapped up, Frank shook their hands and saw them to the door.

Seth pointed to the stained glass window in the transom above the outside door. "It wouldn't take much to fix that."

Frank laughed good-naturedly. "I'm sure you're right, but I've never taken the time to find someone to do it."

"Got a ladder around here?"

Frank looked at Seth in surprise. "Well sure, downstairs, but why?"

"See how there's an outside pane of regular glass on the street side and the stained glass window itself is set in behind it? I could probably pop it out of there without too much trouble. Take it back to my shop and fix both that crack and all the lead between the panes that's starting to deteriorate."

Frank paused, considering this. "Any idea what that'd cost me? Seems anything we touch around here costs an arm and a leg to fix anymore."

"I imagine it does. You know . . . Celia helped me get into stained glass—probably the part of my business I enjoy the most. I won't charge you. I know she'd have appreciated me giving you a hand. And it would also be my way to thank you for helping us clear up this mess."

"Son, you've got a deal," Frank agreed, giving Seth a fatherly pat on the shoulder as he turned away to retrieve his ladder.

CHAPTER 24

Gift of Milestones

"*D*o you want to take this?"

Jess held up the pink stuffed teddy bear that had been living at Whispering Pines on Lauren's bed for the past year.

Lauren cringed, reaching out protectively to the teddy bear. "Do you think my roommate will think it's stupid?"

"I would ask why it matters what she thinks, but I suppose it does since you're sharing one small room. How about this—bring her along in your suitcase. Keep her hidden if you want, but I suspect there may be a time or two that you're going to feel lonesome or overwhelmed, and being able to hug your little friend will help."

"Mom, her name is *Cupcake*. Why can't you remember that? It's been her name for fifteen years."

"Maybe because it's such an *unusual* name for a little girl to pick for a toy?" Jess joked.

She tried to laugh at her own words, doing her best to stay positive. Tomorrow was the day *she'd* dreaded for eighteen years. Her baby would leave for college. Most of her things were already packed and stored in the vehicles. They'd leave early in the morning.

Maybe I shouldn't have told her to take Cupcake . . . I could have snuggled with it when I get lonesome for Lauren.

Jess forced a smile, thinking, *At least I'll have Harper to keep me company.*

***

The three of them were on the road by eight. Lauren followed Jess in her car. Jess's Land Rover was full: the front passenger seat was piled high with new bedding for Lauren's dorm room, Harper was strapped in her car seat behind Jess, and Lauren's hanging clothes took up the rest of the back seat.

When they reached campus, Jess followed the signs, pulling up in the unloading lane next to her daughter's designated dorm. Student volunteers descended on them, helping to quickly unload their vehicles and pile it all in a small area on the lawn. The grass was littered with many similar piles. There was an efficient system behind the chaos. Jess and Lauren took turns parking their vehicles after they were unloaded.

No one was in their room yet when Lauren's RA unlocked the door to Lauren's assigned dorm.

"Since you're the first one here, you can pick whichever bed you want," the frazzled young woman said. "Once your roommate gets here, I'll check you in together." As the RA hustled out of Lauren's room, she yelled to someone down the hall. "Wait . . . you're gonna scratch the wall. You can't move a futon by yourself! Here, let me help."

Lauren began hauling her pile into her dorm room—with help, Jess noticed, from a trio of cute guy volunteers.

"Is that your baby sister?" one of them asked Lauren, nodding toward Harper, giggling in Jess's arms.

"Yeah!"

"I figured it must be—she looks just like your mom."

Jess saw Lauren shoot her a nervous glance. *Wonder what the kid would say if I told him the* real *story,* Jess wondered. But she wouldn't let anything ruin Lauren's big day.

Wait—do I still look young enough to have a baby of my own? This second thought bumped Jess's mood up a notch.

She gave Lauren a reassuring smile despite feeling a little sick to her own stomach; Lauren didn't need anything else to worry about.

When the cute guys turned away to grab more stuff, Jess leaned in and whispered, "You might want to pick the bed by the window."

"I hope that doesn't make her mad, me grabbing the best bed," Lauren said, chewing nervously on a fingernail.

"Lauren, honey, you need to stop worrying so much. The two of you will figure it all out. It'll just take time. Why don't you take the bed by the window but then this closet over here? That way she gets the better closet. A little compromising goes a long way."

Lauren nodded at her mother but her eyes swam with unshed tears.

"Oh no, you don't," Jess warned. "No tears. At least not while I'm still standing here. You'll get me going and we'll look idiotic in front of those guys. Here—take her."

Jess handed Harper to Lauren, knowing the distraction would do her good. The guys had just brought in the eight-by-ten-foot rug Lauren wanted for her birthday. (She'd sent pictures of it to her roommate to be sure she liked it, too.) Jess lined up the roll and cut the tape. The carpet unrolled to cover the ugly tiled floor, instantly making the room feel warmer.

Harper clapped her hands and pointed at the pretty aqua color rug.

"Oh, that's nice!" Lauren said. "You want to see?"

Lauren set the baby down on her bottom and started to unpack her new sheets.

Jess smiled, the crisis of waterworks successfully avoided. "Let's see if we can't get it looking nice in here before your roommate gets in."

***

Jess buckled Harper back into her car seat. The dorm room was coming together and Jess felt good after meeting Erin, Lauren's new roommate. They'd taken a tour of campus, found the girls' classes, and done plenty of damage to Jess's checkbook with a trip to the bookstore. Erin and Lauren were heading to dinner and Jess knew it was time to say their goodbyes.

I held it together pretty well—only a few tears . . . for now, at least.

Her cell rang as soon as she'd started backing out of her parking spot, so she pulled back in and answered.

"Hi, Renee. What's up?"

"Well, *you* sound better than I thought you might."

"I have an audience," Jess replied, glancing in her rearview mirror at Harper. The baby was starting to nod off after their action-packed day and no nap.

"True. So what are you going to do now?"

"I was going to head back to Whispering Pines. I'm beat."

"I have a better idea."

Jess groaned. "What?"

"Swing by Mom and Dad's. Mom said she'd watch Harper. You, me, and Ethan can go out for dinner. Relax a little. All you've been doing lately is working and getting Lauren ready to go. You need to unwind a little."

"I guess it's on the way . . . and I haven't seen much of Ethan this summer, either. All right. If you're sure Mom doesn't mind."

"I'm sure. Meet you there in an hour."

***

Jess relaxed with Ethan and Renee on a patio overlooking the golf course, sipping wine while they waited for their meals. It was a perfect fall evening and Jess was glad she'd agreed to come along.

"So how did it go with Lauren today?" Ethan asked.

"Better than I'd hoped. With everything going on, I was worried she wouldn't be ready to go or we'd forget something important, like her computer. But I think everything she'll need—at least to get started—is now safely stored in her dorm. Her roommate seemed nice, too. She's a bubbly little thing. She can't be more than five feet tall and is as blond as Lauren is brunette. Fingers crossed . . . but I feel good about it at this point."

Renee nodded. "Good. Check that big item off your list. How about your kids, Ethan?"

"Busy, as usual. Elizabeth has it all mapped out, of course, so she'll be done with college in the spring."

"I can't believe this is her fourth year *already*," Jess said with a shake of her head. "Nathan is hoping to finish up soon, too."

"And both boys are playing football," Ethan continued. "So lots of filthy clothes and daily practices. Now that school has started, it'll mean late nights cramming homework."

"Is Dylan big enough to play?" Jess asked.

Ethan gave a big belly laugh at this. "Apparently I need to bring the boys around more often, sis. Dylan's got his big brother by two inches and twenty-five pounds."

"Oh man, three years younger too? Maybe I should have asked if *Andrew's* big enough to play!"

"How often are they with you?" Renee asked.

Ethan shared custody of the boys with his ex-wife. Jess knew it wasn't a fifty-fifty arrangement. "It's supposed to be every other week, but she's been traveling for work—or so she says. But I'm glad. I'd rather they were with me. Then at least I have some idea what they're up to. Especially Drew, now that he's driving and dating."

"Is Stacey pretty lenient then?"

"I would label it more *uninvolved* than lenient. Dylan told me he thinks she'll marry the guy she's been seeing these past few months. I swear, she treats the kids like they're an inconvenience. I don't think Elizabeth has talked to her mother since the end of school last spring. It's ridiculous."

Jess scowled. "That witch. You should have listened to me when I told you she wasn't good enough for you, big brother. Remember? You *assured* me you knew what you were doing. So how'd that work out for you?"

"Shut up, Jess. You can't tell me something like that at my *rehearsal dinner* and expect me to take you seriously. And thank God I didn't listen to you. Unlike Stacey, I *love* being a parent."

A waiter placed their meals in front of them and Renee ordered a second bottle of wine.

"No, no, one glass is it for me," Jess insisted. "I have to take Harper home tonight."

"Why don't we have a sleepover at Mom and Dad's?" Renee asked, bouncing in her chair like a little girl. "I saw that diaper bag you had for

Harper. You have enough diapers, food, and clothes in there for a week. Ethan isn't drinking, *he'll* drop us off!"

"I'm sure that's just what Mom wants. And what about your husband, home all alone? Aren't you two still newlyweds?"

"I already cleared it with Mom, and Matt is working nights this week so he would be leaving about the time I would get home anyhow."

"And your *son?*"

"Robbie's seventeen, Jess! He'll be *fine.* Come on, have a little fun!"

Ethan looked at her like she had horns. "Seriously, sis? You think it's all right to leave a seventeen-year-old home alone all night? I remember what *I* was doing at his age. You might want to think through that."

"Ethan, I trust Robbie. He screwed up pretty bad last year, but he came clean about it. I think it scared him. Besides, if anything happens, I track his phone—and Matt can check in on him, too. We're covered."

Resigned, Jess held her empty wine glass up for Renee to fill. "Looks like the bases are all covered. So, Ethan, what else is new? Dating anyone?"

"When would I have time to *date* anyone? This single-parenting of two teen boys is all-consuming."

"Oh, come *on,* you must at least think about it sometimes. Do you have your eye on anyone?"

Ethan tried to ignore his persistent sister by cutting his steak and buttering his baked potato.

"Come on, bro . . . anything?"

"No, I'm telling you *nada.* But what about you, huh? Anything in the romance department now that ol' Willy-boy is locked up behind bars and you're a free woman? Do you have *your* eye on anyone?"

"Does she *ever!*" Renee interjected, swirling the ruby liquid in her wine glass with a knowing look. Her cheeks were getting a little flushed—the wine was clearly loosening up her tongue.

Jess sent her a scathing glare in return. "Renee . . . be *quiet,*" she hissed. "I do not have my *eye* on anyone." She turned her attention back to her brother. "I'm not technically a 'free woman' yet."

Evan started in on his food, then said, "What? You've got to be kidding! And I thought *my* divorce was a hot mess."

"I know. It's ridiculous. Hopefully it'll all be over soon."

"Despite that technicality, you don't feel like you have to still be faithful to that jackass, do you?"

"No. But just like you, I hardly have time during the day to brush my teeth, let alone date anyone."

"So what did Renee mean, then? 'Does she ever'?"

"Oh, she's just being dramatic. I've had to spend a lot of time—*working*—with Seth Lindell lately. She thinks just because he's cute and single, I should chase him."

"Ha!" Renee jumped back in. "So you admit it—he's cute!"

"What he *is* is stubborn, blue-collar, and too young. The cute can't offset all that."

"Now wait a minute there, sis," Ethan said. "What do you mean he's 'blue-collar'? The guy works with his hands. So do I. Something wrong with that?"

"Of course not! Jeez, don't be oversensitive, Ethan. What I *meant* was his interests are completely different from mine. He has zero interest in things I enjoy, like reading and business."

Ethan laughed. "Business, huh? Well, you thought you had things in common with Will . . . and, to quote you, how'd that work out for you?"

Renee had been enjoying their bickering back and forth. "How do you know he doesn't like to read? Did you ask him?"

"No . . . I guess I just assumed," Jess admitted. "He didn't show much interest in books when we went to see Frank Fisk. All he cared about was the architecture of the old store."

Renee continued to pepper her with questions. "How much younger is he than you?"

"I don't know, like seven years or something."

"That's nothing! You know women peak sexually later than men, so you might be lined up about perfect."

Ethan almost spit his water out at that one.

Jess wanted to scream. "All right, are you two done? I currently have *no* love life. If I ever *do* have a love life again, you will be the *last* to know.

Now, if you want to stop acting so immature—or, in Renee's case, *drunk*—I think there's something else I do need to talk to you two about."

She folded her napkin and laid it on top of her plate, giving herself a minute before getting into details.

"I wish Val was here," Jess said. "She's going to be mad if I tell you guys without her."

"She had back-to-school night for a couple of her boys," Renee said. "I'm sure you can tell her later. What is it? Don't tell me you have more crap to deal with because of your ex?"

"Believe it or not, this has nothing to do with Will. It has to do with Celia," Jess said, her tone conveying the seriousness of what she had to talk to them about.

That sobered Renee up real fast.

Over the next twenty minutes, she told them everything she knew about Patricia and her claims against Celia. She also told them what she'd done so far to prove that Celia couldn't have been the culprit—if there was in fact embezzlement somewhere in the past.

"Is that woman nuts?" Renee asked. "Celia was the most honest, generous, smart woman I ever knew. There is absolutely *no way* she'd have ever done anything like that!"

"I know, I know. I don't believe it either. But I've had more time to think about this, to *process* this, than you have. I can't just ignore Patricia. What if there *is* something? What if someone stole from Homes Sparkle and it gets pinned on Celia because she's no longer around to defend herself?"

Ethan had been quiet, but he sat up suddenly. "You're right, Jess. It's on us to make sure nothing taints Celia's legacy."

"You don't think I'm overreacting?"

Ethan looked grim. "Unfortunately, no."

The waiter came back and cleared their dishes, and Ethan ordered coffee for the table.

"All this is why I've been spending so much time with Seth," Jess said once the waiter had left. "He feels the same way we do. He wants to help make sure no one ever lays this on Celia."

Ethan nodded. "So you feel like we need to figure this out before this Patricia woman takes her claims any further?"

"Absolutely. Seth is going to talk to Jack with me—you know, Celia's lawyer? He's also Seth's uncle. We want to pick his brain a bit. He might know if Celia had any older business records she kept anywhere, too. He gave me some current information when he helped me with all the paperwork to transfer the ownership in the three businesses Celia left me."

"That's a good idea," Renee said, her coffee taming the buzz she'd displayed earlier.

"Jess . . . I wonder if there's anything at the house yet," Ethan said, thinking out loud.

"At *Celia*'s house?" Jess knew her brother had started doing some remodeling work on Celia's old Victorian. The house had passed to him after her death.

"Yeah. I've got workers coming and going now, and I'm not there all the time, so I locked a ton of stuff from her office up in the attic."

"Did she still have much in her office?"

"Yeah, she had boxes and boxes of old paperwork. The closet in her office was piled to the *ceiling*. It took my boys an afternoon to transport everything upstairs.

Jess could picture Celia's attic in her mind. It encompassed the third level of the house. The stairway came straight up the middle and the attic was one big open area. They used to play up there as kids and ride their bikes around when it was cold or rainy outside.

"She never used to have much up there, from what I remember," Jess pointed out.

"She didn't . . . but it's packed now. I knew we'd have to go through it all someday and figure out what to do with everything. If I had to guess, if there is any more paperwork, that's where you'll find it."

"Is there anything we can do to help?" Renee asked.

Jess shook her head. "I'll ask if I can think of anything you can help with, but nothing right now."

"Did you want to come over to the house?" Ethan asked. "See if you can find more records in the attic?"

"I do. I'm supposed to go to Jack's office with Seth on Wednesday. Can we swing by after we're done there? Will you be around?"

"I'll make a point of it. Just let me know the time. Have you talked to Dad about this?"

"I suppose I should," Jess said. "I guess I thought if I didn't talk about it, it might go away."

"He needs to know—as does Mom," Renee said.

Ethan topped off their coffee cups, apparently not quite ready to call it a night. "Well, now that we know what Jess has been up to, how about you, Renee? You and Matt done any more about building a house out at Whispering Pines? When I talked to him a couple of weeks ago, he seemed pretty excited about it."

Renee blew on her steaming cup. "We might have found a spot tucked back in the woods on the south end. We're waiting for the plat drawings to be sure we know exactly where the property lines are—don't want to get started and then run into trouble. I'll have to show you next time you come out. It seems like there used to be something there, before."

Ethan raised an eyebrow. "What do you mean?"

"We're pretty sure it's the foundation to an old building. Maybe an old cabin? Do you remember a cabin back in the woods, from when we were kids?"

Ethan, as the oldest, might remember something. He loved playing in the woods as a kid—even got lost there once.

"Hmm . . . I don't. Maybe if you show me where, it'll jog my memory. Does Dad remember it?"

"He doesn't think so," Renee said. "I asked him about it on the phone, but I haven't taken him out there yet either."

Conversation stalled as all three thought back to visits to the resort as kids.

"Hey . . . do you guys think there's any risk of us losing Whispering Pines, or any of the other things we inherited from Celia, if any of this *does* turn out to be true?" Renee asked, voicing the question swimming around in her brain. "I don't believe a word of it, trust me, but . . . I'm a little nervous now."

"We'll make sure it never comes to that, Renee," Jess assured her sister with a squeeze of her hand.

Renee squeezed back. "Can I tell Matt?"

"Yes, I think you should—but as your husband, not as the sheriff. We don't want him to *do* anything about it. Got it?"

"Of course. I'm just not comfortable keeping this from him. We wanted to maybe start on the house soon, before winter. I wonder if we should hold off. Ethan, pass me that bottle, will you? Tonight isn't a night to let good wine go to waste."

Jess watched as Renee poured the last of the wine into her glass and gulped down the contents. Her sister, not normally much of a drinker, was obviously worried about the claims against Celia, too.

CHAPTER 25

Gift of Anticipation

*A*s Jess waited for Jack and Seth in the outer parlor where Sally, Jack's receptionist, had requested she wait, she thought back to her conversation with her parents about the accusations against Celia and felt a renewed sense of justification for being here. Unsurprisingly, they'd had similar reactions to everyone else.

Celia had been gone for almost two years; Jess hated that it was getting harder to hear her aunt's voice in her mind with every passing day, but that wouldn't stop her from holding onto her memory.

As Celia aged, she'd spent more and more of her time on philanthropic projects. It had always been a bit of a mystery to Jess how her aunt had managed to amass so much wealth during her lifetime. Yes, she was a successful businesswoman. She never married and had no children of her own. She supported her own mother until she died. There weren't too many drains on her finances throughout the years, but Jess had always wondered. Celia's success had been awe inspiring and a little hard to fathom.

What if . . . ?

Jess shook her head to dispel the nasty thought before it fully formed. She had to keep the faith. The Celia she knew was honest, through and through.

Jack entered through the front door, nodded a greeting to Jess, and took a moment to have a quiet conversation with Sally.

"Yes, sir, I'll do that right away," the woman said as Jack turned back to Jess.

"Hello, dear," the lawyer greeted Jess. "I was happy to hear from you. I was also more than a little surprised when you said you'd be bringing my nephew along. I don't see enough of him."

"Is he here?" Jess asked, suddenly self-conscious.

"As a matter of fact, he pulled up outside as I was coming in."

As if on cue, the front door opened again. Seth stopped by Sally's desk for a quick hello and then shook hands with his uncle.

"Now that we're all here, why don't you two come in and tell me what brings you here today?"

Jack practiced in a two-story colonial-style home whose main floor had been converted to offices years earlier. Jess thought he lived upstairs. The house reminded Jess of Celia's in a way she couldn't quite place, although the style was different. Jack led them through his office door—a sturdy, wooden piece with a large frosted-glass window. Jess noticed two similar doors down the hallway.

"Do you have any other lawyers here with you, Jack?" she asked.

"Not anymore. Used to, but they've long since retired. I used to be the young one around here, believe it or not. My two other partners had me by about ten years."

Jess checked out Jack's office. The room looked and smelled like an aged library with its dark woods, chairs upholstered in red leather, and a wall of leather-bound books. It was exactly what Jess would expect as the office of an elderly, well-respected lawyer.

This is the look Will was going for in our house, Jess thought, *but he never* quite *pulled it off.*

"You could have retired ten years ago yourself, Uncle Jack. Why are you still practicing?" Seth asked.

"You can only spend so much time on the golf course, Seth," Jack replied with a wink as he rounded the corner of his desk and sat down, motioning to the two of them to do the same. "Besides, I'd get bored. I don't work as much as I used to, but staying involved helps keep my mind sharp—or at least I *think* it does. So, what can I do for you two?"

Once seated, Seth looked to Jess to start, so she said, "I guess we need some advice. It's about Celia."

Jack nodded. "I suspected that would be the case when you called. Do you need some legal advice for your business, Seth?"

"No, not this time. Something has come up that has us quite concerned, and, well, no one had a better handle on Celia's affairs than you did, Jack."

"Yes, yes, I suppose that's true. Other than Celia herself, of course. She was sharp as a tack. I sure do miss her."

"Jack, in all the years you knew and worked with my aunt, were you ever made aware of any unusual business dealings where she was concerned?"

Jack sat back in his desk chair, eyeing Jess closely. "The word 'unusual' can be taken many different ways. Celia was *creative* and *innovative* in some of her business dealings—it's one of the reasons she was so successful, but you already know that—but *unusual*? What exactly are you asking?"

Jess struggled with how best to articulate the situation, finally saying, "Let me rephrase my question. Were you ever made aware of any claims of improprieties of any kind related to Celia or her business?"

Jack slowly leaned forward, his eyes never leaving Jess. He clasped his hands together on the ink blotter covering the surface of his antique desk. "Why would you even ask something like that?"

Displeasure rolled off of him. Jess knew she'd upset the man with her loaded question. Seth, seeing the same, intervened.

"Jack," he said, also leaning forward in his chair. "We by no means believe Celia would ever have been involved in anything illegal. We are some of her biggest fans. We're here for your help. Someone *else* is questioning her actions. Not us."

Jack brought his hands up, his index fingers forming a steeple as he regarded Seth and Jess. His light blue eyes appeared moist behind his bifocals, tired. He didn't immediately respond. Instead, he rose from his desk, stepped out of his office briefly, and then came back in. Jess met his eye as he came back to stand next to his desk, facing them. She couldn't read the man.

"Actually," he finally said, "a number of years ago, Celia warned me something like this might come up."

"You're kidding?"

"No, Seth, I wouldn't kid about something like this. Why don't you tell me what you've heard and who you heard it from? Then I'll tell you what I know."

Jess started at the beginning. Jack listened without interrupting. She ended by saying, "So ... do you think anything Patricia is saying has merit?"

"No," he said emphatically. "But let's not get ahead of ourselves. A while back Celia paid me a visit. That wasn't at all unusual, she always had plenty of business to keep me busy. But I remember that particular appointment better than most because she wasn't acting like herself. She was agitated about something. When I pressed her on it, she refused to go into any detail. All she would say was she'd tried to help someone and it backfired. She looked me in the eye like I'm looking at you now, swore to me she'd done nothing wrong, and handed me a letter with very explicit instructions."

"When was this?" Jess asked.

"Hm ... the woman would have been in her eighties at the time. She was certainly aware of her own mortality, which would have explained her urgency that day. She gave me the sealed envelope and made me promise that if anything unusual came up around her business dealings—*after* her death, she was careful to remind me—I was to give the letter to a family member. I was not to open it under any circumstances."

Jess felt her hand raise to her mouth, and was surprised to find tears stinging her eyes.

"She had an unwavering trust in me," Jack said, "which I appreciate more than you know, and I worked hard to earn that trust. I took the letter and put it in a safe place, just in case it was ever needed. I feel like your coming here today may, in some way, be related to her concerns."

"So where is the letter now?" Seth asked.

"Me stepping out just now was so I could ask Sally to go to the bank and get it out of my safe deposit box. She should be back shortly."

Jess cleared her throat and said, "Jack, I have to tell you, this may give us the answers we're looking for. I don't know how to thank you."

"Well, don't thank me yet. I could be way off base here. Maybe it's totally unrelated. But based on her wishes, I feel comfortable giving you the letter, Jess. I know she trusted you as well. She *had* to have trusted you to leave her business ownerships and portfolio to you."

There was a soft knock on the door. Sally entered, handed an envelope to Jack, and left again without saying a word.

"I don't want you to open it here. Take it with you now. I don't know if you want to open it along with your father, Jess, or just open it yourself, away from any prying eyes. That's up to you. If there is anything in there you need to discuss with me at any point, please do not hesitate to call." Jack handed the envelope to Jess and sat back down. "Is there anything else I can help you with today?"

"Jack, if—and I'm not saying I think it will be the case, but *if* anything inappropriate does turn up and we find out Celia was involved . . . what could happen now that she's gone? Anything other than a tarnished reputation?"

Jack sighed heavily. "If it would ever turn out she obtained any of her assets through ill-gotten gains, I suppose there could be some risk they would need to go back to their rightful owners."

"What about Whispering Pines? Could the resort ever be at risk? That would devastate Renee. It would devastate all of us."

"I helped Celia with that transaction and, as far as I know, it's airtight. If we do learn anything new, we'll deal with it then. Anything else? I can cancel my tee time if there's more."

Jess shook her head. "No, we'll be going. We've taken up enough of your time. Thank you so much for your help."

Jack nodded grimly. "I hope the letter contains some answers."

Jess picked her purse up off the floor, stowed the letter inside, and turned to leave. Halfway to the door she stopped and turned back to Jack.

"Do you know anything about family law, Jack?"

"No. No, I'm afraid I have very little expertise in that area. But I could refer you to someone, if you like. Someone you could trust."

"I don't need another lawyer yet, but it may come to that. My own lawyer can't seem to push my divorce through, and there's something else

I may need help with too. But I'll save that story for another day, if need be. Go enjoy a round of golf in this sunshine."

Seth followed Jess out to her vehicle. Once there he said, "I'm not sure what I expected . . . but I guess that might have been helpful. Especially if there's anything useful in the letter. What do you want to do about it?"

"I think I need to read it right away. We're due at Ethan's in an hour, and it's lunchtime now. Would you mind maybe picking up some subs and meeting me at the gazebo in the park? Do you know the one . . . over on Elm?"

Seth nodded. "Close to Celia's old house."

"That would give me a few minutes to read Celia's letter, while you're picking up food. I feel like it's something I need to read alone."

"Good. I'm glad you want to open it now, and, to be honest, I'm kinda glad I won't be there when you do. I'll meet you there in a bit."

***

Jess waded through autumn leaves on the path leading from the asphalt parking lot to the white gazebo. The fall air was still warm. A group of little kids—probably a daycare—played on some newfangled equipment at the north end of the park.

Whatever happened to swings and see-saws? Jess wondered, watching the kids run along vibrant-colored walkways high in the air and slide down poles that looked like they belonged in a fire station. Seeing the kids made her miss her own. Harper would be that age soon.

The gazebo was isolated and empty, thankfully. Jess sat down on a wooden bench inside the open-air structure. It was cooler in the shade and she pulled her sweater on. She slid the sealed envelope out of her purse, turning it over, as if that might give her some clue as to what was inside. Across the front, in handwriting she recognized, were the words: *To be opened only as instructed by Jack Poole.* It was signed by her aunt.

Jess slid her finger under the seal, careful not to tear whatever was inside. The stationery reminded her of the letter Celia left Jess when she died, conveying her wishes related to her estate. In a strange way, it was nice to have another letter from her, despite the circumstances.

It only contained one hand-written page. Jess slipped her glasses on and read Celia's words.

Dear Loved One,

I write this letter in the hopes no one will ever have to read it. Unfortunately, since you are reading it now, my intuition was correct. I find it fascinating how we can spend our whole lives striving to live a life of integrity, fighting against the temptations that surround us, protecting our own reputation, only to have our character called into question regardless. Why can't our actions speak louder than a few words from others?

I have spent the last few months battling against the evils of greed and dishonesty. When people feel a sense of entitlement and lack sound moral judgment, they will find a way to accomplish their personal goals, no matter the cost. I pity them.

So why am I leaving you this message? It's not to point fingers or lay blame. Those who have wronged me in the past have sworn to never do so again. I believe in second chances. I believe people can change. Do I believe they will stay true to their word? Perhaps. More than likely, however, they will not.

I've decided against going into specifics. I've personally experienced the pain of being wrongfully accused of something I didn't do. I cannot, in good conscience, do the same to someone else. I'm writing to you today while I still have a chance to make my wishes known to you, while I'm still of this earth, although I will not be by the time these wishes reach you.

Know that I never failed you. If presented evidence to the contrary, dig deeper. My final wish is for my family to know I lived my life in the service of others. The funny thing about one's reputation is it's nothing more than smoke, easily dissipated and then forgotten. Do not waste your time trying to protect something so fragile. Seek answers only if absolutely necessary. Sometimes the price of the answers is too high.

The answers are there, among my possessions, if they still remain like I believe they will. Good luck digging, my Loved One.

Know I love you and I only ever wanted the best for you.

All my love,
Celia

Jess read the words twice. Celia was a wonderful writer, but still, Jess felt more confused now than ever before.

So much for getting some straight answers.

The slamming of a car door pulled Jess's attention back to the park, to the laughter of the children and the rustling of a breeze in the leaves. She watched Seth approach, a white paper bag stamped with the red logo from Ann's Deli, a local favorite, in one hand and two bottles of water in the other. She folded the letter and stowed it back in her purse.

"I hope you like Italian," Seth said, handing her the bag.

"Anything is fine," she replied, distracted. "Thank you."

"From the look on your face I'm guessing you had a chance to read the letter?"

She nodded.

Seth settled onto the bench next to her, unrolled the white paper from his sandwich, and tossed the trash back into the bag. The aroma of freshly baked bread tickled Jess's nose, pulling her attention back to Seth.

"Do you want to talk about it?"

"Sure ... but there's really nothing to talk about. It didn't tell me much."

"Really? Why would she go to all the trouble of leaving a mysterious letter if it didn't tell you anything?"

"That's what I'm trying to figure out."

"Do you want me to read it?" Seth asked. "Because I meant what I said before. I'll only read it if you want me to."

"Actually, I do want you to read it. I'm curious what you think she was trying to get at."

"All right, well, let's eat first and then I'll take a look before we have to head over to meet Ethan."

Jess nodded, smiling. She felt relieved to have Seth here with her. After they'd finished lunch and he'd read Celia's letter, he suggested they take a walk. They gathered their things and headed down one of the walking paths that looped around the park.

"Celia was a complicated woman, wasn't she?" Seth remarked with a laugh. "*God*, I miss her."

"But what do you think it means?"

"Not exactly sure. It was awfully cryptic. But I think it was her way of assuring you that regardless of what you're hearing, she did nothing wrong. She knew she wouldn't be able to defend herself once she was dead, but this was her telling you that she's worth defending. I think someone wronged her in the past, she caught them at it, and they promised to never do it again. For some reason, she gave them a second chance, but she was doubtful about whether they could be trusted. It sounds like there's some kind of answer trail, somewhere, but you have to look for it."

Jess walked beside Seth, listening intently, processing it all. Seth paused to look up at the sky and then continued.

"It seems like she's warning you that if you dig, you might find more than you bargained for, that maybe it wouldn't be worth it in the end. Like she's giving you permission to allow people to doubt her integrity, that maybe it isn't worth defending her. The cost might be too great."

"You know, I underestimated you," Jess finally replied as she paused and placed a hand on his forearm. He turned to face her.

"How so?"

"I'm a black-and-white kind of girl. When I opened that letter, I was wanting to see hard answers to our questions. Since there weren't any obvious revelations, I was starting to jump to the conclusion that there was nothing valuable in the letter. But you, you caught Celia's meaning. What you're saying makes perfect sense."

"You mean I'm not just some shallow jerk who rips up old buildings and lives to irritate you? Is that what you're implying?" Seth took a step closer to Jess, bringing his hands up to rest on her waist, challenging her with his words and his closeness.

"Perhaps."

Seth pulled her closer. "Is it later yet?"

She smiled. "Not quite."

CHAPTER 26

Gift of Childhood Memories

*J*ess pulled up in front of Celia's old house and Seth parked behind her. Ethan was unloading sheetrock from a trailer parked in the driveway.

"Hey, sis," he said. "Give me a sec."

"Need some help?" Seth asked, nodding toward the trailer.

"Sure. Grab a sheet and follow me, and once we set this stuff down I can give you a tour."

Jess held the door as both men carried the building materials into the house. The sounds of construction filled the air. Once both he and Seth's hands were free, Ethan extended his in greeting.

"Ethan Richter, Jess's brother."

"Nice to meet you, Ethan. Seth Lindell. I'm familiar with your work."

"I'm familiar with your work, as well. Jess gave me a little background on why this business with Celia interests you, too. Why you want to help. I'm sure it's been said, but we really appreciate it."

Seth simply nodded.

"Before we go upstairs, I thought you might want to see what I've been up to, Jess. I hope you don't object to any of the changes I'm making to Celia's."

"Ethan, it's your house now. I know you'll only make it better. It's been a few *decades* since this old beauty had any kind of facelift."

"My thoughts exactly, sis. You been here before, Seth?"

"A couple of times, but I've never seen anything other than the kitchen and living room. But I love old homes, as you probably already figured out, so a tour would be great."

Things were in various stages of completion. Jess immediately noticed the small vestibule, once just inside the front door, was now gone.

"Ethan, I love how you've opened this up. Remember how we used to all cram into that tiny entry to take our shoes off before coming in any farther? Celia would have skinned us if we wore them in her house. There was barely room to turn around. This is *so* much better. And . . . oh, man . . . I never realized how incredible this staircase was," Jess said as her eyes traveled upward. She ran her hand over the smooth, dark mahogany of the newel post at the base of the stairs.

"Glad you approve, sis. You haven't even gotten to my favorite part yet."

They made their way from room to room on the main level. Scaffolding flanked the front wall in the living room and the strong smell of chemicals permeated the air. Original trim around the windows was partially scraped clean of what looked to be multiple layers of different colors of paint. Someone was sanding hardwood floors in the dining room.

Jess sneezed and then gasped as she entered the kitchen. The transformation was stunning.

"Ethan, this is *fabulous*! I'm going to have to hire you to update my duplex," Jess said in awe, wishing she could *afford* to fix up her new home.

"I'm glad you like it. Soon as this backsplash is done, we'll move the appliances in and I can check this room off the list."

At that moment, someone came through the back door carrying a stack of tiles. It was a woman in dusty work clothes, a tool belt, and a ponytail.

"Oh, hey, I didn't know anyone was in here," she said, glancing their way before heading back to a corner of the counter where the backsplash was only half complete. She set the heavy tile down on a towel and turned back to them, brushing her hands off on her pant legs.

"What do you think, Ethan? Like it?" the woman asked, facing Jess's brother.

"Hey, Brooke. I do like it. Did that last batch of tile match up all right?"

"Yes, it's fine. Giving a tour?" the woman asked. But before Ethan could reply, she said, "Wait, oh my God, Seth Lindell?" and, skipping around the large new island in the middle of the kitchen, caught a surprised Seth in a hug.

Seth's face quickly lit up as he returned the hug, picking the woman up off her toes and giving her a little spin as he greeted her. He set her back down, took a small step back, and smiled down at her.

"Brooke Olson, long time no see. It's been like, what . . . five years? I thought you moved away."

"I did. I went out to live with my sister in San Diego. The weather was beautiful, but I got homesick. Moved back about a year ago. How about you? What's new?"

"Not much. Still have my shop. Work too much, play too little."

"So nothing's changed, then?" Brooke said with a laugh. "So how do you know Ethan? Are you working together?"

"Actually, no, I just met Ethan today, but I've been doing some work with Jess here, Ethan's sister."

Brooke seemed to notice Jess for the first time. "Hey there," she said, nodding.

Of course you didn't notice me, not with these two in the room, Jess thought, surprisingly irritated by the woman. She managed a single "Hey."

"Well, I should let you three get back to your tour. I've got lots to do yet today," she said, turning back to her work.

"Nice seeing you again, Brooke," Seth said as he followed Ethan to the door.

"Oh, wait, Seth. Hey, do you have any old tile stock out at your shop? I've got a job down at that old mansion on 18th Street—you know, the one the city is trying to renovate and turn into apartments? I'm having trouble matching up some of the tile work. New stock doesn't work."

"Sure, I've got a decent selection. Why don't you stop out?"

"I'll do that," Brooke agreed with a dimpled smile. "Your number still the same?"

"Yep."

"Sounds good. I'll give you a call."

"Looking forward to it," Seth said on his way out of the room.

Ethan continued with his tour. Jess was quiet, responding where appropriate to Ethan but saying little else.

Ethan checked his watch. "Crap, I have to pick Dylan up and get him over to football practice. I can come back. Do you guys want to get started upstairs while I'm gone?"

"Sure," Jess said. "Go ahead, I know the way. See you in a bit."

"Here, I'll unlock the door. If it's too hot up there, open the windows and feel free to take the fan out of Celia's office if you need to. It's been closed up so it might be stuffy. Oh, and Jess, did you warn Seth about Casper?"

***

Jess climbed the steep wooden stairs, heat enveloping her the farther she went up. She groped for the light switch and flipped it on. One naked bulb, hanging down from the ceiling far above, illuminated their path. Dust motes danced in the air.

"Ethan was right, it's plenty hot up here," Seth said, making his way to one of the only two windows and opening it.

Jess headed to the one on the opposite side of the room. Despite her best efforts, she couldn't figure out how to unlock it. Muttering under her breath, she refused to ask for help. Seth must have noticed her struggle. He walked over and got her window open in a few deft movements.

"Tricky locks," he said.

He probably works with them all the time, Jess stewed. *What a showoff.*

Jess's silent treatment must have been too obvious to ignore, because Seth said, "Do you want to fill me in on what I did to piss you off this time?"

"You didn't piss me off. I just have a lot on my mind. I'm going to go grab that fan."

As she made her way back down, she forgot how slippery the wood on the stairs could be, despite having fallen on them more than once as a kid.

Her right foot slipped off a tread and she grabbed for the railing, catching it in time to break her fall but making an awful racket in the process.

"Since I didn't hear a scream or crying, I assume you're either fine or unconscious down there," Seth hollered from above. "Need help?"

Jess chose to ignore him. She left the door to the attic open, hoping the cooler air from below would find its way upstairs.

Why am I such a grouch all of a sudden? Must be the heat and all the crazy smells in here.

Jess unplugged the fan from the office and took it back upstairs, walking more carefully this time and reminding herself to play nice. She needed Seth's help.

"This should help," she said, plugging the old box fan in.

"Glad to see you're all right," Seth said. He appeared to be making his way around the piles.

Jess looked around, dismayed. "Ethan wasn't kidding. There's ten times more junk up here than there ever used to be. As you can imagine, Celia never came up here, at least not in her last few years. Those stairs are a bit treacherous."

Seth shot Jess a look at that statement. "Ya don't say?"

"Shut up. All right, how should we do this? It doesn't look like there's any rhyme or reason to this mess."

"Is all this disorganization going to make you break out in hives?" Seth teased.

Finally, Jess laughed. "It just might at that. Sorry I was a little bitchy . . . I'm just nervous about what we might, or might *not*, find up here."

"And here I thought you were acting like that because you were jealous."

Jess paused in her perusal of the maze of boxes. With hands on her hips she regarded Seth in surprise. "What would I have to be jealous of? Just because an old friend of yours, a *pretty* old friend, suddenly shows up and is fawning all over you, why would I be jealous? She is none of my business."

Jess turned her back on him and walked over to the far side of the cavernous attic.

Oh God, could he be right? I need to watch myself. I have no business being jealous where Seth is concerned.

"Well, that's good to know. As long as it doesn't bother you, I'll have to see if she wants to grab a drink. We should catch up, being as how we're *old friends* and all. And you know, now that you mention it, she *is* pretty . . ."

Jess was down on her knees, peeking into cardboard boxes. Her voice was muffled as she assured him he should go ahead and do that, to which he didn't reply. For the next ten minutes, they both poked around, trying to ignore each other.

"Hey, Jess, come here," Seth whispered. "*Quick.*"

"What? I'm busy over here. I think I found some of the boxes from Celia's office."

"I hear something. Come here," he repeated.

"Oh, that's probably Casper. He won't hurt you."

Seth said nothing more for a minute and then let out a belly laugh. "Oh God, that's the *wind*, isn't it? Some of the pipes in this old place must be situated just so and when the wind is right, it sounds like moaning. Freaked me out for a minute there."

"Huh," Jess said. "It took us about ten years to figure that out. When we were kids, we were sure it was haunted up here."

"I've seen it before. Or, I mean, I've *heard* it before."

Apparently satisfied no one was hiding in a corner, moaning, Seth left the piles he'd been rummaging through to help Jess.

"You finding paperwork over here?"

"Yes, but I don't know where to start."

Seth looked around, trying to devise a plan. "Well . . . there's a big wooden folding table leaning against the wall over there. Why don't we clear an area under that window and set the table up there? I can bring boxes over to you and you can start going through them. It'll be easier to do, sitting at a table in natural light. Better on our eyes, and maybe better on your attitude."

So they began to methodically go through boxes. There was lots of paper but nothing helpful. Jess had little to show for their efforts other than a nasty paper cut. After two hours, she pushed back from the table, stood, and stretched. Her clothes stuck to her. Her hair, caught up in a small messy bun on the top of her head, had come loose, her hair sticking out in every direction.

"I thought it would start to cool off by now. This is *miserable!* How are you holding up?" she asked Seth as he dropped another heavy box at her feet. The line of sweat staining the back of his gray T-shirt proved he was hotter yet, having been doing all the heavy lifting.

"I'm fine. I *do* wonder what happened to Ethan," Seth said.

As if on cue, heavy footsteps echoed up the stairs.

"You two still alive up here? Man, it is *hot*. Good thing I brought some refreshments."

"Beer?" Seth asked, his voice hopeful.

"Nope, no drinking on the job. Blizzards!"

Jess squealed as she took the two large cups full of ice cream from Ethan and handed one to Seth.

"You are a lifesaver, Ethan. We were about out of steam up here. Where's yours?"

He grinned. "Gone. Didn't want to try to carry three so I ate mine on the way over. You two finding anything helpful up here yet?"

"Maybe a little. We found a bunch of boxes of paperwork and Seth's been helping me go through them, see if there's anything in here we can use. These two boxes labeled 'Homes Sparkle'? They were taped shut and I didn't open them yet. I want to take them home with me so I can go through them more carefully—and out of the heat. We set them to the side for now so we can see what else we can find."

"Want some help?"

"Sure, that'd be great. Seth can show you where we were finding the boxes that likely came out of her office."

Ethan followed Seth, glancing at the piles of Celia's things strewn everywhere. "I feel kind of bad about this," he said. "She always kept it so neat and tidy up here. Now it looks like a bomb hit it. My boys have strong backs but no sense of organization. I don't know where they set half the stuff."

After a moment Ethan said, "Well, *this* is interesting . . ."

"What?" Jess asked from over at her makeshift desk.

"This one's from the Corner Market. Either of you remember it? That old grocery store on the corner of Main and Tenth?"

"Vaguely," Jess replied, walking over to look into the box with Ethan. "Didn't it close down a long time ago? I didn't know Celia had anything to do with it."

"Yeah, old man Klaus ran it for something like fifty years. I remember when he died. Massive heart attack. He had no family, so when he died, the store closed. The town lost a landmark. I kind of remember Celia helping him out."

"That woman had her hands in everything, didn't she?" Jess commented, shaking her head. "Is there just the one box? Maybe I should take that one home, too. I don't want to miss something."

"I only see the one. I'll add it to your stack of homework."

Ethan walked the box over and set it down next to the Homes Sparkle boxes, then wandered off in the opposite direction.

"Hey, Jess, remember this?" Ethan asked, moving a pile of old quilts off something up against the wall.

Jess couldn't see what it was from her chair so she joined her brother. He was crouched down next to a wooden chest roughly the size of a forty-gallon cooler, painted a robin's egg blue and beat up. She smiled.

"Oh, how could I forget? We used to play restaurant up here and that was *always* our table. Renee and me, we'd be the customers, you'd be the waiter, and Val always wanted to be the chef. We would sit on stacks of old books. Celia used to let us use her old teacups and that set of doll dishes. I wonder if those are still around here somewhere . . . now *those* would be great to find."

"What's in it?" Seth asked, having wandered over to join them.

Ethan shook his head. "I always wondered . . . but it was always locked. I remember asking Celia one time if she had the key, if I could open it. She looked at me for the longest time, smiled, and said, 'Some things are better left locked away.' If she hoped that would dissuade me from wondering what was in it, she was mistaken—her comment had the opposite effect. I remember coming up here alone one time and trying to pick the lock. I couldn't get it open and afterward I felt so guilty I never tried again."

"I never knew any of that," Jess said, punching her brother playfully on the shoulder. "You little sneak. I guess I never gave it any thought."

Seth said, "Maybe it's time we found out what she wanted to keep locked away. Hell, maybe it's connected to the rest of this mystery."

"That thing has been up here for decades. Since we were kids. I can't imagine it would have anything to do with all this business stuff," Jess said.

"Maybe, maybe not. Just because she didn't give Ethan the key doesn't mean she didn't have it. We have no idea how recently she might have been in that trunk."

Intrigued, Jess eyed their makeshift table; quickly she walked around it, studying it. "Ethan, have you run across any keys?"

"There was a small box of them in a kitchen cupboard, but I have no idea where that might have ended up," he said, his eyes again taking in the mess around him.

"Unlike your brother, I've been known to be able to pick a lock or two in my day," Seth stated, winking at Jess when he caught her eye.

"Do we dare?" Jess asked.

"Jess, think about it," Ethan said. "Celia's been gone for two years. One of us is going to have to open it someday. It's not like it can sit up here forever."

Jess plopped down on her butt and rested her elbows on her knees, still eyeing the chest.

"Good point. Let's do it."

"Got any tools up here, Ethan?" Seth asked.

"I've got a Leatherman in my pocket, will that do?"

Seth laughed. "That'll do just fine." Ethan handed him what initially looked like a large pocket knife until Seth folded it open, revealing multiple tools, all in one unit. He whistled in envy. "I lost mine. May have to pick up a new one. They're pretty handy."

"You two are such geeks," Jess said. "Here, I can hold the light again."

"Have you guys been picking locks together for a while?" Ethan asked, grinning at his sister. "Be careful or you might end up in the pokey like your old man, Jess."

"*Ex* old man, you mean."

"Did the divorce finally go through, then?" Ethan asked, surprised.

"Well, no, not exactly. But he's still definitely nothing more than an ex." Jess glanced in Seth's direction, but if he heard their exchange he gave no sign.

"All right, you two see if you can't get that open, I'll keep looking around, see what else might be up here," Ethan said, wandering off.

"Way to avoid answering him about lock picking," Seth murmured to Jess, and she nudged him with her shoulder. "Careful," he scolded. "Can't you see I'm working here?"

After five minutes, Jess was getting fidgety.

"Hold the light still, I think I've almost got it," Seth said. Not long after, she heard the satisfying snap of a lock opening. "*Got* it."

"Ethan, come back here," Jess called out. "Let's see what's in here."

Ethan grunted as he moved a heavy box out of his way.

"Since you've been so curious for all these years," Jess said, motioning at the blue box with a dramatic flair, "we'll let you do the honors."

"I'm not going to get struck by lightning, am I?" Ethan joked, but his eyes widened a bit when a low rumble of thunder could be heard off in the distance.

Jess burst out laughing. "No, that was *not* Celia warning you off. The forecast called for late afternoon showers."

"I knew that," Ethan said, but Jess thought his grin looked a little sheepish.

He knelt down next to the trunk and lifted the lid. The old hinges grated in protest and a musty odor escaped.

"It doesn't *smell* like it's been opened since you guys were kids," Seth said, waving the stale air away.

"Old and smelly, just like my big brother here," Jess joked, to which Ethan flipped her the bird.

The trunk was full. On the very top was a photo album.

"That shouldn't be in here," Jess said, carefully lifting the album up and opening the cover. "Mom and Dad thought they found all her old photo albums and brought them home to their house to try to keep them safe and out of the temperature extremes. Guess they missed one . . ." She looked at the first few pages of pictures. "These aren't even that old. Look, Ethan. These look like they're from Celia's eightieth birthday party."

"How can you tell?" Seth asked, looking over her shoulder.

"I remember she had a big party when she turned seventy and again at eighty. Here's Lauren and Nathan," Jess said, pointing to a girl and a boy of around six and nine. "They wouldn't have been born yet for her seventieth. I better take this and drop it off at Mom and Dad's next time I'm over there." She set the album to the side. A leather-bound book had been under the photo album. Jess thumbed through it, recognizing Celia's hand-writing. "We might be on to something here, boys," Jess said, setting the journal on top of the album and rubbing her hands together. Next was a layer of white tissue paper. Jess carefully folded back the paper and drew in a breath when she saw what lay beneath.

"What in heaven's name is *this*?"

"Looks like a wedding dress to me," Seth said, stating the obvious as Jess carefully removed the ivory garment.

The elegant dress unfolded as Jess stood and gave it a gentle shake. "I know *what* it is. But I wonder *whose* it was. It's gorgeous."

Jess inspected the dress. It was made of heavy satin and covered with intricate lace and beading. Based on the style of the dress, it had to be very old. "It looks like it's never been worn," she said, more intrigued by this particular find than either Seth or Ethan. They were already looking to see if there was anything the dress had been hiding.

"I wonder who these belonged to," Ethan said as he lifted a tiny, crocheted set of blue booties and a little white dress.

Jess carefully laid the wedding dress across a stack of nearby boxes after checking to make sure they weren't too dusty. She took the small white garment from her brother and examined it. Similar to the wedding dress, this one was also covered in fancy lace trim. Tiny tucks were sewn into a pattern on the chest. "I think this is a christening gown," she said. "I've never seen it before, though, not even in photographs. I wonder if these items have been locked away in here since before you wanted to open it forty years ago, Ethan."

"If I was a betting man, I would put money on it. Seth, grab that piece of paper on the very bottom. Is that anything?"

Seth pulled out the paper. As he unfolded it, he tried to read what was on it. "It's faded, but it looks like it's a receipt for a cemetery plot."

Jess looked over at the paper in his hands. "OK, well, that's a bit of a downer. Please set it with the album and journal. I'll see what I can figure out with it, I suppose."

"What should we do with all this now?" Ethan asked, motioning to the clothing.

"We'll need to show them to Dad, or maybe Uncle Gerry," Jess said. "But for now, I think we should fold them back up—very carefully—and put them back in here. They've been safe up here all this time. I think it's all right to leave them up here for a while longer yet, until we can get some answers."

"I'm fine with that," Ethan confirmed, setting the booties back in the bottom of the trunk and helping Jess get the dresses put back in as well."

"I'll take the photo album and journal. It's almost five and I need to pick up Harper. Would you guys mind helping me get this stuff downstairs and out to my vehicle? I can't wait to see what secrets this journal holds," Jess said, waving the old book in the air.

CHAPTER 27

Gift of Confrontation

"Son, you have no idea how great it is to see you," Will said, sitting across the picnic table from Nathan. It was a beautiful fall afternoon and the prisoners were allowed to meet their visitors in the outside commons area—prison and nature, two things that felt so diametrically opposite.

Nathan didn't crack a smile and offered nothing more than a small nod in greeting.

Will sensed Nathan's displeasure with him, could see the tension in his son's hunched shoulders. But he could only hope that maybe, someday, his kids would understand he'd done what he'd done for them, too, to give them the life they deserved.

"How's your sister? How is Lauren?"

Nathan looked away, checking out their surroundings, his eyes traveling over to the fence and up across the razor-wire along the top, meant to keep dangerous men inside. Will couldn't be sure whether his son was nervous to be in a prison yard or just disgusted to find his father locked inside. Finally, Nathan looked back at Will. "She's fine. Talked to her last night." Will didn't think Nathan would give him anymore than that, but then he added, almost begrudgingly, "The first week of classes went well and she likes her roommate."

Will nodded. "I always knew she'd do great at college. She's a social kid, like me."

Nathan bristled. "But *unlike* me, right, Dad? Is that what you meant to say? Not nerdy and quiet like me? I'm so much more like Mom, aren't I?"

"Nathan, don't be ridiculous. You're not a nerd. You've just always been happier with your own company. Not quite as outgoing. That isn't a *bad* thing."

"Oh gee, thanks, Dad. That's why I came here, after all—for your approval."

Realizing their conversation wasn't going anywhere, Will tried a different approach. "How are your classes? Are you still on track to finish up this year?"

"Yes."

"Good. Then what? Have you thought about it?"

"Of course I've *thought* about it. But we'll have to see. I'm leaving my options open."

Will nodded but kept his mouth shut. He couldn't fathom facing college graduation with no set plans. He'd always known he wanted to be a surgeon since he was a little boy. Surgeons made lots of money. Easy choice.

"I haven't talked to your mother for a couple of weeks. Do you know if there's been any action on the house?"

"I think the realtor has had a couple of showings," Nathan replied.

"Has your mom talked about what she's going to do with everything in the house? I'll have to have her put my things in storage . . ."

Nathan's fingers started drumming on the table top. Will knew this was a sign his son's temper was rising even higher.

"I can tell you have something on your mind, Nathan. Why don't you get it off your chest? What really brought you here today?"

"Yeah, Dad, I do have something I want to say. In fact, I have many things I want to say. I'll keep some of them to myself because you don't deserve to know how I'm feeling about you these days. You lost that right well before you lost your freedom." He paused. "I'm here because of Mom."

"Your mom . . . what do you mean? Is she all right?"

"You're kidding, right? You sit here, lazing your days away, letting the state pay to feed you, clothe you, house you . . . while Mom is out there working her *ass* off to keep all the balls in the air, and you ask if she's 'all right'?"

Will supposed he deserved that. Things had spiraled out of control.

"I'm sorry so much of it has fallen on her. None of this is her fault."

"On that we can agree," Nathan said, leaning forward to make his intentions clear. "I came to warn you. If that *woman* comes around again ... threatens to take Harper away from us again ... you will pay. You may not be in here forever, but you will lose *us* forever. And if there are any more skeletons in your closet that could cause Mom pain, you better bury them so deep they will never see the light of day. We've all had more than enough of your bullshit, Will, and we're not going to take any more. You got that?"

Well, well, well, Will thought. *My son finally grew a set.*

"Nathan, I assure you, all of my dirty laundry has been aired. If it hadn't, I wouldn't be here. And I will do everything in my power to keep Tiffany away from all of you. I know I've made mistakes, and we're all paying the price for those now. I'll do my time, and once I get out of here, we can start over."

"There is no *starting over.* When it comes to 'us,' I suspect our relationship will never do anything more than limp along until one of us is dead and the other can put it behind them. In the meantime, no more screw-ups," Nathan warned.

He stood and turned his back on his father, never looking back.

Will got up and began pacing the perimeter of the fence. He didn't see Nathan drive away. Later, when the prisoners were all brought back inside, Will made a call from a designated phone.

"You need to figure out a way to get in the house," he said into the phone, speaking soft but clear. "I need you to get that box out of the bottom drawer of my filing cabinet. There's also two tubs in the backseat of the Volkswagen in the garage, under the tarp."

Will leaned against the wall, rubbing his left temple with his free hand, listening to the caller on the other end. "I know, I *know,* but I ran out of time. Now, please, listen to me. This is important. The key for the filing cabinet is hanging on the key rack by the back door."

He listened again.

"Because, it was so obvious no one would ever bother to try those keys. I think she changed the locks . . . what if you posed as a potential buyer, had the realtor show you the house? You could sneak the things out then."

More listening.

"Look. You're smart. You're going to have to figure it out. We can't have anyone getting their hands on that binder. Get it done."

Will hung up, handed the phone back to the guard, and ran his fingers through his hair in a nervous gesture, following another guard back to his cell.

CHAPTER 28

Gift of a Gamble

*S*eth placed the last of the boxes in the back of Jess's car. "Do you need me to stop out at the Pines to help you get this stuff inside?" he asked.

Jess shook her head. "Thanks for the offer. I really appreciate it. You have no idea how much I appreciate *all* your help, Seth. But my head's killing me and I need a shower. I think this is going to have to wait until tomorrow. The weather looks a little rough, too," she said, just as another low rumble of thunder sounded as if to illustrate her point. "I'll ask Robbie or Matt to help me bring all this in, and I'll start going through this stuff tomorrow, when Harper is at daycare. Do you want to come over and help?"

"I would, but I can't. I have to head over and start stripping a building tomorrow. I'll be gone for a couple of days. But call me if you find anything interesting, OK?"

Seth seems to be in the habit of suggesting women call him.

"Sure, handsome. Is your number still the same?" Jess asked in a flirty voice, giving him a wink.

"Cute. But hey, thanks for the reminder. Maybe Brooke wants to grab a drink tonight . . ."

***

Jess's mind wouldn't slow down as she went through the motions of picking up Harper and driving back to Whispering Pines.

What would she find in the boxes?

Who had the wedding dress and christening gown belonged to?

I think Seth *was kidding about calling Brooke* . . . Jess thought, rankled by the idea and even more by the fact that she was rankled in the first place.

Big fat raindrops began to fall as Jess pulled into the lodge parking lot. She glanced at the old journal and photo album on the seat next to her. She jammed the journal into her purse to protect it during their run for the house. The album would have to wait.

The smell of fresh rain rushed in when she opened her door. She took Harper out of her car seat and looked for a blanket she could throw over the baby's head to protect her from the weather, but soon realized she'd forgotten to bring one. Harper held her hands up to the sky and babbled, clearly intrigued instead of frightened by the rain.

The cold rain felt heavenly to Jess after their hot afternoon. Instead of running back to the duplex, she took her time, laughing when an especially plump drop landed on Harper's cheek, making the girl giggle. By the time they walked through the door, Jess felt revived. All was quiet next door. Jess remembered Matt and Renee were at something with Robbie and would be home later. "Looks like we've got the place to ourselves, girl," she said to the still-giggling Harper.

As the two settled down for the night, rain started to fall harder outside and Jess could hear the wind pick up, could see it pushing the tops of the pines from the kitchen window.

"It's a good night to stay inside, Harper," Jess said as she corralled the busy girl in her high chair and gave her a small piece of graham cracker to gum while she made supper.

Later, after they'd eaten and bathed, Jess sat down in the old La-Z-Boy with Harper, two children's books, and a novel for herself. She rocked Harper, read her *Goodnight Moon* once . . . and then again . . . and then one more time before the baby finally drifted off in her lap. Jess continued to gently rock the chair, listening to the rain against the window and the sighing of the wind. She read a few pages of her book, but quickly nodded off herself.

***

Something woke her.

She thought at first it was Renee next door, but a light tapping came again. She'd left the front curtains open just enough to see a sliver of someone at her door. Feeling a second of vulnerability, she gripped the sleeping child on her lap a little tighter, scolding herself for leaving the curtain open so anyone could see them sitting there in the living room.

Creepy.

The person standing on the porch shifted—and she could see it was Seth.

Letting out a sigh of relief, she stood up carefully and shifted Harper so the baby's head rested on her shoulder, trying not to wake her. Jess made her way over to the door, opened it, and held a finger to her lips. She stepped back and let him in. He brought the scent of rain and fresh pines in with him.

"Here, you want me to take her up?" he whispered, motioning for Jess to pass him the sleeping child.

Jess must have been sitting weird in the chair because her lower back was killing her. Or, more likely, it was from hauling the heavy boxes down from Celia's attic. She nodded and he quickly kicked his boots off, then took Harper. "I'll put her up in her crib."

Again, Jess gave him a nod and followed him up the stairs after pulling the front curtains closed. The single lamp glowing by her chair provided minimal light. Dusk had fallen outside.

Since he'd been upstairs the one other time, Seth knew which room was Harper's. He went straight to the crib and gently set her down. Jess turned a small table lamp on in the hallway as she passed it—she didn't want one of them to trip in the gloom and wake the baby on their way back downstairs. Not sure if the sleeper would keep her warm enough through the chilly night, Jess crossed over to the crib and pulled a light blanket over Harper's sleeping form. She followed Seth back out to the hallway and gently closed Harper's door behind them.

"I'm surprised to see you," Jess whispered, turning back to the man whose presence, Jess was suddenly hyperaware, seemed to fill the hallway.

"I went back to the shop, loaded my truck for tomorrow, and got cleaned up. I was just going to head home but kept thinking about you, wondering if you were going through the journal or boxes out here and if you were finding anything." He kept his voice low.

Jess shook her head, an internal battle beginning. She knew the wise thing would be to head back to the kitchen and continue this conversation downstairs. At the same time, her open bedroom door—right there, just behind Seth—taunted her. She remembered his warning last time she'd brought him into her bedroom:

Don't ever bring me to your room again unless you mean it.

Did she mean it now?

"Is your headache better?" Seth asked, watching Jess carefully.

"Yes, a cool shower and food did wonders," she said, offering him a tentative smile. "I thought you were going to call Brooke," she teased, unable to help herself.

"No," Seth said, this time taking one step closer to her, as if testing things himself. "I never had any intention of calling her . . . but you already knew that, didn't you?"

Jess shrugged. "I didn't want you to, but I really wasn't sure."

And now here we are . . . and not by accident this time.

"Do you want to go back downstairs, Jess?" he whispered.

This time Jess took a step toward him, holding his gaze with her own. "Not this time."

Seth opened his arms to her and she accepted the invitation. Her arms went up around his neck and she fit herself against him, feeling the roughness of his work coat through her shirt and bra. Her hands could feel the wetness in his hair from the rain outside. She could still hear it droning against the roof. But most of all, she could feel his lips on her own.

They stayed like that for some time, their kisses deepening and hands exploring. The sound of a shutting door through Renee's adjoining wall had her pulling back slightly, contemplating how far to take this.

"Second thoughts?" he asked.

Jess stretched up on her tiptoes and gave him a quick, hard kiss in answer.

"No second thoughts," she said, taking him by the hand and leading him into her room, closing the door behind her.

"Are you sure about this, Jess?" Seth asked, keeping a loose grip on her one hand but giving her space to think clearly.

"I'm sure. I trust you, Seth. I don't know what this is, this *thing* that seems to keep pulling us toward each other, but tonight . . . I'm sick of trying to figure it out. I just want to be with you, to feel your arms around me. Maybe we'll regret it later, but I'm tired of always being sensible. Too much sensibility is lonely."

Seth gave a low chuckle and shrugged out of his damp jacket, tossing it on a nearby chair.

"So I suggest we stop thinking then," he said, taking her into his arms again.

She shivered against the warmth of him, slipping her hands, still wet from his hair, up under his shirt and running them over his warm back. His followed a similar path, exploring her. When his shirt kept getting in her way, she pulled it up over his head and dropped it to the floor. Now her hands could travel over his chest, too. She couldn't see him in the darkness but could feel the strength there; she needed to be near it, to feel it against her, to let it make her stronger.

Seth's fingers found the buttons on the front of her old flannel shirt, fumbling to open them as he devoured her mouth. When he made too little progress, a nervous giggle escaped her lips and she stopped her own exploration to flick the tiny buttons open for him.

As their clothing fell away, Jess slowly pushed Seth backward, their steps bringing the backs of his knees up against her bed. He started to speak again, but she held one finger up against his lips. She didn't want to think, didn't want to chicken out.

She needed this.

She gently pushed against his chest and he tightened his arms around her bare waist, falling back onto the bed, his back landing on her comforter and Jess landing on top of him.

Seth pushed himself farther up onto her bed, easily bringing her along with him. Jess consciously blocked all thoughts out of her mind and let herself relax and enjoy the sensations. She could analyze all of this tomorrow, but now she would stay in the moment. It was time to let go of her painful past and move on.

Her last thought before her mind let her body take over was how glad she was she'd made her bed that morning.

CHAPTER 29

Gift of the Written Word

*J*ess listened to Seth's soft snoring beside her. Moonlight streamed through the window; she'd left it open an inch after her shower earlier in the evening to let the fresh air in. She shivered in the rain-cooled air and snuggled in closer to Seth, his body warm . . . comforting. Sleep eluded her. She'd hoped to put off thoughts of what they'd done until later but her mind didn't work that way. Sleep would be impossible, so she crawled out of bed—hating to leave the warmth, hating to leave *his* warmth—and took care not to wake him. She slid the window closed; fall was in the air and she couldn't let it get too cold inside.

Slipping on her robe and a warm pair of socks, Jess left her room and peeked in on Harper. The child was sound asleep. Thankful for the lamp she'd left on in the hallway as well as the one downstairs, she went down to the kitchen and put a pot of water on. A cup of herbal tea might help. A glance at the clock on the wall showed it was just after midnight. No sound came from next door.

She considered reading a few more pages of her novel—but then she remembered Celia's journal, still in her purse.

I already took one scary leap tonight, Jess thought to herself. *Might as well see what other surprises Celia might have in store for us.*

Jess took her cup of tea and the journal and settled back into her chair. She pulled her old afghan around her, the chill permeating the whole house. She folded back the book's leather cover and began to read. Daily entries walked her through Celia's movements, reminding Jess how busy her aunt stayed, even as she aged. The entries were dated beginning in

2005—Celia would have been eighty-two years old. She mentioned bridge games, business meetings, and even a fundraiser for the historical society.

I wonder if Seth was there with Ruby . . . ?

A few pages in, an entry caught her attention.

June 16, 2005

Something isn't right. Today I received a letter from the IRS. They have concerns about inconsistencies in the tax returns for the Corner Market. It's been five months since Clyde Klaus died and I was forced to close the store. Karen helped me compile the ending financials and filed the final tax returns. I'll take the letter to her tomorrow. I need to figure this one out and fast.

"Karen?" Jess questioned, her voice loud in the hushed night.

June 17, 2005

I called Karen, but she was unavailable today. We have an appointment tomorrow. When I mentioned the letter, she wasn't surprised. She'd received a copy of it as well, apparently, since she was listed as the preparer on the returns. She apologized for not being able to meet today, assured me it was all a simple mistake, and she would see me tomorrow. Feeling a bit relieved.

June 18, 2005

Imagine my surprise when I arrived at Karen's office today and Helen was there! Apparently Karen's assistant had the day off. My friend met me at the door, but she said little beyond a simple greeting before taking me back to Karen. I was in for another shock. Karen, normally dressed to the nines and coolly professional, was a wreck. Her face was streaked with mascara, her clothes rumpled, and I even thought I smelled alcohol, although I couldn't be sure.

Helen took my arm and walked me over to a chair, helped me into it. I don't understand why the woman acts like I'm some fragile egg to break.

She's older than I am! Circles of color stained her high cheekbones, a sure sign my friend was upset about something.

As soon as we were all seated, Helen instructed her granddaughter to explain herself. I remember looking between the two women, knowing I wasn't going to like what either had to say from that point onward. Karen tried and failed to speak, getting a few words out but breaking into tears before she could say anything meaningful. Clearly frustrated with Karen, Helen raised a hand to silence the gibberish.

Helen went on to explain her granddaughter had suffered a "serious misstep" related to her involvement with the Corner Market. She'd been facing astronomical medical bills related to her infertility and, instead of coming to Helen for help, she may have made a few "slightly inappropriate" entries in the Market's financials, justifying her foolish actions by assuring herself she worked hard to help me wrap up Mr. Klaus's affairs, assuring herself she deserved a bit more of what she called "financial compensation" and the rest of us call embezzlement.

Helen went on to assure me she was committed to helping us figure out the whole unfortunate mess without involving the authorities. She would take care of any financial implications. Knowing I value our friendship as much as she does, she told me she's confident I will want to make this go away as quickly and as quietly as possible. After all, her granddaughter and Karen's husband were important people in our community and maintaining their stellar reputation was critical. She actually said that—critical.

I am in shock over all of this. Once Helen filled me in, Karen apologized time and time again. My stomach churns as I think about all the different businesses in town to whom I've recommended Karen's services. I asked her if she has done anything similar with the other companies. She is adamant she has not. The situation with the Corner Market, she says, was a perfect storm . . . an intersection of opportunity, severe financial pressures, and poor judgment influenced by a body pumped full of hormones in an effort to conceive a child.

Can I believe her? I've felt that sense of panic myself. When you know time is running out on your ability to bear a child of your own. It can make one feel irrational.

Tomorrow I will review all the bookwork to determine what exactly happened. I insisted Helen give me time before I'm willing to even listen to her plan for handling this.

June 19, 2005

I am ashamed I gave Karen so much free access to the assets and records of the Corner Market. Poor Clyde is probably turning over in his grave right now, disgusted with me for being so foolish. Nothing Karen did was particularly clever or inventive—or moral.

If I'd taken the time to monitor things, I could have prevented all of this.

In the weeks following Clyde's death, when I was busy figuring out a way to dispose of the perishable inventory of the store, Karen found a couple of different ways to pay herself more than her agreed-upon fee. From what I can see, she wrote out a series of five checks over a three-week time period, drawn on the store's checking account, to herself for a total of $15,000 for what she called "consulting fees." Thinking she could do this and recognize the expense on the Corner Market but not file a corresponding 1099 and recognize the income on her side was a rooky move. Something easily spotted and blatantly illegal. She knows better. Her brain must be befuddled with hormones, as she says.

I believe she took it a step further. I'm seeing current W-2s for two additional employees who left the company years ago. Did she pretend to pay them, maybe for an extended period of time, when in fact she was pocketing the money herself? It certainly looks that way.

How could I be so stupid? Helen may be right. I may need to help her make this all go away. Helen was so good to me, back when I also made a stupid mistake. Perhaps it's my turn to return the favor.

June 20, 2005

I presented my findings to Karen and Helen. Karen disputed nothing. She continues to assure me how sorry she is and promises nothing like this will ever happen again. She seems sincere. Am I being too soft, too trusting? I don't believe so. I think she means it.

Helen wants me to tell the IRS I made a mistake with the records, blame it on my advanced age and pay them any additional taxes owed. Will they buy it? Probably. Why spend their time and resources pursuing a trifling amount (in their eyes, at least) from a scatterbrained old woman who admits to them she is guilty of a stupid mistake?

It pains me to do this, but it is for the best. Helen is right. Karen can't afford to have her reputation sullied. Helen and I are old women, but Karen has little other than her career. Are we more similar than I care to admit? I have to trust that Helen knows her own granddaughter well enough to be sure this was an isolated incident that will never happen again.

I hope I don't live to regret my decision.

She closed the journal, shocked at all she'd read. This didn't sound like the Celia she knew. The Celia she knew would have put Karen through the wringer and made her face the ramifications of her own actions.

Jess jumped, screeching at a touch on her shoulder. She'd been so engrossed in the journal she hadn't heard Seth come downstairs.

"Sorry, I didn't mean to scare you," Seth said, coming around the front of her chair and sitting on an old ottoman so they were eye to eye. He was shirtless but had slipped into his jeans. "I woke up and you were gone."

Jess put a hand to her chest. "I know. I'm sorry. I tried not to wake you, but I couldn't sleep. I came down here for a cup of tea and Celia's old journal seemed to call to me," Jess said, glancing again at the kitchen clock and then at her cold tea. "I came down at about midnight. Seth . . . something happened more than ten years ago that might help us now. It might be the answer we've been looking for."

He arched an eyebrow. "What is it?"

Jess lowered the footrest on her chair, set the journal on the end table, and stood. "I think you should read it yourself. Do you want to read it now or wait until morning?"

Seth stood as well. "I'm going to have to be on the road by six. I better take a look now. I don't want to wait until I get back."

"All right. Come here, let's sit on the couch and you can read it. Do you want a cup of coffee or tea?" Jess asked.

"No, I don't need anything. Thanks."

He picked up the journal and her afghan that had fallen to the floor. He took both over to the couch, sat down at one end, and motioned for her to join him. She sat down next to him. He put a throw pillow on his lap. "Why don't you lie down while I read it? Get some rest. From the look on your face, I'd say you're going to need it."

Without saying a word, Jess did as he suggested, a bit tense at first, but she relaxed as he began reading, his arm resting around her middle. Exhaustion finally won out and she fell asleep.

Sometime later, Seth's shifting woke her and she sat up, disoriented for a moment. When she could grasp her surroundings, she heard Seth say, "So you think Karen might have something to do with what Patricia found over at Homes Sparkle? She's the Fisks' daughter, right? Is she an accountant?"

"She is. Of course I can't be sure, but maybe Karen is also involved in their books. Damn, I never thought to ask who specifically works on the taxes for Patricia. I knew they used the local CPA firm in town, and I'm pretty sure Karen works there. It seems like an awfully big coincidence if there really is money missing and Karen helped both businesses with their financials and their taxes. Do you really think Celia could have been that gullible?"

Seth said nothing at first, clearly trying to process all he'd just read. "I don't know. What I do know is Celia liked nothing better than to help other people. It's how she lived her life. I always thought she was a tough lady . . . but everyone has their weak spots. Maybe this was one for Celia. I wonder what she meant when she said Helen helped her years ago."

"I wondered about that, too . . . but we may never know. Remember, Frank said Helen died recently . . ."

Jess's voice trailed off, her hands rubbing her face, and she let a frustrated groan escape her throat.

"What?"

"I'm a little slow putting two and two together. Patricia said their accountant was out of town for a 'family emergency.' Karen was with Virginia, helping settle her grandmother's estate, and I bet *she* was the accountant Patricia was referring to."

"I forgot about that. Shoot. So what do you want to do now?"

"Tomorrow I'll start going through all the boxes we brought from Celia's. See what more I can find."

"And tonight?"

"Well, there's not much left of the night, but I do think the bed upstairs is much more comfortable than this couch," she said with a smile.

CHAPTER 30

Gift of Fewer Burdens

"*I* noticed a strange pickup in the parking lot when we got home last night. Thought it looked a lot like the one Seth was in when he was out here last weekend," Renee said, her voice trying and failing to sound casual.

"Good morning to you, too," Jess greeted her sister, who'd let herself in as Jess was cleaning Harper up after breakfast.

"Oh, come *on*, Jess. Don't make me wait! I've been dying to talk to you since I saw his truck. Matt told me to mind my own business."

"Matt is a smart man."

Renee sighed. "You aren't going to make this easy, are you?"

"Nope. I don't kiss and tell."

"Ha! But at least you admit there was kissing," Renee exclaimed, a big grin lighting up her face.

Poor choice of words. "I admit no such thing. We were working again. We brought a bunch of boxes of paperwork back here from Celia's attic, and he offered to help me go through them."

Renee looked around. "Where are they?"

"Where are the boxes?" *Crap*, Jess thought. She was trapped. "It was raining so we couldn't bring them in. They're still in the back of my vehicle."

"But you just said he helped you go through the boxes. What, did you go through them in your *car?* Are you trying to pull one over on me, sis?"

"No, technically I said he *offered* to help me."

"That is just semantics and you know it." Renee threw her hands up in defeat. "All right, I'll let it go—*for now*—but you can bet I'll pump you for information the next time we have a bottle of wine sitting between us. In the meantime, did you find anything useful at Celia's?"

Jess turned away to rinse the dish cloth she'd just used to clean Harper's face, exhaling a quiet sigh of relief when Renee dropped the subject about Seth.

"Actually, we did. Do you remember that old blue chest we used to use for a table when we played restaurant? Up in the attic?"

"Sure."

"Did you know Ethan asked Celia to open it for him, back when we were kids? She basically told him no and said some things were 'better left locked away.' "

Renee shook her head. "Let me guess. Now that Celia is gone and there is a mystery to be solved, Ethan thought it might hold some answers?"

Jess laughed. "You know him well. Remember how he loved to read the Hardy Boys?"

"No, I don't remember Ethan ever reading much."

"That was back before he started to think it wasn't *cool* to read. Anyhow, back to the blue trunk. You're right. Ethan wanted to open it, and I think it might have provided some answers."

"That sounds like a story I'll need a cup of coffee in my hand to listen to this morning. It was a late night. I had a hard time falling asleep . . . wondering what my sister was up to next door."

"Knock it off, Renee. Grab a cup and I'll fill you in—on *Celia*, I mean."

Renee filled her cup and Jess took Harper out of her highchair, putting her down on the floor with some of her toys. *Hopefully that will keep her interest for a few minutes at least,* Jess thought. She still needed to get Harper dressed and delivered to daycare before she could get any work done.

"So, what was in the trunk?" Renee asked.

"The most helpful thing was a journal. I was able to bring it home so we started reading through it," Jess said, pointing to the leather-covered journal still sitting on the coffee table.

"What did you learn?"

Jess waved her question off. "That can wait a minute. First, I want to tell you what else was in there, because some of it seems, I don't know, *odd*. I'm not sure what to make of it."

"Oh ... the plot thickens," Renee said, rubbing her hands together then picking her coffee back up.

"The first thing was an old photo album."

"That's not unusual. Celia had lots of them," Renee cut in. "But I thought Mom and Dad brought all of those to their house."

"They thought so, too. They couldn't have known another one was locked in the trunk, I guess. I only glanced at it. The first few pages were from Celia's eightieth birthday party. It's out in my car with the boxes. But the other things in the trunk were what I wanted to ask you about."

Harper was losing interest in her toys and the company. She'd abandoned them and was crawling through the living room, either heading for the door or the stairs. Jess tried bringing her back, but Harper saw her, squealed, and suddenly it became a game.

"Here, give her to me," Renee said, holding out her arms. Harper settled on her lap, content for the moment. "What else was in the trunk?"

"A wedding dress ... a *gorgeous* wedding dress. And a christening gown and blue baby booties. Oh, and some paperwork of some kind, but it's really faded."

Surprise had shown on Renee's face at the mention of the wedding dress. "Were they Celia's?"

"I have no idea."

"Hmm. That *is* weird. Add to that the comment you said she made to Ethan years ago, about keeping some things secret or whatever, and it really makes me wonder. Maybe Dad or Uncle Gerry might have some ideas. Did the clothes look old?"

"Yes, they really did. Of course, all three of those things are kind of timeless ... but the wedding gown looked *old-fashioned*."

"I'm sorry, Jess, but I have no idea what any of those things could mean. Remember, in addition to Celia and Gerry, Dad did have another sister. She died young. I'm not sure how old she was, but maybe they were *her* things."

"Maybe. Her name was . . . Beverly?"

Renee nodded. "Was there anything else in the trunk?"

"No, nothing else."

Renee nodded to the journal. "And what'd you find in there?"

Jess grimaced. "Actually . . . she talked about some problems with a different business. The IRS flagged tax returns back in 2005 and Celia was able to figure out someone had actually helped themselves to a bit more compensation for work done on behalf of the business."

"Is that a nice way of saying someone embezzled?"

Jess snorted. "Yes, that's exactly what I was getting at. The business was the Corner Market."

Renee's brow furrowed and she nodded. "I remember that old place. Honest to God, it was the only place I knew of where you could still get penny candy. And I mean the *good* stuff. Didn't the guy who owned it die or something, and it closed down?"

"Yes. Celia worked with him, too. It fell to her and the accountant to get everything closed out."

"Who was the accountant?"

Jess took a steadying breath and said, "Karen Lark."

Renee blinked. "Karen *who*?"

"Karen Lark. She was Karen Fisk as a kid. Her folks are Frank and Virginia—you know, from the bookstore."

"Oh sure, I remember her now. So . . . if it was Celia and Karen left . . . and the owner was dead . . . was there something in Celia's journal that implicated Karen?"

"Yes, very clearly. Helen Arbuckle was Karen's grandmother. And Helen was one of Celia's best friends, ever since they were kids."

"That had to be awkward . . ." Renee said as she ducked her head to the side to avoid Harper's fingers, which were currently intent on seeing what might be in Renee's nose.

"You'll have to read it. See what you think. I don't want to say any more until you read it. See if we think the same thing."

"Sure. Have you read the whole thing yet? The whole journal?"

"No," Jess said. "Not yet. I got through about half of it last night, but it got late."

Renee started to say something about it "getting late," but the look Jess shot her must have made her think better of it.

"I need to get Harper to daycare, put a strong four hours in on work, and then I can switch back to Celia's stuff," Jess said. "What does your day look like?"

"I wanted to sketch out our retreat calendar for this coming fall and winter. We probably should have already done all that, but I've been distracted with the possibility of building a new house."

"Do you want to read the journal today, while I'm busy with everything else, and give it back to me later this afternoon so I can finish it, too?"

"Sure. Now that you've told me this much, I doubt I'll be able to concentrate on much else until after I have a chance to read it." Renee went to hoist Harper up out of the chair with her, but then something occurred to her. "Oh, hey, what did you do with the other things in the trunk—the clothes? Are they here?"

"No, we talked about it and decided, since the trunk had kept them safe for who knows how many years, it could keep them safe for a while longer." Jess's cell phone rang. "Just a minute," she said. "It's my realtor."

"Sure, go ahead, I'll take Harper up and get her dressed."

Thank you, Jess mouthed to Renee. "Hello, this is Jess Rand."

***

Moments later Jess ran upstairs and found Renee in Harper's room, trying to wrangle the child into a long-sleeved shirt.

"She—is—a—*worm*. I think she'd rather be naked," Renee said with a laugh.

"I *know* she'd rather be naked," Jess agreed. "Hey, change of plans. That was the realtor and she has an offer on the table."

"Really? That's *great*, Jess!" Renee said, settling a now dressed Harper on her hip.

"Well . . . it's an offer, yes, but it's a little on the low side. I'm not sure what to do. Do you think I should talk to Will about it first?"

"Jess, I honestly don't think you owe him that courtesy. What do *you* want to do? If the offer is enough to pay off the mortgage, maybe even leave you with a little bit of equity, accepting the offer means one less headache for you to deal with going forward. Is the offer ridiculously low?"

"No, I don't think so. Will might be mad, though," Jess replied slowly, considering her options. "He tends to have an overly inflated idea of the value of anything he owns."

"Oh, really?" Renee asked, her voice laced with sarcasm. "Do you have the legal authority to accept the offer without his signature?"

"Yes, I do. We set it up that way, given the circumstances. Neither of us wanted to miss out on a potential sale because we couldn't physically get Will's signature in a crunch."

"Then I wouldn't worry about Will. Do what you think is best. Selling means you're done paying interest on the mortgage that much sooner. It might end up being a wash anyway."

Renee's right . . . screw Will, Jess thought. *I don't want to take a chance on messing this up.*

"Thanks, sis," she said out loud. "The realtor said the buyers are anxious to find something and close as soon as possible. I'll go accept the offer."

Renee smiled. "Once the house is gone, that's one less tie you have with that ass."

Jess returned her sister's smile, but it faltered when her eyes fell on Harper, still in Renee's arms. *But when it comes to untangling this mess, the house is nothing compared to you, is it, little one?*

CHAPTER 31

Gift of Partnerships

*J*ess signed the papers. Closing was in five weeks, meaning that now, on top of everything else, she had four weeks and six days to clear the house out.

I'm going to need help ... lots of help. And I can't afford to hire movers.

She called Nathan and Lauren first. Together, they agreed on the weekend they would pack. She hated the idea of the extra cost, but they agreed that she'd have to rent a storage unit for Will's things.

Now that the house was sold, there were a few things she wasn't ready to part with yet. It had been easy to pretend she didn't care about the items when she moved to the duplex, but it was another thing to actually sell them off. She wanted the kids to have a few of the pieces, too, but neither had room for bigger items yet. Nathan was sharing an apartment in an old building with a bunch of guys and Lauren only had her dorm room at school. At least Jess had an empty basement at the duplex. Storing as much down there as she could was her best option—she couldn't think of any other storage areas at Whispering Pines.

Jess had hoped she could count on her extended family for some muscle and pickup trucks, just as Renee had when moving into Whispering Pines, and she was right. She got commitments from all three of her siblings that they would help and recruit their own kids as well.

I can do this, I can do this, Jess kept telling herself. *Now I just have to tell Will I sold the house. But he can wait. I have too much to do to drop everything and go visit him. And I don't want to tell him over the phone.*

On the other hand, maybe a phone call would be better. I'll hear his snotty disapproval but won't have to see his anger.

Once all the arrangements related to moving out of the house were handled, she needed to get back to Celia's mess. Karen would be home in a few days, and Jess needed to meet with Patricia, find out if Karen worked on Homes Sparkle.

She didn't get back to the journal until after ten that night. Renee left it on her kitchen table, but Jess didn't get a chance to talk to her before her sister left for a chamber event.

Jess sat down and picked up where she'd left off.

June 21, 2005

They believed me. I called the IRS this morning. Apologized for my error and committed to filing an updated return, removing the expense and paying additional taxes. It was the quickest way to make this go away. While it galls me to pretend this was all me, I just want this whole ugly mess to disappear. We're crossing our fingers nothing ever comes to light regarding the W-2s. That would be harder to explain.

I'm going to have to watch Karen like a hawk. Helen may be sure Karen made a stupid mistake just this once, but I'm certainly not. I don't think she'd steal from her own parents, and I want to believe there are no other improprieties, but I'm not going to assume that's the case.

Entries over the next couple of weeks rehashed the steps Celia took to check over things.

July 15, 2005

Maybe Helen was right. I'm finding nothing else. I did catch Karen alone yesterday. I sat her down for a heart-to-heart and made it clear I'm watching her. She remains contrite. She's appreciative I've said nothing to her parents.

Hopefully all of this is behind us. I'm too old for this drama.

Celia was right. She shouldn't have had to deal with that situation. *I wish she'd asked me to help her,* Jess thought, thinking back to what she would have been doing twelve years earlier. *Juggling motherhood, my own career, and trying to live up to Will's expectations as the wife of a successful surgeon.* While Celia and Jess often discussed business, Celia probably hadn't wanted to bring her into this mess. Maybe part of her hated the fact she'd been duped and she didn't want anyone else to know about it.

Too late. It's come out now.

The journal didn't reveal anything else.

***

Jess spent the next two days reviewing the rest of the records they'd brought from Celia's. She could see the entries in the Corner Market discussed in Celia's journal. She didn't notice anything unusual for Homes Sparkle.

She also checked everything over from Frank and the bookstore. She could see the decline in business when she went back through their older records. It was disheartening, but otherwise, things looked accurate.

Maybe the incident with Karen and the Corner Market had been isolated.

It was time to meet with Patricia and find out.

***

Do I tell her or don't I? was the internal battle Jess faced every day since reading the journal. By now, Jess had almost convinced herself Karen was the CPA working with Homes Sparkle, but she needed to confirm if this was true with Patricia. If she was right, Patricia might be more cooperative if she was told Karen had screwed up before. On the other hand, maybe Patricia was wrong and there hadn't been any new embezzlement. If there was no embezzlement, Jess had no right to air Karen's dirty laundry.

They agreed to meet at one o'clock the following day and would spend the afternoon combing through things. Jess decided she wouldn't mention the Corner Market unless it became apparent this was a similar situation and Karen was indeed involved.

It was a beautiful fall day when Jess stepped outside, two hours before she was due at Patricia's. The resort was quiet. They had renters in one cabin for the week and would be full for the weekend, but no one was outside now. Jess wasn't sure if Renee was home. She hitched her laptop bag up on her shoulder, walking out to the lodge parking lot.

The crunch of gravel signaled someone's arrival. Butterflies jumped to life in her stomach when she saw the large white pickup. She hadn't talked to Seth since he'd left at dawn days earlier. She'd tried not to think about him or what they'd done behind closed doors, doing her best to tuck it into the back of her mind.

Looks like it's later, Jess thought, her mind going back to their earlier agreement to hold off on any kind of romantic involvement for the time being. She clicked her doors open and placed her bag inside her vehicle.

He parked next to her, turned off the noisy diesel engine, and got out.

"Hey," he said, coming around to the passenger side of his truck to stand beside her.

"Hey," Jess said back, nervous. "How did things go with the building?"

"Good. I was able to pull out lots of nice pieces. Filled my trailer *and* truck. There was an impressive staircase, and if I can find the right buyers, it'll have been worth my time."

"You pull all of that out yourself?"

"Sometimes, but this project was too big. I hired some help."

"Glad it went well."

Seth seemed a bit hesitant, maybe nervous, too. "How about around here? Find anything? I'm sorry I didn't get a chance to call."

I wasn't sure if you would want to, Jess thought.

She shrugged. "I was able to corroborate what Celia said in her journal with the actual records for the Corner Market. But I didn't find anything unusual for Homes Sparkle or the bookstore. Is that why you stopped out? I could have told you that over the phone. I know you're busy."

Now it was Seth's turn to shrug. "I guess. But I knew you wouldn't have time to come out to the shop this week, with everything you're working on, and I wanted to show you something."

Butterflies fluttered again. "Really? What?"

"I remembered the bad spots in that old tin ceiling at the bookstore and Nathan digging through my pile at the shop."

Jess laughed. "Don't you mean knocking your pile *over* at your shop?"

Seth waved that off. "It's great the kid notices things like that. Anyhow, I found these in the old entryway of the building I worked on this week. Do you think Frank might want to use them to repair the ceiling?"

He'd wandered back to his tailgate as he was talking, and Jess followed. He dropped the gate and rolled back a tarp that had been strung taut over everything. A pile of ceiling tins filled one corner of his truck bed, held securely with straps. Jess doubted there'd been any shifting given how neatly Seth had packed everything in. The box was full but orderly.

"Oh, Seth, these are *great*! I think they look like they might match, too. I honestly don't know if Frank wants to incur the expense, but we could ask him."

"He's probably going to have to spend a bit to clean that place up if he hopes to find a serious buyer. Old buildings can be money pits. He doesn't want to scare buyers off with *obvious* problems. Besides, I wouldn't charge him much. And maybe Nathan would help me get them up. That way Frank wouldn't have to find someone else."

Jess stared at him. "You'd do that?"

He shrugged again. "Sure, it's what I do."

"I know it is . . . but you normally charge for your services."

"I'm like you. I don't want to see any of Celia's businesses struggle."

"And here I thought you were a heartless jerk, back when I first met you."

This had Seth turning to Jess, taking a step toward her. "Oh, you did, did you? It could be that you infuriated the hell out of me, coming in and telling me I should change this and that, clean up my messy paperwork. Or maybe it was you snooping through my stuff. You were a bit more, dare I say, *bossy* than Celia ever was with me. You might have rubbed me the wrong way. I'm usually known for my charm."

Jess laughed. "I somehow doubt anyone has ever accused you of being charming, Seth."

"I missed you, Jess," Seth said, his teasing tone gone as he put his hands on her hips and shifted her stance, her back up against his tailgate, his body gently brushing the front of hers. He put his hand behind her neck and angled his mouth down to hers, his fingers applying light pressure.

The butterflies were fluttering like a gale storm now.

She'd started questioning what they'd done, thinking it might have all been a terrible mistake. But here, in his arms, her body questioned nothing. She sank into the kiss, forgetting they were out in the open. She squealed when Seth picked her up and sat her down on the very end of the tailgate, putting them eye to eye and hip to hip.

She felt something scratchy on her side. Looking down, she noticed the white tape encompassing his left thumb. She pulled his hand up so she could inspect the bandage.

"What did you do?"

"Smashed my damn thumb," he said, disgusted with himself. "And I have *you* to blame for it."

"How could I possibly be responsible for this?"

He used his hand's position—Jess was still holding it up between them—to lightly caress her breast through her sweater with the back of his hand. "Well, you see . . . pulling out hundreds of old nails and screws gets a bit monotonous after a while, gives the mind plenty of time to think. I kept going back to the other night, in your bed, and I might have gotten a little sloppy. I'll probably lose the nail."

Jess leaned ever so slightly into the back of Seth's hand. "You were thinking about us?"

"I'm here, aren't I? By the way, it looked like you were leaving. Am I holding you up?"

She checked her watch. "I'm OK yet. I have an appointment with Patricia at one o'clock. It's why I've worked so hard to review everything since you left. Karen will probably be home any day."

"Are you going to tell Patricia about the problems Celia had with Karen before?"

Jess shook her head. "I've thought about it, but I think I'm going to hold onto that card, at least for now. I'll only reveal it if it becomes absolutely necessary."

Seth nodded. "Smart."

"Oh, I forgot to tell you—the day after you left I heard from my realtor. I got an offer on the house!"

"You did? Was it a decent offer? And are you sure you still want to sell it? I know you said you couldn't stand the thought of living there with your ex, but he has different living arrangements now. It might be more convenient for you than living out here. You could have the place to yourself now."

Seth's observation made her pause. She'd said all along she never had any intention of moving back in there, after everything that happened. Was she being too rash? *Should* she consider it?

"Maybe it's a terrible idea . . . forget it," he said.

"No, it's actually a really good question. Things are moving pretty fast these days and I don't want to do anything I'll regret later."

"I hope you aren't referring to us . . . ?" Seth said, a questioning note in his voice.

Jess laughed. "I *promise* I wasn't referring to us. Honestly, though, I never really liked that house much. It was always too fancy, too big for our needs. It was all about the *show* for Will. So while I appreciate the question, I guess my answer is still no. I have zero reservations about selling it. I *love* living out here at Whispering Pines," Jess said, looking around them, inhaling deeply and appreciating the smell of pine trees and fall leaves—and Seth. "I feel revived from my year out here. I know my duplex is shabby and small, but it's mine, you know? Well, *technically* it's Renee's, but I rent it from her."

Seth chuckled at her clarification. "There's nothing wrong with 'shabby and small.' Just consider it *cozy* and *comfortable*. But seriously, I've only been out here a few times and I already understand why you wouldn't want to leave this place. Most people would consider themselves lucky to be able to spend a week or two of vacation out here. You actually get to *live* here."

"I'm lucky to have so much support from my family, too. And speaking of support, they've already agreed to help me get everything moved out of our old house, so you don't need to worry about injuring any more fingers. I need to be out in a little under four weeks now."

"You *are* a busy woman, aren't you?" Seth said, pulling Jess up tight against his body. She was still sitting on his tailgate but wrapped her legs around his waist. A few more kisses and Seth picked her up again, turned, and set her back on her feet next to his truck. "Any chance I can schedule a date with you somewhere in that crazy schedule you keep?"

Jess tucked her hands in the pockets of her jeans, rocking back and forth on the balls of her feet, grinning like a school girl. She couldn't remember the last time she was invited out on a date. "You want to go out on a date with me?"

"I want to do all kinds of things with you," Seth said with a wink. "But a date would be a good start. I do have one condition, though."

"You do, huh? And what would that be?"

"We spend the whole night *not* talking about work or Celia."

"But then what would we find to talk about?" Jess joked.

"Anything else would be fair game."

"Deal. But I can't go for a couple of days yet. How about Saturday night? That gives me time to find a sitter for Harper, too."

He kissed her cheek softly. "It's a date."

***

Patricia met Jess out in their front lobby at Homes Sparkle and ushered her back to her office, shutting the door behind them.

"Thanks for agreeing to see me, Patricia."

"I'm glad you called, Jess. I've been trying to figure out where the problem is in the books, but ... I'm going to be honest with you. I haven't been able to find anything. Not a thing. I'm mainly acting on intuition here, but I'm certain our expense load is out of balance somewhere. We should be showing more growth. We've been adding new customers and not losing many old ones. I thought it would be easy to figure out, but . . ." Patricia's voice trailed off.

Jess understood why Patricia was hesitant to ask her for help. "Maybe if we put our heads together we'll be able to figure something out. I promise I want answers as much as you do. If we find something wrong, even if it involved Celia, I'll work with you on it. We need answers. You want to better understand the dynamics of this business so you can help grow it, and I want the same thing—plus, I also want to be sure Celia's reputation is protected if she's an innocent in this."

"I have to admit I might have been premature in pointing fingers," Patricia said, dropping her eyes from Jess's.

"I'm working on instincts here too, Patricia. And my instincts tell me your initial suspicions were way off-base. But let me work with you to prove it. I've blocked off the rest of my day," Jess said, pushing up the sleeves of her sweater. "Where can we start?"

And so the digging began. For the next three hours Patricia showed Jess old reports prepared through the years, new spreadsheets she'd created to spot trends with the intention of building her business case for expansion, and even payroll records and underlying journal entries. Jess jotted down notes and attempted to keep an open mind as she looked through all the information. Patricia was still irritated about not having any records further back than eight years. Jess didn't tell her some of the old records were sitting in her kitchen at Whispering Pines. She knew she might need to tell Patricia she had found them, but she wanted to take another evening, now that she had insight into more recent records, to see if she could find anything in there first. Then she'd show them to Patricia. She wouldn't have to reveal she'd taken time to review them before showing them to the other woman.

"What is 'Temp Angels'?" Patricia asked.

"I'm not sure ... sounds like a service for placing temporary employees. Why do you ask?"

"I'm seeing some payments to them."

"Do you ever use temp agencies?" Jess asked.

"I didn't think we did, but I should ask Wendy. She'd know for sure," Patricia said, pushing back from her desk and heading out into the hallway. Jess could hear her talking to someone, and then she was back. "Wendy said we've used temp agencies once in a great while, when we were desperate for cleaning teams, but not often. She's never heard of Temp Angels, though."

"Here, let me check if they're listed," Jess said as she pulled out her phone.

"I'm reviewing 2012 now," Patricia said. "It looks like one or two checks a month to them."

"I'm not finding anything, but maybe, after five years, the business isn't around anymore."

Patricia nodded and continued to review.

Jess decided to use this moment to do a little detective work of her own. "Patricia . . .who does your taxes?"

Patricia looked up from the box she was combing through. "A woman by the name of Karen Fisk. Do you know her?"

Jess nodded. "Yes, actually, I do. What all does Karen do for you in relation to your bookkeeping? Just your tax filings?"

"No, there's more to it. Let's see. She makes our monthly deposit of our payroll taxes and she prepares and files our quarterly and annual tax returns. She also reconciles our monthly bank statements. She'll make the occasional general ledger entry—you know, to keep everything in sync. For example, she makes the payroll tax entries to support the deposits she makes. Why do you ask?"

Should I say anything at this point? Jess wondered. *I don't like what I'm hearing, but just because she has access to things doesn't mean she's done anything wrong . . . again.*

Jess shrugged. "Just curious who is doing what as far as some of that standard stuff every month. Hey, it's getting late and I need to head out. Can we do this again tomorrow morning?"

CHAPTER 32

Gift of Reminiscing

*J*ess picked up Harper from daycare and headed over to her parents' house for dinner. George and Lavonne liked to have everyone over at least once a month. Unless it was a holiday, it was rare everyone could make it, given busy schedules, but on this night all Jess's siblings made it work.

There was a crispness to the fall air as Jess took Harper out of her car seat and headed inside. She could hear kids playing in the backyard, and the house smelled homey when she let herself in the front door. An instant connection to her childhood. She smiled and held Harper closer.

"Hey, everybody," she greeted her family in the back of the house. "It smells *great* in here."

"That would be my famous chili and your mother's sugar cookies," George said, taking little Harper from his daughter and settling the baby on his hip. He tickled the little one under her chin. "Hey there, kiddo, have a good day?"

George was always good with the grandchildren, and babies never made him nervous. Jess grinned at her father. Harper wasn't *technically* his granddaughter, but George would never be one to worry about something like that.

Val was at the counter, tossing a salad.

"Hey, sis," Jess said, making her way over to Val's side and giving her a quick hug. "Haven't seen you in ages."

Val hugged her back but gave her a questioning look.

"What?"

" 'Hey' yourself. What's gotten into you? You're not much of a hugger," Val said pointedly. Her right eye teared up and she flicked the moisture away, the partially chopped onion in front of her the likely culprit.

"I know, but I've missed you. Boys keeping you busy?"

"Always. Three out of four of them are playing football this year. They're all on different teams with different practice and game schedules."

Jess shook her head in amazement. "I don't know how you do it."

"We've been known to miss a pick-up time here and there, but so far, we get everyone home ... eventually," Val replied, making light of what Jess knew had to be a scheduling nightmare. "How are things going with you? Is it going OK having Harper?"

"That is actually going really well. We've settled into a routine of sorts, believe it or not, with all the other crazy stuff going on."

Val used her knife to scrape the chopped onion into a large bowl of lettuce then set it to the side, giving Jess her full attention. "I admire you for taking her in, sis. You know most people wouldn't do that for a skanky ex-husband."

"It's definitely a unique situation," Jess agreed, uncomfortable with the compliment.

"What about her biological mother? Mom said she did come back around, at least for a little while. Jess, what if she wants Harper back? Do you have any legal grounds you can use to prevent it? I worry that would break your heart. I can see how much you love her already, and it's only been a few months."

"I worry about that, too. The short answer is 'no.' At this point, I suppose if Tiffany showed up again and insisted on taking Harper, I might not be able to prevent it. *Will* might not be able to prevent it, either. She is, after all, Harper's biological mother. But I'm hopeful that won't happen. When I last spoke to Tiffany, she claimed to be working at a new job in Chicago and needing to 'get on her feet,' " Jess said, emphasizing her words with air quotes. "I haven't heard from her since. I got the impression she had no desire to be a single parent if Will couldn't give her any financial support. I think maybe Harper was just a paycheck to her, as cruel as that sounds. Who knows, maybe she's already found herself a new sugar daddy in Chicago."

Val laughed. "There are days when a handsome, wealthy sugar daddy and no little boys running around and messing up the house sounds like a *dream*. But only for a minute. I wouldn't give up my circus for any amount of money or peace," she said, rubbing at a spot near her armpit.

The motion caught Jess's eye. "Dry skin?"

Her question caught Val by surprise. She lowered her hand, glanced around the room as if to check if anyone else was listening to their conversation, and said, "Nah. I had a little procedure yesterday, and it itches."

"What kind of procedure? Is everything all right?"

"I'm sure it will be. I just found a little lump and they wanted to biopsy it."

"Oh my *God*, Val, why didn't you *say* anything? Do Mom and Dad know?"

A scene from last winter flashed into Jess's mind: Nicole Lee, the speaker at their January retreat, talking about losing a sister. Jess remembered thinking at the time how awful it would be to lose a sibling. *Don't even go there,* Jess scolded herself.

"No, only Luke knows—and you aren't going to say a word to anyone. Promise? It's nothing to worry about. I'm supposed to hear in a day or two, and I'm sure it's *fine*," she said again, more forcefully.

Jess thought she saw a flicker of fear in her baby sister's eyes despite her trying to sound confident. Val never worried about her own health, but this seemed to have her a little spooked.

"OK, I promise I won't say anything . . . but you have to let me know what you find out *right away*, you got it?"

Val gave her a little salute. "Yes, ma'am. Now help me get the food on the table."

Jess took the salad bowl from Val's outstretched hands, giving her an encouraging smile.

***

Later, after they finished eating and the grandkids took their sugar cookies outside, the adults sat around the dining room table with coffee and their own plate of cookies. Robbie took Harper out back with the rest of the kids.

"So, what's new, everybody?" Lavonne asked, glancing around the table at her children and her two sons-in-law. "You're all so busy these days, I hardly hear from you anymore."

Renee laughed. "Mom, don't try the guilt-tripping. You know you talk to each of us almost every day."

"I know, but a quick phone call isn't the same as sitting down over a cup of coffee and really *talking*. So, Renee, you seem talkative—you go first," Lavonne instructed.

Renee smiled at her new husband and then back at her mother. "Well, OK, I guess we *do* have news . . ."

"Don't tell us you're *pregnant*! At *your* age?" Val said, drawing laughs from around the table.

"Cute, sis," Renee said. "We've actually decided to start on our new house now, before winter sets in."

Exclamations echoed around the table.

"That's *great*, honey," George said. "Have you picked out a spot and a floorplan yet?"

"We have, Dad. Come out this weekend and I'll show you. There's this great spot in the southwest corner of the property that should work perfectly. It's where we found what we think is an old foundation. Remember, I called you to see if you remembered any other cabins or structures out there, tucked in the trees?"

George sat back in his chair, his eyes angled up to the ceiling as he searched his memory banks. "Oh, man, I remember you asking, but . . . I don't remember any old buildings like that. Maybe it's been gone since before we started going to Whispering Pines. We'll come over and you can show me. Maybe seeing the spot will jog my memory."

"That's exciting, guys," Jess chimed in. "I loved that spot back there. I even . . . I mean . . . do you think you can get it done before winter? Did you check on the property lines?"

Jess had almost mentioned showing Seth that spot, but doing so might have steered the conversation in a direction she didn't want to go.

Renee nodded. "Seems like it'll work, too. We have someone lined up to come out tomorrow so we can be sure. We won't be able to get it *all* done before winter, but hopefully we can get a shell up with doors and windows—and a furnace, of course. The finishing work can be done over the winter."

"There isn't a road back there now," Jess pointed out. "Won't it be hard to get back there, not only now with all the construction materials and equipment, but later, too?"

"We're looking into building a second road in, along the back side," Matt said, pulling a pen out of his shirt pocket and sketching it out on a napkin to help everyone visualize their plans.

"Will the county let you do that?" Ethan asked, all too aware of the headaches associated with zoning.

"It's looking like we can get it approved," Matt confirmed.

"You guys have been busy," Lavonne said. "That's exciting."

"Hey, Jess, did you get a chance to ask Mom or Dad about that stuff we found in Celia's attic?" Ethan asked. "Renee's question to Dad about an old cabin reminded me of it. As long as we've got him going down memory lane, you might as well ask about that stuff, too."

Jess shook her head. "No, I hadn't had a chance yet."

"What were you guys doing up in Celia's attic?" George asked. "My sister never kept too much up there."

"Well, *she* didn't," Ethan said, looking sheepish. "But *I've* managed to fill it up. I couldn't remodel the downstairs rooms when they were full of furnishings. The boys helped me move a lot of it upstairs."

George nodded. "Makes sense. Are you going to keep all that old stuff?"

"No, not forever. I suppose we'll want to talk about a sale or an auction someday, but for now, it works to store it all up there. I'll want to incorporate some of Celia's things back into the house once it's updated. Of course, anything any of the rest of you want to take, too, feel free. After we've all made use of what we can, we can figure out next steps."

"So why were you digging around up there, Jess? I can't imagine you have any time to help Ethan with his remodel project," Lavonne asked.

Jess laughed. "You're right, Mom. No time to paint a wall or tile a floor. I just needed to see if I could find some of Celia's old paperwork."

"So did you find something interesting when you were digging around up there?" Lavonne asked.

"We *did . . .*" Jess went on to tell the story of the blue trunk and its contents.

It was obvious from the look on Lavonne's face that she didn't know the story behind the items. George was a little harder to read, sitting back in his chair, his arms crossed over his chest, listening as Jess described the wedding dress, christening gown, and other items.

"Does any of that sound familiar, Dad?" Ethan asked after Jess finished.

"I remember the old trunk you're talking about. You kids used to play on it. So you took the journal and the photo album, huh? And left the rest in the trunk?"

"We did," Jess confirmed.

"Was there anything in the album or journal to give a clue as to the other items? Do you think they were maybe all locked in the trunk around the same time?"

Jess shook her head. *Figuring out the mystery behind the gowns hasn't been my top priority these days.* "No. The album is more recent. I haven't looked through it much yet, but it starts out at Celia's eightieth birthday party. So we're in it," she said, motioning around the table. Then, smiling at Matt, she added, "Most of us, at least."

Matt gave a little nod, clearly interested in the conversation even though he was a much newer addition to the family.

"And the journal seems more recent, too. The entries are dated, and they start in 2005. While I can't be certain how old the clothing is, it looks more like it's from the early 1900s to me."

"Well, as most of you know, Celia and I had different fathers," George said. "Celia's father's name was Charles Middleton. He was killed in some kind of work-related accident in his mid-forties. He was the father to Celia and Beverly. Celia must have been around five when he died, so she didn't really remember him very well, and Beverly was even younger. Mom had to raise Celia and Beverly alone—at least until she remarried."

"How much later was that? I forget," Lavonne said. "I'm familiar with that story, but we haven't discussed it in *years*, George."

"About ten years, I'd say. Margaret, my mother, married Clarence Richter in 1937. Then they had Gerry in 1938 and I was born a few years after that."

"That explains why Celia was so much older than you," Matt said. "I'd wondered about that."

"Right," George said with a nod. "She was eighteen when I was born. Beverly would have been fourteen. It was kind of like having two separate families, the age difference was so large. Honestly, Celia often acted like our mother, despite Mom living to be seventy-four."

"So George, I've met your brother Gerry," Matt said, working to piece the family puzzle together, "and I've heard all about Celia. But what about Beverly? What happened to her?"

"That's the thing," George said, rubbing his forehead in concentration. "No one ever talked too much about Beverly. She died in 1944, when she was only eighteen. I'd have only been three, so I don't remember her at all. Mom and Celia always said she'd been sickly her whole life. They were never willing to say much more about her than that, and eventually I stopped asking. Gerry would have been six when she died, so he never knew much about her, either."

"Dad," Ethan piped up, "one time when I was younger, I asked Celia if we could open the trunk."

"You did? What did she say?"

"Something like . . . 'It's better to leave some things locked away.' I can't remember her exact words, but, the way she said it, I knew better than to keep bugging her about it."

"I don't know who the wedding dress belonged to," George said. "I doubt it was my mother's. She always said how she was dirt-poor growing up, and I don't think Charles came from money, either. She married my dad at the Justice of the Peace. As far as I know, Celia was never engaged to anyone, and obviously she never married. Maybe it was Beverly's . . . maybe she was engaged but died before she could be married. I've been to her gravesite. The headstone reads Beverly Middleton."

Lavonne left the dining room for a minute and returned with a second plate of cookies and the coffee pot.

"What about the christening gown or booties? Could those have been for you and Gerry?"

"No. I know sometimes babies, regardless of whether or not they were girls or boys, were dressed in those fancy little gowns for baptism, but we weren't."

Val, who'd been unusually quiet for someone usually so outspoken, finally joined the conversation. "Dad, how could you know that?"

"Because Gerry and I weren't actually baptized until we were older."

"You're kidding?" Lavonne exclaimed. "You never told me that."

George shrugged. "Dad didn't believe in baptism. He didn't believe in organized religion. He believed in God, and the wrath of God against sinners, but he didn't allow Mother to have us baptized. It wasn't until after he died that she did. So we were almost teenagers by then."

"Wow . . . that's crazy, Dad. I had no idea your father was like that. He sounds awfully controlling."

"If you guys came around for dinner more often, you'd know these things," George said, grinning. "But seriously, I'm not being much help here. I suppose the booties could have been for us. What about the receipt for a cemetery plot?"

Jess shook her head. "Unfortunately, it was written in pencil and is barely legible. I've tried, but I can't make out the dates or anything."

"Can you read the name of the cemetery?"

"Yeah, but now I can't remember what it was. I suppose we could try to follow up on it that way. It might be nothing. Maybe it was for Celia's father's grave, or even Beverly's."

"You do have me curious now," George said. "Tonight has stirred up lots of old memories. If you figure anything out about that stuff you found, let me know. And if I remember anything useful, I'll call. Celia lived a long, productive life. I'm sure there were a few skeletons in her closet we'll never know about."

The slap of the back screen door and running of feet served to redirect the conversation.

"Mom!" a voice yelled from the mudroom. "Can you come here? Dylan threw a bomb and Noah tried to catch it but it smacked him in the face. There's blood everywhere!"

Val sighed heavily and pushed back from the table, grabbing up any paper napkins still lying on the table, and shoved them into the pocket of her sweatshirt. "Duty calls," she said. "At least we had time for a bit of conversation before they drew blood again."

CHAPTER 33

Gift of Hindsight

"Tiffany ... this is a pleasant surprise," Will said, trying to keep the *un*pleasant surprise at seeing the woman from showing on his face.

When he was told he had a visitor, he'd expected it to be Jess. She'd called and left him a message about the house selling but hadn't bothered to get any more details to him yet, so he was irritated with her; knowing Jess, she probably gave it away at a ridiculously low price just to spite him. He knew Jess had never really liked the house—and she certainly didn't like him much these days, either.

Pulling his attention back to the woman waiting for him at a table in the visitor center, he sat across from her. She looked different. Better. Like she'd put extra effort into her appearance—something she hadn't done as much of after the baby was born.

"Hello, Will. I hope it's OK, me just showing up like this. It's not like I can just pick up the phone and call you at any time."

"True. So, what brings you by? Have you visited Harper yet?"

Tiffany looked away, first glancing at the other inmates and visitors in the room and then at her feet. She slipped her cardigan off and set it on the bench next to her. When she again lifted her head and met his gaze, her eyes sparkled with unshed tears.

She looks good. The extra baby weight is gone. Maybe if she hadn't shown me this same act too many times in the past, I might actually believe those tears are real, he thought to himself, waiting to see what she was up to this time.

"No, Will, I haven't gone to see our daughter yet. It's too painful. Seeing her with that woman. It wasn't supposed to be like this. We were supposed to be a family—you, me, and Harper. We were supposed to be raising her *together*," Tiffany said, putting extra emphasis on the last word and wringing her hands as if distraught. "Now I'm trying to build a new life for her and me in Chicago, without you ... and you're stuck here behind bars, instead of with us where you belong."

Will did his best to tamp down the frustration he felt rising in his chest. What did he ever see in this woman? She was a whiner and a manipulator. He was quite sure Tiffany was missing his money more than his daughter.

"How are things going in Chicago?" he asked, hoping to shift the conversation and get to the heart of why she was there.

"Challenging," Tiffany replied. "I told you about my job at the hospital, but the hours were *so* demanding. All I did was work. Work and pay rent. I have *no* social life. I haven't made any new friends. It's not at all what I expected."

Will picked up on Tiffany's reference to her nursing job in the past tense.

"Oh? How so, Tiffany?" Will asked, losing interest fast in this conversation but trying to feign it anyway. He had bigger things to worry about now that Jess had sold the house. They'd be cleaning out his office—and he didn't want anyone finding that box in his filing cabinet. Earlier efforts to get it out of there had failed. His contact on the outside refused to break into his house ... didn't want to attract attention. He was running out of options.

Tiffany must have realized she wasn't scoring any sympathy points with Will, complaining about her boring life full of nothing but work while he was stuck in jail. "I'm sorry, honey," she said, looking contrite. "I came today because I *miss* you. My heart is breaking for you. And all I do is complain ... I shouldn't do that."

Will said nothing. He tried to keep a pleasant look on his face while he waited for her to get on with it.

"I drove by the house today. Do you know, not only is there a For Sale sign in the front yard, but it also says SOLD! I was so hoping, someday, the three of us could live there again. I still have some of my things in there, too."

Now Will shook his head. "Tiffany, we've been over this. I told you I can't afford to keep the house now that I'm not working. We have to sell it."

"I was hoping you might have been exaggerating a tiny bit about the money being all gone," Tiffany said, angling her body toward Will to give him a slightly better view of her cleavage. "You are such a successful man. Money was never a problem before."

Will bit the inside of his cheek, doing his best to remain civil.

"When you make the kind of money I do—or *did*—money shouldn't be a problem," he reminded her, gritting his teeth to keep from raising his voice. "But we screwed up. Remember that? And if I didn't work so hard to keep your name out of everything when it was all coming down, you'd probably be laying your pretty little head on a lumpy, piece-of-shit pillow, just like mine, at the women's prison down the road."

Tiffany recoiled from Will's scathing words. She met his eyes briefly and then hung her head. "You're right. I'm so sorry. I owe everything to you. No one has ever taken such good care of me as you did. I shouldn't pester you now."

For the first time in a long time, Will suspected she was finally being sincere. *Too bad it's too late for that.*

A bell rang out, signaling the end of visiting hours.

"You have to leave now, Tiffany. Where will you go next? Are you going to go see Harper?"

Jess was not going to be happy with him if Tiffany kept popping in and out of their lives, raising hell.

Tiffany stood, buttoning her sweater. "I'm still trying to decide."

"Please think of Harper. Our little girl. Don't keep disrupting her life. Tiffany, figure out what you want before you barge in on Jess again."

Tiffany froze, clearly bristling at Will's mention of his wife. She pulled her shoulders back and stood tall, all signs of remorse gone.

"Actually, Will," Tiffany said, finally looking him directly in the eye. "You've helped me decide *exactly* what I want."

With that, she gave him a broad smile that did little to dispel the cold glint in her eyes and turned away, leaving him to his own imagination.

And his imagination scared him.

CHAPTER 34

Gift of Reaction

"*H*ere, put these on so you don't cut your hands," Seth told Nathan as he handed him a pair of work gloves. "You know, I was glad when your mom called and said you wanted to help me with these today."

Nathan shrugged. "I think that old building is pretty cool. The Fisks are trying to fix it up so they can sell the bookstore, right? Besides, I never get the chance to do this type of thing. You know—work with my hands. Dad was never handy, never showed me how to do anything around the house or on the cars. So I apologize in advance if you ask me to hand you a wrench and I hand you a pair of pliers."

Seth laughed. The sarcastic nature of some of Nathan's comments reminded Seth a bit of Jess. *And he doesn't sound like a huge fan of his dad, either.*

"Don't worry about it. I appreciate having a strong young back to help out on something like this. These panels might not feel heavy right now," Seth said, giving the old piece of tin he'd carried out to his truck a slight shake, "but believe me, they start to feel a lot heavier when you're trying to hold them above your head and secure them to a ceiling."

"Glad to help."

"Let's finish loading these and we'll see how glad you are."

Nathan laughed.

"Too bad your mom didn't have time to meet us at the bookstore today," Seth said. His comment earned him an odd look from Nathan, so he added, "I just mean because she's the one who knows the Fisks so well."

Need to be more careful, Seth, he told himself. Just because he was having a hard time getting Jess off his mind didn't mean her kid had to know that.

***

Frank held the door for Seth and Nathan as they wrestled Seth's awkwardly long ladder into the store. It took a bit of maneuvering to get it in place without knocking things over. Virginia was in another corner of the store, engaged in an animated conversation with another elderly woman.

"Never mind them," Frank said. "They'll be back there debating who the best new up-and-coming romance authors are for the next hour. It's a weekly practice of theirs. I really appreciate you guys helping me out with this today. That ceiling has been an eyesore for ten years."

"Happy to help," Seth said. "Nathan was digging around in my shop a while back and mentioned you had damage. I noticed it when I was here last—maybe because he'd said something. Anyhow, when I pulled these out of that old building, I thought they may have matched."

"I suppose you start to develop kind of a sixth sense about things like that, don't you?" Frank said. "I mean, old buildings and all. Have you always been interested in them?"

Seth shrugged, one foot on the bottom rung of his ladder as Nathan waited, holding a ceiling tin against his leg. "I think our dear friend Celia and my grandmother Ruby can take a lot of the credit for my current fascination with old buildings. They were both big in the historical society. I went to a few meetings with them, in fact, when I had to give Grandma a ride, and something just ... sparked. The rest, I guess, is history."

"I liked Ruby."

"I did too. She was good to me. Now, I suppose we better get these tiles up so we aren't in your hair all day," Seth said, anxious to get to work.

"I apologize, young man, I'm holding you up. You two go ahead. I'll quit bothering you now."

"You're not a bother. Stay close, we might need a hand," Seth said, climbing up.

For the next two hours Seth and Nathan wrestled down the old, stained tiles surrounding the hole in the ceiling and got the new ones up in their place. Nathan proved to be a worthy sidekick. Just as Seth was screwing the last tile into place, the little bell over the front door jingled.

"Hey, everyone! I brought lunch," Jess announced, carrying a bag from a local deli.

"Hello, Jessica," Frank said, coming out from behind the sales counter to take the sandwiches from Jess.

"Hello, dear," Virginia greeted her. She'd been resting in the back reading nook with a novel and a cup of tea, tired out from her weekly debate with her old customer.

Nathan gave his mom a grin and held up his grimy hands to her on his way back to the bathroom to clean up. Seth stepped down off the ladder, stowed his drill, and turned back to Jess.

"Well, this is a nice surprise. I thought you were tied up with Patricia," Seth said.

"We were. I think we may have made some progress on our little *mystery*," she replied with a wink only he could see, adding in a low voice, "I'll fill you in later."

Turning back to Virginia, she took both of the woman's hands in hers. "Virginia, I was so sorry to hear your mother passed away. I know Helen was good friends with Celia. I bet they're playing a hot game of bridge in heaven right now."

Virginia squeezed Jess's hands and then gave her a brief hug. "Thank you for your condolences, dear. Mother was blessed to live a long life."

"When did you get home?" Jess asked, more curious than Virginia would have reason to suspect.

"Last night. It was exhausting. Thank goodness for Karen. She did all the strenuous work. I think it helped her get through her grief. You may not be aware of this, dear, but my mother and I seldom saw eye to eye. We weren't very close. My daughter, Karen, on the other hand, thought the sun rose and set on Mother. This has been quite the blow for her. At least she will be well provided for. Mother left her entire estate to Karen."

This surprised Jess, but she tried not to show too much of her shock.

"The whole thing? Does that bother you?"

"Me? No, dear. As I said—Mother and I seldom agreed on things, and many of our disagreements stemmed from her near obsession with material goods. I never understood it. As long as we had enough money to buy food and books, I've always been content."

Frank overheard this last comment and let out a snort.

"My dear Virginia, no one would ever accuse you of being materialistic. A little bit of that woman's money might have helped us get out from under *this* place," Frank said, motioning around him, with emphasis at the new patch in the ceiling. "But I understand you wouldn't have wanted any of her money, even if she'd have left it to you. At least it stays in the family . . . and maybe Karen can use it to redo her kitchen—*again*."

Jess bit the inside of her cheek to stop from laughing.

"Now be nice, dear," Virginia scolded her husband, patting him on the shoulder as she walked back toward the reading nook. "I have bottles of water and paper plates back here. I don't know about the rest of you, but lunch sounds delightful to me."

***

"What time do you want me to pick you up tomorrow?" Seth asked Jess after they'd stowed his gear in his truck. Nathan had run back inside to grab his cell phone. He planned to catch a ride home with Jess.

"Tomorrow?"

"Don't tell me you've already forgotten about our date?" Seth asked.

Nice job, Jess, she thought to herself. *A hunky man asks you out for the first time in* decades *and you forget?*

"Of course I didn't forget," Jess insisted, hoping he'd buy it. "There's just been so much going on . . . I forgot today was Friday."

"Did you find someone to watch Harper?"

"I was going to ask Nathan if he could stay with her. He's coming home with me now, has the weekend off for a change. He said he was just going to do homework, anyway."

Seth nodded, but Jess sensed he had more to say.

"What?"

"Are you going to tell him *why* you need a sitter?"

This gave her pause. She hadn't thought that far yet.

"That's a good question. And yes . . . *yes*, I'll tell him."

"Damn," Seth said.

"Wait, don't you think I should?" Jess folded her arms. "Are you embarrassed to be going on a date with me?"

Seth reached for her hand—discreetly, even though it was doubtful anyone could see them standing between their vehicles. Frank, Virginia, and Nathan were all inside. He tugged her a little closer.

"No, pretty lady, I am not embarrassed. Why would you even say that? It's just . . . I get the impression Nathan was thinking I was kind of a cool guy, you know? He seems to like my shop, and I'd swear he's actually starting to have an interest in old architecture. When he finds out I'm taking his mother out on a date . . . I'll go from cool to jerk, just like that."

"Now why would you say that? He *might* still think you're cool," Jess said—although she had to admit he was probably right.

"If your kids don't like the idea of you dating, will that be a problem for us?" Seth asked, stroking the palm of her hand with his thumb.

"They'll just have to get over it," Jess assured him, giving him a quick, stolen kiss, hoping no one was looking. "It's not like I'm crazy about either of them dating, but I still *let* them."

Seth laughed. "Good point. I guess we all get a little worried when our loved ones let other people in."

Jess inched closer for another, longer kiss. "And with good reason."

***

Nathan wanted to drive and Jess was happy to let him. They picked Harper up from daycare on the way out to the resort.

"Is Lauren coming home for the weekend?" Nathan asked. "I haven't talked to her all week."

"She can't. She has a couple of big tests she's pretty nervous about."

"I remember my first round of tests in college. You don't know what to expect."

Jess nodded, thinking back to her own first year at college. She'd been so young, so naïve. She'd met Will in one of her business classes; he was two years older and pre-med, but he was also getting a minor in business. She could still remember how she felt when he first bothered to talk to her, a lowly freshman.

"Did you?" Nathan asked.

Jess pulled her attention back to their conversation. "I'm sorry, honey. I was thinking back to my own college days. I didn't hear your question."

Back to when your father was a likeable man, she thought with a sigh.

"Never mind," Nathan said as he adjusted the rearview mirror. Then, as if he could read her thoughts, he continued. "What year were you in college when you met Dad?"

"I was a freshman, just like your sister. He was two years older and he swept me off my feet."

Nathan focused on the road ahead, chewing on his bottom lip, a habit since he was young. "I'm sorry, but I just can't imagine you and Dad, all happy and in love in college."

"Believe me, all the years in-between have left the memories pretty fuzzy for me, too. But we truly were in love back in those early years. We both had big dreams."

Nathan glanced at his mother and then back at the road ahead, passing a farm truck as it shot black smoke out of its tailpipe. "That guy needs to get his truck tuned up."

"Some of our dreams *did* come true. It wasn't all a disaster. We got the two of you out of the deal, and I kind of like you."

"I was under the impression Dad was always more focused on his dream of becoming a successful surgeon than on his family. I still can't believe he was stupid enough to screw that up. Screwing up our *family* wasn't as big of a surprise."

Jess debated how best to respond, looking out her window at the passing trees, now taking on the colors of fall.

"I agree with you, Nathan. Over the years, your father . . . he *changed*. I don't know why. He wasn't like this at first. If he had been, I would have walked away. *Stuff* has never been important to me. Status. Money. But thank God I didn't leave him in the early days. If I had, I wouldn't have you and Lauren."

Nathan nodded, but he didn't seem to want to pursue the topic further. He flipped the station on her radio. They listened to music, both lost in their own thoughts. Harper whimpered in her sleep in the backseat. Jess glanced back at her. The baby's pacifier had slipped out, but she settled again, not coming fully awake.

"Say, Nathan, I have a favor to ask. Would you mind watching Harper for a while on Saturday night? I wanted to go out."

"Sure. But will I have to change a diaper?" he asked, grimacing.

Jess laughed. "Probably, but I promise you can handle it."

"Are you and Renee doing something?"

"No. I actually . . . hmm . . . I'm going out on a date."

"Really?!" Nathan asked, turning to look at Jess in surprise.

It all happened in an instant. A motorcycle flashed in front of them, cutting Nathan off. Nathan swerved to miss the bike, but his front right tire got too far onto the shoulder of the road. He fought the steering wheel, trying to get the vehicle back up on the road, but the soft ground gave way. The momentum tipped the vehicle up precariously on the two wheels on the passenger side. For a split second Jess feared they were going to roll, but gravity intervened, slamming them back down the other way. Nathan inched a little farther onto the shoulder so they were off the road and put the car in Park.

Jess quickly checked Nathan and Harper. Thank God everyone had been buckled in. For once she was glad she'd caved when Will insisted on buying her this vehicle. She'd thought the price tag ridiculous, but the roll stability control feature the salesman bragged about may have just saved their lives. At first glance, both kids looked fine. Harper was awake, wide eyes taking in her surroundings as if trying to decide what just woke her. Jess was surprised there were no tears. When she looked back at Nathan, she noticed a small trickle of blood inching out from his hairline, down his forehead.

"Oh no, honey, you're hurt!" she said, fishing a napkin out of the pocket in her door panel and reaching over to blot at the blood.

Nathan captured her wrist and took the napkin from her, dabbing at his forehead himself. "Holy *shit*. That was scary. I'm fine. I think I just banged my head on the steering wheel. Did you see that guy? Where did he come from?"

"I saw him about the same time you did," Jess said, leaning forward to peer through the windshield. "But I don't see him now. He must have kept going. Who knows if the jackass even saw us?"

As the adrenalin wore off, she started to shake. They could have been hurt. Or worse. "Stay put," she ordered, opening her door.

She couldn't see anyone else on the road. There was never much traffic out here. They weren't far from the turnoff to the resort.

The front right tire was flat and the front end was sitting at a weird angle. She couldn't tell if it was because the ground had sunk or the axle was bent. Either way, they wouldn't be driving out of this today.

"I better call Matt," she said, climbing back into her seat. "Front end is messed up."

"I am so sorry, Mom," Nathan said, his face still white. She'd need to have his head wound looked at, too, whether he liked it or not.

"Honey . . . that was *not* your fault. If you wouldn't have swerved, we might have hit that guy. He could have been killed—*we* could have been killed. A wrecked tire is nothing in comparison. You handled it great. I don't know if I'd have been able to do as well."

He nodded, looking slightly reassured.

She called Matt. He'd be there as quickly as he could, he told her, along with a wrecker.

As they waited, Nathan dabbed at his head, but the bleeding had stopped. "So, Mom, what's this business about a date? Who's the lucky guy?"

Deciding to be direct, she looked him square in the eye to watch his reaction.

"I'm going out with Seth."

"Oh . . . I thought you meant you had like a *real* date," Nathan said with a laugh. "Mom, you shouldn't work on a Saturday night. You need to have some fun *sometimes*."

"Nathan, it is a real date."

His smile fell away. "You can't date Seth. He's too young for you."

"No, not really."

"Isn't he closer to my age than yours?"

"He most certainly is not. You are twenty-two. He's thirty-seven and I'm forty-five. You're a senior in college—do the math."

"Ha-ha, Mom. I thought he was younger than that. But still . . . that just seems, I don't know, *weird*."

Jess understood—better than Nathan probably thought she did.

"Honey, I don't know that it matters if it's Seth or some other guy. I understand it's weird to think about your mother going out on a date with someone. But don't you think it's time I *maybe* try to put myself out there a little? You said it yourself—I don't have enough fun."

"I guess," he replied, clearly less than thrilled with the idea.

They were saved from further conversation on the topic when a tow truck pulled in ahead of them. Matt rolled up behind them in his patrol car.

"Everybody OK?" he asked again, although Jess had already tried to assure him they were when she called. He opened up Harper's door and checked her over as well as he could while she was still strapped in her car seat. She babbled at him in recognition and tugged at his hair. "Yep, she's fine," he said with a laugh, taking her out of the seat. "How about you two?"

Nathan got out and joined Matt and Harper on the shoulder of the road, holding his arms out to show he was fine. Jess got out, pointed to the little cut on Nathan's head. Matt inspected the wound, looked him over, and asked him a few questions. Matt thought Nathan would be fine, but if he developed a headache, he said, they should go in.

Matt handed Harper to Jess and walked around the vehicle, inspecting the damage.

"So what happened?"

Nathan gave his recount and then Jess did the same, but Matt didn't recognize the description of the motorcycle. "Hate to say it, but we may never know who pulled out in front of you."

Jess shook her head. "It probably doesn't matter. No one got hurt. That's the important thing." Jess reached over and squeezed Nathan's shoulder then kissed Harper's forehead. *Thank God the kids are all right.*

CHAPTER 35

Gift of Romance

What does a girl wear out on a date these days?
Jess wasn't even sure where they were going.

She was so nervous she could die.

"Mom, Seth's here!" Nathan hollered up the steps.

Crap!

Instead of guessing what she should wear, she decided to just go ask him what they were doing. She found Nathan and Seth out on the front porch, talking. Seth turned toward her when she let the screen door slam.

"Hi, ready to go?" he asked.

She took in his jeans, boots, and blue button-down, sleeves rolled up; then she looked down at the sweatshirt and ratty jeans she still wore. "I just need to get dressed real quick, but I wasn't sure what we were going to do."

Nathan looked between Seth and his mom, gave a little shake of his head, and left them to figure out their date night without him.

"Is he all right with this?" Seth asked once it was just the two of them still on the porch.

Jess grimaced. "You were right. He thought it was weird at first, but I think he'll be fine."

Seth took a step toward her, a wicked grin on his face. She took a similar-size step backward, keeping a respectable distance between them. "Don't push it."

"I know, I was just kidding."

"So? What are we going to do tonight? I'll run in and get dressed so we can go."

"It's a surprise. But we have reservations for 6:30, so you better hurry. Why don't you just go with jeans and a sweater, maybe comfortable shoes? It'll be cool, too, so grab a jacket."

"Interesting. Now you have me curious. OK, I'll be right back."

True to her word, Jess was back in five minutes. She'd slipped her lucky arrowhead into her jeans pocket. Lauren had told her it would protect her from further heartbreak. She could use some protection in the romance department.

Seth gave her a hand into his pickup and he drove north.

"*Now* do I get to find out where we're going?"

Seth spared a glance at her as he drove. "Do you have your sea-legs with you this evening?"

Jess looked down at her jean-encased legs in confusion and back at Seth.

"I've been known to be pretty sea-worthy," she replied, "but there isn't a sea within driving distance tonight."

Seth laughed. "Well, it's the best I could do, OK? I heard about this riverboat cruise they do at sunset and thought it might be fun. I enjoyed our canoe ride, and this seemed like a logical next step."

Jess beamed. "That *does* sound like fun! The leaves are turning, too, so I bet the scenery will be great."

Seth reached over and took her hand. "I bet it will be," he said.

Her hand felt right in Seth's, which was much larger, rougher. She glanced down at the scars crisscrossing the back of his hand.

"What did you do to your hands to get them so scarred up?" she asked, tracing the finger of her other hand over one of the more prominent scars.

"Too many jobs without bothering to put on gloves, I guess. Stained glass is not forgiving, either."

She nodded and sat back, trying to relax. *Why am I so nervous tonight? I've spent lots of time with Seth lately.* Maybe because she couldn't help but remember what those scarred hands felt like against her bare skin—hands so different from Will's.

Stop comparing Seth to Will, she scolded herself. *Seth is nothing like him.*

"Everything OK?" Seth asked. "You're awfully quiet."

"Just a little nervous," Jess admitted with a shrug.

Seth brought the hand he still held up to his lips, kissing each of her fingers gently.

"It'll be fun," he assured her.

She smiled. "I know."

***

After one wrong turn, they found the boat landing. The parking lot was full—not a surprise on a beautiful September evening like this. It wouldn't be long before the nights were too cold for riverboat cruising. Seth found a parking spot and they hurried to the loading dock, boarding the double-decker vessel with only minutes to spare.

"Good thing you told me to wear comfortable shoes, or else I wouldn't have any sea-legs," Jess laughed.

Seth led her to the bar below. "What would you like to drink?"

A few minutes later they stood on the upper level against an iron railing, enjoying a blood red sunset. The sun lit up the burgundy- and crimson-colored oak leaves lining the riverbank, tempered with golden asp. Jess sipped her glass of white wine while Seth nursed his red.

"This was a wonderful idea, Seth. Thank you."

"You are very welcome, Jess," Seth said, dropping a light kiss on her nose. "It is pretty up here, isn't it?"

"Hard to imagine how much this will change in the next couple of months."

Seth nodded. He started to chuckle.

"What?"

"I was just remembering the look on your face when you fell onto your backside in the lot out at my shop last winter. It was glare ice. God, you scared me. You could have broke your neck."

"As I recall, you didn't seem too worried. You had some kind of smart-alecky comment, of course, but it never occurred to me you might have *actually* been concerned. How sweet!"

"Yeah, well, I did still think you were a pain in the butt back then. So bossy."

"And when did that change?" Jess asked, bumping him gently with a hip.

"I'd say when you barged in on me in the shower."

Jess laughed, raising a finger to object. "*Technically* you were out of the shower by then."

Seth looped his arm loosely around Jess's waist and together they enjoyed the last of the colors as the sun quickly dipped below the horizon. A bell chimed below.

"That would be dinner," he said. "Shall we?"

Together they headed down to the dining room below. Their table for two was on the perimeter of the room, along the glass windows. A few fading smudges of pink and coral were still visible on the horizon as the moon and stars started to wink on.

"Wow . . . Seth, you know how to spoil a lady," Jess said, holding Seth's gaze. His blue shirt made his eyes appear a brighter green than usual behind his glasses, the lenses reflecting the light from the candle between them. It had gotten cool upstairs in the open, but it was warm and cozy in the dining room. The smell of freshly baked bread rose from the basket of rolls on the table.

"I had to order our meals when I made the reservations. I hope you don't mind, but I picked the walleye for us both."

"Sounds perfect. So, Seth . . . I've been dying to update you on what Patricia and I found when going through the books yesterday. But," she added, "I understand if you don't want to talk business tonight."

"Are you kidding? You've had me curious ever since the bookstore. Let's hear it!"

Jess set her wine glass down and leaned in slightly. "We found a pattern. I agreed with Patricia when she showed me the trending information she'd pulled together. They'd been adding new customers and growing their revenue over the years, but it just seemed like their expenses were *also* increasing, and more than they should have been, so their bottom line didn't grow much. We started finding checks, written out once a month or so, for various amounts, to a business that sounded like a temp agency. Homes Sparkle paid them almost $100,000 over a seven-year timespan. Individual checks were never over a thousand dollars—I think that's why it didn't hit anyone's radar. It's such a labor-intensive business, payroll costs are high and can vary quite a bit. There were also a few checks to a different temp agency."

"So why are you thinking the payments weren't legitimate, if they used temp agencies?"

"The checks in question were all made out to a place called Temp Angels. I tried to find a local business under that name, but I couldn't find anything."

Jess paused when a woman brought their meals, setting a plate of food in front of each of them. It smelled delicious. As the waitress stepped away, Seth asked, "Is it possible the business just isn't around anymore? Maybe they closed."

"I thought that at first, too, but now I don't think so. There were checks made out to them as recently as *this year*."

Not wanting their food to get cold, Jess paused in her storytelling so they could start on their meals. "This tastes as good as it smells," Jess said, savoring the lightly breaded fish, likely caught in this very lake.

"It *is* good," Seth agreed. "So who wrote the checks out?"

Jess laughed. *The man wants answers as much as I do.*

"Guess."

"Karen?"

"Karen."

"Wow . . ." Seth set his fork down and sat back in his chair. "That almost seems too easy."

Jess shrugged. "Sometimes the most brilliant plans are the simplest. Because Homes Sparkle is such a small operation, Karen, as their outside accountant, helped them pay some of their bills. Remember, until recently, this was a mom-and-pop-type operation. It's not like they're big enough to have a bunch of internal controls. I'm sure they trusted Karen."

"So it's looking like Celia had nothing to do with it?"

"That's right. Celia died in October of 2015. This has been going on for years, but it continued *after* her death."

"And Patricia . . . what is she thinking about all of this?"

"I convinced her to keep it between us for now. I want to see if I can get a copy of a few of the checks to see where they were deposited. Wendy, her sister, handles most of the staffing for Homes Sparkle and had never heard of Temp Angels."

"What's next?"

"Like I said, we want to see if we can figure out where the checks were deposited. Then I suppose we'll need to talk to Patricia's parents, decide if we should involve the authorities."

"At that dollar amount, you'd almost have to. Besides, Karen works with lots of businesses in town. What if this isn't the only one she's stolen from? If this all turns out to be true, of course. We already know she stole from the Corner Market years ago."

Jess nodded. "I know. This kind of feels like a small piece of what could be a bigger problem. I feel sorry for Frank and Virginia. This could devastate them. Their only daughter . . ."

They ate in silence for a bit. Neither wanted to see the kind old couple suffer because of their daughter.

"I'm glad you've made some progress in untangling this mess," Seth said. "It sucks Patricia was right and someone probably has been stealing from their business, but I'm relieved it's looking like Celia wasn't involved. Glad Karen never got her sticky fingers in *my* business."

"Right? I'm still surprised Celia continued to work with Karen. There must be something more to it—but with both Celia and Helen gone, we may never know the whole story. Maybe, after the Corner Market episode, Celia always had a bit of a trust issue where Karen was concerned. That's probably why she never had you use her accounting services."

Seth raised his wine glass. "Cheers, Celia."

"And I would hope Karen wouldn't steal from her own parents' bookstore. I didn't see anything unusual there."

Seth set his glass down and picked a roll out of the basket on the table. Jess handed him the butter dish.

"Speaking of the bookstore, any leads on a buyer for Frank? I know you said he wanted to be out before the end of the year, and it's already September." Seth tore the roll in half, setting part of it down on his plate. He buttered the other half and handed it to Jess.

"Honestly, I haven't had any time to help him look. Got any ideas?" she asked, accepting the bread with a smile of thanks.

"Let me think about it," Seth said. "Are you guys set on wanting it to continue as a bookstore? Because the building itself has some potential. It could be repurposed."

"I would hate to see the bookstore close. There just aren't enough places like that around anymore. I understand the appeal and convenience of eBooks and online shopping, but can you imagine not being able to actually walk through a physical bookstore, to see and hold the books in your hand, talk with a real live sales clerk who can make recommendations of favorite new books? Local authors can get a bit of a start through indie stores, too—book signings, that kind of thing."

Seth grinned at Jess's enthusiasm. "I get it. I do. But what about the bigger box stores, like Barnes and Noble? How can a place like the Fisks' compete with both online giants like Amazon and local mammoths like Barnes and Noble?"

Jess took a sip of the hot coffee brought with their dessert. "It's tough. But it can't be easy for the Barnes and Nobles of the world either. They have a higher overhead. Nathan works at one. He said the inventory they carry is unreal, and they have to turn those books to keep the lights on. Other big chains have already closed."

"It's not going to be easy, that's for sure, but I do hope you find someone to take over for the Fisks. Whoever does will probably have to do more than just sell books. They might need a new angle in order to keep *their* lights on."

Their conversation drifted off into lighter topics, and their two-hour cruise passed quickly.

Once back in Seth's truck, Jess called home to check on things. Seth got the impression, based on Jess's end of the conversation, that Nathan might be having a little trouble with Harper.

"Need to call it a night?" he asked when she hung up.

"I really don't want to . . ." Jess said. "But she's fussy. I think she's cutting teeth, maybe running a low-grade temp."

"Why don't we go back out to the resort? You're going to be worried if we don't."

She sighed. "I'm sorry, Seth. I really am."

"No problem. But it's still early. Maybe I could come in for a night cap?"

She looked at him. "Seth, Nathan is there."

At this Seth laughed. "I know that, Jess. I wasn't implying anything. What do you take me for? Actually, don't answer that . . . I'm just not quite ready to go home yet. I haven't been out on a date on a Saturday night for a long time."

As Seth started up his pickup, Jess placed a hand on his forearm. "Thank you, Seth."

He paused from shifting into Reverse. "For what?"

"For reminding me there's more to life than work and kids."

In the darkened cab, Jess clicked her seatbelt off, leaned over the center console, and kissed him. He turned off the truck, put his arms around her, and kissed her back. The divider between the bucket seats proved problematic, not allowing them to get comfortably close.

"This is when I miss my old Ford," Seth said with a groan. "A bench seat is much more conducive to making out."

Jess gave up and plopped back down in her own seat. "I suppose we could wait for all this traffic to get out and crawl in the back," she suggested—mostly kidding. What was it about this guy that made her think like a teenager again?

Seth gave a belly laugh. "Tempting as that sounds, I don't think that would be much better. I had thought about stopping out at the shop and showing you my new shipment of stained glass, but we better get you home. The old couch upstairs *is* comfortable, but . . ."

Jess started to giggle, and once she started, she had a hard time stopping. Seth backed out of their parking spot and drove out of the lot, heading back toward Whispering Pines.

Her laugh was contagious. "What's so funny?"

"No guy has ever offered to show me his *glass collection* to entice me over to his place."

"Another time, perhaps," he teased. "You'd love the new green shades."

***

Nathan was pacing the floor with Harper when they got back, relief evident on his face as he handed his fussy little sister over to Jess.

"We had fun at first," he said, shaking his head. "She loves that baby swing you hung up in the backyard. But then she started getting tired, and when we came in and I tried to give her a bottle, she wouldn't take it. Been fussing ever since."

"Oh, poor baby . . ." Jess placed the palm of her hand on the baby's forehead. "She feels a little warm. Let me see," she said to Harper as she tried to look into her mouth. Harper wasn't about to let her do that, throwing her head from side to side. Jess quickly ran her finger over Harper's gums. "Yep, I can feel a tiny bit of sharp on the bottom," she said, letting the baby bite down on her finger and walking over to the freezer. She pulled her finger out, wiped it off on the leg of her pants, and dug a teething ring out of the inside door, handing it to Harper. The baby popped it in her mouth, intuitively knowing what to do with it.

Harper stopped fussing almost immediately.

Seth and Nathan watched, both clearly in awe.

"How did you do that?" Nathan asked.

"Years of practice, dear," Jess assured him. "Thanks for watching her."

"Where did you guys go?"

"Seth actually lined up a riverboat dinner cruise. It was fun."

"Really?" Nathan asked in surprise. "I wouldn't have thought of something like that. I might have to steal that idea . . ."

"Feel free," Seth said, grinning at the younger man. "You seeing someone?"

Nathan shrugged. "Not really."

This was news to Jess. *Not really,* in Nathan's language, wasn't the same as *no.*

"But . . . ?" Jess tried to encourage him to continue, but Nathan had always been notoriously close-mouthed about any relationships he might be in.

"There's nothing to tell yet, Mother. So don't try to weasel anything out of me. When there *is* something to tell, you'll be the first to know."

Jess laughed. "I bet."

"I have an online quiz I need to do this weekend, and I know you said we have to go over to the house and start packing things up tomorrow. Mind if I go take it now?"

"Of course not, go ahead," Jess said. "And thanks again, honey, for watching her. It was nice to get out a little tonight."

"No problem. It was a good reminder, though, that I am *so* not ready for kids and all that yet. They're a lot of work. See ya later," he said, and he headed upstairs.

"He's a good kid," Seth said after Nathan was out of hearing range.

"He is. They both are. That's one area I got *really* lucky in. Other parts of my life may be a hot mess, but at least Lauren and Nathan don't give me too much trouble."

Seth nodded and made his way over to the fridge. "Got anything cold to drink in here? A beer, maybe?"

"Sure, help yourself."

Voices out on the front porch caught their attention.

"Sounds like Renee and Matt are home. Do you feel like company? I could invite them over."

"Yeah, OK. Here, I can take the baby if you want to go talk to them," Seth offered, setting his unopened beer bottle down.

Jess nodded and handed Harper over to him, relieved to see he seemed perfectly comfortable with the little girl. Harper continued gnawing on her frozen toy but reached up with her other hand to touch Seth's glasses. He caught her hand, effortlessly distracting her before she could try to grab the glasses off his face.

Renee and Matt came over when Jess popped her head out the front door to invite them in. Introductions were made, the two men shaking hands. Renee and Seth had already met.

Renee explained that they'd been at a potluck for parents of the kids wanting to play basketball in the upcoming season. They'd met some fun people and Renee was hopeful Robbie would get to play this year, after missing last year with a broken arm.

Jess told them about their dinner cruise and coming back a little early because Harper was fussy.

"So Nathan's feeling OK after your accident yesterday, then? No headaches?"

"What accident?" Seth asked, both surprise and concern in his voice.

Jess groaned. "Oh! I'm sorry, I forgot to tell you. After we left the bookstore yesterday, we had a little incident on our way home. It all turned out all right—other than a couple of lost hours today getting my tire fixed. No one got hurt."

"Jeez, Jess, I can't believe you forgot to tell me you had a car accident," Seth said. There was an awkward pause in which the others realized he was genuinely upset.

"With so much going on," Jess said, "I guess I forgot about it. Or, more likely, I blocked it out of my mind. Nathan was driving and a guy on a motorcycle cut him off. We almost rolled. It could have been much worse. Seeing as how I have plenty of drama in my life these days, I'm just thankful we were all fine. Nathan bumped his head on the steering wheel and there was a little blood, but no other damage . . . other than to my tire."

"Girl, you never have a dull day, do you?" Seth asked Jess, shaking his head.

"If you're going to hang around this family, you better get used to it," Matt said, chuckling. "They certainly keep *me* on my toes."

"Speaking of keeping you on your toes, Matt . . . did Renee mention the issue with Celia? We probably need to pick your brain a bit."

The rest of the evening was spent updating Renee on what they'd discovered and getting input from Matt regarding how they should handle things with Karen.

CHAPTER 36

Gift of Moving On

"Mom, what am I going to do with all these old clothes?" Lauren asked, staring into her large walk-in closet in dismay. "Most of this doesn't fit anymore."

Jess came to stand beside Lauren and peered into the closet. "When you grow six inches in your last few years of high school, that's what happens," she said, looking up at her daughter. "If you'd asked me that question three years ago, I would have said to donate it all. You should still donate some of it, but you probably need to go through and pull out the things you think you can sell at that teen store down on fortieth. You know, the one that buys higher-end clothes and resells them?"

"I love that place. Do I get to keep the money?" Lauren asked.

"You do, but it has to go toward school. Got it?"

Lauren nodded. "So I *don't* get to keep the money. Got it."

With Lauren facing a few hours of work on her closet, Jess went to check on Nathan. The three of them planned to spend the day at the old house, packing up as much as they could; then everyone else in the family would help them move out the following weekend.

She found him in the garage.

"What are you doing out here, bud?"

"Oh, hey, Mom. I thought I would pack up Dad's tools. Remember when he bought this big red Craftsman tool chest and filled it up that summer? Said we'd work on my bike and maybe build a tree fort? Never happened. Most of these tools have never even been used. What should we do with 'em?"

Jess pulled open one of the drawers in the chest. It slid open easily to reveal a vast array of different-size screwdrivers neatly arranged inside. She shook her head. What a waste. She remembered that summer. Nathan was around twelve, desperate to do something with his dad. Will was all in at the beginning, making big promises but never following through.

She said, "I'm going to rent a storage unit for most of his things so he has them when he gets out. But he never used any of this. Got any ideas? Should we sell it? It's probably worth quite a bit."

Nathan shrugged, the idea of selling all the tools not seeming to sit well with him. "I wish I had somewhere to store them. I'd love to have these," he said as he pulled open the various drawers and gazed at the tools.

"If you want them, you should keep them, Nathan. We'll figure out somewhere we can store them until you have a place of your own. Deal?"

"Deal. I'd appreciate that, Mom. Maybe I can build a tree house for my own kid someday," he said, grabbing a packing box from the pile just inside the garage in Jess's old parking spot. "Hey, what are you going to do with Bugaboo?"

Jess turned to her old Volkswagen, hidden under the tan tarp in the far stall. Nathan had called it *Bugaboo* for as long as she could remember. Each kid had begged to be allowed to drive it when they got their license, but Jess couldn't let it go. What would she do with it now? She couldn't afford to pay to store it anywhere—she was already facing a bill to store *Will's* things.

"I haven't figured that out yet . . ." She was starting to feel overwhelmed again with all the decisions she'd have to make over the next couple of weeks.

"Here, let's take the tarp off," Nathan said. "See if she'll still start."

Together they wrestled the heavy covering off, stowing it in a corner. Jess still loved the sky-blue color of her old car. She ran her hand over the fender, thinking back to when she'd helped her dad paint it. He'd taught her some basics and let her pick the color. The blue complemented the ivory interior.

"Where are the keys?"

"They should be hanging on the hooks in the mudroom," Jess said. "Just a sec."

She went in through the door from the garage into the back entryway. Sure enough, the keys were hanging there, her old key-ring from her college alma mater making them easy to spot. Other keys hung there as well. She'd need to figure out what they were all for at some point.

"Found 'em," she said, tossing them to her son. "Give it a try."

The driver door creaked in protest as Nathan climbed in. It took a couple of tries, but the engine turned over, coughing and firing black smoke out the tailpipe. It had sat a long time.

Waving her arms to try to dispel the exhaust, she pointed out to the driveway. "Back it out before we get asphyxiated!"

Nathan popped it into Reverse and moved the old car. His stick-shift driving abilities were rusty—the car died once, but he got it going again and moved out of the garage.

"Let's put the top down," Nathan said, climbing out. "You could probably convince me to take it to pick us up some lunch."

"Oh, I could *convince* you, could I?" Jess laughed. "Do you remember how to put it down?"

Together they figured it out, even though she hadn't messed with the top in years.

Even though it was technically *her* car, Will had taken it out once or twice a year, but Jess hadn't driven it in a long time. She was surprised to see two tubs stacked in the small backseat. She reached in and took the plastic lid off the tub on top. It was full of what looked like Will's old medical books.

"Weird," Jess said, trying to wrestle one of the tubs out of the backseat. "Looks like your dad stuck some stuff in here. These should go to his storage shed. Nathan, help me get these out of here, will you? They're heavy. Can you set them up against the wall there?"

"Sure. Books? Do you think he'll ever need these again?"

Jess shrugged. She'd decide by next weekend what would stay and what would go. She had too much to get through today to worry about it.

Once they'd emptied the car of Will's tubs, Nathan said, "You know, Mom, maybe Seth would have room for Bugaboo out at his shop. He has some extra buildings out there that look like garages. I wonder if he'd have a spot for her. She doesn't take up much room."

"I hate to ask him to do that . . ." Jess replied, eyeing her old vehicle. God, she loved her Bug. It was the one thing from her early days she wouldn't dream of parting with. "Maybe you're right, maybe Seth wouldn't mind. I'll give him a call."

***

Hours later, Jess was feeling good about their progress. The kitchen was packed up, as were the kid's bedrooms, both family rooms, and the dining room. She had yet to tackle her old bedroom or bathroom, though, and it was nearly five o'clock. She knew she'd been stalling, getting everything else done first.

A vehicle pulled into the driveway and a door slammed, giving her another excuse to avoid the inevitable. She could hear the kids down in the basement, presumably packing up the movie room as she'd asked them to. She went outside to see who'd pulled in.

"Hey, Jess," Seth greeted her as she opened the garage door. "So where's this old car you called me about?" He whistled when he caught sight of it, now parked back in its regular spot. "Sweet!"

Jess laughed as she met him beside the car. "Me or Bugaboo?" she teased, pushing her hair back from her face. She knew she was a mess from packing all day.

Seth didn't seem to mind, pulling her close for a kiss. "Why, *you* of course. But the car is pretty cool, too." Then, giving her a funny look, he said, " 'Bugaboo'?"

She laughed, pulling back. "Isn't she pretty?" Jess said, pride in her voice. "I've had her since high school. My dad bought her for me and we fixed her up together. Painted her and everything."

Seth circled the convertible, its top still down from Nathan's earlier food run. "I can't believe how good of shape she's still in. What is it, a '79?"

"No, '78. I know, I'm surprised I was able to keep it this nice. She was my main mode of transportation all through high school and college, even up until Nathan was born. Then I needed something bigger."

"I can't believe those two kids of yours didn't talk you out of it when they started driving."

"Oh, believe me, they tried. But I stuck to my guns. It doesn't get driven much anymore. Will used to take it to the golf course once or twice in the summer, just to run it and keep things working."

"When was the last time it was driven?"

Jess checked her watch. "Five hours ago. Nathan talked me into letting him drive it to pick up lunch."

"Nice. Well, at least we know she'll start. You're more than welcome to move it out to my shop. I have a garage in the back with an open stall. I haven't had any trouble with people breaking in, but I suppose there aren't any guarantees. As long as you're OK with that, feel free."

"Seth, you have no idea how much I appreciate that. And I can pay you to store it, too."

He waved away the notion. "Jess, the stall is empty. Don't worry about it. Just keep storage insurance on it, just in case. How is the rest of your packing going?"

"We've had a productive day. The kids are in the basement now, but I better send them on the road. They both have class tomorrow and it's getting late."

"Are you ready to call it a day, too?"

"Not quite. I still need to pack up our bedroom and bathroom. To be honest, I've been avoiding it. Too much baggage, I guess."

Seth nodded in understanding. "Why don't you get started on it and I'll run and pick us up a pizza? I'll come back and help you finish so you aren't here all night by yourself."

"If you don't mind, that sounds great. All this physical labor has me hungry again."

"Should I get enough for the kids, too?"

"No, I'll give them each some money and they can pick something up when they get back to their places. Unlike me, they've been snacking all afternoon."

"Great," Seth said, giving her a quick kiss before turning for his vehicle. "See you in a bit."

Jess stretched her head side to side and rolled her shoulders. She was stiff from all the work but did not want these last two rooms hanging over her head. Now the task before her didn't seem quite so daunting. She talked to Nathan and Lauren, helped them load a few things into their cars, and sent them on their way.

She took a stack of empty boxes back to her old bedroom and dumped Will's clothes into them, labeled each one as "Will's clothes." He could sort through them later—she wasn't going to bother now. She'd already taken most of her clothes. She did find a section of hanging clothes and a few pairs of shoes on the floor—women's clothing—that didn't belong to her.

"And there you have it," she said out loud. The presence of *the other woman* she'd been dreading.

"Talking to yourself back here?" Seth said, coming into the bedroom with a pizza in one hand and two cold beers in the other.

"Oh God, you scared me!" Jess said, her hand over her heart. "I didn't hear you come in. Look," she said, pointing to the only clothes left hanging on the rack. "Looks like Tiffany forgot a few things."

"Ouch," he said. "That's kind of rough. I'm sorry you have to deal with this, Jess. Every time you turn around you have reminders of your ex."

"I figured there'd be something in here. Let's hope this is it. If I find a drawer full of sexy lingerie, *you* can deal with it."

Seth shot her a look, obviously not comfortable with that idea. "Why don't we eat first, and then we can tackle this last bit together?" He found a towel in the adjoining bathroom, laid it down on the carpet, and set the pizza on top of it. "We can pretend we're on a picnic," he joked.

"I can honestly say I've never eaten pizza in my bedroom," Jess laughed. "Thank you, Seth."

"For what?" he asked, flipping the pizza box open.

"For distracting me so I can get this done without too much drama." Jess sat down next to Seth, picked up a beer, and popped it open, taking a sip. "I don't normally like beer, but beer and pizza sounds perfect. Will would *flip* if he knew we were doing this in our old room."

Seth set his beer down on a bedside table and took Jess's can from her. He set it next to his, walked back on his knees to her side and pulled her up against him. "What would upset him more . . . me or the pizza?"

"That is a *great* question. I suspect it would be you."

Seth cut off their conversation with a kiss, his hands running up and down Jess's body. The pizza was forgotten. As need began to course through her, Jess pulled back.

"Is it childish of me to want to fool around with you in here, just to get back at him for everything he did to me, to our family?"

Seth shook his head. "No. It's perfectly understandable. My only hope is that he isn't the *only* reason you want to fool around with me."

Jess laughed and proceeded to show him her feelings went well beyond a little jab at her ex. "Just let's stay off the bed. I'm going to burn that thing."

CHAPTER 37

Gift of Inquisitiveness

*P*atricia managed to get copies of some of the canceled checks Karen issued to Temp Angels. She showed them to Jess first thing on Thursday.

"I kind of expected to see the checks deposited into an account at Karen's husband's bank."

"Her husband has a bank?" Patricia asked, surprised.

"Well, his family owns the bank, he runs it. But per this stamp on the back, the checks were deposited at Eastern Hills State Bank over in Alexandria. I suppose if she was doing something funny with checks made out to a business, trying to deposit them at a bank where everyone knows you would be risky."

Patricia handed one of the copies she'd been studying back to Jess. "I finally found an address listed for Temp Angels in our records last night. I thought that said Alexandria, too. Let me check."

She fired up her laptop. Jess studied the rest of the check copies while Patricia opened her notes.

"These were all deposited at the same bank," Jess observed.

"Yep, here it is. Same town as Eastern Hills State Bank. About half an hour from here."

Jess pulled her phone out again and, peering over Patricia's shoulder, typed the street address into Google Earth. She zoomed in as far as she could. "Well, *that's* not going to be very helpful."

"What?"

Jess handed Patricia her phone. "Looks like that might be one of those mailing stores. The sign says 'Going Postal.' "

"What if we drive over there, talk to some people at both the mailing address and the bank? Someone might be able to tell us something. I just feel like we need a little more evidence before talking to my parents, and especially before we talk to Karen."

"It might be worth a shot," Jess agreed. "Do you have time this afternoon? I'm going to be tied up tomorrow and over the weekend, but I know we need to get some answers here soon."

"I could go. I just need to be back by six."

"And *I* need to be back by 5:15, or I'll have to pay extra at daycare."

Patricia paused, surprised. "Oh, I didn't know you had a little one. Or is it a grandchild?"

Lady, you just lost any points you'd managed to build up since we started working together on this, Jess thought. She wasn't old enough to be a grandmother. Maybe a really *young* grandmother, but Patricia should have known better than to say that.

"I'm watching a baby for a . . . friend."

I need to practice how to respond to questions about Harper.

Jess's face must have given her away.

"Oh God, I'm sorry, Jess. I didn't mean to imply I thought you *could* be a grandmother. It's just . . . I thought your kids were older," Patricia stammered.

"Forget it. Come on. I'll drive." Jess gave her a wry smile. "Unless you're worried I'm too *old.*"

***

Jess's GPS took them straight to the bank. As she pulled up, she thought it *looked* like an old bank. Inside, the tall ceilings and tile flooring made sounds echo like they were in a cavern. Jess's heels clicked across the floor as they made their way to the bank manager's desk, after receiving directions from someone at the teller line.

Jess extended her hand to the elderly man who stood at their approach. She didn't give him their real names. She kept her explanation brief as to the reason for their visit, stating only that they were attempting to get in contact with someone from Temp Angels. They needed to pay them for their services but, unfortunately, they'd misplaced their address and were not having any luck finding the information. They were hopeful someone at Eastern Hills might be able to help, since they could see their last check was deposited here. "Do they perhaps have an account here?" Jess asked.

"Now, dear, I'm sure you understand the need for us to protect our customer's privacy," the man said, giving her a stern look. "I'm not at liberty to share that type of information."

"Oh, I hadn't even considered that," Jess said, trying to keep her tone light. His condescending tone set her teeth on edge, but she knew better than to let it show. "We just really want to get in touch with the woman we've worked with in the past. We feel terrible, not being able to get a check to her."

The man paused, seeming to consider how best to address the situation. "I understand, dear . . . since I can't divulge account ownership information, why don't you leave your name and number, and the next time he stops in, I can give it to him."

So much for not being able to tell me whether or not Temp Angels has an account here, Jess thought, pleased with herself.

"While I appreciate the offer, sir, I'm afraid we can't wait that long. We'll try another avenue," Jess said, standing to make their escape. Patricia did likewise. "Thank you for your time today."

They clicked their way back across the marble-tiled floor and out into the fall sunshine.

"Jeez, playing Nancy Drew makes me nervous," Jess commented as she climbed back into her vehicle. "If that old coot called me *dear* one more time . . ."

"Well, that was a bust," Patricia complained, slumping in the passenger seat. "But what's with the fake names? I have to admit, that was brilliant."

"I don't think it was a total bust," Jess said, grinning at what she thought was an actual compliment from Patricia. "Did you notice how the bank officer said he would give *him* our contact information the next time *he* stops in? He pretty much told us they have an account there. I wonder if the 'he' was a mistake or if it really is a man doing their banking."

"I didn't even catch that. Interesting. Do you want to stop by the other place now?"

"Sure," Jess said, starting the vehicle and putting the next address in her GPS. "It's only a couple of blocks away. Maybe they won't be quite so close-mouthed there."

***

"I'm sorry, I can't talk about our customers. I could lose my job," the young woman behind the counter said when Jess asked who normally picked up mail at this address for Temp Angels. "Company policy is very specific about that."

"We would never want you to do or say anything that would put your job at risk," Jess said, trying to come up with an angle she could use to get any type of information out of the woman. She was determined not to go home empty-handed. "Have you worked here long?"

"Three years," the woman replied. "It's the longest I've worked anywhere. It can be kind of boring most days, but some of the customers keep it interesting."

"I bet," Jess said. "What type of clientele do you see most days?"

"All kinds, really. Business people, young people who don't have a permanent address, some people who seem a little shady . . . you know, the kind you don't *want* to know what they're sending and receiving in the mail . . . that kind of thing."

"Oh, I never even thought about that," Jess said, doing her best to sound fascinated and keep the woman talking.

Patricia shot her a look, probably wondering why Jess was making idle chitchat with the woman.

Jess ignored her and continued. "I was so hoping we might be able to figure something out today. You see, me and my friend here, we're in trouble at work and we're desperate for answers. We don't want to lose *our* jobs."

"What does that have to do with Going Postal? You seem like nice ladies. I wouldn't want you to lose your jobs either."

"Well, it wouldn't have anything to do with your store, not directly. You see, we work in bookkeeping, and we're afraid something happened with the last check we sent to Temp Angels. I thought I made the check out for $1,000 . . . but it was cashed for *ten thousand dollars.* I'm trying to figure out if I made a mistake or if the check was altered on their end."

The woman's eyebrows shot up. "Oh, it *had* to have been a mistake, there's no way he would change your check. He wasn't like that."

"He?" Jess prodded.

"Darn it. I've probably already said too much," the clerk said.

"I promise we won't tell anyone you helped us. Don't worry. Can't you help us save our jobs?"

"Look, I'm not going to give you a name. But the guy who picked up the mail for Temp Angels did not seem the type to cheat anyone. He was way too nice. Pretty cute, too. How long ago did you say this happened?"

Jess's mind raced. She noticed the woman kept referring to whoever the guy was in the past tense.

"Last month. The problem with the check just surfaced now when the owner did the bank statement. I'm so scared . . . what if I messed up?"

The woman seemed to buy this timeline. "Well, you know, I noticed the guy who was picking up their mail hasn't been around for a while. He used to come in every Wednesday. I was kind of hoping he was going to ask me out. But lately some lady has been coming in instead. She doesn't say much, not nearly as friendly. I only noticed her because one week she got a package delivered here that didn't fit in her box so she came up to the counter to sign for it. I asked her what happened to the guy, but she didn't say much. My Wednesdays aren't nearly as fun anymore."

"And you're sure you can't give us the man's name?"

"I'm sorry. I have a kid at home. I can't risk my job. Besides, I only ever knew his first name."

Jess opened her mouth to ask one last time for a name, but a phone rang behind the counter and the woman gave them a little wave as she answered it.

She's not giving me any more, Jess thought, feeling like they'd been so very close to getting some answers.

***

Patricia and Jess debated about what they'd learned during their drive back to Patricia's office. Were they wrong about all of this? Based on comments made by both the banker and the store clerk, a man was involved. Did Karen have an accomplice? That was something they'd never even considered.

It was almost five by the time they got back. Jess only had a few more minutes, but something was bugging her. She just couldn't quite put her finger on what it was yet.

"Here, will you hand me those?" she asked Patricia, pointing to the check copies on her desk. She took the five pieces of paper and laid them all out on the table in Patricia's office. "Do you guys always use the memo line when you make out payments to vendors?"

"I usually do. If there's a customer number or invoice number on the bill, I'll list it. It just gives a little more tracking info if there is ever a question about a payment later. Why do you ask?"

"Because all of these have some type of number listed on the memo line, that's all. It's probably nothing."

Patricia leaned over the table and studied the checks. "I'm not sure what those are. To be honest, Dad used to do a horrible job filing receipts. I haven't been able to find any underlying invoices from Temp Angels, if they ever even existed."

"Hmm . . . all right. Well, I feel like we might have learned something important today, even though it raised more questions than answers. When did you plan to talk to your folks about this?"

"They're coming over for dinner this weekend. It's probably time for me to loop Dad in."

"I understand," Jess said. "We can't keep this a secret from him forever. Maybe he might even have some answers. I wish I could be with you when you talk to him about it, but I'm moving this weekend and my whole family is helping me. I won't be able to get away."

"That's fine," Patricia said. "If I get a chance to talk to Dad alone, I will. I don't want to involve Mom at this point. Between you and me, she's battling some health issues, and she's such a worrier. I'll call you Monday and let you know what Dad has to say, if I get a chance to tell him."

"All right. Hopefully we can figure all this out soon. In the meantime, watch things really closely. Make sure Karen isn't writing out any more checks. We need someone other than her doing your monthly bank reconciliations, too."

"Agreed. I'm nervous what Dad will have to say. He has a terrible temper."

CHAPTER 38

Gift of Family

Saturday morning arrived, and Jess's house became a hub of activity. The goal was to have the house completely emptied out by evening. She'd clean what she could on Sunday, and the carpet cleaners were scheduled for Monday. Tuesday, October 1, was closing day. She wouldn't walk away from the sale with much equity, which still boggled her mind after more than ten years of mortgage payments, but she couldn't wait to be out from under the pressure. Financially, no more mortgage payments would be a huge relief, but she was also glad to not have to worry about clearing snow in the winter or any of the other headaches that came with maintaining a vacant property.

She found Lavonne in the kitchen, handing out donuts.

"Thanks for coming over today, Mom. Dad says your back has been bugging you—promise me you won't lift anything," she said, selecting a maple Long John from the donut box.

"Don't worry, Jess, no lifting for me. I'll help direct the troops. Why don't you tell me your game plan and I'll try to make sure things get where you want them to go?"

"Sounds good. Last week I went through and labeled everything I could think of. Will's things need to go to the storage unit I lined up for him. Ethan said to go ahead and load his trailer and he'll take it over there. So, like, the things in Will's office, his clothes in our closet . . . that kind of thing. Some of the furniture, too."

Lavonne nodded and Jess moved on.

"We can put all the items I plan to donate out on the northwest corner of the lawn. The thrift store is sending a truck over at three this afternoon.

Yesterday Renee and Matt helped me get some of the old furniture out of the duplex to make room. I'll take a few things from here to replace those items. Most everything else will have to go into my basement at Whispering Pines. Good thing that was pretty much empty."

"What are we going to use to move things out to the duplex?"

"Luke is picking up a U-Haul for me."

"I should have known you'd be well-organized today, honey. But how are you feeling? Are you OK with all of this? I know it's been hard. Do you feel bad about the house?"

Jess took a bite of her donut and smiled. "I honestly don't, Mom. It'll be a relief to be done with it. Another tie I can cut from Will. You know, I never really liked this house in the first place. This was Will's deal."

"Well, good. Let's get this show on the road, then," Lavonne said, topping off her coffee cup and closing the donut box.

***

Thank God for family, Jess thought several hours later as she wandered from room to room. It was only four o'clock, but most everything was gone. Seth even had a buddy drop him off so he could drive her Volkswagen out to his shop.

She'd forgotten to talk to Will about his Lexus, but she didn't think he'd want to pay for a second storage unit to house the car. Nathan's old pickup had been acting up lately, and while a Lexus for a college kid might be a bit much, it made more sense for him to drive that than to pay to buy him something else. Will would probably balk at the idea, but as far as Jess was concerned he had no say in the matter. She mentally added it to the list of things to mention to her ex. She'd purposely avoided him, handling the move on her own. All he'd be able to do from prison was try to boss her around, and she'd had more than enough of that through the years.

George offered to let Nathan store the tools in his garage for safekeeping. Ethan had made multiple trips to Will's storage unit, and now his trailer was filled with the last of the items from the house. The next challenge would be to fit everything stowed in the U-Haul and Ethan's trailer into Jess's duplex. She started sending everyone in that direction. Renee was already at Whispering Pines, ready to feed the hungry crew, and Harper and Val's two youngest boys were with her. They would have been more of a hindrance at the house, given all the commotion.

Jess needed to talk to Val but hadn't been able to catch her alone all day. She saw her sister climb into the U-Haul with Luke. Jess ran across the yard to catch them before they drove away.

"Hey, Val, can you come here a minute?"

"What's up?" Val asked through the open truck window.

"Why don't you ride out to the Pines with me? Keep me company? Luke gets you all the time," Jess said, giving her brother-in-law a little finger-wave.

"Sure," Val said, climbing back down from the vehicle. "See you boys out there," she said to her husband and son, slamming the door.

Luke drove off, leading a caravan of other vehicles, and Ethan brought up the rear. Val and Jess were the only ones left at the house.

"Val, do me a favor and back my car out of the garage, will you?" Jess asked, tossing the keys to her sister. "I have to run through the house quick and make sure things are locked up and the lights are off. Leave the garage door open and I'll come out that way."

Jess went in through the front door. She started in the basement, clicking off lights as she went, and was just about to head upstairs when she heard a buzzing. A phone sat on the bar. She scooped it up and answered the call, her father's picture showing on the screen.

"Hey, Dad. Who forgot their phone?"

"I'm glad we caught you. It's Robbie's."

"I'll bring it with me. Tell him I'll be sure to only respond to the texts that come in from girls while I'm in possession of his phone," Jess teased. She could hear yelling in the background.

"Robbie is begging you not to do that, Jess, so naturally I'm begging you to do that," George said, apparently in the same car as his grandson.

Jess laughed. "See you in a bit. I gotta go. Val's waiting for me outside."

She dropped her nephew's cell in her jeans pocket and checked the rest of the house. She locked the front door and headed out through the garage, stopping at the site of the two tubs, still sitting against the garage wall where Nathan had set them after taking them out of Bugaboo.

"Crap. These got missed. I should've labeled them," Jess said, stopping in front of the tubs. "Val, can you help me lift these things into the back of my Land Rover?"

Val got out of Jess's idling car and came over to help. A black pickup slowly drove by, catching Val's eye.

"That's weird . . ."

"What?" Jess asked. "These tubs?"

"No. That truck. I swear they drove by two or three times since I've been waiting for you."

Jess glanced down the street, but the pickup was gone. "Are you sure? Maybe it was a neighbor?"

"Probably. So what's with these?" Val asked, motioning to the tubs. "They look heavy."

"I know. They were supposed to go to the storage facility. Some of Will's old books."

"Can't you just ditch 'em?"

"I considered that, but I better not. I've gotten rid of lots of his stuff already in this move. I think these might be important to him. He had them stashed in the back of my convertible. I'll just put them out at the duplex for now. I need to have everything out of here."

Together they wrestled the heavy tubs up and into the back of her vehicle, next to the last few boxes from inside. Before shutting the garage door, Jess made sure the alarm system was turned on—she didn't think the black truck was anything to worry about, but you could never be too careful.

***

"So, did you hear back from the doctor yet?" Jess asked Val as they made their way back to Whispering Pines, eventually catching up to the rest of the family.

"I did. The tests didn't show anything definitive. Doc wants to keep an eye on things, though. She wants me to come back again in three months."

"What are they concerned about?"

"I'm not exactly sure. I suspect they're just being careful. The biopsy didn't show any cancer cells."

"Well, that's a relief. Do you feel better about it?"

Val shrugged. "I guess."

"You don't sound very convincing."

"To be honest, I was pretty scared. Of course I wanted the news they gave me, it's just . . . I don't know. I wish she would have said something more like 'See you in a year for your annual checkup.' This doesn't feel like a completely clean bill of health."

"Try to think positively, Val. Do you *feel* all right?"

"Yes, for the most part. Kind of tired, but that could just be from all the running around we do."

"What does Luke think?"

"He says he's sure I'm fine, but he has been a little more *attentive* lately. I think it rattled him, too."

"I'm sure it did. Luke's crazy about you, you know."

"What's not to be crazy about? Plus, I'm the mother to his *four* children. He needs me around for a few more years yet."

"Val, don't even joke about that!"

"I know. I'm sorry. That wasn't funny. I'm sure it's nothing. But other than this moving business, how are things going for you?"

"Well . . ." Jess grinned. "I had a date last weekend."

"Oh, you did, did you?" Val asked, but she didn't sound surprised at all.

"Let me guess . . . Renee already told you?"

"She might have mentioned something about it. So you went out with Seth, huh? Do you happen to remember our discussion in Minneapolis, back when we were dress shopping with Renee? I suggested way back then that you go out with him, and you claimed it was a terrible idea. What happened to change your mind?"

Now it was Jess's turn to shrug. "I guess he just kind of grew on me."

***

By the time they got back to Whispering Pines, Renee was feeding everyone in the lodge.

"Hey, sis, thanks for having supper ready for us," Jess said, giving Renee a high-five. "I'm sure everyone's starving. I worked them hard today."

"Did you starve them, too? Some of the kids are already on their second round of burgers." Renee laughed. "Did you get everything done that you needed to?"

"Almost. After we're done eating, I'll just need one last push by everyone to get the trucks unloaded. I'm thinking maybe we save the cake until later. You know, bribe 'em a little. What do you think?"

"I think you are a master manipulator, Jess, and I should take notes," Renee said.

"Is Harper all right? How about Jake and Noah?" Jess asked.

"They are all just fine. The boys had fun playing with Harper for a while, but then they lost interest. She should sleep well tonight. We kept her busy. Grab a plate and get something to eat. You'll want to get those trucks unloaded before it gets too dark out."

"Good point," Jess agreed.

Twenty minutes later, supper was devoured and cleaned up, and the last push was on. The back door into Jess's kitchen was right at the top of the basement stairs, so most things went down relatively easily. Lavonne was positioned downstairs to make sure things were placed as strategically as possible. By the time they were done, there was little room to walk in the basement, but everything fit.

"Now as long as you don't get water down here, you should be good," Lavonne declared, looking around with satisfaction.

"Mother, why would you even *say* such a thing?" Jess asked. Water down here would be a disaster. She thought back to the mess the Fisks had at the bookstore after that summer storm. *God forbid that happen here.*

They headed back upstairs to the kitchen where most everyone was gathered.

"Thank you, everyone, for all your help today," Jess said, loud enough for everyone to hear. "We couldn't have done it without you. Please, grab some cake and relax. Kids, take your cake and go play outside. It won't be dark for another half hour. You've earned it."

Those staying inside helped themselves to dessert and found a place to sit in Jess's combination kitchen and living room. The furniture they'd brought over from her old house helped provide more seating. Lauren took Harper upstairs for a bath and bedtime.

"So, Jess, what's this I hear about you having a date last weekend?" Lavonne asked with a grin.

"OK, Renee, you have a big mouth," Jess said, shooting a look at her sister. "Yes, Mother, as you obviously already know, I went out with Seth last weekend."

"Seth, huh? The same Seth we talked about in Minneapolis last spring?"

"Oh, hush. Val already gave me that line in the car on the way back here."

"I saw him stop by the house today," Ethan pointed out. "Why isn't he here tonight? Didn't he want to help his new girlfriend move?"

"God, you guys are all *so funny*. Yes, he stopped by the house. He's going to store my convertible for me out at his shop. Yes, he wanted to help today, but I didn't think that would be a good idea. All of you at once might scare him away."

"All right," Ethan conceded. "I just wanted to make sure you weren't dating a slacker."

"I wouldn't say we're *dating*. We've only *officially* gone out one time."

"Doesn't matter," Ethan said. "Glad to know he didn't duck out because he's lazy."

"All right, how about we change the subject?" Jess suggested.

"Jess, where's that photo album you found at Celia's? I'd like to see it," George asked.

Thankful for the distraction, Jess went up and grabbed it from her room.

"I haven't had time to look at it either, Dad," she said, handing it to him.

George opened the album and started thumbing through it. "I remember this party," he said with a nod, pointing at a spread of photos. "It was at Celia's, in the backyard. It was a ridiculously hot day, if I can recall." He turned the book so Jess could see. "Oh, look at this, Jess. Look how young the kids are in this one."

Maybe it was exhaustion after a full day of moving—maybe the reality of selling their family home was settling in—but the snapshots made Jess tear up. Jess was *not* a weepy kind of girl. She squeezed in on the sofa between her mom and dad to look with George.

"Nathan was eight and Lauren five. This actually might have been the summer we bought our house," Jess said. "Ironic."

Lavonne leaned over Jess's shoulder to peek at the book, too. "I love how Celia wrote the names under the pictures . . . ooh, look at *that* shot. That's her band of crazy lady friends."

"I remember how they used to go out for dinner every single Thursday night," George said, nodding. "Celia usually drove that big silver Cadillac of hers, and while I loved her dearly, I think we can all admit now she wasn't the best of drivers."

Jess laughed. "I remember her friends now that I see their faces again. There's Celia, Helen . . . but I don't recognize that one." She pointed to a woman wearing a hat, shading her face from the sun. "It says *Eleanor* under the picture. And look, there's Ruby, Seth's grandma. Jeez, I wonder if *Seth* was at the party . . ."

"I doubt it. Seth's parents would have still been alive then. Eleanor was another one of Celia's good friends. These pictures are great. I'm glad they don't seem to be damaged from being up in the attic for all those years," George said.

A photo in the bottom corner of the page caught Jess's eye. "It's nice to see Lauren actually smiling at her father," she said, pointing. In the photograph, Lauren was sitting in Will's lap, smiling up at him. Will was talking to a woman sitting next to him. "Who's that?" Jess asked, squinting to better see the woman.

"It says *Karen*," Lavonne said, pointing to Celia's note.

"Oh . . ." Jess was surprised to see a much younger picture of the woman she'd been investigating lately at her aunt's birthday party. But it shouldn't have been surprising. Karen knew Celia—and Helen, Karen's grandmother, was at the party, too. "Looks like the guy on the other side of Karen is Stuart, her husband."

Renee came to stand behind the sofa, looking over their shoulders at the album.

"Check out that polo on Will, collar flipped up and the whole nine yards," Renee pointed out. "And are those *jelly* shoes on Lauren? Those were so darn cute, but the plastic didn't breathe. Their little feet would get *so* sweaty. And there's Julie . . . wearing yellow jellies, too. We must have caught a sale on them, Jess."

The picture Renee pointed out showed Julie pulling her own father across the yard by the hand. Renee didn't mention Jim. Jess quickly did the math in her head, realizing Jim would be dead within two years of this photo.

Julie and Robbie lost their dad. Now Lauren and Nathan need to go on without Will, too. Almost like another death.

"Where are all of us women?" Renee asked, noting plenty of pictures of kids and husbands, but not many of Lavonne, Renee, Jess, or Val.

"Val was probably on a hot date with Luke, and the rest of us were likely slaving away in the kitchen."

Val heard this from across the room. "Can you blame me?" she asked, giving her husband a quick peck on the cheek, causing him to blush all these years later.

George flipped the page and together they checked out the other pictures. After the ones from the party came various pictures of different holidays, family gatherings, and what looked like vacation pictures with Ruby.

"I wonder if there was a reason Celia stowed this album up in the attic instead of with all her others?" George said.

"No idea," Jess replied.

"I guess it doesn't matter. I'm just glad you found it so we could keep it somewhere out of the temperature extremes. Do you want to keep it here, Jess, or do you want me to take it home and keep it with the others?"

"Go ahead and take it, Dad. That way all her albums are in one place."

The conversation drifted to other topics. Jess noticed a yawn here and there around the room. Everyone was beat. She stood and started cleaning up the dessert dishes. Her signal prompted others to start the process of heading home. It didn't take long for her kitchen to empty out. Nathan took two big bags of trash out back. The old screen door slapped shut behind him. He came back in a minute later as she placed the last of the dishes in the dishwasher.

She needed to get to bed. She'd be up early on Sunday to head back to the house to clean. But then she remembered the boxes and tubs in the back of her vehicle.

"Darn it. I still need to get stuff out of the back of my car. I forgot about it. I'll need the back to be empty tomorrow so I can bring the vacuum and cleaning supplies back here, after I'm done cleaning the house."

"I can go grab it, Mom," Nathan offered as he flipped the deadbolt closed on the back door.

"Thanks, honey. I don't know if my back would let me lift one more thing today. Lauren can help. You'll still have to make a couple of trips, though. Can you just set the stuff in here, by the door? I'll figure out where to put it in the morning. We're about out of room downstairs."

"Sure. Why don't you go up and go to bed?" he suggested.

There are some advantages to the kids growing up, Jess decided, giving her son a quick hug and thank-you on her way upstairs.

***

Despite feeling bone weary, Jess couldn't sleep.

She tossed half the night. Her mind kept racing. She was overtired. She kept going over her visit with Patricia earlier in the week, to Alexandria. Jess was now fairly certain Celia had nothing to do with any of it, but she still needed to deal with Karen. She hated the impact it would have on Frank and Virginia when the truth came out. She only hoped it didn't extend beyond Homes Sparkle. The fear it very well could was keeping her up.

That, along with something else she couldn't quite put her finger on.

CHAPTER 39

Gift of a Helping Hand

*D*espite her restless night, Jess was awake early, before anyone else. She wanted to get over to the house and get her cleaning done so she wouldn't be stuck there the whole day. Lauren had offered to keep Harper while Jess cleaned. She suspected her daughter thought spending the day with Harper would be easier than cleaning, but Jess doubted it. Harper was crawling all over the place now and starting to pull herself up to a standing position—she was a handful.

Jess popped two ibuprofens before even getting out of bed. The previous day had taken a toll on her body. She dressed in her favorite sweat pants and an old hoodie with a T-shirt underneath. It would be a messy day, and she wanted to be comfortable.

Halfway down the stairs, she groaned at the sight of the boxes her kids had brought in the previous evening. They were exactly where she told them to put them; the problem was, she didn't know where to put them now so they were *out* of the way.

The two tubs were too heavy for her to move far by herself, even dragging across the floor. She would take the other four cardboard boxes downstairs and add them to one of the piles. She'd already made three trips to the basement when she heard someone else coming downstairs. Her son came around the corner, also dressed in grungy clothes.

"Good morning, Nathan."

"Hey, Mom."

"I figured you'd be dressed for work already. I thought you had to be there by ten."

"No. My boss sent me a text and said he didn't need me today," Nathan replied, wandering into the kitchen. "That's been happening quite a bit lately. It's slow. I suppose it'll pick up in early November for the holidays. I'm not getting many hours in now. I might have to pick up a second job to make rent."

Jess hated to see him have to do that. Two jobs during his senior year of college would be challenging.

"Maybe you should quit at Barnes and Noble and find something where you can get more hours."

"I suppose I could," Nathan said, pulling a box of cereal out of the cupboard and pouring himself breakfast. "But I like working there. Don't worry, I'll figure it out. And since my day opened up, I can help you over at the old house before heading home."

"I won't argue with an extra set of hands. I'll take this last box downstairs. Would you mind putting those two tubs up in the spare bedroom? There really isn't any more room downstairs, and I can't just leave them by the door. I probably should have taken Val's advice and ditched 'em."

Nathan hoisted one up off the floor with a grunt and headed for the stairs.

"Try not to wake the girls up," Jess warned.

***

Nathan followed Jess back over to the house in his own car so he could leave from there when they were done. Together they started on the second floor, dusting and vacuuming as they went. Nathan stood on a stepstool and cleaned off the light fixtures and other hard-to-reach spots as best he could.

They were partway through the main level, following the same routine, when Jess's cell phone rang. Glancing down at it, she was surprised to see Frank calling.

"Be right back, Nathan," she told her son, leaving the room to take the call.

He'd just finished vacuuming the living room and was moving into his dad's old office when Jess returned.

"Well, *that's* a tough deal," she said, coming back in the room with a broom in her hand.

Nathan turned off the vacuum so he could hear Jess.

"What's that?"

"That was Frank. I guess Virginia's been feeling more tired than usual lately, so she went in to see her doctor. Apparently they're afraid she might have a blockage in her heart and they want to do a procedure on Wednesday. Frank wants to be with her, but the timing is terrible. He has a book signing scheduled at the store for a new local author. They've been doing quite a bit of promoting, and Frank was excited about it. He's always been passionate about helping new authors."

"That does suck . . . doesn't he have anyone that can watch the store?"

Jess shook her head. "He doesn't. He had a part-time high school girl, but she quit after school started. So he doesn't have anyone now. He was letting me know he'd probably have to close the shop for at least a day, if not the rest of the week."

Nathan fiddled with the vacuum cleaner while Jess swept out the corners of the ceiling with her broom. He left to dump the tank, and when he came back with the empty canister he said, "Maybe I could help out."

"What do you mean?"

"Wednesday is my light day for classes. I'm done by eleven. I usually go into work, but I'm sure someone would take my shift. Everyone's wanting more hours right now."

"You would be willing to do that? It's quite a drive for you from school. Has your pickup been working any better?"

"Well, once in a while it has a hard time turning over, but so far I haven't had to get it jumped again. Made it here OK, didn't I?"

Jess remembered her idea to offer him the use of Will's vehicle. It seemed ridiculous to have a perfectly good vehicle sit while his was giving him trouble.

"Why don't you use your dad's car for a while? I don't want you stranded somewhere with a broken-down truck."

Nathan stopped what he was doing to stare at his mother in surprise. "Seriously? I can take the Lexus? Is Dad OK with that?"

"Don't worry about your father. I'll handle him."

"I don't think he'll like it . . . but OK, if you insist. Do you want to call Frank back to see if he could use my help? Or should I call him?"

"He's already met you a couple of times. Here. Use my phone. If you guys can figure out the logistics, that would be great."

Nathan went outside and called Frank. Jess got down on her hands and knees to dust the baseboards. He returned twenty minutes later.

"I think we figured it out. He's going to be at the shop tonight until about eight. I guess their daughter is gonna go stay with Virginia, so he's going in to work on paperwork. He asked if I could swing in so he could show me how things work. It'll be a little tough, him not being there for the book signing, but it's better than canceling. It's scheduled from four until seven on Wednesday night. My first class isn't until three on Thursday. Frank suggested I stay in the apartment upstairs, open the shop for him on Thursday morning, and he might be able to be back by early afternoon. Even if he can't make it and I have to lock it up early, at least they can stay open most of the time."

"That is great news, Nathan. Thanks for suggesting it. Maybe helping Frank could be your second job this year. I know he'd be super flexible and would just appreciate any help you could give."

Nathan seemed to give it some thought before joining her in cleaning again. "Yeah . . . maybe."

CHAPTER 40

Gift of Disclosure

"Thanks for calling, Dad. We haven't done lunch, just the two of us, for ages," Jess said, pulling out a chair across from her father.

"I'm glad you could make it," George said, looking up from the menu he'd been studying. He stood and gave his daughter a quick hug. "I figured we needed to catch up."

He and Jess sat down and she accepted a glass of water from a waiter.

"Thank you again for your help this past weekend. It's so nice to have everything out of that house."

George laughed. "I didn't do much. I can't lift things like I used to."

"Are you kidding? You made sure everything got to the right place. I also saw you lifting quite a few things . . . but I won't tell Mom."

"I appreciate that. She won't listen to my complaining about aches and pains if she knows I brought them on myself."

They placed their orders and then sat back to visit while they waited for their food to arrive. Jess had missed this. They used to squeeze lunch in at least once a month, but life had gotten in the way ever since her split from Will.

"So how are things with you, Dad?"

"Oh, fine. I've been a little worried about all of you, though," George said.

Jess snorted. "Dad, you always worry about us."

"That's not true. You guys haven't given me much to worry about, and I know that when you do have things come up you'll usually ask for help if you need it. But it seems like everyone has lots going on these days."

"Maybe it's where we're at in life. I'm not sure. Our forties have been challenging."

"So I know better than to ask *you* how your brother and your sisters are doing. You never gossip. But what about you? You probably have the most irons in the fire of anyone."

Jess had to agree. Almost every facet of her life seemed to be filled with *something*. At least she felt like she was making progress, but it was a long climb.

"Having Harper around has been the biggest adjustment, but she is such a sweet baby. I had huge reservations about taking her . . . but what choice did I really have? That mother of hers is a flake."

"What was her name? Tonya?"

"Close. Tiffany. She worries me, Dad. She's already come back once, threatening to take Harper. That woman is not equipped to be a mother. It would make me sick if she took Harper. What scares me is if she showed up and wanted to take her, she could. I don't have any legal grounds to stand on. I'm just the *nearly* ex-wife of the baby's father. *She's* the biological mother."

"Do you think she'd do that?"

"I worry about it all the time. The sad thing is, if she does, I don't even think it'll be because she wants to be Harper's mother. I think it's more likely she'd do it to try to stay in Will's good graces."

"But won't he be in prison for years yet?"

Jess nodded. "Yes. I suppose there's the possibility of early release. I don't know much about that stuff. But Tiffany is the type of woman who needs a man to take care of her."

"The opposite of you, then?" George pointed out in a teasing tone. "Seriously though, you may want to get a lawyer involved, Jess. See if there's any way Will can legally convey his parental rights to you, given his situation and the fact the woman deserted them. That has to count for something."

"You're probably right. I've been crossing my fingers and toes, hoping for the best where Harper is concerned. I may be at the point where I need to do more, though, but between selling the house, working, and helping out with Celia's other businesses, I'm stretched thin these days."

"I can help you find someone, if you'd like."

"Oh, I just remembered—Jack Poole knows some good family law attorneys . . . he said he'd give me a referral if I decided I wanted one."

George nodded. "There you go. You certainly are stretched thin, dear, and you probably need to be a little careful. Don't try to do *too* much. And take Jack up on his offer."

Jess didn't take offense at her father's directive. He'd been telling her to slow down for years. While she usually bristled at being told what to do, she knew her dad meant well. But she did what had to be done and couldn't see herself slowing down any time soon.

"So, Dad . . . I should probably talk to you about something else I've been working on."

"What's that?"

"It has to do with Celia."

George put down the sandwich he'd been about to take a bite out of.

"Did you learn more about those ridiculous accusations?"

"Maybe. As you can guess, I was furious at Patricia for even suggesting such a thing." At George's raised eyebrow, she added, "Patricia—she's the old owners' daughter at Homes Sparkle."

"Ah," George said, nodding. "I'm angry as well."

"Seth was mad, too. He's been helping me prove that there was no way Celia would ever do anything like that."

"Wait, Seth? The guy Ethan was teasing you about last night? What's the connection?"

"Yes, that Seth. Remember, Celia helped him with his architectural salvage place and that was one of the business interests she passed on to me? Ruby was Seth's grandma—Celia's best friend?"

"Oh, yes, yes. Now I remember the connection. Go on, sorry to interrupt."

"Anyhow, we've been researching old records and stuff, trying to figure out if someone really has been stealing from Homes Sparkle, and if so, who might be behind it. That's why we were digging around in Celia's old attic."

"That makes more sense now. I'd wondered why in heaven's name you'd be up there, going through all that old stuff. So, have you been able to figure things out?"

"We're getting close . . . and of course it isn't looking like Celia played any part in it."

"Damn straight. Celia had a spotless reputation. It was the most important thing to her. That and her philanthropy."

"I feel like I should tell you about something we *did* discover related to Celia."

"That sounds ominous. I thought you said you're sure she wasn't involved in anything illegal at Homes Sparkle?"

"She wasn't. This was something that happened earlier. Back in 2005. Remember how I told you there was a journal in that blue trunk in her attic? The one where we also found the album we looked at last weekend and the vintage wedding dress?"

George nodded, his lunch all but forgotten now. Jess went on to relay the story to him that she'd first discovered by reading Celia's journal and been able to at least partially verify by studying old financial statements.

When George had soaked it all in, he said, "Well, I'll be damned. She never said a word. But, knowing Celia, for her to shoulder the blame for something like that when she didn't even do it seems really out of character. What would ever have made her do that?"

Jess nodded in agreement. "That's exactly what I thought."

"So . . . you said Karen *was* involved? Helen's granddaughter? I've known Helen for years. She really wasn't a very pleasant woman. I never understood what Celia saw in her, why they remained friends through the years. Didn't she pass away recently?"

"She did. In fact, Karen and Virginia just got back from trying to take care of Helen's things after her death. Do you know Virginia? She's Helen's daughter and Karen's mother. She's a sweet woman, runs the bookstore I'm involved with too."

"Sure, I know Virginia. Not well, but I know who she is. She always seemed so different from Helen. In a good way."

"Virginia told me they were very different and never got along well, but Karen was very close with her grandmother."

"So, back to your story about that old grocery store. Do you have any idea why Celia would have let Karen get away with that?"

"No . . . there *has* to be a reason, but we may never know why—unless Karen will tell us."

"I suppose you're right, Jess. And maybe it doesn't even matter now. Hopefully you've managed to keep Celia's name out of the mud—which, by the way, I truly appreciate. Celia would turn over in her grave if someone tarnished her reputation."

Jess took a few bites of her lunch, debating whether or not to mention her strong suspicions about Karen's involvement in possibly stealing from Homes Sparkle. The topic wasn't just buried in the past, as her dad assumed, but still ongoing. Before she could speak up, though, he continued.

"You know, Celia's generosity did have a downside."

"What do you mean?"

George laid his napkin over his half-eaten lunch and pushed his chair back far enough to allow him to cross his legs.

"People were always coming to her with their hand out, looking for money. When Celia felt people were deserving, she'd try to help. But sometimes I worried she'd let herself be taken advantage of."

Jess nodded, waiting for her Dad to go on. Celia's generosity was legendary. Jess wondered why he thought it necessary to point it out; a fluttering of unease started in the pit of her stomach.

"There's something that's been bugging me for years, but I never wanted to tell you about it. Didn't want to say anything that might hurt your relationship with Will."

It was Jess's turn to push her plate away, her appetite deserting her.

"With Will? What does *he* have to do with Celia? Wait—he did tell me, not long ago, that he asked Celia for money when he wanted to buy our house and she turned him down. Is that what's been bugging you?"

George crossed his arms over his chest.

"Well, that was part of it. He did do that. But it went beyond that. He approached her a few times for money. He went to her when he had a new business idea. Another time, he even asked her to foot the bill for his schooling, like she'd done for you. It got to the point where she finally talked to me about it. His sense of entitlement concerned her. Celia helped people who she thought couldn't help themselves. In Will's case, she knew he was perfectly capable of fending for himself—he was a surgeon, for Christ's sake. But when he wouldn't back off, she asked me to talk to him."

Jess could feel her face flush. She was embarrassed to learn Will made a habit of going to her family for handouts. She'd had no idea.

"I wish you would have told me this sooner, Dad."

He nodded, his face somber. "I was tempted to, especially over the last year or two before you guys split up. He was obviously pulling away from you and the kids. It made me so mad. But you were an adult and I had faith in your ability to deal with your husband how you saw fit. I do admit, though, I was relieved when you finally kicked him to the curb."

"You and me both. How long ago did you talk to him?"

"Oh, probably at least ten years ago now. I called him and asked him to meet me out for a drink. He was none too happy when I explained to him that Celia had talked to me about his requests for money and that he needed to stop. As I'm sure you can imagine, he got really indignant, insisting it was none of my business. I basically told him to man up and take care of his own family instead of asking for charity where it wasn't deserved. Needless to say, it wasn't a long conversation. He stormed out and neither of us ever mentioned it again. After that, we both tried to keep up appearances when we were around each other, but it wasn't easy."

George paused and took a drink from his water glass. Jess struggled with a myriad of emotions at her dad's words.

"I am so embarrassed . . ." she confessed. "I feel somehow responsible."

"Oh, knock it off, Jess," George said, setting his glass back down and leaning toward her, his palms on his knees. "I'm tired of you shouldering the blame for that man's mistakes. I understand that part of the reason you always tried to mask Will's indiscretions and failures was because you thought they reflected poorly on you, but believe me, *you* were not the problem."

"So why did it take me over twenty years to figure that out, Dad?"

"Because, honey, you don't give up easily. You fight the good fight. I'm just glad you're fighting for yourself and the kids now. Will doesn't deserve any more from you."

CHAPTER 41

Gift from Beyond

*J*ess normally picked Harper up shortly after five o'clock each afternoon, but she decided today would be an early one. Her discussion with her dad over lunch was bothering her, she couldn't concentrate, and Patricia wasn't picking up her phone.

When they got home to Whispering Pines, she decided to bundle Harper up for some outside exploration. Fresh air would do them both good. They didn't have any renters during the week, now that it was late September, so she guessed there would be little to no traffic on the gravel road between the resort and the highway. The gravel had been worn nearly smooth over the years, so it shouldn't be hard to push a stroller on it.

"Come on, honey, let's go for a walk," she said to the little girl, stuffing the child's arms into the miniature pea-coat Lauren had found for her at a vintage store. Harper tolerated the jacket, but her hat was a different story—the little escape artist did all she could to avoid it. "Come on, baby girl, I don't want you to get an earache."

Finally, Jess was able to distract her with a toy and get the cap tied on, a secure bow under her chin. Harper looked adorable in her red wool coat and hand-knit ivory beanie. Jess couldn't resist snapping a few pictures of her in her stroller. Fall leaves made for a pretty background.

As they started on their way, the colorful leaves conjured up the dream Jess had months earlier of the young Native American woman down by the water, holding a bundle in her arms. It had been autumn in her dream, too, a day much like today. The woman had looked so forlorn. What could have made her so sad on a beautiful fall day?

Get a grip, Jess scolded herself. *It was a dream, for crying out loud.*

But it felt so real at the time. She reached into her jacket pocket and touched the arrowhead she'd stowed there. Ever since Lauren had found it in the lake right after the wedding—the same moment in which Jess had realized she would indeed take Harper—Jess thought of it as a good-luck talisman and carried it with her when she thought she needed it.

Harper let out a squeal, pointing to something up in the trees and babbling in delight.

"What is it, babe? What do you see?" Jess followed her tiny finger and saw a beautiful cardinal, its red plumage striking against the golden leaves. "Oh, Harper, that's a cardinal!"

Harper continued to babble, clearly excited over her bird sighting.

"Did you know some people believe red cardinals are messengers from heaven, a sign from a loved one who has died? I'm not a big believer in that kind of thing, but . . . maybe Celia is trying to tell us something."

I wish Celia would give me some guidance. Why do I feel like I'm missing something?

Harper watched in wonder as the beautiful bird flew up and away, out of sight. Jess watched the little girl's eyes scan the forest surrounding them. She stopped walking, hoping if they stayed still, more wildlife might appear for Harper to see in the peacefulness of the late afternoon quiet.

As they waited, Harper relaxed in her seat—still watching, but Jess noticed her eyelids start to droop. She'd missed her afternoon nap when Jess picked her up early. Jess stood beside the stroller and closed her own eyes, trying to focus. She needed to open her mind to let something in . . . whatever it was that had been floating around at the edge of her conscience, trying to get her attention.

There was something about the checks . . . the checks Karen signed.

What about the checks?

She concentrated further.

Then her eyes popped open.

The numbers. The numbers on the memo lines.

I've seen numbers like that before . . . but where?

Harper sat straight up in her stroller again, suddenly wide awake, pointing and giggling. Her red cardinal was back. This time it was sitting on something closer to eye level, a few feet off the road. Jess slowly pushed the stroller ahead to give Harper a better view of the bird.

Now Jess could see the cardinal was sitting on an old metal mailbox. The pole supporting the mailbox was tipped at a crazy angle—probably clipped by a snow plow at some point. Jess had never noticed it there before.

"That's *it*! Harper, I know where I've seen numbers like that!" Jess said, the excitement in her voice scaring off the cardinal.

Harper watched the bird fly away, then snapped her head toward Jess in surprise, her eyes filling. Her face crumpled and she burst into tears.

"Oh, honey, I'm sorry, I didn't mean to scare the birdie away. Come on, let's turn around and go home. It's getting late and I need to check something. Just sit back. We'll be home in no time. Maybe we can hang a feeder in the backyard—then you can watch lots of birdies all the time."

The combination of the trundling stroller and Jess's soothing voice calmed Harper, her cries reducing to small hiccups as they made their way back home.

Jess felt energized. It was as if the critical piece in a jigsaw puzzle had fallen into place, the one so many others hinged upon. She sent a text to Seth.

I might have figured it out.

Once back at the duplex, Jess knocked on Renee's door and tried the knob. It opened and the smell of cooked meat wafted out at her.

"Hello? You guys home?"

"Hey, Jess! In here," came her sister's voice.

Jess walked in with Harper on her hip. "What are you doing?"

"We just finished dinner," Renee said, coming out of her kitchen, a dishtowel in her hands. "Robbie is helping me with dishes and then he has to go to an evening practice. Matt stopped in, so we ate early. He's upstairs but has to leave again in a minute. What are you two doing? Did you just get home?"

"Actually, we just got back from a walk. Renee, I need to check something quick. Would you mind taking her for a little while? She's tired and hungry. I'm sorry to dump her on you like this, but it's important."

Renee tossed the towel on her kitchen table and reached out to take Harper. "Of course I don't mind," she said, breaking into a grin when Harper stretched her arms out to her. "I can never get enough time with this little love. I was going to start brainstorming the details for our November retreat, but that can wait. Matt will be late and I like to wait up for him. I can work on it later."

"Thank you, I appreciate it. I'll grab her diaper bag quick so you have what you need."

"Don't worry about us, we'll be just fine—won't we, Harper?" Renee sat down on the couch and took Harper's jacket off, then looked back up at Jess. "Do you mind me asking what's up? You seem more intense than usual."

Jess grinned. "I better not say yet, in case I'm wrong. But I have an idea. If it pans out, you'll be one of the first to know."

***

Jess finished getting Harper settled next door and was about to run upstairs to her bedroom when a knock came at her door. Surprised, she peeked through the front window. Seth stood there. She pulled open her door.

"*This* is a surprise," she said to him with a smile, stepping back to let him in.

"I got your text, but when you didn't respond back to me, I wondered what was going on. Are you okay?"

"Oh! I'm sorry. Yes. I was out for a walk with Harper when I had an idea. I needed to drop her off with Renee so I could check it out. My phone's in my jacket pocket. I mustn't have heard it."

"Don't worry about it, I was in the area. Been pulling old barn wood about fifteen miles north of here. The barn collapsed this past summer and I convinced the owner to let me take it off his hands before it gets buried in snow. I'd just loaded the last of it in the back of my truck when I got your text. Sorry if I stink—it was a dirty job."

Jess laughed. She *could* smell him, but she appreciated the fact he wasn't afraid of hard, physical labor. "Don't worry about it. Come with me. I was just heading upstairs to check out my theory."

"Upstairs, huh?" he said, wiggling his eyebrows at her as he stooped to untie his work boots. She headed upstairs, confident he knew the way. She went back to her bedroom and dropped down on her hands and knees to look under the bed.

"What are you doing?" he asked as he came into her room.

"Getting out Will's box," she said as she pulled the metal container out into the open.

"Here," Seth said, reaching down and taking the box. He set it on Jess's bed and offered her a hand up.

"Let's take this downstairs," Jess said, scooping up the box and heading back out in the direction they'd just come, Seth not far behind.

Back in the kitchen, Jess snapped open the metal box. She took the binder out, laid it on the table, and flipped the cover open. Then she went back out by the front door and grabbed her leather computer bag where she'd set it when she and Harper first got home before their walk. She brought the bag into the kitchen, too, and set it on a chair so she could see as she dug in it for something. She pulled out a manila envelope and took out copies of the checks.

"What are those?"

She glanced his way, so intent on her mission she'd nearly forgotten he was there.

"Oh, sorry, you probably think I'm acting nuts here. These are copies of a few of those checks I told you Karen wrote out to that mysterious temp agency. Patricia let me make copies of them. Something about them has been bugging me, but I couldn't quite put my finger on it. Then we saw a cardinal in the woods—Harper and I on our walk, I mean—and something clicked."

Seth put a hand on Jess's shoulder. "I don't think you're acting nuts, but now you're starting to lose me. Why don't you slow down a little? What does a bird have to do with this?"

Jess reached up and squeezed the hand resting on her shoulder, taking a deep breath. "Right." She pulled out two chairs and indicated for him to sit with her. "I'll back up. Patricia ordered copies of the checks we thought looked suspicious. We've been researching some of the information on them, like the endorsement and bank stamps on the back, but these numbers down here on the memo line meant nothing to us."

Seth examined the copies Jess handed to him and nodded for her to go on.

"Patricia didn't put any importance on them. I knew the numbers had to mean *something*, but what? They looked vaguely familiar, but I couldn't put two and two together. The synapses weren't connecting."

"But something changed today? On your walk?" Seth asked, still clearly lost as to where this was going.

Jess nodded. "Are you familiar with what some people believe about red cardinals?"

"Sure," he said. "Ruby used to point them out to me, say that was Mom trying to give us a message . . . you know, after the accident."

"Really? Did you believe her?"

He shrugged. "Who knows? Like I've told you before, I've worked in old buildings where I've felt . . . something. Always subtle, but enough to catch my attention. I suppose there could be some truth to it. But how does that apply here?"

"Harper kept seeing a bright red cardinal on our walk and she was getting a kick out of it. At one point it flew off, so I stopped moving. I hoped if we stayed still, it might come back. It did, but this time it landed on this old metal mailbox and just looked at us. I know this may sound silly, but it had been minutes after I wished Celia would give me some kind of sign to help me figure this out. Like I said, sounds absolutely bonkers, but seeing that old metal mailbox made something click. I remembered the binder full of numbers I found in Will's box. They might be similar."

Seth gave her a look. "You're kidding, right? Why would checks written out by Karen have numbers on them that match up with numbers in a box you took out of your ex's office?"

"Bear with me. I'm not sure if they do. Just a hunch. But I can't shake this feeling . . ."

Jess took the copies of the checks back and compared the numbers on the memo lines to those in the spreadsheets in Will's binder. "Look . . . they *do* seem to follow the same pattern."

"But I don't understand. What's the connection between Will and Karen? Do they even know each other?"

"I wouldn't have thought so . . . but remember that old photo album we took from Celia's attic? When everyone was over here the other day, after helping me move out of the old house, we were sitting around relaxing and Dad asked to look at it. Here, I'll show you," Jess said, getting up and walking over to the photo album that still sat on the end table next to the couch.

"By the way, the new furniture looks nice in here," Seth said, looking around.

"Thanks. Not quite so shabby, huh?"

Jess set the album on the table in front of Seth and flipped a few pages in.

"Here. So that's Karen and I think her husband, but he's looking in the other direction. I can only see half his face. But she's talking to *Will.*"

"That's Will?" Seth asked, looking closer.

"Yep. And Lauren is on his lap. Looks like Will and Karen *do* know each other."

"It looks like they've at least met, sure . . . but it's a pretty big leap to go from a picture at Celia's birthday party, almost fifteen years ago, to possible collusion on an embezzlement."

"I completely agree. Patricia and I talked to a couple of people, though, and both mentioned a guy when we asked them about these checks. It made us start to think that maybe Karen had help . . . but of course we had no clue who that might be."

"And now you think that guy might be Will? I don't know, Jess, that's still a huge stretch."

Jess nodded. "I know, but there's more. I had lunch with my dad today. He finally told me something he's been wanting to tell me for years. I guess Will went to Celia multiple times and asked her for money."

"You didn't know he'd done that?"

"I knew he'd done it *once*, and even then I had no clue until this past summer when he told me he'd asked her for help when he wanted to buy our house. He was furious she'd turned him down. But according to my dad, he asked more than once, and she was starting to feel harassed. She asked my dad to step in and tell him to back off. Unbeknownst to me, Will was *really* bitter about all of it. Caused a rift with Dad, too, but they hid it pretty well from me."

"So you think this could mean Will and Karen not only know each other but teamed up to steal from a business Celia was part owner in?"

"I know, I know . . . but remember, based on what we've heard about Karen, she sounds a lot like Will, as far as being obsessed with money and the appearance of wealth. And both somehow had ties to Celia and Celia's money. It's all just a crazy theory right now, I haven't had time to confirm anything yet, but it feels to me like I'm getting close to some answers." Jess motioned at all the things lying on her kitchen table. "And if I can actually match up the numbers on these checks to any in the binder . . ."

"Maybe I should let you work on that and head home," Seth said.

"I wish you wouldn't go," Jess said. "I like having you here to bounce all this off of."

"Jess, I'm filthy and starving."

"Why don't I pull something together to eat while you take a shower here? Do you have any other clothes in your truck?"

"Yeah, I guess I do. So you want me to stay?"

"I do, if you want to."

Seth pushed back from the table and stood. "Sounds like a good plan to me. I'll be right back." Seth went outside and came back in a few minutes later with a duffel bag.

"There are clean towels in the hall closet," Jess said. "Make yourself at home. How does chicken and rice sound?"

"Sounds like real food. Thanks."

Seth went upstairs and Jess heard the shower turn on. She pulled chicken breasts out of the fridge, put them in a cake pan, added rice and soup, and popped it all in the oven. Then she sat back down, jotted the numbers off each check copy onto a piece of scrap paper, and started running her fingers down the columns of similar figures in Will's spreadsheets. About twenty pages in, just when her eyes were feeling like they might start to cross, something caught her attention and she backed up a line.

"There!" she said to an empty kitchen.

The number in one of the columns matched one on her scratch paper. She found the copy of the check bearing that particular number on the memo line. Following the row across on the spreadsheet, she could see the far left column included a date that matched the check and the next column included the dollar amount. The final column on that row in the spreadsheet included another series of numbers, along with some letters, but she didn't know what those meant.

Excited now, she opened the clips in the binder and pulled out the page where she'd found the entry that matched one of the checks. She gathered the piece of paper and the check copy, wanting to show Seth right away. The shower had turned off upstairs. A glance at the timer on the stove showed dinner wouldn't be ready for another thirty-five minutes.

The bathroom door was still closed when she reached the top of the stairs. Not wanting to burst in on Seth *again* when he was finishing up in the shower, she glanced around, looking for something to occupy herself with to give him another minute or two of privacy. Her eyes fell on the two tubs of Will's books she'd asked Nathan to put in the spare bedroom. He'd put them in the closet but hadn't closed the closet door. Maybe she should check to see if they contained anything more than books.

She snapped the overhead light on in the bedroom—it was getting dark. She set her papers down on the bed and pulled one of the tubs out of the closet, across the carpet, just far enough so she could sit down next to it.

The tub was black plastic, so she couldn't see through the sides. She started removing books, dropping them into piles around her.

The bathroom door opened. Seth came in, wearing jeans but no shirt yet, toweling off his hair. "I thought I heard someone in here." When he saw all the books, he laughed and said, "What are you doing *now*?"

Jess suspected she looked a sight, seated next to the tub surrounded with books.

"I came up to show you something, and when you weren't out of the bathroom yet, I decided to check something else real quick."

Seth draped the white towel around his neck and came farther into the room, peering into the tub she'd been digging in. "Let me guess. These are Will's, too."

"They are. But so far all I'm finding are books. Do you want to go back downstairs? I can look through these later. Supper will be done before too long."

Seth shook his head. "How much longer?"

"How much longer for what?" Jess asked, her attention split between the half-empty tub and the half-dressed man in the room. The way he was looking at her made her forget about the tub.

"Before dinner is ready?" he said, reaching a hand down to again help her up. This time he didn't release her hand but instead pulled her close. "You could have interrupted my shower, you know. It wouldn't have been the first time."

Jess reached her arms up to encircle his neck. His skin still felt damp from the shower, and he smelled *much* better. She let her fingers wander up into his hair, now dark red and curling from the towel-rub. She pressed herself up against him as he caught her up in a kiss that curled her toes.

"Twenty minutes," she said between kisses.

He chuckled. "Twenty minutes to stop kissing you, or . . . ?"

"No, twenty minutes until dinner is ready," she said, grinning up at him.

He rested his forehead against hers. "I don't want to distract you from figuring this thing out with Karen and your ex. Do you want me to help you finish looking through the tubs?"

"The tubs can wait."

Jess took Seth by the hand and led him back to her bedroom. He shut the door behind them and allowed Jess to pull him over to the side of her bed. There was little light, only enough to see silhouettes.

"I've missed you," he said, carefully lifting her shirt up over her head. His work-roughened hands gently caressed her breasts through the lace of her bra, then reached around to remove the barrier. Jess shivered as Seth's hands roamed over her back. "Are you cold?" he asked, feeling her tremble.

"Only the parts of me that aren't touching you," she said, pressing herself up against his warm body.

"Well, let's see what we can do to warm you up then," he whispered, lifting her up so she could wrap her legs around his waist. He sat down on the edge of her bed, Jess cradled in his lap, her feet on the bed behind him. They stayed that way, their kisses deepening. Seth moved his lips away from hers to trail light kisses across her cheek and down her neck. Jess leaned backward to give him access as his mouth trailed down to her breast.

"Who needs dinner when I have you?" he asked, making Jess squirm with need.

Eventually she had to pull first one leg and then the other out from behind him. "I'm not quite as flexible as I used to be," she said with a little laugh, moving to stand between his legs, dropping her head to continue kissing him. "If I stay like that too long, I'll get a cramp."

He laughed and lay down fully on the bed, pulling her with him. "Now we wouldn't want that, would we?" he said, rolling them both over so he had her body pinned below him.

"Still cold?" he asked.

"Not even a little."

CHAPTER 42

Gift of Revealing

*J*ess killed her engine in the prison parking lot, pausing for a moment to get her thoughts in order before going in to confront Will.

She'd eventually finished going through his two tubs the previous evening, after Seth had gone home and Harper was asleep. Near the bottom of both tubs, she'd found damning evidence against Will. She missed it at first, but then one of the piles of books she'd removed from the tub toppled over when it got too tall and a book fell open. Shocked, she saw the thick book had been hollowed out and a short stack of envelopes, secured with a rubber band, was tucked inside.

The envelopes contained bank statements—statements from the bank she and Patricia had recently visited. The accounts showed lots of activity, both in and out. Setting the statements aside, she'd dug further, finding four additional books converted to hiding spots.

Jess was now convinced, after finding those books last night, that Will was the man helping Karen. She hadn't yet told anyone else what she found in the tubs.

Light tapping on her vehicle brought her out of her own thoughts and back to the prison lot. A stiff wind was blowing, knocking dying leaves and cold rain into the Land Rover. Looping her purse straps around her neck and shoulder, Jess flipped up the hood on her rain coat and made a dash for the front door.

Inside, she paused to repair damage the rain and wind had done to her hair. The heavyset guard manning the front desk watched her with bored eyes. She couldn't recall seeing this particular guard before. Between the weather outside and the sea of miserable humanity locked up behind him, the man likely had little to enjoy about his job, and his face reflected it. Jess gave him a bright smile, trying to cheer him up. After today, she didn't plan to be back here for a long time, if ever. The poor guard probably spent half his life here.

He returned her grin with a tired one of his own. "And who might you be coming to see during visiting hours today?" he asked her, his voice a slow drawl, marking him as someone from somewhere south of Minnesota.

"Will Rand," she replied, handing him her identification.

"Huh," the guard grunted, referring to his computer screen as he began the process. "So what's the deal with this Rand character? This is only my first week on the job and you're the third woman to visit Will Rand since I started. Lucky s.o.b. has more women after him than I do, and *he's* doing time." He gave her an appraising look. "Bad boys turn you on?"

The man's rudeness rendered Jess temporarily speechless. Ordinarily, he would have found himself on the sharp edge of her tongue, but her attention was still snagged on his earlier comment about three woman stopping to see Will in a week.

Three?!

If she wanted to get any answers out of this crass man, she needed to appeal to his nature.

"Well, you seem like a smart man to me," Jess said, hoping she sounded flirty and not sarcastic. "Will's my husband, which you probably already figured out since we have the same last name. I thought, with him in here and all, that maybe the cheating would end . . ." Jess tried to sound bitter and a little heartbroken. She suspected the guard would respond better to a helpless, whimpering female than her usual straight-talking self.

She reached into her purse—the one he'd be searching shortly—and pulled out a tissue. She wiped at pretend tears, stowed the Kleenex back in her purse, and removed the photo of Karen and Will she'd pulled out of the album last night. She'd planned to use it to get Will to admit what he'd done if he tried to deny it, but it might come in handy now, too.

Tangled Beginnings | 383

"Was this one of the women?" she asked the guard, making her voice quiver ever so slightly.

He took the picture from her and glanced around to see if anyone else was in earshot. He studied the picture, handed it back to her, and shrugged.

"Might be, but her hair is different. Shorter and darker. Here a couple days ago. Bossy thing, that one. Didn't much care for her."

So Karen had likely stopped by. Jess hated to consider who the second woman might have been. Was Tiffany back again? She didn't have a picture of Tiffany to show the man, but that one was easier to guess at.

"Sounds like the bitch who was sleeping with my husband," she whispered to the guard.

"That first one *was* a bitch," he said. "If you're feeling too bad about your husband, I'd be willing to take you out on the town, get your mind off him. You're probably plenty lonely these days." The guard hoisted his pants up higher and arched his eyebrows at her.

Is this guy for real? Jess thought with disgust, hoping she wouldn't gag before she found out what she needed to know from him.

"You said there were *two* other women," she said. "Do you remember what the other one looked like?"

"Sure do. Sorry to tell you this, honey, but that one was a real looker. Bit younger than you, blond, built. Now *that* one looked like 'the other woman,' if you know what I mean."

Crap! The guard's description sounded like Tiffany, all right.

An older guard came through a heavy metal door behind the desk, and based on the way the first guard reacted, she suspected the guy who'd just come in was his superior.

"Got a problem up here, Stu?"

Jess's information source stood up straighter and stammered a bit as he replied.

"No . . . no, sir, no problem here. Just checking Mrs. Rand in here so she can go see her husband."

***

Since she hadn't let him know she was coming, Jess waited at the table while someone went to get Will. She was still mulling over the guard's comments about Will's two earlier visitors, sure the women had been Karen and Tiffany. *Karma is circling back to bite him now.*

Will didn't keep her waiting long.

"It's about damn time you came, Jess," Will said as he sat down across from her.

"What, you can't even spare me a proper hello?" Jess asked.

She suspected it wouldn't take him long to read the disgust she was feeling toward him on her face. He rubbed his own face with both hands. She recognized his effort to get a grip on his own emotions. Did he have some reason to suspect she might be on to his games? She decided to let him take the lead, see where this would go.

"I'm sorry. *Hello*, Jess. Are you here about the house? I was none too pleased when my lawyer brought me the papers to sign. Why would you accept such a lowball offer? We damn near *lost* money on that deal."

"Will, I told you before, I just wanted the house out of my hair. It was a good-faith bid, and I knew the buyers had cash in hand. I couldn't take the chance of waiting for a higher offer."

And without that mortgage hanging over my head, I'll be able to help the kids with their college costs. No thanks to you.

Will treated her to his signature eye roll she'd become so accustomed to over the years. It now had zero effect on her. She waited to see where he would take their conversation next. *Nothing like a little cat and mouse,* she thought.

"So, did you get everything moved out of the house? What did you do with all my stuff?"

"Don't worry. It's all safely stored in one of those temperature-controlled units out on 45th."

All except your tubs and your binder full of numbers, she thought. *But I'm not about to tell you that. Not yet.*

He looked at her suspiciously. "Everything?"

"Pretty much," she confirmed. "Oh, by the way, Nathan's pickup has been acting up. I let him drive your Lexus. He needs a dependable car, and it's not like you're using it these days."

Jess watched a light flush creep up Will's neck, but, surprisingly, he didn't say anything about his car. "All right. I may need a friend of mine to get access to my things in the storage locker. Can you give me the key, just in case?"

"Probably. Although it's not like I can just hand it to you here, right? Something tells me you aren't allowed to walk around with metal keys in your pocket."

Will pinned her with another one of his looks—but if he thought she would be intimidated, he better guess again. Jess pondered where she wanted to go first with Will—Tiffany or Karen?

Will decided for her.

"Jess, I have some bad news. I had a visitor this week," he said, pausing for her response.

She waited.

"Tiffany is back. Things got a little rocky for her in Chicago. She's considering moving back here, raising Harper herself."

Jess felt like she'd been punched in the gut. She couldn't keep doing this. Harper deserved a stable home, not a flakey mother who came and went on a whim.

"Jess, you *have* to know I want *you* to keep Harper. Despite all our other issues—and I admit most of our problems were my fault, not yours—you have always been the best damn mother to our kids."

"But Will, Harper isn't *our* child."

"And you have no idea how much I regret that fact," he said. For once, he looked sincere. But so much about their relationship had been a lie. What could she believe from this man?

"So where do things stand, then? With *her*, I mean. Do you think she's serious?"

"I think she's *unstable*. I think she lives in a fantasy land where someone is always expected to take care of her. I'm afraid she would have no clue what it takes to properly raise a child, nor do I think she has what it takes to stick it out."

Jess had to admit she enjoyed hearing Will say these things. "Do you think she sees Harper as a way to hold on to you?"

"I have no doubt. She's hoping I get out early and we can go back to being a happy little family. She seems to forget she bailed on me and Harper when the going got tough."

"What do you think the odds are of you getting out early, Will?" Jess asked. She'd never talked to him about his sentence. She hated to acknowledge her ex was a convicted criminal, even when visiting him in prison.

"My lawyer says if I keep my nose out of trouble, act the 'model inmate,' I could be out in two years."

If I'm right about you and Karen, Jess thought, watching the man she used to think she'd spend the rest of her life with as he sat across from her in standard-issue prison attire, *you're going to be in here for longer than you think.*

She would need to figure out what to do about Tiffany. No way could Jess give Harper back to her. She'd find a lawyer specializing in family law. There had to be a way.

But she'd come to see Will to find out about Karen. A glance at the clock behind Will's head showed visiting hours were winding down.

"I had lunch with Dad yesterday," Jess said, knowing her abrupt change in topic would throw Will off. He never liked it when a conversation shifted away from being all about him.

Will snorted. "How is old George doing?"

"*Old* George is great. It was nice to have some one-on-one time with him. It gave us a chance to really *talk* . . . to talk about some things we probably should have talked about years ago. It might have saved some heartache, but that can't be helped now."

Will said nothing but eyed her warily.

"Imagine my surprise," she continued, "when he told me you'd made it a bit of a habit to ask Celia for money."

The flush was back, this time reaching his cheeks. "Look, Jess, I told you. I went to that old bat and asked her for help when I wanted to buy our house. If she'd helped me out with the down-payment, I could have gotten a cheaper rate."

Jess nodded. "You did tell me that . . . but only recently. What you failed to mention was that it wasn't the *only* time you asked the 'old bat.'"

Will visibly squirmed. "There might have been one other time."

"One? And when she told you no, suggested you were capable of raising the money yourself and you didn't need handouts, how did that make you feel?"

"Oh no, you don't," he said, leaning toward Jess as he spoke. "You aren't going to get me to speak ill of the dead. All I'll say is she wasn't nearly as generous as she wanted people to think."

"Speak ill of the dead? What, like referring to her as an old bat?"

Will didn't respond to this.

"Did you think she owed you, Will?" Jess prodded, knowing it didn't usually take much to keep Will talking.

"Let's just say she could have done more."

"And when she didn't?"

Will shrugged. He wasn't taking the bait. Jess was going to have to try another angle.

"I'll admit I was surprised to find you'd been storing some of your old books in my convertible."

This got his attention. "Your convertible? Oh . . . yeah, an old buddy of mine from med school died and his wife called me. She was cleaning out his things and asked if I wanted his textbooks. I really didn't have a need for them, but I wanted to help her out, you know, take them off her hands so she had one less thing to worry about."

Always so concerned about helping out women in distress, Jess thought mockingly. *The fact one of the books had your name written in the front cover probably doesn't mean anything either.* Jess had to hand it to him, though—he was good at making things up on the fly.

"Did you put the tubs in my storage unit?" he asked.

She chose not to answer him directly. "Oh, by the way, I went through the filing cabinet in your office, too. I hated to put it away in storage without checking to see if there were any important papers in there, things I might need related to the kids or the house or anything else, you know?"

"My filing cabinet?" he asked, the flush of anger quickly draining away and being replaced by a look of fear. "You had a key?"

"Of course I had a key. Why wouldn't I have a key? I *bought* the thing. I've always had a key. I just never bothered to look in there before. Didn't think I had a reason to."

"Did you find anything important?"

She again chose not to directly answer him. *I probably shouldn't get such a kick out of playing with him like this . . . but he's earned it.*

"I kept a few things, locked it back up again, and hauled it to the storage unit."

A short, loud burst of sound came over the loudspeaker, indicating visiting hours would be over in five minutes. It was time to get to the point behind her visit.

"I found the binder and the bank statements, Will," she finally said, watching his reaction closely. She could almost hear the wheels grinding away in his mind as he tried to figure out how best to respond, how to find out how much she knew.

"What are you talking about? What bank statements? What binder?"

"Will, you should know by now that I'm not stupid. Naïve, maybe . . . too trusting, for sure . . . but not stupid. When you tried to tell me the money was all gone, it made no sense. It didn't compute."

"What are you implying, Jess?" Will's face appeared set in stone as he asked the question.

"I'm not implying anything. I'm simply telling you what I've discovered. The money isn't *gone*, it's just been *redirected*. So, tell me, have you and Karen been working on your little scheme for long? And just how many businesses have you hit?"

Will scoffed. "I always knew you suffered from a vivid imagination, Jess, but this takes the cake. What, did you read about something like this in one of those little novels you always have your nose buried in? Because I sure as hell don't know what you're talking about. Karen *who?*"

"Oh, please," Jess said with a sigh, in no mood to play any more games. "You know perfectly well what I'm talking about. What I don't understand is why you thought it was necessary. We didn't need the money. Celia never did anything to you. Did it start out as an affair, you and Karen? Or was it all about the money?"

Will watched her closely as she spoke. He must have reached the conclusion she wasn't going to let this go and she wasn't buying his innocent act. His voice got deadly quiet as he said, "Jess, I swear to God, if you tell *anyone* about this, you will regret it. You might think you know what happened, but you have no idea."

Poor Will. He had no idea things were already moving along, well out of her control. Patricia had called her on her drive over to the prison to let her know she'd had a chance to speak to her father, John, about their concerns with Karen. John was furious and refused to wait to contact the authorities. For all Jess knew, they might even be questioning Karen right at this very moment. Jess hadn't personally named Will as a possible accomplice to anyone but Seth, but she couldn't know if Karen would rat him out.

"Will, don't threaten me. You don't have a leg to stand on. How about this? How about you figure out a way to make Tiffany leave us alone, *permanently*, and let me raise Harper? You make that happen and I'll consider keeping your involvement in Karen's little scheme to myself. Of course, I can't vouch for whether or not *she* will implicate you, but you know I'm good for *my* word. Something you can't say for yourself, and neither can your partner."

Jess stood up. The one thing she knew would never change was Will's extremely strong sense of self-preservation. He *would* figure out a way to make sure Tiffany didn't take Harper, even if it was only to save his own skin.

"Figure out a way for me to keep Harper or you won't see the light of day for another ten to twenty."

***

Jess felt lighter as she crossed the prison parking lot. The rain had stopped and the sun was emerging through broken clouds. Answers were helping to loosen the tangled mess that had held her to Will for so long. Things were starting to make sense. Their money wasn't gone simply because of their lifestyle. She'd known for a long time that Will couldn't be trusted, but in this moment she finally felt free from him. Free of his manipulation and even free from her own guilt over their failed marriage.

Free to start over.

Her phone vibrated in her hand as she reached her vehicle. Glancing down, she saw a text from Lauren.

Tiffany is here! She's threatening to take Harper!
COME HOME NOW!

CHAPTER 43

Gift of a Refuge

$\mathcal{L}$auren had called her mother the previous evening.

"Mom, both my classes were canceled for tomorrow. I was thinking maybe I'd come hang out at Whispering Pines with Harper. You know . . . keep her home from daycare for the day. I didn't get to see her much over the weekend with all the packing and moving."

"But Lauren, that's a lot of driving. You just got back to school yesterday. Besides, you'd need to be here before eight if you were going to watch her. I've got a teleconference first thing."

Good old Mom, ever practical, Lauren thought. Aloud she said, "I was looking at my schedule and I have lots of tests coming up starting next week. I'll barely get to see you guys. Come on, Mom, it's just one day. Let me have a little fun with Harper."

Lauren eventually managed to get Jess to agree. She'd been prepared to admit she was feeling a little homesick, a card she knew she could use to gain her mom's sympathy, but it wasn't necessary.

She was awake by six. Jess was getting Harper up for the day when Lauren arrived. Their morning passed quickly. Jess worked from the kitchen table and left at ten, telling Lauren she needed to go visit Will at the prison. Lauren shivered at the thought. She did miss her dad a little, but there was no way she'd ever go visit him in prison. She was sure one trip inside would give her nightmares for life. Nathan had told her he'd gone to see their dad, but Lauren had no plans to do the same.

By eleven, Harper was rubbing her eyes. Lauren laid the baby down for a nap, deciding to take her on a walk after lunch, much as her mother told her they'd done the day before. Lauren hoped they'd find the cardinal Jess told her about. She would have liked to take Harper down by the beach to play in the sand, too, but it was too cold.

While Harper was napping, Lauren pulled out her computer. She needed to take an online quiz for her anthropology course before midnight. The quiz was harder than she'd expected. By the time she finished, she could hear Harper upstairs in her crib, calling out for attention. Once her sister started talking in a way the rest of them could understand, Lauren suspected they were going to have a real chatterbox on their hands. She shut her computer down and headed for the stairs, stopped short by a quick rap on the door.

She peeked through the peephole and saw Renee standing there.

"Hey, auntie," Lauren greeted Renee as she pulled open the front door. "What's up?"

"Hi, Lauren. Your mom texted me that you were going to be hanging out here with Harper today. Listen, I just wanted to let you know I need to run into town for a meeting. Are you going to be all right out here, just the two of you? The only other people around today are the folks starting to clear the land back on the far corner of the resort. Just FYI—if you see some strange guys around, don't worry, they're supposed to be here. Matt had the early shift this morning, so he should be home by four or so. I probably will be, too."

"So you guys decided to go ahead with the new house?" Lauren asked.

"We did! I hope we won't regret it. My meeting is with our architect. Someone Ethan suggested. Just an initial meeting, so I can give him some general ideas as to what we're thinking and he can come out here to check on things like the elevation of where we're going to build, that type of thing."

"That's exciting!" Lauren said, and meant it. She liked Renee's new husband, Matt, and was happy her aunt had found someone after so many years. Hopefully Jess would do the same someday. She hated the thought of her mom being all alone. Maybe her mom and Seth would turn into something more . . . "Don't worry about me and Harper. We'll be fine."

An indignant little shout from upstairs made them both laugh. "I think she can hear us and wants up. We'll have lunch and then I'm going to take her for a walk. I'm sure the afternoon will go fast."

"Sounds fun. Keep an eye on the weather, though. There's a chance for heavy rain this afternoon, and it's not very warm out," Renee cautioned.

"Will do. I'll throw an umbrella in the stroller, just in case. If it starts to rain, there's a canopy on the stroller, too. We won't melt."

Another screech from upstairs sent Renee on her way so Lauren could attend to Harper.

***

"Renee was right," Lauren said, talking to her little sister in the stroller as they made their way down the gravel road. "It's *cold* out here."

She probably should have dressed warmer herself, but she had been focused on making sure Harper was all bundled up. The poor kid had so many layers on she could barely move in her stroller. At least she'd thought to grab her mom's jacket off the hook by the front door and put it on. She wasn't used to the weather being cool and had left her own coat back in her dorm room.

"Where's your cardinal, sweetie?" Lauren asked, hoping to spot the brightly colored bird for Harper. Beyond the treetops, gray clouds rolled in. "Maybe your bird is staying out of this weather."

Lauren continued walking, pushing the stroller and pointing things out to Harper as they went. Harper communicated back as if Lauren could understand her, which of course she couldn't. It didn't matter. Lauren was enjoying the company.

A cold, fat raindrop plopped on Lauren's nose, causing her to stop and laugh. Harper looked up at her, pointed, and giggled too. Scurrying sounds in the brush off to their left caught both their attention and they gasped in awe when a small deer stepped out onto the path near them.

Harper's little eyes popped as wide open as they could and her pretty little mouth formed a perfect circle. She pointed a chubby finger at the deer but stayed quiet, as if she could sense that any sound might frighten the animal away. The three of them all stood perfectly still, watching, barely breathing.

A flash of color swooped in front of them, and a bright red cardinal landed gracefully on the road, feet from the deer. The deer looked lazily at the bird and back at the sisters, seemingly unconcerned. The bird squawked, loud and clear, hopping aggressively toward the four-legged animal. Now the deer shuffled back a few steps, unsure of the bird's aggression. One more squawk and the deer turned tail and ran, disappearing back into the forest.

"Now why did you have to scare the pretty deer away, birdie?" Lauren asked, curious about the bird's actions. "He wasn't bothering you."

Now the bird flew up and over their heads, landing again on the road, but this time in front of the girls, almost as if blocking their path forward. It let out three loud squawks, taking tiny little hops in their direction.

Harper looked from Lauren to the bird and back to Lauren again, clearly wondering about the crazy bird too.

Lauren laughed. "Maybe Auntie Renee sent her, telling us to turn around and go home before we get rained on."

The red bird tilted its head slightly, as if listening.

The crunch of tires heading toward them surprised Lauren. She quickly scooted Harper's stroller over to the side of the road. She hadn't expected to encounter anyone on their walk—except maybe their cardinal friend.

The cardinal flew away.

Lauren could tell the driver was moving slowly but was still heading in their direction. Maybe someone had taken a wrong turn. They wouldn't be able to turn around on this narrow road until they reached the parking lot at Whispering Pines. A chill ran down Lauren's spine. She suddenly felt vulnerable as the thick pines pressed in on both sides of the lane. Maybe bringing little Harper out here wasn't such a good idea.

The slowly approaching vehicle made the curve up ahead and a navy-colored, four-door sedan came into view. A few scattered raindrops found their way through the treetops above, smattering the windshield. The driver flipped the wipers on, then off. Lauren tried to make out the driver but couldn't. When the car was still a couple of yards in front of them, it slowed further, then stopped. Lauren could hear the transmission shift into Park and the driver-side door opened with a squeak.

What the hell? Lauren thought, shocked at the face she could now see clearly, the blond hair, and even the white jacket she recognized from before.

"Tiffany?"

"*There's* my baby!" the woman said in a high sing-song voice, her gaze locked on Harper in her stroller. "Oh, how I've *missed* you, my sweet little petunia. How's Momma's little girl?"

"Tiffany," Lauren said again, louder this time. "What are you *doing* here?"

The woman looked from Harper to Lauren, as if noticing her for the first time. Lauren thought Tiffany's eyes looked odd, unfocused. Her grip tightened on the stroller's handle.

Something isn't right here.

Lauren hadn't seen Tiffany since last spring. Her mom had told her Tiffany had left her dad high and dry with the baby, ran out on both of them. Since it had been so long ago now, Lauren had assumed Tiffany was gone for good.

Tiffany didn't seem to recognize her. "Why, I came to take my precious little baby home with me. I've missed you so much, Harper. We need to go home and get everything ready. Your daddy can't come home quite yet, but when he does, we'll be waiting for him. The three of us will make the perfect little family."

Lauren stepped between the stroller and Tiffany, who was coming closer and closer as she talked to Harper in that sickening voice. The drizzle picked up. Lauren considered turning the stroller around and making a dash back toward the duplex. But that would be slow going, and Tiffany had a car. She looked over Tiffany's shoulder at the vehicle, considering whether or not she could safely get Harper into it and get away from this crazy woman. Doubtful.

Tiffany stopped three feet away, tearing her gaze away from Harper as Lauren blocked her view of the child with her body. The older woman squinted at Lauren, as if trying to place her. This close, Lauren could see how glazed and confused Tiffany's eyes looked. *She's really messed up* was all Lauren had time to think before Tiffany tried to push her out of the way.

"Move!" Tiffany grunted as she reached for Harper, but Lauren was taller and Tiffany wobbled on her high heels. Lauren shoved back, causing Tiffany to shuffle back three steps.

The sky opened, rain quickly drenching all three of them.

"Oh, this *rain!*" Tiffany said, holding her hands over her head. "It'll ruin my hair. I need my umbrella." She turned and jogged back to the sedan. The fact she said nothing about the baby getting wet spoke volumes to Lauren about the woman's state of mind.

Lauren saw an opening and took it. She turned to Harper, quickly snapped her little seatbelt off, and scooped the child out of the stroller. Seeing no other options, Lauren took Harper and slipped as quietly as she could into the woods rimming the road, leaving the stroller behind. She needed to put distance between her and Harper's mother as quickly as possible. Would Tiffany try to follow them?

It didn't take long before Lauren could hear Tiffany yelling for Harper. She even yelled Lauren's name. *So somewhere in that mess of a brain she remembers me,* Lauren thought, stepping as carefully through the dense underbrush as possible while carrying the baby. Harper wrapped her little arms tightly around Lauren's neck, as if she sensed the need to stay quiet and hold on tight.

Eventually, Lauren could no longer hear Tiffany. She must not have followed. A fallen log, covered with brush and all manner of forest debris caught up in the tree's dead branches, promised a measure of shelter. Lauren crawled underneath it, careful to hold Harper in such a way that she wouldn't get scratched by the sharp branches. Lauren sat on the relatively dry ground and held Harper in her lap. Their temporary shelter kept most of the rain out and Lauren was able to rest for a minute. Running through heavy brush with a crazy woman behind you and a nine-month-old on your hip was hard work.

When her heartbeat slowed a bit and she could breathe normal again, Lauren pulled out her cell phone. She couldn't get enough of a signal to call her mom, so she tried sending her a text. Seconds later her phone flashed *Not Delivered* in red letters.

Dammit!

Harper started to squirm in her arms. The baby didn't cry, but Lauren thought her lips looked a little blue. They'd freeze if they stayed out in this weather too long. Lauren dug in the pocket of her jacket, hoping Jess had a tissue stashed there so she could wipe Harper's nose. She pulled out a tissue and something hard and sharp poked her hand. As she shook out the tissue, she was surprised to see a rock fall to the ground. Bending down and picking it up, she realized it was the arrowhead she'd given her mom last summer, the one she'd pulled out of the lake. Her mom had called it "lucky." Maybe it would keep them safe today.

We need all the luck we can get, Lauren thought, dropping the arrowhead back into her pocket.

Tiffany had seemed so focused on Harper, she was afraid the woman wouldn't simply drive away and leave them alone. She was probably waiting for them at Whispering Pines. Lauren didn't want to chance it. Maybe she could make her way through the woods, steering clear of the resort itself, and find the guys Renee said were working on their lot, take the long way around to them. She'd keep trying to get a signal on the way. While she hated to leave the shelter of their tree, she was afraid she didn't have a choice.

"Hold on, honey," she said to Harper as she crawled out from under the tree.

She set off in what she hoped was the right direction. The trees were so thick she was afraid she was getting a little turned around. She walked and walked, pausing once in a while to rest and check her phone. Finally, she thought maybe one of her texts to her mom went through. She prayed it did. The rain, which had slowed to an annoying drizzle, was freezing cold. The wind picked up and Lauren would have sworn she heard a rumble of thunder.

In October?

Lauren was starting to lose hope. Harper dozed fitfully in her arms. Lauren was so tired she didn't know if she could walk much farther with her little sister. Maybe she should have chanced going back to Whispering Pines right away. Dashing into the woods had been stupid.

As she stepped carefully around another fallen tree, a sound caught her attention.

What was that?

She thought she'd heard a clanging of some kind, but she couldn't tell over the rising wind.

She heard it again. It sounded like metal on metal.

Curious, she forked a little to the left toward the sound. The wind sighed above them. Despite the persistent drizzle, the sun peeked through the clouds above and the sun's rays shone down. The light glinted off something up ahead.

Is that water?

Had her wanderings brought them back out to the lake?

No, it looked like something solid. As she got closer she could see it was an old, dilapidated camper. She slowed. What if some weirdo lived out here?

The way our day is going, it wouldn't surprise me, she thought.

It didn't look like anyone was around. She heard the sound again, and could see an old lantern, hanging from what looked like a clothes line, swing in the wind and bang against the metal pole holding the clothes line upright.

"Hello? Anyone here?" Lauren called out, despite her fear someone might be home.

Nothing other than the sighing of the wind met her question. The drizzle again turned into a downpour. Left with no other options, Lauren made a dash for the camper.

Please let the door be unlocked!

CHAPTER 44

Gift of Reinforcements

*J*ess slammed on her brakes and her tires skidded on the last few feet of gravel as she pulled into the lot at Whispering Pines. Lauren's car was there, as was a blue four-door she didn't recognize. There were no other vehicles in the lot, meaning neither Renee nor Matt were home yet. Renee didn't answer her phone—she must still be meeting with their architect. She'd also tried to reach Matt on her frantic drive home from the prison but got his voicemail. She knew he'd come as soon as he could.

Maybe she was overreacting. Tiffany probably just wanted to see Harper. It was unfortunate she'd shown up, out of the blue, and obviously scared Lauren based on her daughter's text. Lauren wasn't answering her phone. Maybe the battery died, but Jess had a nasty feeling in her gut.

She hurried toward the path that would lead her to the duplex but pulled up short when she saw Harper's stroller sitting abandoned on the sidewalk.

She called Lauren's name but there was no answer.

Another sense of foreboding flashed through her mind. She left the stroller where it was and jogged toward home. A cold rain still fell here, making the scattered leaves on the path slippery under her feet. She slowed so she wouldn't fall.

As she broke from the cover of the trees into their front yard, she slid to a halt. Someone, probably Tiffany, was rocking in the old Adirondack rocker on the porch, sitting back in the shadows away from the falling rain. Jess approached at a measured pace, trying to see who it was through the gloom.

"Hello?" she said loudly enough that whoever was there surely heard her; but the figure said nothing, only continued to rock. Jess made it to the bottom of the stairs. Now she could see it was, indeed, Tiffany, albeit a bedraggled Tiffany.

"Jess," she said with a small nod.

"Tiffany? Are you all right? You're soaking wet."

Tiffany shook her head side to side, slowly at first but then faster and faster. Jess saw a hard shiver shake the woman's whole body and then the head movement ceased. Tears were flowing down her cheeks.

"I'm afraid I scared Lauren off."

"What do you mean, 'scared Lauren off'? Tiffany, where are Lauren and Harper?"

"In the woods."

"In the woods," Jess said, as if repeating what Tiffany said would force it to make sense. "What in heaven's name would they be doing *in the woods*?" After Tiffany didn't respond, Jess said, "Why don't we go inside? You're freezing, and I'm starting to feel the same."

"Are you sure you want me inside? I think I'm losing my mind, Jess."

Maybe I should wait until Matt gets here, Jess thought, but changed her mind when she saw Tiffany suffer another violent shivering attack.

"Of course you aren't losing your mind. Come on. We need to find the girls. They shouldn't be out in this weather."

Jess climbed the stairs and unlocked her front door. Tiffany pushed out of the chair, slowly shuffled her way over to the door, and followed Jess inside.

"There's no way you'll get warm with your clothes soaked like that. Do you want me to get you a dry outfit?" Jess asked.

Tiffany took her jacket off and hung it on a nearby hook, her movements robotic. "No, that's OK. You're right. We have to find the girls. There's no time to worry about me."

Jess nodded and pulled out her cell phone, walking back to her kitchen. "Why don't you come back here and sit down? I'll get us coffee and try my brother-in-law again. He's the sheriff, he should know what to do."

This time Matt picked up.

"Jess, I just got your message and was about to call you back. Tell me again what's happening. Your message was a little garbled."

"Never mind that. I'm home now and I'm afraid Lauren and Harper are out in the woods. They might be lost. And Matt, Tiffany is here."

Matt swore softly. "Sorry, that's unprofessional," he apologized, "but what the hell would they be doing in the woods in this weather? We only have a few hours of daylight left, too."

"I was just going to find out more when I called you. I'm not exactly sure *why* they're out there, but I don't think we want to waste time trying to figure that out right now. We need to find them."

"I agree. I'll bring a couple of deputies with me and we'll be there as soon as we can. Don't go out looking for them by yourself. I don't want to have to find three people instead of the two already out there."

Jess hated to make that promise, but she did. Waiting would be excruciating, but she knew Matt was right.

"All right. Sit tight. Oh hey, Jess, do you track Lauren on her cell?"

Jess smacked her forehead. "Why didn't I *think* of that? Yes! Oh my God, maybe it won't be so hard to find her."

"It should help, as long as her phone is on and there's enough of a signal," he confirmed. "I have to go. Remember, stay put."

Jess occasionally used her phone to check up on Lauren but now when she tried, all she got was *Location Unavailable*.

Damn . . .

She set her phone down on the counter and brought a cup of coffee over to Tiffany. It would be at least twenty minutes before Matt could get here. She'd keep trying to locate the girls with her phone, but she might as well get the story out of Tiffany now, too, in case it would help find them.

"Help is on the way. Here, use this towel to at least dry your hair," Jess said, handing her a dish towel out of the drawer. "We're supposed to wait for them. Why don't you tell me what happened?"

Tiffany raised the coffee cup to her lips with shaking hands and took a fortifying drink of the hot brew. "Jess, I was serious when I said I'm afraid

I'm losing my mind. I think something's wrong with me. I keep having these episodes . . . like I black out or something."

Sure looks like you lost your mind, Jess thought. She was starting to understand why Lauren ran.

"Do you think you had one of these episodes and it scared Lauren? Is that what you meant about scaring her?"

"Maybe. I should back up." She paused to take another drink, and Jess noticed that her shaking was already beginning to subside. "I don't know if you remember from when we talked before, but I was trying to make a life for myself in Chicago. I realized I wasn't in any shape to try to raise Harper on my own then, when I barely had any money and Will wasn't able to help. I went back there, and Jess, I *swear* I tried. I worked hard and saved my money. But then . . . I don't know . . . it's like something comes over me and I can't control myself. I go out, drink too much, party with strangers, and when I come out of it, I'm right back at square one again. Broke and alone."

And you think you can raise Harper now? Jess thought, but kept quiet, needing to understand where Tiffany's head was at on all of this. Tiffany still held the trump card when it came to Harper. Maybe Will was wrong about her intentions.

"Tiffany, I'm sorry, but I have to ask. Did you take anything? Any drugs? Either street drugs or prescription?"

"I do have antidepressants, but sometimes I forget to take them and then things get worse."

Jess nodded. "Consistency is so important with antidepressants. So things weren't going well in Chicago. What brings you here? Today? I just visited Will and he told me you stopped to see him."

Mentioning Will was a bad idea. Tiffany's shoulders began to shake and the tears started to flow again. Between hitching breaths she said, "I thought if we could just . . . go back to the way we were *before* . . . before Harper was born, before he was sent away to prison . . . I'd be OK. But *with* Harper now, of course, we can't go back to life without her. I know Will still loves me . . . we could be a *family* again."

Jess pitied the woman sitting beside her at her kitchen table. Her grip on reality, like her grip on the coffee mug, was shaky at best.

"Tiffany, we need to talk about Will . . . but now is not the time or the place. You need to tell me what happened this afternoon with Lauren and Harper."

Tiffany nodded, took another long drink of her coffee, and told Jess how she'd driven to Whispering Pines with the hope of seeing her daughter. It had been months, and she'd felt as if she'd die if she didn't see her again. Lauren had Harper out for a walk in her stroller. When she said she'd come upon them on the road, Jess gasped.

"No, no, don't worry," Tiffany said, reaching across the table to squeeze Jess's hand. Jess had to stop herself from ripping her hand away. "I saw them in plenty of time. I stopped and got out. It was so overwhelming to see Harper again, it was almost too much for me. I scared Lauren. It started to pour down rain so I went to my car to get an umbrella, and when I turned back around . . . the girls were gone."

"Gone? What do you mean, *gone*?"

"The stroller was there, but they weren't. I knew Lauren must have run into the woods with Harper. I wanted to go after them, but . . ." Tiffany hesitated, pointing to the high-heeled ankle boots sitting next to the door. "I knew I wouldn't get far in those. I'd break an ankle for sure. I honestly thought Lauren would just run with Harper back here, to the resort, so I followed the road the rest of the way in my rental and walked around, yelling and looking for them. But they never came. Everything was locked up tight, so finally I sat out on the porch here to get out of the rain."

"How did you know this is where we live? And not in one of the other cabins?"

Tiffany shrugged. "I didn't. Like I said, I just needed to get out of the rain."

"Why was the stroller sitting out by the lodge?" Jess asked. "If you saw them out on the road to the highway, and Lauren ran into the woods, why isn't the stroller still out there?"

Another shrug. "I couldn't very well leave it out there. I brought it back. I couldn't figure out how to fold the damn thing up, though, so I just left my trunk open and drove slow."

Jess could accept that. One mystery solved. "Now, Tiffany, this is important. Do you remember what time it was when you saw the girls?"

Tiffany picked up the towel she'd ignored up to this point and used it on her now-drying hair. Her eyes took on a faraway look, as if she were struggling to remember. She shook her head slowly and said nothing.

A shuffling out on the deck had Jess up and out of her chair in an instant.

"Lauren?!" she yelled, relief flowing through her.

"No, sorry, Jess, it's just me," Renee said as she came through Jess's unlocked door. "I saw a missed call from you but before I could call you back, Matt called and told me the girls were missing. I came as quick as I could. He should be here any minute. I take it they haven't shown up yet?"

Jess shook her head as she hurried over to her sister's side. Renee saw the despair on Jess's face and caught her younger sister up in a hug, trying to reassure her everything would be all right. Matt would find them. She caught a glimpse of the woman sitting in Jess's kitchen.

"What the hell is *she* doing here?" she asked. "Does Matt know she's here?"

Jess nodded. "Tiffany came to see Harper. Things didn't go well and she's afraid she scared Lauren into the woods."

"Were they still on their walk when she got here?" Renee asked.

"Well, yes . . . but how did you know they went on a walk?" Jess asked, confused.

"I talked to Lauren just before I ran into town. She told me they were going to have lunch and then go for a walk."

"How long ago was that?"

Renee checked her watch. "It's almost 4:30 now. That must have been about 12:30. My appointment was at 1:30 and then I stopped to pick up groceries afterward."

"So if they ate before they went out, it was probably two o'clock or so by the time they left the house. Hopefully Lauren's found some way to stay warm. They've still been out there, what . . . maybe two hours?"

Renee hadn't closed the inside door when she came in; they could hear male voices through the screen, heading their way.

"There's Matt and his guys," Renee said, releasing Jess and heading back outside.

***

The next ten minutes were a whirlwind of activity. Matt couldn't pick up Lauren's phone through Jess's tracking, either.

"Not surprising—she hasn't called or texted. But I *did* get one text from her," Jess said. "That's how I knew to come home."

"Maybe she just found a fluke signal for a minute. But don't worry. We'll find her." Matt turned to Tiffany, still in her chair in the kitchen. "I need you to go out on the road with us, show us where you last saw Lauren and Harper."

The three women followed Matt and his men. Tiffany thought she remembered the spot, and they searched the immediate area to determine whether or not it was where Lauren ducked into the woods. Jess let out a choked cry when she saw something bright in the grass.

It was Harper's favorite pacifier.

"Well, at least we know they came by here," Matt said. "But we can't be sure this is where Lauren ran in."

Luckily the rain had moved on and weak sunlight was now finding its way down through the treetops.

"I'm pretty sure this is the place," Tiffany said, although she didn't sound very sure.

"I'd say it's our best option," Jess said, turning to Matt. She was done talking. They needed to get in those woods and find her girls. "Can we split up and start looking?"

Matt studied Jess for a moment. "You're right. We aren't going to have any way to know for sure. So yes, let's get moving."

Renee was standing off to the side, looking shaken. Jess noticed her first. "Renee, come on—don't you want to help?" When Renee didn't respond, Jess walked over to her side. "What's up, sis? Something wrong?"

This seemed to snap Renee out of her trance. "God. I'm so sorry, Jess . . . it just felt like déjà vu, Matt organizing search parties and another one of our kids missing."

"This is different. Come on, Renee. That was a nutcase stalking your Julie. This is just Lauren and Harper, getting a little lost in the woods. No one is going to hurt them. We just have to find them before they get sick from the cold."

"You're right. I'm sorry. Let's go find them."

"But what about me?" Tiffany whined. "I can't go off traipsing around in the woods in *these* shoes. My feet already hurt from walking this far."

Matt eyed the spineless woman, clearly irritated with her. "Fine. Wait here or walk back to the resort and wait there. We have to get going."

Matt had brought two deputies with him. The men checked that their walkie-talkies were working and then split up, one deputy going with Renee, the other with Jess, and Matt set out on his own. Jess was less than thrilled to see her brother-in-law head out alone, but she bit her tongue when he shot her a look that was non-negotiable.

Almost an hour into their search, Jess fought off despair. She was cold, hungry, and her feet hurt. She could only imagine how miserable the girls must be by now, wherever they were.

Just then the radio the deputy walking beside her carried crackled and Matt's voice came through.

"I got 'em."

***

Jess couldn't stop fussing over the girls. They were cold and hungry, but it was nothing hot baths and some food couldn't take care of. Lauren wanted to drive back to school so she wouldn't miss class in the morning, but Jess put her foot down. Lauren would sleep under her roof tonight, and if she was fine in the morning, she could drive herself back then.

Missing one class wasn't the end of the world. It was dark out and she'd had a traumatic day.

Jess could still hardly believe the story Matt shared when they were all back safely in the duplex and he'd sent his deputies home. One of them took Tiffany back to her hotel. Before she left, Tiffany was allowed to hold Harper for a few minutes. Jess hovered close by, conflicted over whether or not to even let the woman touch the little girl. But Harper put up a fuss and it wasn't long before Tiffany was handing the baby back.

Once the girls were both in bed, and it was just Jess, Renee, and Matt, Matt shared the story of how he'd managed to find the girls.

He'd heard something, something out of place. When he'd gone to investigate, he started to take the right fork in a path but stopped when a red cardinal landed in front of him, blocking his path. When he stopped, he heard the sound again, but it was farther to his left.

"Celia," Jess whispered.

Matt paused in his recount of what happened to give Jess a confused look. She motioned for him to continue. He went on to report he decided to instead follow the other path to the left. It took him to a deserted campground, complete with a derelict camper. He yelled the girls' names and was shocked to see the door fling open to reveal Lauren standing in the doorway. Harper was inside, asleep on an old cushion.

"And now your daughter thinks I'm a hero," Matt said, giving Jess a wink.

"*I* think you're a hero, too, Matt," Jess said, winking back. "And here I thought you were bad news the first time I saw you here with Renee. Guess I was wrong."

"You thought I was bad news?" Matt asked, clutching at his heart. "I'm shocked."

"Oh, shut up," Jess said with a tired laugh. She stood. "Should I throw in a pizza?"

"Sounds great. I've gotta call in the serial number on that camper, see who it belongs to. It looked abandoned to me. If we can't find the owner, which I suspect will be the case, I'll get it hauled out of there. It was a safe haven for the girls today, but the next time someone stumbles across it, it might be utilized for something less desirable."

CHAPTER 45

Gift of Awareness

*J*ess scanned the hotel restaurant for Tiffany. They'd arranged to meet for breakfast to discuss things. Jess's stomach roiled. She'd never be able to eat. She was more convinced than ever that Tiffany wasn't fit to raise Harper. Jess needed to convince Tiffany of this, and she wasn't sure she'd be able to. Tiffany might still be living her fantasy about building a life with Will and Harper.

She'd tossed and turned most of the night, debating what to say to Tiffany. Should she convince her Will was scum and she shouldn't waste another minute of her life waiting for him? Jess suspected Will had been having an affair with Karen for at least a decade, although she hadn't yet been able to prove it. Should she pretend she knew this for a fact and convince Tiffany that Will loved Karen? Maybe she could mention that Karen had been visiting him in prison, too. Would that shatter the woman's ill-founded illusion?

Or should she try to blackmail her? Convince her Will would implicate her in the case that landed him in jail in the first place if she didn't sign over her parental rights to Jess?

Jess didn't like to fight dirty. It was why she'd slept very little and why she felt sick to her stomach now. She wasn't looking to destroy this woman's life. She only wanted what was best for Harper.

***

In the end, whatever Jess decided she'd say to Tiffany was irrelevant. The hostess approached Jess, a questioning look on her face.

"Are you Jess Rand?" the older woman asked.

"Why, yes, I am. I'm supposed to be meeting someone here."

The woman nodded and turned her back on Jess, walking around a counter and pulling an envelope out from beside the cash register. She handed it to Jess. "I'm afraid your party won't be able to join you this morning, but she left this for you. Would you like to stay for breakfast?"

Jess, again caught off guard by the unpredictable Tiffany, shook her head and turned away, walking back out through the lobby and out to the parking lot, all the while holding the envelope by the corner, afraid of what it might contain. Once she was cocooned in the privacy of her vehicle, she inhaled deeply and broke the seal, vowing to herself she would figure out how to deal with whatever curveball Tiffany was throwing her way this time. She unfolded the single page of hotel stationery to find a handwritten letter.

Dear Jess,

I'm sorry for all the heartache I've caused you and your family. You are a decent person, so much better than I could ever hope to be.

I finally realized something yesterday. I'm not fit to raise a child, especially on my own. Harper is a beautiful baby, inside and out. Thank you for letting me hold her again. I'll hold that memory close to my heart forever.

You must believe me when I say I only want what is best for my daughter. I've thought long and hard about this, except when I'm incapable of thinking at all of course. I may be her biological mother, but you are her true mother. You can give her what she'll need to grow to be a beautiful young woman, just as you have done with Lauren.

Will is her father but he doesn't deserve her. There is something fundamentally flawed with that man. It's taken me until now to realize it. But his one redeeming quality is that he truly loves his children. He's morally corrupt, but he's not stupid, and he also knows you are the best person to raise Harper.

Below you will find the name and phone number for my lawyer. Get yourself a good family lawyer and have him contact mine. I want to sign over my parental rights to you and I want it done in a legal and binding way. I know myself, and I have to completely sever all ties or I will spend the rest of my days seesawing between knowing I'm bad for her and wanting her back. I need to remove those options.

Thank you, from the bottom of my heart, for being willing to give so much of yourself to care for that which means the most to me.

Sincerely,
Tiffany

CHAPTER 46

Gift of Justice

The case against Karen took on a life of its own. Once the authorities were involved, it didn't take them long to put all the pieces together.

Karen and Will had been at it for years, finding creative ways to steadily steal first small amounts of money and then growing sums from small businesses around town. They targeted smaller companies with lax internal controls. They were smart in that they didn't take huge amounts at once, instead keeping it small at each business and stealing over months and years instead of in big hits. They had an elaborate system for tracking what they were doing.

As Jess suspected, their relationship went beyond their embezzling scheme. Their affair began shortly after they met at Celia's birthday party, around the time of Jess and Will's tenth wedding anniversary. Both Karen and Will were jealous of Celia's success and disgusted by her unwillingness to share her wealth directly with them. Their feelings of entitlement and jealousy provided a common ground off of which they built their twisted relationship.

Will did not choose well when he picked Karen to partner with in their endeavors. When things heated up with the police, she was quick to tell everything. Will, on the other hand, said little.

Jess was interviewed due to both her relationship with Will and her assistance in uncovering the fraud. She turned over the items she'd found in his office as well as the tubs from the garage. One of the detectives interviewing Jess found it hard to believe she had been ignorant to her husband's scheming for over a decade. She didn't appreciate his leap to judgment.

"I put my husband through medical school, raised our two children—not to mention raising his illegitimate child now—and worked hard to build a life with him," Jess said, struggling to control her anger at this stranger's audacity to question *her* character. "He loved to spend money, yes, but the man was a *surgeon*. He *made* lots of money. I knew he cheated on me with at least one other woman, and I eventually left him because of it. But I never had any reason to suspect he was stealing. The first indication I had that he was funding his lifestyle on something other than his salary was when he was indicted for the prescription-fraud ring at the hospital that landed him in jail. How *dare* you sit here and judge me."

The detective, a man at least ten years younger than Jess, squirmed under her direct gaze and reprimand. His partner, a woman of around fifty, held up her hand to stop him from saying anything else that would further infuriate Jess.

"Look, Ms. Rand, I feel your pain," the woman detective said. "Men like your husband are master manipulators. I applaud you for taking steps to get out from under his hold. I also understand you've been raising a child he fathered with a younger woman he had an affair with while still married to you. That's some serious shit, woman. I'm sorry if my partner here is a bit over-zealous in his assumptions. He has a lot to learn."

The woman glared at her partner then turned back to Jess.

"That will be all. Thank you for your help on the case."

***

Karen took a plea deal. There was no hiding what they'd done, so the time and cost of a trial wasn't warranted. She cooperated with the forensic accountants in compiling summaries of how much she and Will stole from each business. Every penny of Karen's inheritance from Helen went to pay back what they'd taken.

What goes around comes around, Jess thought, not missing the irony of the situation.

Will's sentence was extended as well due to his involvement. Harper would be starting college by the time he had any chance of release, whether he was a "model inmate" or not.

Jess was able to keep Celia's name out of everything. Her aunt's journal, containing the account of Karen's earlier theft from the old Corner Grocery, was once again locked up in an old blue trunk in Ethan's attic. Perhaps they'd uncover the story behind the other items in the trunk later, or maybe the mystery would remain unsolved. One of those things that, unlike the memory of Celia Middleton, would fade away with time.

CHAPTER 47

Gift of Continuity

*J*ess kept in close contact with Frank and Virginia when the world came crashing down on their daughter. No one wants to see their child go through something so terrible even when they bring it on themselves. Everyone worried about Virginia, given her heart condition, but she handled things better than most expected.

Jess asked her about it one afternoon as they sat in the reading nook at the bookstore, drinking coffee.

"Karen is a complex woman, Jess," Virginia said. "On the one hand, she has taken good care of us as things have gotten more difficult with our advancing age. She took good care of her grandmother, as well. Most of the time she's attentive and pleasant, but she's never seemed truly happy. Her and her husband weren't able to have children, and I think that damaged their relationship. Her best friend was my mother, who was perhaps not the best influence on her. Some days I wish I'd kept Helen away from her. Perhaps Karen would have found more joy in life if she hadn't always been so concerned about wealth and status. Look where that got her."

Jess nodded. She'd never understood why Will came to approach life much the same way. It hadn't been like that when they were young. Could Karen have been that bad influence on him?

"Of course," Virginia said, "given everything that's happened, I feel we owe *you* an apology, too, dear."

"Why in heaven's name would you owe me an apology, Virginia?"

Virginia's eyes became sad. "Because of what Karen did to your marriage."

"Don't be ridiculous. What Karen and Will did or did not do is on them. None of it is *your* fault, and none of it is *my* fault. I'm sure we'll all struggle with the repercussions of what they did in the months and years ahead, but we're not to blame."

Virginia sighed deeply. "I suppose you're right, dear."

Voices floated over toward them as Frank and Nathan came back up to the main level of the shop from the basement.

"I think he's still living in the area," Frank was saying. "Do you want to reach out to him to see if he'd be interested?"

Jess couldn't make out Nathan's reply.

"Hey, do you guys want to join us back here?" Jess called. "What were you two up to downstairs?"

Frank set a book he'd been carrying on the front counter and the two men came back to the nook.

"I wanted to find out more from Frank about the books in that back room," Nathan said. "You know, the ones by local authors we saw when we helped them clean up from the flooding this summer?"

Jess remembered that day, certainly. It had come to her mind often lately. She wondered if Nathan remembered meeting Karen down there. Another one of his father's mistresses.

"Speaking of local authors, Nathan," Jess said, "how did that signing go? The one you helped out with a while back?"

"Great," Nathan said, grinning at the memory. "We probably had about thirty people stop by over the course of the three hours. It was lots of fun, and I think it'll help give the author a boost."

Frank shook his head, chuckling. "This kid of yours is certainly coming in handy, Jess."

"How so?"

Frank gave a look to Nathan as they sat in the two remaining chairs in the reading area. "Do you think now is as good as any to tell your mom what we've been talking about, Nathan?"

"Sure, why not?"

"What are you two cooking up?" Jess asked, although she had a pretty good idea where this was heading.

"Why don't I start?" Frank said. "Jess, I know I was pushing you hard to find a buyer or I'd threatened to close up shop come the end of the year. I'm actually reconsidering a little now, though, given everything that's happened."

Jess smiled, relieved. She'd had zero time to seriously look for a buyer, and Halloween was only two weeks away. "So, why have you changed your mind?"

Frank glanced at Virginia. "The main reason is what's happened with Karen."

This surprised Jess. "Not sure I follow . . ."

"Ginny and I have been talking," Frank admitted. "I explained to my wife my concerns with her health, but she assures me she's feeling better now that she had that stent put in her heart. She wants to continue to spend time here, at the shop, to keep busy. Neither of us want to sit home and dwell on everything, nor do we want to leave town and look like we're running away . . . ashamed."

"All valid points," Jess said. She'd probably feel the same in their shoes. She wasn't about to hide away in embarrassment because of all of Will's scandals, either. She almost told them as much, but instead she allowed Frank to continue.

"And then there's this young man of yours," Frank said, motioning toward Nathan. "I think we've found ourselves someone with the ability to enjoy this bookstore as much as we have through the years."

Nathan nodded. "I think I'll take it from here, Frank, if you don't mind," he said.

"Sure, son, be my guest."

"So, Mom, you know how I told you they were cutting our hours at Barnes and Noble, and I thought maybe I would need to get a second job? We've found a better solution."

"Oh, you *have*, have you?" Jess said, trying to contain her grin.

"We have. I really enjoyed helping Frank out that first week when Virginia was doctoring. Spending time here meeting their clientele has been *great*. Plus, I have some ideas of new things Frank and Virginia might be able to do to drum up more business. I've been bouncing some of these off Frank, and I've got him thinking."

"So . . . ?" Jess prompted.

"Frank has offered me more hours here than I could get at Barnes. I could quit there and wouldn't need a second job. Frank will be flexible, too, which will help during my last semester and a half."

Jess nodded to her son, delighted to see him so encouraged about helping Frank out. But she did have some concerns. "Frank, do you think you can afford part-time help? Things *have* been slow . . ."

Frank took it over from Nathan, saying, "You're right to ask, Jess. Could I afford just any old part-time clerk? Probably not. But two big things make me think this is the exact path we need to follow. First of all, I don't want us to be here so much anymore. We shouldn't have to work as many hours, at our ages, as we'd need to if we wanted to have our store open like it should be. So I need someone if we're going to keep the doors open. The second thing—and this is what *I'm* excited about—is this: Nathan wouldn't just be part-time help. He'll help us grow. I predict he'll bring in enough new business and revenue to more than pay for himself."

Jess raised her eyebrows, pleased. "Some of those ideas must be pretty great, son, if you've got Frank excited about trying new things. That's a hard sell—believe me, I know."

"Got some cool ones," Nathan confirmed, nodding excitedly. "And, Mom, here's the kicker. Virginia offered to let me move into the apartment upstairs. They'd charge me rent—but less than I'm paying now, to help offset the cost of having to drive farther than before. We register for spring sessions soon, and I'll be careful how I set up my class schedule. I'll probably even do one of my last classes online."

Frank, Nathan, and Virginia all looked at Jess expectantly. She was part owner in the bookstore, after all, and they all knew she felt a strong sense of responsibility to the ongoing success of the businesses Celia passed on to her.

Jess glanced around the store. In her mind's eye, she could see the store decorated for Christmas and holiday shoppers browsing the aisles. The little bell above the door would ring, followed by the ringing of the cash register as her son helped a customer purchase a stack of books for presents. She had faith he could add value.

Besides, Celia would have loved this!

"Well, it sounds like the three of you have been doing some scheming on this behind my back," Jess said, looking to each of them in turn. "I like it!"

EPILOGUE

"What a difference a year makes," Renee said to her sisters as they carried trays of sandwiches and treats out to the buffet table set up in the main room of the lodge, just outside of the kitchen. "Here we are at our *second* annual Whispering Pines Halloween party. And ladies, let's keep this one drama free!"

Jess couldn't agree more. Last year's party had nearly ended in tragedy when Julie disappeared.

"I'm glad it's just us this year. Last year's open house was a great way to kick things off, but this is more relaxing," Jess said. She looked Renee up and down. "By the way, what are you supposed to be?"

"Come on, can't you tell? I thought this was pretty great," she said, adjusting her red bandana and rolling up the sleeves of her denim shirt.

Jess shook her head. "I have no idea."

"Rosie the Riveter!" She flexed an arm at them and said, "You can do it!" then added, "And Matt is coming as Bob the Builder! Is that great or what?" At Jess and Val's blank expressions she sighed. "You know, since we're building our house."

"You are such a dork," Jess replied.

"How about you in your Dorothy costume and ruby-red slippers?" Renee said with a laugh.

"Hey, I thought it was perfect. 'There's no place like home' seemed appropriate this year. Old home is gone, and *this* home is where I belong," she said, executing a quick spin. "Besides, Harper loves my stuffed Toto."

"Speaking of Harper, how are the legal proceedings going?" Val asked, her Princess Leia wig looking a bit like big brown cinnamon rolls on each side of her head. Her white gown would probably be sporting food stains before too long—Val was never far from the kitchen, and Halloween treats were one of her many specialties.

"Actually, they're going great," Jess said, turning to Val. "Since Tiffany was the one who suggested involving lawyers to transfer over her parental rights, things are moving right along. And . . . drum roll, please . . . my divorce will be final on November first!"

"About damn time," Val said, shaking her head and dislodging her wig in the process.

Renee clapped. "That calls for a bottle of wine! Val, I can't take you seriously in that wig."

"Maybe if we drink enough vino, it'll grow on you," Val replied, readjusting it.

The main lodge door opened and George and Lavonne came in, carrying more food.

"Look at you two hippies," Jess said, grinning at her parents' flower children getups, complete with tie-dyed clothes and headbands.

"Everybody here?" Lavonne asked.

"No, not yet," Renee said. "The younger kids are upstairs playing. Luke and Matt are on a beer run. The older kids should be here any minute.

The door opened again and Jess recognized Seth's "Hello," hollered from the entryway.

"Be right back," she said, setting her tray down.

Seth was bringing his daughter Kaylee along; she was in town for a visit. Jess was beyond nervous to meet her.

"Hey, you two," she greeted them.

Seth stood there in regular street clothes while the girl next to him was dressed all in black, complete with a cape and witch hat. A broomstick was clutched in her hands—maybe Jess wasn't the only one nervous.

"See, Dad, I *told* you to wear your costume," the thirteen-year-old scolded her father. Jess recognized that tone and felt pity for Seth. She knew he'd struggle with the teenage attitude.

"Yeah, Seth, where's your costume?"

"I wasn't sure I believed you that the adults dressed up, too," Seth replied with an embarrassed grin. "But I can see you were serious . . . Dorothy."

"Oh, we take Halloween *very* seriously around here," Jess replied, laughing.

"Jess, this is Kaylee, my daughter. Kaylee, this is Jess, my . . . *friend.*"

Ouch.

"Hi, Jess, nice to meet you," Kaylee replied, giving Jess a little curtsy with her witch cape. "Dad here has a hard time talking about relationships, so don't feel bad that he can't actually say *girlfriend* out loud yet."

Oh yes, he is going to have his hands full, Jess thought, grinning pointedly at Seth.

"Why don't we head back toward the kitchen? We're just getting the food out. Val's boys and Harper are upstairs, and the older kids will be here any time. I suspect you'll want to hang out with them when they get here, Kaylee."

They hadn't made it very far when the door opened for a third time and five more bodies piled through.

"Speak of the devil," Jess said, turning back to check out all their costumes. "Robbie, where's your costume?" she asked her nephew.

"I'm wearing it," he replied with a grin.

"Isn't that Nathan's college sweatshirt? Not real creative, bud."

"Hey—I'm dressed like Nathan and Nathan is dressed like me. We thought it was pretty brilliant!"

"In other words, you two didn't feel like dressing up tonight," Jess said, "so you just swapped outfits."

"You can't be mad, Mom," Nathan said, coming to stand next to Robbie. "Seth isn't dressed up, either."

"Hey, man, don't drag me into this," Seth replied. "I'm the newbie. I get a pass."

"Where's the food?" Robbie asked, pushing past them toward the kitchen, Nathan on his heels.

Julie, Lauren, and Grace stood behind them, hanging jackets up on the coat rack next to the door. Their skimpy costumes wouldn't have been enough to keep them warm on this chilly night.

"Now *that's* better, ladies," Jess said, delighted they'd chosen to participate. Julie and Grace looked great in their 1940s flapper costumes and Lauren made the perfect Indian princess. Her long, dark hair had probably suffered some extra straight-iron time but now hung in a perfect curtain, nearly to her waist. She wore a pretty light-brown fringed dress and moccasins. She reminded Jess a little of the young woman in her dream, way back last New Year's Eve, except Lauren's hair wasn't braided.

"Great costume, Lauren," she complimented her daughter.

"Your arrowhead gave me the idea, Mom."

"I love your costumes, too, girls," Jess said to Julie and Grace, standing there looking elegant. "Grace, is Grant coming?"

"Yes, he is. Dad was just talking to Matt and Luke outside. I think they're having a beer in the parking lot."

"Figures. They'll be in around the time the food's ready. Come on in, let's get this party started, ladies!"

Jess ushered everyone down the hallway toward the food. Someone had turned on the old jukebox, its disco lights now flashing and "Monster Mash" blaring. The lights were turned down and the decorations Jess and Renee hung earlier added to the festive atmosphere.

"Hey, Dad, would you mind running upstairs and letting the rest of the kids know the food is ready if they're hungry?" Jess asked. "Seth, can you help me in the kitchen for a minute?"

Jess was happy to see that Renee was visiting with Kaylee as she walked by, back to the kitchen. Seth followed her.

"What do you need help with?" Seth asked as the swinging door closed behind them, muffling the noise from the party. No one else was in the kitchen.

"Can you help me open a couple bottles of wine?"

"Sure. But do you have any beer?" Seth asked, taking the corkscrew Jess handed him and starting on a bottle sitting on the counter.

"Yep, don't worry, the guys have it outside. I'm sure they'll bring it inside in a few minutes. But first, I want to make a toast."

Seth gave a little grunt as he pulled the cork out of the bottle. "All right . . . what are we toasting?"

Jess set two plastic wine glasses next to him and he filled them both. He set the bottle aside, handed her one of the glasses, and picked up the second one for himself.

"I wanted to toast *us*," Jess said, smiling up at him.

"As in, you-and-I, 'us'?" Seth asked, clearly not sure where Jess was going with this.

"Yes. Us. This has been a crazy year, and I want to thank you for sticking by my side and helping me get through it all. You're loyal, and not nearly as annoying as I initially thought, not to mention you're . . . *hot*," she said in a teasing voice, going up on her tiptoes in her ruby slippers to steal a quick kiss.

"Oh, is that right?" Seth asked, pulling her closer with his free hand.

"That's right—even if you suck at costumes. But wait, I'm not done. I also wanted to toast the fact that, as of Wednesday, I'll be officially divorced . . . and very soon I'll also be the official mother of kid number three."

Seth laughed and took his turn stealing a kiss.

"You are just full of surprises, aren't you?"

The door swung inward and Val cruised in, carrying an empty tray. Seth and Jess jumped apart.

"There you two are, hiding back here and acting like guilty teenagers," Val said in mock disgust. "You better get out there. The guys are all here and I bet Seth would rather have one of their beers than that wine he's holding. Come on," she said, heading back out to the party after setting down her tray.

"She's almost as bossy as you," Seth said, looping his fingers through Jess's and pulling her back toward the party.

***

Jess took Harper from George so he could fill a plate. The nine-month-old looked adorable in her Toucan Sam costume.

"She looks cute," Seth said, checking out the multi-colored beak poking out from the top of the baby's head. "I'm surprised she's leaving that thing on."

"Me too," Jess agreed, laughing as she balanced Harper on her hip. "It was the closest thing I could find to a red cardinal costume. Every time we're outside, she points at the birds and gets really excited when she can spot a red cardinal. I knew she'd like dressing up like a bird. I hope your daughter has fun tonight. I'm glad you brought her."

"I'm glad she agreed to come for a visit," Seth said, watching as Kaylee laughed about something Robbie said to her. She seemed to be fitting right in.

"I'll have to introduce you to Grant, too," Jess said, motioning toward the man talking to her son. "Nathan's probably trying to get him to agree to come do a book signing at the store this winter. Grant just self-published his first novel and Nathan's going to work for the Fisks."

"Oh, that's great!" Seth said. "Frank seems like a nice guy. And I know Nathan was interested in the bookstore when we were there fixing the ceiling."

"It'll be a great partnership," Jess agreed, turning at the sound of another round of hellos. Her dad was welcoming Ethan and someone he'd brought along. When George stepped out of the way, Jess could see there was a woman on Ethan's arm—a pretty woman dressed in an attractive outfit, but not a costume. Jess suddenly felt ridiculous in her *Wizard of Oz* getup. She watched as the woman's eyes scanned the crowd.

"Look, Seth," Jess said, pulling his attention from Harper. "Ethan brought your friend Brooke."

Jess gritted her teeth when she saw Brooke notice Seth, the woman's face lighting up with a brilliant smile.

This is going to get interesting.

Did You Enjoy
Tangled Beginnings?

Thank you for reading *Tangled Beginnings*. I am so grateful you selected it and I hope you enjoyed the second book in my Celia's Gifts series.

If you missed *Whispering Pines*, the first book of the series, I invite you to go back and follow Renee on her journey from corporate employee to resort owner. It's a story of heartbreak, second chances, and personal growth. You can find it on Amazon.

Celia's Gifts follows a tight-knit family as they navigate the challenges and celebrations of modern life.

There are many adventures yet to come for this family. If you enjoyed *Tangled Beginnings* and would like to read about other ways Celia managed to leave a legacy for her family, please visit my website to join my Reader's Club for updates on future books in this series and my other writing projects. To thank you for joining, I will send you a copy of *First Summers at Whispering Pines 1980*, a free novella. I hope you'll enjoy this trip back to a time of innocence when Renee, Jess, and the rest of the family first visit Whispering Pines as kids.

Did you notice the chapter headings in Tangled Beginnings? I believe life offers so many gifts. These chapter names also provide a writing prompt for my blog. You can also find my blog and other projects on my website:

Visit my website at www.kimberlydiedeauthor.com
Or email me at kim@kimberlydiedeauthor.com

Finally, if you enjoyed this book, I'd like to ask you for a big favor: Please post a review for *Tangled Beginnings* on Amazon and Goodreads. As an indie author, this is the best way readers can help me!

Your feedback and support is invaluable in helping me not only improve this book, but my future writings as well.

All the best,
Kimberly Diede

ACKNOWLEDGMENTS

What a year it's been! The support I've received from family, friends and strangers as I embarked on my author journey has been phenomenal! Your encouragement is the fuel behind my continued pursuit of my dream to entertain and inspire others through the written word. I cannot thank you enough.

Of course, it all starts at home. A huge thank you to my husband, Rick and our kids, Joshua, Alecia, and Amber for helping me honor my commitment to this endeavor. Our family provides me with wonderful examples of how, together, we can all live our best lives. I also want to welcome my new daughter-in-law, Taylor, to our family. I hope to encourage you to explore your own writing dreams.

Dad, thank you for helping introduce my first book, *Whispering Pines*, to the world. You proudly wear the sweatshirts you designed bearing the title of my book. You are a walking billboard and always quick to explain the story behind it when asked!

Mom, I may never have hit "publish" if not for your love and encouragement. I'm so glad you were able to help me celebrate the early days of *Whispering Pines* and now you are my very special angel, continuing to work your magic in my life. I will keep working to make you proud.

It didn't take me long to realize writing the second book in a series presents its own unique challenges: how much do I share again, which story lines should I continue developing, and how do I stay true to the magic that is Whispering Pines? Many thanks to my book coach, Ramy Vance, for helping me develop the outline for what would become Tangled Beginnings. You amaze me with your ability to not only pick up on a thread of an idea and help writers weave it into a full story, but also your talent at offering encouragement and advice to keep our focus on what is most important - writing our books.

A big thank you to Spencer Hamilton, my editor on both Whispering Pines and Tangled Beginnings. You are a talented *wordsmith* and you know how to make me dig deeper to bring out my best. You are helping me grow as a writer.

My continued involvement with the Self-Publishing School community is an ongoing source of invaluable information related to the publishing process, but even more than that, it allows me to be part of a group of talented leaders and aspiring writers that band together to support each other's lofty ambitions. It doesn't get better than that!

A huge thank-you to all of the amazing, selfless people on my *Tangled Beginnings* book launch team. Thank you for your careful review and suggested corrections. Writing a book begins as a solo project but getting it out to the world takes the work of many.

And finally, as with any "gift," the beautiful wrapping is important, and I want to thank my cover designer, Cakamura DSGN Studio, for sharing your talent with me. You created a thing of beauty with your cover for *Whispering Pines* and I'm so excited to partner with you again on this book!

ABOUT THE AUTHOR

 Kimberly Diede's first novel, *Whispering Pines*, was inspired by her real-life "Aunt Celia," Mary K. Nierling. Aunt Mary was a generous, extraordinary, slightly formidable woman who excelled in a "man's world" in the mid-1900s. The Celia's Gifts series is Kimberly's way of honoring her great-aunt and the legacy she left behind.

An avid life-long reader, Kimberly would occasionally read until the sun rose, before adult responsibilities made the habit unsustainable. Her love of reading has evolved into a love of writing as a creative outlet from the demands of thirty years in corporate America. She is currently at work on future novels in her Celia's Gifts series.

Kimberly lives in North Dakota with her family and spends as much time as possible at the lake in the summertime.

You can visit her website at www.kimberlydiedeauthor.com.

54133824R00257

Made in the USA
Columbia, SC
26 March 2019